The Captain

By Ryan M. Shelton

Martin Sisters Publishing

Published by
Martin Sisters Publishing, LLC
www. martinsisterspublishing. com
Copyright © 2015 Ryan M. Shelton
ISBN: 978-1-62553-082-0
Christian Fiction/ Young Adult
Printed in the United States of America
Martin Sisters Publishing, LLC

DEDICATION

For my students, past and present, and for all educators, like my wife, who work hard to give everything they have.

ACKNOWLEDGEMENT

I owe everything to God, from whom all blessings flow. I also owe much to my wife Angela, who won't let me settle for less than my best effort. She is my first editor, and a mighty fine one at that. I want to thank my three wonderful children, Andrew, Ezra, and Neesa. Despite all my flaws, they love me unconditionally with the love of the Lord. What more can a parent ask?

I thank my mother who has always been there for me and always believed in me. As the rejection letters piled up over the years, Mom never lost faith in me. She kept me strong. The same could be said about my brother Chris and my sister Lori. They both inherited that same trait from Mom, backed up by their better halves Holly and Marty, respectively. I swear that Chris and Lori are more excited than I am each time I call with news about my writing. Special thanks goes out to my in-laws, Pamela, Steve, Irala, and Rosemary Magee, all of whom supported my first book. In true philanthropic spirit, they gave away many of the copies they bought. They are great examples of Christianity at work.

I would like to thank Melissa Newman and Denise Melton of Martin Sisters Publishing. First, they took a chance on an unknown, then they decided to double down with this sequel. They are wonderful to work with, and I appreciate their expertise and dedication to publishing great novels. Author Mark D. Williams is always busy with a new book, a research trip, mentoring his own students, and being a family man. With all of this on his plate, he still found time to take me on as a project to help me get started in this business. For that and for the continued encouragement, I will always be thankful. I would also like to thank my editor for this book, Kathleen Papajohn. It has been a pleasure to work with her over the course of this series, and I thank her for her insights. It takes a careful eye to mold a fine novel out of a mess of words and ideas.

Rachel Rhodes and Betsy Easley are two special ladies. Rachel, an undiscovered author, is trying to push through college in three years to be a teacher, and Betsy is the best teacher at Ponca City High School. Both of them were very busy when I asked them to be my first readers, but neither so much as hesitated when asked. Both gave valuable input that helped me see things from different perspectives. Thank you so much.

Considering the college setting for this novel, I wanted to know what all had changed in the fifteen years since I left, so thank you to my former student Reese Larmer for filling in the gaps. I also needed a parent's perspective, because after all, the parents so often have to fit the bill. In this regard, thank you to Diane Jeans for being so forthcoming with the entire list of special fees a college student has to pay (Yikes!) I also want to thank my former student Alyssa Neufeld for her valuable insights when I was crafting the "Belly of the Beast" moment. An old curmudgeon like me can really screw things up when it comes capturing the thoughts of a teenager. Enter Alyssa. Thank you for your contributions.

I would like to thank Jason Hicks of Jason J. Hicks Photography for the head shots. Jason is a member of my church, the Agape church of Christ. They are a loving body of believers, all of whom are there for me when I need them. They supported me in my first book, and I am ever grateful. I would also like to thank the faculty and staff at Ponca City High School. The individuals are nearly too numerous to mention, but they supported me in so many ways and continue to support me. The one exception to anonymity that I will make is librarian Debbie Shelton who was very proactive in her approach to making sure the students had an opportunity to buy my book. Thank you, all.

Finally, I would like to thank all my fans who read and enjoyed

The Mentor. *The Captain* would never have come to life without all of you. I hope and pray that my books touch you. My prayer has always been that my books make it into the hands of those who need them. If you know of someone who can benefit from one of my books, please do everything in your power to get it to him or her. For anybody I might have forgotten, please forgive me. I'll catch you next time.

DISCLAIMER

In the spring of 2014, I was brought to my knees when I found out that a former student of mine committed suicide. This young man had a bright, ardent spirit and a real zest for life. I so enjoyed working with him day-in and day-out because he was a perfect blend of creativity, intelligence, and fun. When my lessons were finished, I smiled because I just knew he would change the world. Then the unimaginable happened.

I heard suicide described by one of my students as a permanent solution to a temporary problem. How true. Would my student have done this if he had just remembered that he had hundreds of family, friends and teachers who loved him? Would he have done this if he knew that we would be left with so much pain?

At the time I was still writing *The Captain*, and I heard God's voice loud and clear. This is a problem that everybody in each community must fight. The topic of suicide had to be broached in the book, to show that there is always a way out of whatever problem *seems* insurmountable. If you have considered suicide, or are considering suicide, know this one thing; YOU ARE NOT ALONE. This is a battle you should never fight alone. There are many people out there who understand what you are going through. Please seek professional help. Visit suicidepreventionlifeline.org or call 1-800-273-TALK (8255) twenty-four hours a day, seven days a week. God bless.

Chapter One

A THIN LIGHT filtered in through the window blinds from the street lamp and illuminated the ceiling that Vincent stared at as he daydreamed. It also cast slight, broken shadows, and it was then that Vincent noticed that one of the ceiling tiles drooped a little, casting a longer shadow.

Turning the light on, Vincent scooted a chair over to the middle of the room and stood on top of it. He propped open the neighboring tile, reached in, and pulled out a bottle of whiskey, the same one he had had up to his lips the other day.

He sat back down on his bed with the bottle in hand and the lights off and tried not to think. Images of his drunken father came to mind but then were replaced by images of his roommate, Evan. Evan with his pretty girlfriend. Evan with the girls from the tennis team. Evan with any one of his girls. What was it about Evan that attracted girls to him?

It's alcohol, idiot. Evan is fun. You're not. There's a reason for that.

Vincent frowned and unscrewed the top to the bottle. He

took a whiff, winced, and thought of his father yet again. Were there any times in his life when he loved his father? Respected his father? Surely there was something endearing about his father? Surely Vincent held something in common with the man who provided half of his DNA, the man who provided half of the equation to the Punnett square that was Vincent Preston.

The sinister smell of the liquor beckoned him. "Who am I?" Vincent heard himself say out loud.

You are a Punnett square of your mom and your dad. That's who you are.

"I am my father."

The bottle was at his lips.

Standing on top of the pitcher's mound, Vincent stared at his assistant coach, who called for a curveball. Vincent never liked curveballs. Slow, loopy, and bad on the elbow, they were an invitation for a power hitter to crank a pitch out of the park. That's what Vincent was taught, and he considered himself a good pupil, only because he was taught by the best.

His mentor that past summer, a man who Vincent affectionately referred to as "Grandpa Dean," had spent his entire life studying the game of baseball, since way back in the thirties when he was playing youth ball, and through the rest of his working life as a big league scout after the war took his pitching arm. So when Grandpa Dean told Vincent that curveballs belonged in a category with drugs, curse words, and other sinful vices of the weak, Vincent took him at his word.

Now the fastball, on the other hand, was a thing of beauty, a topic worthy of poetry. A good fastball pitcher could deliver the same pitch and make it go straight, left, right, up, or down. Same arm motion, same delivery, all the pitcher had to do was change the grip on the ball and try not to smile at the poor sucker in the batter's box swinging in vain. Grandpa Dean had taught Vincent all of his secrets.

So when his coach called for the curveball, Vincent decided to surprise him with a fastball instead. He was about to make some jaws drop with his first college pitch. Vincent went into his windup. Lightning shot out from his trusty right arm, and the thunder followed.

Lightning!

Thunder!

POP!

Coach Bailey nearly caught his balance with his right hand before his feet came out from under him and he rolled to his back. He lay there a second, shaking his head before he took the ball from his catcher's mitt and flipped it back to Vincent from the seat of his pants.

"Well, that wasn't a curveball!" Coach Bailey laughed out loud as he looked over at the stoic head coach who stood motionless at the top of the dugout.

This was the first time one of the coaches had the privilege of catching Vincent, so he had put a little extra mustard on the first pitch, something to remember him by when making out the lineup card. Vincent, his coach's misfortune prompting a little smile on his face, lifted his glove to hide his grin and took in the aroma of leather and saddle soap. It was possibly the best smell in the world. Combined with the fastball and the fresh early morning air, Vincent couldn't hold his smile.

In the previous year, he had learned to be a morning person. Rise before the sun and enjoy as much of God's day as possible. Besides, after 10:00 it was insufferably hot in northern Arizona. It was a different hot than he was used to. He was used to a sweltering heat that was so humid; it made him feel like he was breathing underwater. But that was Oklahoma. Here in Arizona, the dry heat was, well, just different.

He looked all around. New place. New faces. New uniform. New start. He could remember longing for a chance to start over, and this was it: college. College was a new experience for him. A rebirth. He couldn't believe there was a world outside of the small western Oklahoma town where he grew up. This fresh start was intoxicating.

"Vincent! Anytime you're ready!"

Vincent broke out of his trance and looked toward the dugout where Coach Johnson was looking at him. Vincent looked back to his catcher, who had regained his feet and refocused on the signs, calling for an inside fastball. A million miles away from the world outside of baseball, Vincent went into his windup, grunted, and released.

Lightning!
Thunder!
POP!

The catcher managed to hold his own this time and flipped the ball back to Vincent. Around the diamond the players worked their various skills, turning double plays, covering different bags on simulated bunts, and doing all this with the precision of robots. One difference Vincent had discovered about college baseball was that everybody on the team was the best player on their respective high school teams. That was one unfortunate thing about living life in a small town in the middle of nowhere. Vincent had had virtually no competition in high school, and thus no barometer to measure his skills in comparison with that of other gifted baseball players. He had been a big fish in a small bowl. Now he felt like a minnow in a school of minnows.

Now that the sun was over the horizon, the baby blue sky slowly turned a darker shade of indigo. Thin cirrus clouds swept the roof of the world, and in the short amount of time Vincent had been at Page, Arizona, he had not seen a single cloud capable of producing a single drop. If it weren't for underground sprinkler systems, there would be no grass to speak of.

Johnson Field lay at the top of San Antonio Hill. The field's dimensions were perfectly symmetrical, 330 feet at both foul lines from the plate to the fence, 375 in both left center and right center, and 400 in centerfield. The prevailing winds blew out of the west from left field, making home runs down the third-base side difficult, but not impossible. As for centerfield, anyone hitting a ball 400 feet was surely headed for the majors. From what Vincent had been told, only two people had ever parked a ball beyond the 400 foot sign, and they both eventually wore big league uniforms.

Just outside of the outfield fence was a cliff that dropped off a couple hundred feet. Anyone wanting to retrieve a home run ball would have a better chance of parking down below the hill and waiting for the ball, and probably a small avalanche of falling rocks, to cascade from up above.

The stands stretched from the right field foul pole, curving around home plate, and all the way to the other foul pole. Twenty rows high, it allowed for all of the population of Page, Arizona and its outlying communities to support the team. This included about 7,000 people, not counting the 3,500 college students who called North Central Arizona State University home from September to May.

The view from the top of the stands was breathtaking. One of the first things Vincent had done when he arrived in Page was go to the ballpark and sit on the top row, above home plate. The view revealed perhaps the most beautiful lake ever made by man, Lake Powell. From Vincent's view, a person with mediocre eyesight could make out the beautiful red bluffs rising out of the crystal blue water a mile past the centerfield wall. Add to that the beautiful American West landscape spreading to the Pacific, and it was enough to inspire poets, artists, and athletes alike. Exploring the lake and Glenn Canyon Dam where the Colorado River held thousands of trout (bullet points in the college brochure Coach Johnson had given him) were on his list of things to do, once Vincent found the time. School hadn't started yet, but two-a-day practices would consume all his energy, and staying inside during the heat of the day was a must.

Vincent readied himself for another pitch, this one a sinker, and let loose. His shoulder felt great, his body felt great, and his mind was at peace when he was on the mound. Off the mound, he was as scared as a pheasant in short grass looking at a line of hunters waiting for the sunrise on opening day of hunting season. He didn't really know anybody here, he didn't know how hard college courses would be, and he didn't know how he was going to make ends meet, since college governmental regulations stipulated that he couldn't even have a part-time job.

His college was paid for with the scholarship, which included tuition, room and board, but not the fees, which were steep. Since he didn't have a car, he didn't have to worry about gasoline, but the cafeteria served only three meals on the weekends: Saturday breakfast and lunch, and Sunday breakfast. Clearly he had some obstacles to overcome.

As Vincent looked around at the other players on the infield, he noticed that a few eyed him suspiciously. He took off his hat and wiped his forehead with the brim. It wasn't like he was sweating; it was a dry heat, but it was a habit that he had picked up the year before. He looked under the bill to read the inspirational bible passage that he had written there in ink:

Phil. 4:13.

Vincent made a mental note to write to Mrs. Dean after

breakfast. He figured she must be lonely without her husband around anymore. Mrs. Dean was the only one who had ever believed in him. She was the one who had introduced him to Grandpa Dean. Vincent still hadn't fully recovered from the loss of his mentor. It was tough, watching a man he loved waste away with cancer. It was a terrible set of memories, seeing Grandpa Dean coughing and spasming while trying to teach Vincent how to pitch, holding Grandpa Dean's hand as he lay on his deathbed, attending Grandpa Dean's funeral.

It hadn't been a month since Grandpa Dean's passing, and Vincent had a lot of thinking to do. He kept to himself as much as possible and constantly sought to lose himself in the wonderful world of baseball.

Vincent readied himself to throw another pitch and gave himself the luxury of another quick peek around. Sure enough, a few of the players seemed to be checking him out. There was one group of about four players in particular, one whose arms were so muscular that it looked like he had blown them up like balloons. They stood around with their gloves to their faces, obviously hiding what they were talking about. Since they were staring at Vincent, he figured he must be the topic of conversation and decided to ignore it and just throw. He was used to people gawking.

Vincent continued throwing, and once he hit forty pitches, Coach Johnson cut him off and sent him to the outfield to shag fly balls with the rest of the outfielders. Vincent didn't know if he would break into the starting lineup as a freshman. He certainly hoped he would. He felt faintly confident that he could be in the starting rotation during fall ball. Where in the lineup? He did not know. Maybe the third pitcher? Fourth?

Every year rumors would surface about Coach Johnson's impending retirement, but he never acted upon any of these so-called "impulses." The people of Page and North Central Arizona University dreaded the day he would hang up his whistle. As successful as NCA baseball had been, it sure was the popular sport in northern Arizona and southern Utah area. The fact that NCA competed with the big west coast teams added to both the excitement and classic underdog mentality. Plus, NCA had no football program and a basketball program that had never made the national tournament. Baseball fans abounded. The baseball players at NCA enjoyed a celebratory status amongst the students in this quiet little town, something Vincent would have to get used to.

After two plus hours of practice, Coach Johnson called everybody in. Vincent saw Grandpa Dean when he looked at Coach Johnson: the way he coached, the way he talked, the general air of quiet confidence about him. Coach Johnson was a wise old man, much like Grandpa Dean. The two had been good buddies during Coach Johnson's days in the big leagues. As an old friend, Coach Johnson had spoken at Grandpa Dean's funeral. As a last act of good will, Grandpa Dean let Coach Johnson in on the best kept secret in Oklahoma. Consequently, Vincent now had a place to go to school.

Coach Johnson always ended a practice with parting words. These always included a quote for his pupils to chew on. It was the players' job to return with an application to the quote. Upon return, Coach would call upon one player to talk to the team. Some reveled in this responsibility, some prayed they wouldn't be called on. But they all prepared a short inspirational speech every practice regardless, because they all respected Coach Johnson.

Once they were seated around home plate, Coach Johnson cleared his voice and said, "Gentlemen, what I see on the field is good. Many of us are improving. Many of us, though we came into camp overweight, are shedding those pounds and getting in shape. The good news first: today is our last two-a-day practice. The bad news is that we aren't ready for our first game yet, and it's coming up just around the corner, next Tuesday, right Coach Pantangeleni?"

"Yes, sir. Southwest Utah, sir."

Coach Johnson shifted his feet as he spat in the dirt. "Okay, gentlemen. That means we have four days to prepare for our arch rivals. As you know we have an inter-squad scrimmage tonight. Now this is the first chance the public will have to see this year's edition of Bulldog baseball. So there will be a little pressure on you guys not only to perform well for us coaches who will decide on final lineup for SWU, but also to give the public a little something to hope for after a season that went sour last year. Sunday we will take off for the Lord's Day, but on Monday, something big is happening. Anyone?"

"First day of class, sir," the players said, almost in unison.

"Okay, gentlemen. 'Whatever you do, work at it with all your heart.' Colossians 3:23. Remember we aren't here to just play baseball. Be sure to have your school business taken care of before Monday. In the meantime, I have the starting lineups for the red team and the blue team posted in the dugout. Feel free to peruse them when dismissed. The only thing I haven't listed is tonight's starting pitchers. That's because they will be giving the words of wisdom tonight. Whichever two I select to speak tonight will be the starting pitchers, and 1-2 in the rotation. Okay, gentlemen, today's quote: Will Rogers once said, 'Always drink upstream of the herd.'" The team let out a nervous chuckle that lasted five seconds. "Get some carbohydrates in your body and drink plenty of fluids for tonight, gentlemen. Meet here, ready to stretch at 4:30. Dismissed."

The team nervously filed their way to the dugout wall to see who would be playing where. Most positions were three players deep or better, so the odds of being on the Red Squad, which was the #1 lineup, or the Blue Squad, which was #2 were pretty good. Vincent waited behind so as not to get caught up in the stampede. Once the players thinned out, he too made his way to the dugout and laid his eyes on two sheets: the first, a blue one, had eight names listed in Coach Johnson's fancy cursive, but Vincent's name was not one of them. Taking a deep breath, he looked at the red sheet and disappointment settled in the pit of his belly.

Chapter Two

NORTH CENTRAL ARIZONA'S campus was open for business in 1975, and was small for the upper-level collegiate division it was in, but to Vincent, between the size of the campus and the student population, it was a culture shock, too big to comprehend, at least right now.

NCA mandated that all freshmen live in the dormitories their first year. On top of that, Coach Johnson made sure all his baseball players also lived in the dorms, regardless of their classification. That way their mischief could be kept to a minimum. Other sports had players suspended because of keg parties at their houses, and this was a problem he wanted to prevent, not solve. All of the players except Vincent roomed with a fellow teammate. Since Vincent was a late scholarship addition, the odd man out, he got the short end of the stick. He just didn't realize it yet.

After practice, Vincent walked down the hill from Johnson Field, through the campus toward Newport Hall. Vincent loved

NCA's campus design. NCA was set on essentially three levels. At the bottom of San Antonio Hill were the dorms, half-way up the hill was the campus, and on top of the hill was the baseball field. He had looked at the design from a satellite view on the computer at the library, and the campus looked like God had used a compass to draw a bull's-eye. The center of the bull's-eye was Brookfield Library, a circular building. Five sidewalks extended out from the library to a circular sidewalk that looked like a wagon wheel from the satellite view. Outside of this circular sidewalk were the five main buildings where most of the classes took place.

Each of the five main buildings was the shape of a trapezoid, short end toward the middle of the bull's-eye, long end on the outside. These included Burtner Hall for history classes, Green Hall for the math classes, Easley Hall for fine arts classes, and the aptly named Science Hall. Then there was McSorley Student Union. It held the campus bookstore and an arcade along with some eating places and a bowling alley.

The only grass on campus was in the outfield of Johnson field. Everywhere else was a Southwest theme of rocks, cactus, and a host of rock-dwelling flowers for building borders: yellow primrose, orange poppy, and azaleas in various shades of red with primrose dominating. There were also some dwarf shrubs that Vincent couldn't identify. Taking care of the Dean's yard back in Oklahoma that past summer gave him a passion for flowers, and he found the Southwest array fascinating.

All the buildings on campus were tan stucco, made to look like elaborate adobe dwellings. Brookfield Library, the center of the bull's-eye, looked like a doughnut with caramel frosting, giving it its nickname "The Doughnut." It stretched three stories high and was, in Vincent's opinion, the ugliest building he had ever seen. At night it looked like an adobe spaceship ready for launch.

The cool thing about the Doughnut was the Doughnut hole. It was a space twenty yards in diameter set outside with benches surrounding a huge water fountain in the very center that shot water ten feet in the air. Vincent had been told by his advisor that the water in the center, which was the very geographical center of campus, was supposed to be symbolic of something, maybe the center of life. Vincent couldn't remember. He did know that the mist from the fountain cooled off the shaded area, making it more comfortable than sitting anywhere else on campus. With the three-story high walls, even the summer's noon-day sun didn't penetrate the center of the Doughnut. It was a popular place on campus to study, but one had to get there early to procure a seat.

There were five dormitories for the students at NCA. Vincent lived in Newport Hall, which was reserved for the male athletes. Looking back up from in front of his dormitory, it was easy to see that Johnson Field was the crowning jewel of the campus, given that it was 200 feet above the physical buildings that made up NCA. No matter where you were on campus, you could look up the hill and see Johnson Field, or at least the outfield fence and lights. Vincent really loved that.

Since Vincent didn't live with another baseball player, he felt like the odd man out, but this was not a new feeling for him. To add to this, none of the other players had invited him to their rooms for so much as a bag of popcorn and a movie. Again, nothing new. It was almost a comforting feeling.

Tired and dirty, Vincent resolved that the first thing he was going to do was take a shower, then head to the cafeteria for some breakfast. On the way to his room, he overheard someone talking sternly in another room with the door cracked open.

"…and you better not let me catch you with alcohol in here.

And don't be snickering! This is serious. With one word from me, the head resident will kick you out of here faster than you can wipe that smile off your face. So you better..." Vincent hurried past and caught only a glimpse of two scared freshmen sitting on a bed and looking up attentively at someone whose figure was obscured by the half-closed door. Vincent figured it was the resident assistant doing all the barking. He had overheard stories about the guy, a fifth-year senior who wasn't good enough to walk-on to the basketball team his freshman year. He had lived in the sports dorm all four years and became an RA when most upperclassmen in his predicament would have moved off campus. Vincent knew not to cross the guy who apparently had let his position of authority turn him into a dictator.

When Vincent opened the door to room number 12 D, the first thing he noticed was a stack of boxes taking up any of the available walking space in the already cramped dorm room. It must have been his roommate, but the guy was nowhere to be seen.

He didn't know much about the guy. All he knew was that his name was Evan Gilchrist, and that he was a tennis player from a private high school somewhere in Los Angeles. The trepidation Vincent felt at meeting a guy from Los Angeles was enough to put a whole new round of butterflies in his stomach. After all, Los Angeles was a big city, and surely he and Evan would have nothing in common. A week prior Vincent had chosen the bed farthest away from the air conditioner, as a sign of respect to his upcoming roommate. He also kept his meager belongings in his own closet and made sure everything was spick and span for the new arrival. Being in a new place with no friends left him plenty of time to tidy up what wasn't there. But Evan had apparently brought his entire house with him, and from what Vincent could tell, half of it was on his side of the room.

"Hello?" Vincent said as he dropped his bat bag and slipped into the room. There was no reply from behind any of the boxes. Right now Evan was nowhere to be seen. So Vincent slalomed his way around all the junk his roommate had brought and went straight for the shower his room and the other three rooms with the number 12 shared.

Twenty minutes later Vincent returned in fresh clothes, but there was a tan colored dress sock on the door knob. He took it off, examined it, and opened the door to find that his roommate's bed was cleaned off, but now there was a guy and a girl laying there. They both sat up, startled. "What the heck, man?!? Haven't you heard of knocking?"

Vincent was startled by this and jumped back. "Uh, sorry!" He looked on the door, saw that he was in the right room, and stepped forward again, not sure of what to say.

"Uh, I'm Vincent. This must be your sock. You must be…"

"BUSY!" the guy on the bed exclaimed, but the girl pushed him away.

"Stop it, Evan!" she said playfully. "You're being rude."

She headed for Vincent, holding out her hand. "Hi, I'm Mandy, Evan's girlfriend. It's nice to meet you." Vincent shook her hand and felt that it was very soft to the touch. He looked into her blue eyes, then down at the floor, embarrassed. She was beautiful, and he didn't really know how to react to a woman his age being friendly. The man on the bed stood up, shook off the wrinkles in his khaki pants and collaredshirt, and then stepped over some boxes. Vincent took quick appraisal of him. He had a full head of bleached blond hair and a dark tan complexion. Vincent figured he'd been spending time on the beach. To complement his hair, he sported a small strip of dark hair from his lower lip down around his chin. Vincent's first impression was *Surfer Dude.*

"Vincent, eh? Well, it's good to meet you. I'm Evan, your roommate." He held his hand over Mandy's shoulder toward Vincent. They shook, rather awkwardly. "Looks like you just took a shower."

Vincent looked at him in bewilderment, still not knowing whether he was invited into his own room or not. Finally the joke hit him and he cracked a smile.

"Aha, see sweetie, my roommate has a sense of humor. You should feel safe leaving me with him. You know, it's not that I'm complaining, but they really don't give us a lot of space in these rooms, do they?"

"No, it doesn't seem so," Vincent said, looking back down at all the boxes.

"Heck, I don't know where I'm going to put my racquet stringer." He pointed to a machine on a stand about chest high that looked as if it belonged in an interrogation room for aliens. Presently it was standing on top of two boxes and almost reaching the ceiling. "Hey, where's all your stuff?" Evan asked.

Vincent looked around and then motioned to the closet. After all, all he had brought was a blanket, a pillow, and enough clothes to get him through a few weeks without having to do the wash, all packed into his mother's old blue leather suitcase. In Vincent's opinion, it was the best thing his mother had given him, about all his mother had ever given him. Vincent also brought his baseball equipment, including his old burlap bag of fraying baseballs. There was still plenty of space in his closet.

Vincent still had plans on going to the office supply store to get a few notebooks and ink pens for class. "Uh, my stuff?"

"Yeah, did you pack light?"

"I guess you could say that." The three were bunched so close in together that Vincent felt awkward, yet with all the boxes, there was no place for him to go.

"So, pal, where do you hail from?"

"Oklahoma."

"Oklahoma! You don't say! Check it out, Mandy. The first person I have ever met from Oklahoma!"

"Well, it's just been a full day for you then, hasn't it? You better take a nap!" she remarked and elbowed him in the gut. He turned her around and planted a big kiss on her. Now Vincent was really feeling awkward. A third wheel.

"I can come back later, if it's better for you. I was just going to—"

"No, pal. Come in and sit down. We're going to spend a lot of time together, so we might as well get to know each other. Hey, how long have you been here?"

"'Bout a week."

"Good! I suppose you've gotten the bar scene all figured out. That'll take some of the guess work out of it for me. Hey, are the girls here hot?" Again, Mandy elbowed him in the ribs, this time harder. "Just kiddin'! You know I'll be a good boy! You won't have to worry about me." Evan turned to Vincent, "Mandy's just here for the day. She's supposed to be helping me unpack, but, well we got a bit sidetracked. She's going to be a freshman at UCLA, which is why she has to get back so soon. She's already rushed and all, so she has the sorority thing to do when she gets back. Tell you, it's quite a trip. What was it Mandy, six hours from LA?"

"Probably."

"Well let me tell you, you can really fly down the road up here. It's nothing like LA, or even around Palm Springs where the highway patrol will nab you for going five miles over the speed limit. Shoot, I didn't even see a cop once I hit Arizona. Of course we kinda took the back roads when we crossed the border. Great idea to see wild, rural Arizona. I was expecting to see dinosaurs, but I didn't even see a buffalo. Of course it was all night driving, so I'm sure they're out there. The only part we got to see was the Grand Canyon. But I suppose that once you see the Grand Canyon, what else is there to see in Arizona? Definitely no ocean out here! What about teepees? I know there's Indians here. Hey, you're from Oklahoma. You live in a teepee?"

Vincent looked at his new roommate sideways and wondered if this guy was for real. Was he just joshing Vincent, or did Evan think Vincent rode in on a horse? Besides, Evan talked about 100 miles-per-hour. Vincent didn't say anything, just stared blankly at his new roommate.

There was a pause in the conversation. Evan and his UCLA sorority girl sure monopolized the conversation. While Vincent was looking for something to say to break the silence, Evan started up again. "Okay, no teepee. Hey pal, have a seat and tell me about yourself."

Vincent looked for a seat as Mandy went back to her boyfriend's bed. The two guys found sturdy boxes and sat down. Evan looked at Vincent and nodded, almost excitedly. Vincent hadn't known what to expect from his roommate, but this was as far off-base as he had imagined. At least the fellow was nice, almost overbearingly.

"Well, I'm from a small town in western Oklahoma."

"What's it like in western Oklahoma? Different from eastern Oklahoma?"

"Uh, maybe? I've barely been east of I-35. But where I'm from is kinda like this, except there's grass, and rolling prairies. No trees or mountains. Just kinda boring."

"I don't know. Sounds interesting to me. So what do you do in a small western Oklahoma town? You know, for fun? Drink whiskey and shoot up the town with six-shooters?"

"Well, to be honest, most of the high schoolers find an older brother who is twenty-one to buy them a keg. They then take it out to a farm and have a party."

"Partying out on the farm! That's wild. Sounds a lot like Malibu! Ha! Hey, you got cows and pigs and stuff like that too? And buffalo! You gotta have buffalo, right?"

Vincent chuckled. "Yeah, we have plenty of cows and pigs in Oklahoma. I even think we may have a few buffalo, though I've never seen them."

"Well you gotta hunt the buffalo, am I right? I saw it on a movie once. You sneak up behind 'em with a fifty caliber, then skin 'em right then and there. How 'bout the pigs and chickens? I'm sure they don't mind you guys getting rowdy though."

"I guess not." Vincent was too embarrassed to admit to his new roommate that he had never been to a party. That he had no car, and had no friends until about a month before he left for college. Even then he wouldn't have called his teammates *friends*, though some were nice. They still didn't hang out after practice.

"Well, it sounds like a hip-happening place to be. We'll have to road-trip it sometime. You know, show me the ole stompin' ground. How long of a trip is it?"

"About a day."

"Holy cow! A day! Twenty-four hours of driving! Man, I bet you were exhausted when you got here, huh?"

"Well actually, I took a bus."

Evan looked up and popped a smile at Vincent, until the smile wasn't returned. Then Evan turned red. Vincent actually did hop on a bus and twenty-four hours later landed in Page, Arizona. "Wow! No kidding? How you going to get around without your ride?"

"I suppose I'll walk. I've been doing it my whole life."

"No car? Well, just as well. The price of gas these days is ridiculous. It took $200 in gas to get the ole Hummer out here.

Took half that to get her BMW out here. There goes my spending cash for this week and next. Mom and Dad gave me their plastic, but I had to promise not to go over $400 a month. Guess they're not going to get a Christmas gift this year," he said and chuckled, patting Vincent on the back. He got back up and jumped on the bed next to his girlfriend. Vincent decided he had been in their way long enough. After all, how long did they plan to stay away from each other? They probably needed the time alone.

"Well, I had an early morning practice."

Evan looked up. "What's your sport?"

"Baseball."

"Good sport. Mine's tennis. Maybe I can get you out on the court sometime, smack the ball around."

"Uh, sure." Vincent looked around for an escape route. "But anyway, I'm hungry, so I'm going to head down to the cafeteria and get some breakfast, leave you guys alone for a while." This interlude had helped Vincent forget about not making either of the starting lineups for tonight's scrimmage, but all that came back to his mind as soon as he was out the door.

"Well, Mandy will probably be gone by the time you get back, so we can hang out, you know, really get to know each other better. Cool?"

"Sounds like a plan," Vincent said. He waved to Mandy who didn't see him because she was giggling with his new roommate, so he felt stupid for the effort. He reached down, grabbed the tan sock off the floor and put it back on the door knob before closing the door.

The Cactus Café was awesome. There were three amazing things about this cafeteria. First and foremost, the food was excellent. Now it wasn't as good as Mrs. Dean's spaghetti and meatballs, but it was good in its own right. The sheer quantity of food was enough to make Vincent salivate just thinking about it.

On one side were all the different sugar cereals. Vincent's parents never had money for fancy cereals, so he grew up on regular oatmeal. Icky, gooey oatmeal. They always had oatmeal around the house. God's oats. Generations and generations of fine Americans growing up on oats. Surely nobody ever complained about eating oatmeal before him! Surely he should have been thankful to have oatmeal sticking to his ribs all day! It was the modern day equivalent of manna falling from the sky to feed the Israelites lost in the Desert of Sin. He could never bring himself to like it, no matter how much butter or sorghum he added. Eating it was like taking a pilgrimage on his knees to Mecca. It was just something he knew he had to do. He would eat his oatmeal every morning, slowly smacking, making sucking noises like a carp slurping mud off the bottom of a silted pond. Vincent would try to pretend it was apple pie or something better, and he'd suppress the gag reflex in the process. But, here in the cafeteria, was a world of all the sugary cereal he could eat, and he swore he would never eat oatmeal again!

There were juice machines and a machine that dispensed five different kinds of milk, including chocolate and strawberry. On another side were the hot foods: biscuits and gravy, bacon, sausage done two ways, links and patties, and eggs galore, anyway he wanted them. There were omelets, breakfast burritos, pretty much anything a person could want. Also there was a cook on hand to take requests. He would make darn-near anything within reason. Vincent watched some of the more bold students from the basketball team request Eggs Benedict one day, and darned it if the cook didn't start separating the egg yolks for the Hollandaise sauce.

Finally, there was a small section at the end of the line with a tub of oatmeal that was always full. Vincent held his breath as he passed it.

Breakfast was only part of what was amazing about the Cactus Cafe. Lunch and dinner were grand in their own rights, with all the food groups present and accounted for. Hamburgers were grilled upon request, and Friday night was steak and shrimp night. Whenever Vincent went to the cafeteria, he felt like he had stepped into heaven. He never left there hungry, and he had taken to the bad habit of overeating. He almost felt that the ride might be over too soon, so he should get all he could when he could, like a bear packing on fat before hibernation. Back home, all his father kept in the fridge was beer and an open box of baking soda. Back home, he battled malnutrition.

But the most amazing thing about the cafeteria was that hardly *anybody* ate there! Whether they all went out for fast food, or ate snacks in their rooms, Vincent usually shared the dining hall with no more than twenty others at a time. He figured that would change now that the regular students were arriving for the start of school. By dinner tonight the place would probably be hopping.

Vincent ate a modest meal, downing a bowl of puffed corn and eating a short stack of pancakes with imitation maple syrup. He didn't mind eating by himself, since he really had no friends there, but feeling self-conscious, he chose to take that time to read novels. Presently he was finishing *Of Mice and Men*. Mrs. Dean had given him twenty-five paperback novels she thought he would like to read to keep him out of trouble in the dull moments that accompany college. He liked Steinbeck's simple style. As much as he liked Steinbeck, he couldn't wait to finish so he could get to Hemmingway's *The Old Man and the Sea*. It's not that he wasn't enjoying this first book she gave him, but it's just that he felt a little too close to the character Lenny, and

Vincent knew it wasn't going to end well for him.

Part of him wanted to go back for seconds, but he had made other plans. As soon as he wiped the last of the maple syrup off his plate, he went on a walk. He knew he should give his new roommate and his girlfriend time to themselves. Plus, he wanted to ponder Coach's words. It was obvious that he wouldn't have to give a response, after all, the starting pitchers would be doing that, but he didn't want to be caught with his pants down. Besides, if there was anything he had learned from Mrs. Dean, it was to never take the easy way out.

Walking through the door outside, Vincent thought about the mountain of food he was leaving behind. He wondered how much it must have cost for the cafeteria just to make it, and how much of it would be thrown away since the place was nearly empty. It was more money than he had; he knew that. His checking account had just over a grand from his summer job. That had to last him all school year. The bus ride itself cost him sixty-nine dollars. He wondered how his roommate could ever spend $400 a month! Vincent had school supplies to consider, and they were going to be expensive. He had first made a trip to the campus bookstore to buy his school supplies, but when he saw the prices, he decided he would find a dime store. He did buy a little journal notebook, a six-pack of cheap pens, and a box of envelopes. Despite his frugalness, he still felt he wasted four dollars and ninety-two cents!

It took him forty-five minutes, but he arrived at Glenn Canyon Dam with wide, feasting eyes. It was amazing! He had seen shows on how Hoover Dam was built, and this dam wasn't as big, but it was still an amazing thing for him to witness in person. All that concrete holding back all that water! The immensity boggled his mind.

The mid-day sun was pressing down on him, and

remembering what Coach Johnson had said, he found a shady spot under a tree and sat down. From his angle he could see the face of rock on the west side of the Colorado River tail water, stretching for what seemed like an eternity before it hit the water below. He decided it might be fun hang gliding down to the bottom, but how on earth would he ever get back up?

He peered down at the white water below and saw two fly fishermen way down at the bottom. They were facing upstream, gracefully heaving their lines in synch back and forth, back and forth, before letting the invisible fly on the end float down naturally and become part of the river for but five seconds before being yanked back off the river and whipped around again. Vincent saw this, saw the peace and solitude the two at the bottom of the canyon were obviously enjoying, and even though they weren't catching fish, Vincent was in love. He felt a warm fuzziness in the pit of his belly that made him feel at peace. He promised himself that he would learn this hobby. To the north was Lake Powell, and even though the view of the lake was better from Johnson Field, he still felt better for being there. He watched the two fly fishermen for ten minutes before opening his journal. The pen didn't work at first, so he pressed harder into the paper until the ink finally came out.

"Always drink upstream of the herd." -Will Rogers

Fairly ironic that today's quote would have to deal with a river. Despite the bad news after practice, the day was shaping into perfection. He pondered, looking out at the lake again, and scribbled furiously for a few minutes, feeling totally inspired. Nothing would ruin his day. Turning to the next page, he started a letter to Mrs. Dean.

August 25th

Dear Mrs. Dean,

How are you? I am fine. Just to let you know, I will try my best to write with proper English so you won't be disappointed in me. Please forgive me if I do mess up though. You've graded enough of my papers to understand what I mean. Also, I hope you forgive me for writing on journal paper and sending it. The prices at the bookstore are outrageous, and even though I would like to send you this on stationary, I'm sure you'll appreciate the thought anyway. If I win the lottery, I'll buy a cell phone and just text you.

Just as you suggested, Arizona is a world apart from Oklahoma. I can't even begin to tell you the differences. Right now I am sitting at the top of a huge canyon with the mighty Colorado River rolling underneath. Just to the north within a stone's throw is the prettiest lake in the world. It almost looks like something that should be on Mars, not earth. There are plateaus rising out of the water everywhere. I should think that if I look to one direction or another, I would see Wyatt Earp ride around a bluff on his horse. The land really is amazing. I sometimes feel like I have stepped back in time, into the Old West. I would just love to go exploring, but this is the first chance I have had to make it over here, despite it being only a mile or so from campus. I do know now what it's like to be inspired.

College is good, but I can say that because we haven't started classes yet. Once I do I will be really busy. We have our first scrimmage tonight. I was hoping to make either the first team or the second team in left field, but it appears I will have to wait my turn. I have been practicing real hard, and I hope I can get some playing time. Time and patience. I'll just have to trust in the Lord.

I am about to finish Of Mice and Men. I don't like the boss's son Curly, but I guess that was Steinbeck's purpose. I have an overwhelming feeling I am not going to like the ending of the book, but I have resolved to finish it before getting to The Old Man and the Sea. Sitting here watching two fly fishermen, I am inspired to fish now. We'll see.

Well, I should be getting out of this heat and into the air-conditioning of my dorm room. I met my roommate today, and his girlfriend, and it seems they needed some alone time. To tell you the truth, I am dreading going back there. It's not that he isn't nice, because he is, but I don't think we'll have anything in common. He's a tennis player from Los Angeles and he's really rich. Right now the entire room is filled with boxes. Well, I guess I better go face the music. I hope all is well back home, and please write when you get the chance so you can catch me up on what's happening.

With Respect,

Vincent Preston

Vincent read over the letter, placed it in the envelope and licked it, then remembered he had no stamps. That was just another expense he would have. He wished he had a cell phone to call or text her, or at least a laptop to e-mail her, but at least he would have access to computers and Internet access as soon as school began.

He looked back down at the river and saw that the fisherman on the right was battling a fish.

Chapter Three

WHEN VINCENT RETURNED to the dormitory, it was just after noon. Half of the boxes were now gone, mostly from Evan's side of the room, and Evan was nowhere to be found. On the walls were posters of bands he had never heard of, most of them grotesque in appearance. One such poster had a man dressed up like an ugly woman with a leash around his/her neck, clutching what appeared to be a human femur bone in his/her mouth. At the bottom of the poster it read "The Brillo Pads." Another one had a nuclear war scene above a city with a chicken trying to escape the mushroom cloud. It was titled "The Nuclear Chickens." Vincent cleared off his bed and decided to take a nap, as long as he could get out of the glare of the bone-munching monster staring at him. As he laid his head down, he looked up at the top of the wall and saw a new border consisting of human skulls to match the chicken poster. It was disturbing, and he had a little trouble going to sleep.

He woke up peacefully, until he opened his eyes. His new

roommate was a foot away from his face. It made Vincent jump, frightened. Vincent pulled his comforter up to his neck and adjusted his mind to fit the time and place, then remembering that he should be right where he was, he looked questioningly at Evan. "Uh, hello?"

"Not too early for a sudsy one, is it?" Evan took a bottle of beer out from behind his back and offered it to Vincent. Vincent recognized what it was right away. After all that was his father's favorite dinner. Vincent's mind went back to the moment he walked by those freshmen's room as they were being read the Riot Act by the RA. If that guy came in here at that very moment, Vincent could kiss his scholarship and room goodbye.

That very second the alarm clock blared. 3:45 P.M. Vincent shut it off.

"Uh, I don't think so," Vincent said in response to his roommate's question. He could think of nothing better to say.

"I figured we could get to know each other over a few brews."

Vincent shook the cobwebs out of his head. He had never had a drop of alcohol in his life. He didn't plan to start now. Vincent was really beginning to think this roommate thing was a bad idea. "Uh, you sure that's a good idea? If we get caught with that stuff, we'll get kicked out of school."

"Relax, dude. Nobody is going to catch us. You just need to loosen up a bit. Go ahead," and he offered Vincent the beer again. Vincent was too overcome by peer pressure to tell him that he had never drunk a drop in his entire life. Instead he said the first intelligent thing he could think of, "I have a game I have to get ready for."

"Oh, man dude, I'm sorry. You can't be getting tanked before a game. What time is your game?"

Vincent shook his head again as Evan put the beer back in the little dorm refrigerator under the desk that Vincent had overlooked when he came in. Evan looked to be about half-way through his own beer. Who knows how many beers he had gone through before this? Vincent started getting dressed. "We play at 5:00 tonight. Actually it's just an intra-squad scrimmage." He didn't know how to tactfully tell Evan to get that stuff out of the room. He had to live with this guy for the next year. He didn't want his first day to get off on the wrong foot, but it kind of already had. Judging by the first day, it would be a long year.

"Well, cool. I'll be there. Then we can go out on the town later. What do you say? I hear the Red Pony is opening up a keg of off-brand beer and giving it all away. From what people tell me, you just stand in line and take two glasses to your table at a time until the table is full. Of course one guy has to stay behind to guard the beer. I also heard they don't ID. Be a good way to meet some chicks. If there's one thing I know, it's that free beer attracts hotties. Whadda ya say?"

Vincent pulled on his shoes, and grabbed his bag. It was plenty early to get out there, but he had to get out of the room. He said, "Yeah, we'll see how tired I am after the game, okay?"

"Yeah, sure thing. Hey man, good luck! I'll be cheering you on!"

Vincent smiled. "Well, don't get your hopes up. I don't think I will even play."

Of course he was the first one there. Despite this only being an intra-squad scrimmage, he felt the same old butterflies in his stomach. He had hoped that butterflies were only from immaturity, that when he was in college, they would go away, but he was wrong. They were worse than ever. If there was one thing he had learned though, it was that exercise was a good remedy. As soon as he got his spikes on, he was jogging laps under that hot high-desert sun.

Somewhere around lap three, about the time the butterflies subsided, other players showed up. He didn't want to be seen as an extra-achiever by running laps without the coaches ordering him to, but about the time he decided to stop, a few others joined him, running two-by-two. The guy next to him was perhaps the biggest, strongest guy on the team and looked like he belonged in the Marine Corps with his buzzed haircut and block head, the same guy with the balloon arms Vincent had noticed when he was throwing for the coaches. He hadn't talked to any of his teammates yet. He didn't know anyone's names yet either. Apparently sensing this, the big one spoke up. "So man, what's your story?"

Vincent turned. He was nearly out of breath and hoped the guy had been talking to somebody else, but his face was fixed on his. "I'm Vincent," Vincent breathed. He didn't like to talk while he ran, but he didn't want to be impolite either.

"Vincent," the same one said, and looked away. At this point they were at the centerfield 405 mark. Vincent was wishing he had sat this last lap out. He was quickly losing energy. "So Vincent, where you from?" The nameless guy was having trouble talking and running at the same time also. He was very stout, with a huge barrel-chest, and he towered over Vincent.

"I'm from Oklahoma."

"So you're the one from Oklahoma," one of the guys from behind quipped.

"Of course he's the one," Barrel Chest said, looking back. "Haven't you seen him throw?"

Vincent didn't know what to make of this comment.

"Anyway, it's nice to have you on the team." The big guy caught his breath again. "I'm Brian Redmond, but you can call me Tank. That's what everybody calls me." Again he paused for breath. They neared the dugout, and as of yet, nobody else had shown up.

When they all stopped, Tank reached out his hand for Vincent to shake. "If you need anything, just let me know. I am the team captain, and I am a senior, so I pretty much have it all figured out by now." He smiled and let go of Vincent's hand, which was a good thing, because Tank's grip was like a tourniquet. He turned to the two others,

"These two are also seniors," the captain continued. "Van Roberts and Ray Salinas. We call them Hoover and Steinbeck. Hoover is our starting shortstop, and Steinbeck is the starting second baseman."

Vincent shook each offered hand and was pleased they didn't have Tank's grip. After all he had to protect his pitching hand.

"You'll find that everybody has a nickname on this team," the captain continued. "It's kind of like a secret fraternity handshake. We go by our given names in public, but around the guys, we use our nicknames. The other students here will also pick up on the nicknames and call us by them. Think you'll remember all this?"

"No, probably not. Maybe we should wear name tags," Vincent said in between breaths.

The three others laughed at this. Freshmen were also at another disadvantage. Coach Johnson's philosophy did not allow for putting the player's last name on the back of the jersey, and if it were legal, he would also do away with the number. He believed in teamwork and anonymity. But Coach Johnson also knew about the age-old tradition of ballplayers being superstitious. Each had a number that meant something to him, and the majority of the players were very superstitious about their numbers. In the big leagues, when a big gun is traded to another team, if a person of lesser skill has the star's number, he is usually asked to give it up. Most of the time this is no problem, but many players have blamed their poor hitting on not having their lucky number. Superstitions are a funny thing. Superstitions can cause entire franchises to lose games. It's easier to blame bad fortune on a material vice than to just admit that the team really stinks.

Coach Johnson hand-selected his captain, so Vincent felt confident that Tank was an upstanding man. All indications pointed that way so far. Tank seemed to be the kind of guy you would want on your side if you ever found yourself in a fight. One look at him and the toughest man would run away!

"So what's his nickname going to be?" the man identified as Hoover asked Tank.

"That's another thing, Vincent," Tank said. "It's the captain's job to pick out the freshmen's nicknames. So you better impress me!" Tank chuckled, but Vincent wasn't so sure it was a joke. "You don't want to get stuck with a nickname like Sandy. One of our pitchers got the name Sandy because his fastball didn't top seventy! Plus all his curveballs hit the dirt, so only a girl's name would do." Tank paused and then said, "I know it's sexist to say women throw slow. Ever tried hitting a fast pitch softball? Crazy how fast those girls can throw." Tank paused again. "But it's a tradition. We also had a Rebecca, but he graduated last year. His was a bit undeserving, but that's how it is. Whatever you're given, that's what you are stuck with the whole four years. If you redshirt, you will be stuck with it for five years, like poor Rebecca. But I doubt you will be redshirting."

Vincent's thoughts briefly sidetracked to his encounter with his roommate and his roommate's girlfriend, Sandy. Or was it Mandy? He quickly pushed the whole episode out of his head. "Why are you two named Hoover and Steinbeck?" Vincent questioned the other two who were stretching. He didn't feel the need to ask about Tank's nickname. That was pretty obvious. Many of the other players were showing up at this point, and the stands were quickly filling.

Tank answered for them. "Well Hoover got his name because he doesn't let anything through the infield. He's like a vacuum cleaner. And old Steinbeck here is a nerd!"

"Ha, Ha. Very funny," the one identified as Steinbeck said and tried to shove Tank with one hand. Just like his name, Tank didn't budge an inch.

"He's an English major," Tank continued. "He's going to be an English teacher after college. His last name is Salinas. Of course you know who John Steinbeck was, I'm sure. Since John Steinbeck lived and wrote about the Salinas Valley in California, the name stuck." Between the name Sandy and Steinbeck's Of Mice and Men, the irony was thicker than the swarm of gnats that Vincent had to swat away from his face as he stretched.

Tank continued, pointing at certain players as he scanned the field. "There's Dallas, and talking to Dallas is SoCal. Oh, and then there's Seattle, and Vegas, and Nawlens. He's from New Orleans, but that's how he pronounces it with his Cajun drawl, so that nickname was easy enough."

Tank continued to point out teammates. "There's T-bone, and Rhino—his name is Ryan, so that one's easy. Then there's Rabbit, because he's fast, not to be confused with Turtle who we also call Plow because he's so slow that it seems like he's pulling a plow."

"So, what's it going to be?" Hoover asked again, impatient.

Tank broke out of his train of concentration. "Chill out, man. I don't know yet. I haven't had a chance to catch him yet. Due time. Besides, Oklahoma doesn't sound like a good nickname."

"How 'bout Okie," Steinbeck opined.

"Naw," Tank said, shaking his head. "Doesn't fit."

"Do I get a say in this?" Vincent asked.

"No," the others all said in unison.

42

The coaching staff was making their way down the steps now, and the players started to assemble. "Anyway, like I said, if you have any questions, or just need to talk, let me know. That's the captain's job, and I take this job very seriously." Then to the rest of the team, he shouted, "Let's go! Get in your circle!" Everybody snapped to attention. Vincent knew right then that Tank was indeed worthy of wearing the big letter C on his jersey and that he better not cross Tank.

Vincent whispered to either Hoover or Steinbeck, as he couldn't remember which was which now, "Tank looks a little older than us."

The player responded with only one word, "Marines."

Vincent considered this one-word response. So Tank was much older than the other guys because he was in the military? It would explain the high and tight haircut and the nickname.

The players formed a circle which parted like the Red Sea for the coaches to enter. There was no snickering or joking. Tank walked over to Coach Johnson and whispered something to him. Coach patted Tank on the shoulder, and he joined the rest of his teammates. Everybody was silent, waiting for Coach to speak. The stands were half-capacity and filling fast. The whole town couldn't wait to get a first glimpse of the team.

"Okay gentlemen," Coach Johnson said and cleared his throat. "All of you know your positions except for the starting pitchers. Now each of you will get an opportunity to play tonight. If you were not on one of the starting rosters, you will sit on the blue bench. Red team will play the entire game at their positions. If we make any changes for the Southwest Utah game, they will be posted tomorrow. So play hard tonight gentlemen. Give the crowd something to cheer about, but remember, we are a team no matter if you're starting, or think you should be. So support each other out there."

"Now, today's quote was from Will Rogers, 'Always drink upstream of the herd.' Please give your undivided attention to our blue team pitcher, Dave Austin."

A slender man rose from the circle to applause and chants of "Sandy! Sandy! Sandy!" The team listened intently to the words of the wise junior.

"Well guys, this is the way I see it. Cows are ugly and not too smart. They sure taste good though. So if you're upstream of them, and they try to run away or something, you can just get in your boat and paddle after them. If you're downstream, you would have to paddle harder against the current, and nobody wants to do that. Well, that's about all I have to say." Sandy was on his way back to his seat before he even finished.

Chatter arose and a few had to squelch their congested giggles at such a ludicrous response. Vincent was appalled. The speech made no sense whatsoever, and Sandy managed to misinterpret the meaning of the whole passage. How utterly ridiculous. The guy apparently had no formal training when it came to speaking in front of a group of people. You never sit down before you are done speaking, and you never finish a speech with the words, "Well that's it," or "That's all I have to say." It made him wonder about the legitimacy of higher education if this guy could be passing as a junior. He hoped the next guy would get it right and inspire the team.

"Thank you Dave," Coach Johnson said. "Now for your starting red team pitcher, the first freshman to ever start number one in the rotation for our annual kickoff game, please give a round of applause to Vincent Preston."

Vincent looked up with shocked astonishment. All that running he did was for naught because the butterflies returned like an unwanted houseguest.

The eager teammates applauded as Vincent found the

strength in his wobbly knees to stand and move to the middle of the circle. Too many thoughts rushed at him to comprehend anything. He didn't know if he would even make the starting rotation, and here he was the number one pitcher! He looked around at his teammates and did practice breathing to try to still his heart. Coach Johnson, who had moved back to the circle's outer edge, now walked back over to Vincent and whispered in his ear, "You earned this kid. All these gentlemen are looking to you for leadership. Can you handle it?"

"Yes, sir," Vincent managed to squeak out. He reached for his back pocket and pulled out the piece of paper he had scribbled on earlier in the day while contemplating the quote. He was so startled by the nomination and nervous that he couldn't even remember the quote, much less who said it. He didn't expect to even sniff the field, and here he was the starting pitcher! He unfolded the paper and read the quote over in his head. He took off his hat to wipe the sweat from his forehead and read the scripture he had written on the inside bill.

Phil 4:13.

Suddenly, his confidence grew, and he addressed his teammates with clear candor. "I hope you all don't mind, but I'm not a very good public speaker, so I made a cheat sheet in case I left something out." He looked around the group and Tank, arms folded at his chest, nodded at him in approval with a very serious look. Vincent was the mystery man on the team. Everybody wanted answers about who this guy was. Amazingly, the words came easily to Vincent.

"'Always drink upstream of the herd.' I am just a freshman, a newcomer in this new world. I am not a wise man, nor somebody who people come to for answers. I'm not the old man on top of the mountain who will give you the meaning of life." He stopped, looked at his cheat sheet one last time and folded it up and put it back in his pocket. "But on the other hand, I'm not stupid either. I come from Oklahoma, where the color of the wheat is yellow, and the color of the sky is blue. I'm not fancy, I don't think outside of the box, and I would make a bad shrink."

Everybody laughed politely at this.

"But I am a straight-forward kind of guy. If I eat a cheeseburger and get fat, I don't sue the restaurant for making it. If I go outside without a shirt on and get a sunburn, I don't waste my breath yelling at the sun. And I think Will Rogers was the same way. He was also from the Midwest, my state to be exact, and he had many good quotes that bordered on common sense. 'Don't kick a cow pie on a hot day.' 'If you get to thinkin' you're a man of some influence, try orderin' somebody else's dog around.' 'There are two theories to arguing with a woman. Neither one works.'" Once again, the team laughed. From the stands it must have appeared the players were loose and confident.

"I guess I can just associate with Will Rogers because he thought with common sense. Common sense is something we need a lot more of in this world. And from the stories I hear about extra-curricular activities in college, common sense is something we all have to practice. So when it comes down to it, what I am trying to say is that the answer is never out of reach. Issues can be black and white if you let them. Right and wrong are right and wrong, and there is no grey area. So if somebody is peeing in the stream, drink upstream. Don't let anybody pollute you."

His butterflies resting, he sat back down next to a few other guys he didn't know, but they stood with the rest of the team and gave him a standing ovation, making him blush. This was as good a first impression as Vincent was hoping for. No matter how fickle the crowd back home was when he pitched, and no matter how much they cheered for him when he did well, he never truly felt appreciated till this moment, and he didn't want the moment to end, but his thoughts soon drifted to preparations for the game.

Chapter Four

A HALF HOUR later, standing on top of the mound wearing his red hat with the big white B on it, Vincent allowed himself one quick glimpse of the setting before finding his zone. The red team took the ball around the horn as he looked up at the stands filled to capacity. Lines of people stood by the chain-link fence past the stands on either baseline. Just beyond the left field fence was Harris Cliff that dropped fifty feet from the summit of San Antonio Hill to Johnson Road below. A home run to left could do serious damage to a car below on the road. Hoover flipped the ball back to Vincent, and the first batter stepped into the box. The man on the loudspeaker might have called out Vincent's name, but he wouldn't have known any better. His entire world of concentration consisted of the fingers on the right hand of possibly the strongest man Vincent had ever met. Only the index finger showed, then was replaced with a catcher's glove.

Fastball. Sure, I can do that.

Vincent peered hard at the catcher's glove until he spied a

small discolored scratch right in the middle of the palm to focus on. He made a mental note to ask Tank to take a magic marker to the glove and make a small dot.

Grandpa Dean had taught him the secret of lightning and thunder. The lightning was his throwing motion, and the thunder was the sound of the ball slapping the leather. The closer together the two were, the harder he was throwing. It gave him a confidence that was hard to shake. He knew this batter had no chance.

Vincent went into his windup, paused for a brief moment at the apex, balanced his left leg just as his old mentor had taught him to, and in one lightning quick moment, strode forward and released the ball.

Lightning!

Thunder!

"STRIKE ONE!"

The ball hit its intended mark in a hurry. The batter let the ball go by, trying to time it, frowning after it slapped leather. Vincent saw this, and knew he had the guy. When he turned around he looked at the scoreboard. It read:

MPH

100

Vincent repositioned himself on the mound and focused in again. Tank lowered one finger again, but this time, made a sweeping motion from outside to inside. Vincent made the necessary correction in his grip to a two-seam hold, went into the windup again, and released with as much energy as he had.

Lightning!

Thunder!

"STRIKE TWO!"

This time, the batter had tried to swing, but besides being hopelessly behind the ball, it had moved from the middle part of the plate to well inside. The scoreboard read the same.

Vincent kept his focus on his catcher, saw the stone cold look on his face. Vincent didn't know if he expected the catcher to be smiling or giving him a long-distance high five or what, but he chided himself for letting his mind wander. If there was one thing he knew he must do, it was keep his focus.

Tank called for a changeup. Vincent knew the key was to vary his speeds, so he didn't argue. He offered his palm ball and the batter never took the bat off his shoulder. The slow pitch froze him in place.

"STRIKE THREE!"

Vincent smiled and came out of his trance. He noticed that the entire crowd was on its feet applauding him. It gave him the warm fuzzies, until he looked toward Tank who had his mask off, giving him a stern look. Vincent quickly decided he could enjoy this feeling later.

The rest of the first inning went much the same. Vincent threw in a slider and a sinker to complement his two other fastballs and his changeup. He didn't waste any time throwing balls. He knew he could strikeout every batter on three pitches. He walked to the dugout, pleased with his performance, and with the infielders patting him on the back with their gloves in obvious appreciation. But when Vincent got to the dugout he had two surprises waiting for him. The first was Coach Johnson.

"Tell me son," he started out as an elderly gentleman speaking to a presumptuous youth, "did you learn anything from your outing?"

Vincent thought a moment. Coach Johnson had his arm around Vincent. As Tank walked by, Coach grabbed him by the arm also. "I was just asking young Vincent if he learned anything from the first inning of work, and I will ask you the same thing. Did you, Brian?"

Tank lowered his head in submission. When Tank and Vincent were silent long enough, Coach continued. "Because it occurred to me that you two are throwing against our second team, and while you were certainly impressive out there, don't you think you should be conducting business like this were a real game and not a scrimmage?" Tank nodded in approval. Vincent didn't know what the coach meant and looked at him with a question in his eyes.

"What I'm trying to say is simply that if you plan to be a strikeout pitcher, you're going to have a short, losing career. 100 isn't going to scare everybody off. Plus, you're going to wear out your arm trying to strike everybody out. Look down this bench."

Vincent looked down the bench like he was asked.

"What do you notice?"

"Seven guys."

"That's right. There are seven other players on this bench, and when they're out in the field, they are the best at their respective positions. Your job is not to strike everybody out. You'll kill that young arm of yours or wear out early into a game. Use your infield to get ground ball outs. Don't be afraid to use that sinker ball more. If you want to be my number one pitcher, you have to use your head. Now do me one more favor. Look up in the stands. What do you see?"

"Fans."

"Not entirely true. There are scouts up there. Not major league scouts, but scouts from other college teams. And what they are writing down in their notebooks right now is the number 100. You are going to be type casted as nothing more than a fire baller, and that's what they are going to expect from you when we play them. So basically you've given your number one weapon away before we've played a single foe."

Vincent sunk his head along with the team captain. Just when he thought he was brilliant, he was actually pitching dumb. It was very obvious to him now, just as Tank knew as soon as Coach Johnson pulled them over. "Well, don't sulk about it. I'm giving you two more innings before I pull you, so I am sure you will show a little more versatility and throw a few more outside the strike zone."

As Vincent considered this, Coach threw a second surprise at him. "Grab a bat and helmet. You're leading off."

Vincent's butterflies invaded his stomach again, but he didn't have much time before he was standing in the batter's box facing a guy with the nickname of Sandy. Despite this, he tried to be serious. He knew this guy would not be the number two pitcher if he didn't have good stuff. Besides, it was a matter of pride for Sandy to strikeout the pitcher who supplanted him in the rotation. Since Vincent was conferencing with Coach Johnson, he didn't have time to watch Sandy warm up. All he knew was what Tank had told him before the game. A fastball under seventy and a curveball that didn't reach the plate. That was two years ago though. Maybe his stuff was better now. Heck, it had to be.

Vincent twisted his cleats into the soft soil of the right-handed batter's box to get a good grip and made the sign of the cross with his bat on the plate. Biblical verses played in his head, helping him restore a bit of confidence that was chipped off during Coach Johnson's speech.

Vincent looked up and met the pitcher's eyes with his. Sandy was a picture of concentration. Seriousness. Possibilities played about Vincent's mind. Surely Sandy would want to get ahead in the count, so he would throw a strike. What was his best pitch? That is what he would open with, right? Stretching his mind, Vincent decided the upcoming pitch had to be a fastball, probably on the inside or outside corner. As Sandy went into a very abbreviated windup, the pitch came right down the pipe and Vincent swung for all his worth, but ended up empty.

"STRIKE ONE!"

The catcher threw the ball back. Vincent had been fooled by a curveball. It looked good until it broke clean outside of the plate. Not only that, but Vincent was way ahead of the pitch. He heard the crowd cheer.

Vincent stepped back into the box and tried to clear his thoughts, but he could hear everything around him. His focus was not there. Before he had a chance to formulate a thought, Sandy went into his windup and threw a tailing fastball right by Vincent. He hadn't had a chance to get mentally prepared to hit. The pitch was eighty-seven miles-per-hour, hardly unhittable, but Vincent felt too rushed. His confidence sunk to a new low.

Knowing he had to do something different, Vincent stepped out of the box as Sandy was just about to go into his windup, hoping to disrupt the opposing pitcher's flow. Sandy worked very fast. Vincent had never encountered someone who could work so fast. He and his catcher were on the same page. As Vincent stepped back in, he held up his right hand to the umpire to let him know he wasn't ready yet. He wondered if Coach Johnson approved of this tactic.

Vincent didn't know what pitch to expect, so he decided he must react to the pitch. Once the ump was ready, he motioned to the pitcher and the windup ensued. The pitch came right down the pipes again, and Vincent tried to check his swing, but it was too late as the pitch curved out of the strike zone again.

The catcher and umpire appealed to the first base umpire, who in turn held up his fist in the air.

"STRIKE THREE! BATTER'S OUT!"

Vincent hung his head and walked to the dugout. He snuck a peek out to the mound, but Sandy wasn't looking. He was turned to the outfield, readying himself for the next batter. Vincent knew the guy got the best of him and wasn't going to show any emotion in an obvious victory.

The second batter patted Vincent on the back on the way to the plate as he took off his helmet. Coach Johnson held him up at the stairs to the dugout and said, "Vincent, as I am sure you know now, there is no guessing on this level."

Good to his word, Coach only let him pitch three innings. He was dominant, using the sinker more as Coach suggested and induced a few groundouts. In three perfect innings he had five strikeouts. Nobody reached base. Sandy also pitched perfectly, not allowing a single base runner in his three innings of pitching. Vincent knew he should be happy about his performance, but two things bothered him. One, he knew he could have pitched more responsibly, despite his production. Coach Johnson had been around long enough to know what he was talking about. Two, he was upset about striking out in his only plate appearance. In high school he hardly ever struck out. It was something he took pride in, and yet tonight he felt totally confused and beaten at the plate. He only got that one at-bat because Coach made him put an ice pack on his shoulder. By the end of the game, the only scoring was from a two-run home run by none other than Tank. Vincent longed for another chance at the plate, but he knew he wouldn't get it.

When the last pitch was thrown, the crowd gave a standing ovation and the team met in the middle of the infield for Coach's post-game speech. Once attention was on him, he said, "Gentlemen, today we learned a lot about where we are as a team, and I think some of you learned some valuable lessons. That's good. That was the intent. You all played hard. That's what really counts. We have some good pitching, and good pitching always beats good hitting. Hence, the score. Go back to your dorms and get some sleep. Tomorrow get all your school affairs in order, if you haven't done so already. If you're a freshman, you have been assigned an upperclassman called your big brother. Upperclassmen, it is your responsibility to help out the freshmen. Each of you knows who your little brother is, so make sure they are doing what they are supposed to be doing, and freshmen, listen to everything your big brother says. Understood?"

"YES SIR!"

"Okay. Tomorrow you can come by my office to check the depth chart. Sunday get yourselves to church. No practice until Monday when we prep for Southwest. Good job gentlemen. Our new quote, and the last one since school is starting: 'It's not the size of the dog in the fight. It's the size of the fight in the dog.' Paul Bear Bryant. Dismissed."

Vincent made his way to the dugout, and Tank caught up to him. "Hey Vincent, just so you know, I am your big brother. Do you have any questions about class on Monday?"

"No, I think I'm ready."

"Okay. If you need anything, remember to come to me." Then in a slighter tone, "Don't worry about your performance tonight. I know you're hard on yourself, but you did pitch a good game. The first inning calls were my fault. We'll get it together for Southwest. Oh, by the way, do you go to church?"

"Uh," Vincent started.

"A few of us go to this non-denominational church on the east end of town," Tank continued. "We would love to have you come along."

Vincent thought about this for a moment. "Sure, that would be great. We'll have to do that sometime."

Tank resumed his rock-hard face when the others came by and most of the team's members walked back to the dorms together.

Tank hung around to wait on Coach Johnson. Coach was in high demand, between having to talk to the radio guys, to shaking hands with the public who wished to congratulate or give him tips on how he could have coached better. He was even known to stick around after a game and help the custodian sweep between the aisles and pick up trash. At that very moment, the stadium was practically empty but for him and Coach Johnson who was sweeping the spent sunflower seeds out of the dugout.

Tank descended the steps into the dugout and said, "Here, Coach, let me take that from you." Tank held out his hand, and Coach Johnson reluctantly handed his captain the shop broom.

As Tank finished up what Coach Johnson had started, Coach sat down on the steps and put his hands behind his head, looking out at the field, perhaps thinking about his present lineup, perhaps reliving past glories. As old as Coach was, he surely had plenty of memories. Still, Tank tried not to stare.

"Well?" Coach Johnson said, continuing his gaze at the field.

Tank considered this question as he swept, knowing exactly what Coach wanted to know. "Don't know," Tank finally responded as he tried to uproot a seed that had adhered itself to the base of the bench.

Coach Johnson nodded. "It was fun though, wasn't it?"

Tank smiled. "Actually, my left hand is pretty sore, but, yeah, it was fun to catch him. Never see anything like him before."

Coach Johnson shook his head. "Raw," he said under his breath. "So raw." He shifted his feet a little before standing up and stretching his old bones. "Can you bring him along?"

This was a loaded question, and Tank knew it. "Sir?" He questioned his coach.

"No, not just as a pitcher," Coach Johnson replied. "Can you keep an eye on him, make sure he toes the line?"

"Is he going to be a problem?"

Coach Johnson coughed a little as he took off his ball cap and scratched the top of his head. "He's had it rough. Rougher than most. Matter-a-fact I can't believe he's been able to get to this point." Coach Johnson stopped short and shook his head again. "Rough," he said again, this time under his breath.

"I think he's got a problem with authority, stubborn," Tank replied. "Kept wanting to shake off my signs. Pretty stubborn." Tank made it to the corner of the dugout and had a considerable pile of spent sunflower shells. He leaned on the broom and considered if he should ask the next question, the particulars being important and all but still possibly a breach of confidentiality. Finally he just asked it. "What exactly am I dealing with? Tell me about his past."

Coach Johnson sat down again and crossed his legs. "Bad home life, bad grades, bullying, lack of support, raised himself, lost his mentor to cancer. How's that for a list?"

Tank wondered about the first point of contention: bad home life. He wondered just what Vincent had to deal with. Abuse? Neglect? Both?

"I'm not so concerned about bringing him along as a baseball player," Coach Johnson continued. "That much should take care of itself. It's everything else. You remember what it was like to be a freshman?"

Tank said, "But I was much older."

"Still tough, right?"

Tank conceded. "Yeah, it was. It would have been much tougher if I hadn't gone into the military first. That life really sticks with you. Makes routines and hard work seem a lot easier." Tank gave it a little more thought. "Yeah, it wasn't easy, even starting in my twenties."

"Imagine being eighteen and having no discipline," Coach Johnson said.

"On top of his other problems like home life?"

"So what do you think?" Coach Johnson said without replying.

Tank scooped up the massive pile of shells and dumped them into the trash can. He looked up in the stands at Elmo, the custodian, who smiled and waved as he swept. Tank waved back. "My schedule is tough, but I can keep an eye on him. I invited him to church, but I don't think he was interested."

Coach Johnson inhaled and put his hands back behind his head. "That's a start."

Tank finished scooping the shells into the trash can and replaced it at the end of the bench. "I'll check with him on his classes, too."

Coach Johnson nodded, the old man's version of a thank you.

Tank took the broom with him to the other dugout to clean it up, hoping Coach Johnson would take it as a hint to go home and get some rest. When Tank got to the opposing dugout, he turned around and saw Coach picking up empty pop cans from the first row.

When Vincent got to his dorm room, nobody was there. He didn't know if his roommate made it to the game or not. About 2:00 that morning, Evan finally came in, with a female friend who wasn't his girlfriend, Mandy, or Sandy. Vincent turned over and faced the wall and tried to go back to sleep.

Chapter Five

VINCENT AROSE AT 6:30 with an extra hop in his step. Excited for his first day of college, he stumbled through the dark and flipped on the switch, only to hear a groan from the other bed. Remembering the night before, Vincent quickly switched off the light and fumbled around in the dark for a towel. At least he was able to shower with the light on, but by 7:00 when he left his dorm room, he had no idea if the outfit he had chosen matched. As luck would have it, he didn't look too bad when he surveyed himself in the reflection from the dormitory's front door window in the early morning sunlight.

Vincent's Monday/Wednesday/Friday schedule was going to be tight in the morning: 7:30 Speech, 9:00 Principles of Biology, 10:30 English Comp I. He and his advisor had set the schedule to accommodate his baseball schedule in the afternoon, but he soon discovered that in order to eat breakfast, he was either going to have to get up earlier or skip his shower. Either way, he had already resolved to set out his clothes the night before. It was easy for Vincent to see that living with Evan was going to be an adjustment. They were oil and water. Then there was the alcohol thing with which to contend.

Vincent power walked to Easley Hall where all the fine arts courses were and was the first to arrive to class. The teacher wasn't even there. The first difference he noticed from high school was that the classroom was plain looking. No posters, no pictures, nothing that gave the room any character at all. The walls were gray. The floor was gray. The mood of the incoming students was gray.

The second thing he noticed was that the students dressed differently than he had expected. Vincent had made it out of his dorm room with a nice-looking pair of jeans and a polo shirt, one of the few he had. When the sleepy-headed students started rolling in, most showed up in sweats, tee-shirts, and flip-flops. One thing they all had in common were individual travel mugs of coffee.

Vincent felt out of his element. Apparently he hadn't gotten the memo to dress down. He had this idea of college as being a sophisticated place, where the brightest minds were all assembled and the students, when put together, formed a think tank and solved the world's greatest problems. Maybe they were all supposed to be in suit and tie, or even better, tuxedos. What accumulated in this room appeared to be more of a collective hangover than a gathering of the minds.

At exactly 7:30, the only non-gray feature in the room, the professor, arrived. Despite hot weather, she wore a professional-looking pant suit with jacket and appeared acute with a frosty demeanor, a stark contrast to the zombies in the room. Half of the students had their heads on their desks, drooling. She laid her briefcase down on the floor next to the podium, stood behind it erect, cleared her throat, and stared out at her students.

"Good morning," she said in an even tone that extended neither warmth nor an olive branch of invitation. "The first rule in speech is to wait until you are at the podium and looking at your audience before speaking. The rest of the rules you will learn as we go."

She scanned the room, and her smile turned to a frown. Vincent looked where her eyes lasered in and noticed one particular student, a male with a hoodie over his head and no coffee on his desk, was fast asleep. The lady asserted herself, walked over to the young man's desk, and tapped him on the shoulder.

He rose his head and squinted. "What?" he bellowed and stretched his arms.

Without flinching, the lady pointed to the door and said, "You may try it again the right way on Wednesday. Have a good day young man."

As the rest of the class sat up straight, the boy yawned as he apparently tried to comprehend what was said to him. When the connection was evidently made, he rose, grabbed his white three-ring binder and said, "I'm dropping this class anyway. No way I'm getting up this early for this bull all semester!" He trudged to the door, his shoes dragging on the berber. To add emphasis, he slammed the door in his wake and was gone.

Everybody woke up at the same time and the class was all in a whisper now. The lady regained her poise and walked back to the podium. With the same procedure she used the first time, she frowned and said in a staccato rhythm, "My name is Dr. Vonnegut, and I believe in not listening to my own voice so much as I believe in listening to yours. You see, you are in this class because it may be the most important course you take your entire college career." She pushed up her black-rimmed glasses and continued.

"A poll was taken not too long ago and from the results, we found out that people are afraid of public speaking more than death." She paused as that fact sunk in Vincent's mind. "So my job is to get you over that fear," and she paused, staring at her captive audience for dramatic effect before finishing, "but it won't be easy."

Again she paused. "How many of you have already bought the book for this course?"

Half of the class raised their books. Vincent didn't have one yet. His advisor had told him not to get a book until the professor said so, and he was glad he listened.

"Well," the lady said, "go back to the store and get your money back, or whatever percentage they will give you. You'll not need a book here. I don't believe in book learning. I have a Ph.D. for a reason, and it's to give you my knowledge, not to read to you out of a book." She paused for a moment while looking at some papers she pulled out of her briefcase. After five seconds, she said, as stoically as ever, "Today's topic is how you got here. First up, Michelle Smith."

Vincent, as well as the other twenty students in attendance, looked around until he found a short brunette with dessert plates for eyes. Her medium-length hair was back in a ponytail, and she wore a shirt that had NCA Cheer in big block letters. After a bit of deliberation, she stood and approached the podium. Dr. Vonnegut found one of the many open seats in the front row, crossed her legs professionally, and folded her arms across her chest.

Michelle stood behind the podium and leaned on it for support, surely her knees buckling behind the wooden blind. She took a wisp of hair and curled it around her finger as she searched for the words that weren't coming. Finally, syllables found her lips. "Well, um—. "

"Thank you Michelle," Dr. Vonnegut said in an icy voice. "You may step down now."

The poor girl looked about ready to cry as she took her seat.

Dr. Vonnegut said, "The second rule in public speaking is to always look confident, even if you're not." Without expression she turned in her chair toward Michelle, who was now beet red, and said mechanically, "Oh, don't worry sweetie. You'll have plenty more grades in this class."

This put the poor girl over the edge as she ran from the room crying, forgetting to close the door behind her. Dr. Vonnegut didn't even flinch. "Next on the list, Caleb Adams."

Again everybody looked around the room until one of the dunderheads walked up to the podium, his hoodie still on his head.

"And, I thank you," Dr. Vonnegut said in an even tone.

The guy held both palms up in the air.

"Next on the list is Vincent Preston."

Vincent summoned up all his courage just to stand. To say that he was scared of Dr. Vonnegut was to put it mildly. He was petrified! He didn't know what mistake he was going to make to be sent back to his desk in shame, but willing all of his power, he walked to the podium. Caleb was still standing there, a shocked look on his face. His palms were still face-up. When he saw Vincent standing next to him, he relented reluctantly and took his seat, shaking his head the whole way.

Vincent tried to copy everything that he saw Dr. Vonnegut do at the beginning of class. He was wishing he had run by the cafeteria for a cup of java. He faced the audience, cleared his voice, smiled in defiance, and said, "Hello, my name is Vincent, and I got here by walking."

A few people snickered, thinking Vincent was joking, and Dr. Vonnegut shifted in her seat, looking like she was about ready to make another point, but Vincent quickly continued, "Seriously, I don't even have a car. A few weeks ago, I didn't have a college to go to either." He paused, collecting his thoughts and hoping whatever next came out of his mouth was more astute than sophomoric. Dr. Vonnegut shifted in her seat again and waited.

"I'm used to walking everywhere. In my hometown, I pretty much walk everywhere because my parents didn't want to take me anywhere." Now, feeling more comfortable with a direction, he continued. "My walk in life hasn't been easy, and I've failed more than I've succeeded, but no matter what, I continue to put one foot in front of the other. I guess that is why I walked here."

Vincent smiled and went back to his seat. The students in class clapped for him, and Vincent felt good about himself. Dr. Vonnegut didn't clap at all. She merely shuffled her papers and said, "Beth Davis."

After class all the students slipped out as fast as they could. Vincent caught a look over his shoulder to see Dr. Vonnegut scribbling on her pad. Frankly he didn't want to know what he did wrong, but he was pretty sure it was everything.

He had half an hour before his biology class started, and the walk was all of five minutes, if he took a leisurely pace. To waste some time, he walked over to the student union to peek inside. With backpack strung over one shoulder, for he had noticed that was how all students wore them in college, he opened the big glass doors and surveyed the scene.

On the left was the bookstore. The first time he went in there was a bad experience for him. The registrar's office has a representative in the back of the bookstore. They wanted it to be more convenient for the students to pay for their classes, all their fees, and then buy books or laptops, if they so choose.

The lady who manned the desk really didn't appear as if she liked her job. She wore a frown on her face that no amount of smiling on Vincent's part could cure. Vincent soon found out why. When he was given a list of extra fees, he about fell over backwards. Two pages of fees ranging from ten dollars to fifty dollars: paper fee, computer usage fee, parking fee, bicycle fee, cafeteria fee, street maintenance fee, electricity fee, water fee, sanitation fee, health fee (with 3 free visits to the clinic!) sidewalk fee, grass fee, safety fee, escort fee, tutor fee (with no free visits,) and his favorite, a solar fee. He didn't know how he was responsible for paying for the sun to shine! The list went on and on, and Vincent couldn't figure out how on earth he was going to take advantage of everything he had to pay for. He was sure Evan's parents just paid the bill, but Vincent would have no such luck. It was a huge draw on his checking account.

Just past the bookstore was a large room with pool tables and ping pong tables, pop machines and arcade games. On the right was a little short-order restaurant with open seating. It was plenty busy with most of the college now up and awake. It appeared that breakfast in Arizona looked much the same as it did in Oklahoma, that is, greasy.

Next to the greasy spoon was a coffee shop called Jumpin' Joes Java. That appealed to him, so he walked by the strong smell of sizzling bacon and stood in a line with more sleepy college students. Again he was by far the best dressed among them. As the line slowly moved, Vincent looked at the menu on the wall and couldn't believe what he saw. The cheapest cup of coffee was two dollars and fifty cents, and there were plenty of specialty coffees that he had never heard of that were much more expensive. He quickly computed his finances and how many times he would be able to get a cup of coffee at this place before he drained the rest of his checking account, and he figured he would be broke before Thanksgiving.

"Welcome to Jumpin' Joes Java. What can I get you?" The

girl behind the counter broke his concentration.

Vincent tried to smile and said, "Uh, uh," looked up at the menu again in hopes of there being something cheaper. He didn't want to sound…poor, but that was exactly what he was, so to save face, he came up with a lie on the spot.

"Thank you, but I have to run off to class," Vincent quickly glanced at his watch to make the lie seem plausible.

"The next class isn't for another half-hour," the girl said, but Vincent apologized again and ducked out of line, embarrassed, a few people snickering in line behind him.

On the way out of the store he caught a glimpse of a brunette with a white bow in her hair sitting alone at a corner table. She was looking at him, and when her big brown eyes met his, she smiled, showing off her red lipstick. Still embarrassed, Vincent half-smiled back, and then lowered his gaze to his feet and exited the shop the way he had come. Halfway down the walkway, he looked back and saw that the brunette was still watching him.

Vincent had made it a point not to date to this point for many reasons, chief amongst them the fact that girls typically weren't interested in him. At his high school, he had a reputation as a loner. If a girl had feigned interest in him, as Betty Franklin did in junior high, she would die a slow social death at the hands of the fickle mob. She had become so ostracized by her friends that she left the school to be home-schooled.

Now that Vincent was in college, he had no reputation. He could even change his name if he wanted to. It was a fresh start, and that girl's angelic smile was enough to make him feel as if he were floating on a cloud. Just thinking about her made the butterflies he experienced the other night come back in full force. He had no idea of how to act around girls. None whatsoever. Maybe that was something Evan could teach him. Evan seemed to have that skill down pat.

Vincent reached the glass doors to the outside and considered for a moment going back to introduce himself to the girl in the corner of the coffee shop, but he noticed a stairway leading to the basement just to his left. Curiosity got the better of him, and choosing the path of least embarrassment, he descended into a large room with a bowling alley, ten lanes in all. Nobody was bowling at the moment. Vincent checked his watch again, remembered that he had no money whatsoever to waste on foolish stuff like this, and wished he had an allowance from wealthy parents that he could blow like Evan. His frugal side was all too much a guiding spirit for him, and with decision, Vincent ran back up the stairs.

Five minutes later he found himself waiting in a seat in the middle of the lecture hall in the science building, twenty minutes before class were to begin. Again he was the first person there. To make the time go by more quickly, he counted seats one-by-one and was midway through the right half of the auditorium at 120 when the next student showed up. Slowly the seats began to fill, and the room became quite congested. Vincent had never been in such a large classroom with over 100 students and couldn't fathom how the professor was going to learn all of their names.

Just like his first class, the professor came in right when class was due to start. He was a young-looking man with an unruly red beard who appeared very robotic, laser focused on his task. The lecture hall was quite noisy until he spoke into the microphone, looking down the whole time, his voice as rushed as his appearance.

"Good morning, students. My name is Mr. Stillwell. This is Principles of Biology 1029." Mr. Stillwell grabbed a huge stack of papers and said, "If anyone in here took this course because I am the new instructor, and I don't have a doctorate, and you think it's going to be easy, then there's the door. I suggest you take it and enroll in something else."

He looked up from his papers and pointed to the double doors at the top of the stairs, just past where Vincent sat. Vincent felt a lump in his throat and swallowed it down as everyone stared in his direction.

After nobody headed for the exit, Mr. Stillwell continued, "That's a common misconception. If anything, I plan to grade even tougher than the tenured professors at this university, because I believe in the importance of this class. So again, if anyone wants out, there's the door."

Vincent looked around for the student that got booted from his speech class that morning, but apparently he wasn't in this class.

Mr. Stillwell waited a few more seconds then continued, "No, I'm not a doctor. YET." He emphasized the "Yet." "But if you have to retake this course next semester, that's what you'll call me." He surveyed the students' faces, none of which showed any emotion. He shook his head and said, "I'm required to tell you that if you have any disabilities, you need to inform me in writing so I can provide accommodations in compliance with ADA regulations." He shook his head and whispered something under his breath that Vincent couldn't make out, then continued. "Here's your course syllabus. There will be a quiz over this on Wednesday, so study it. I want you to know everything in this syllabus by heart."

Vincent gulped as the syllabi made their way around the room. The hour ran by very quickly from that point on. Vincent was so busy writing down everything Mr. Stillwell said that when the period was up, it felt as if only fifteen minutes had gone by. He had taken down five pages of notes and wished he had a laptop like so many other students around him. Typing was so much faster than writing. He received confirmation that he needed to buy the textbook. The syllabus had it listed at seventy-five dollars. Vincent sweated bullets over that one. He hoped he would be able to find a used copy.

Back across the small campus in five minutes, Vincent found himself waiting for another thirty minutes for his English professor, this time in a classroom that only held twenty-five seats. Vincent quickly decided he needed something to do in between classes. Hiding in the classroom and waiting wasn't good for his image.

Finally this was a class he was excited about. He figured that English Comp I should be right up his alley. The biology course was obviously going to be tough, and he didn't know what to make out of the speech class. Both seemed to be X factors toward making a 4.0 GPA, but he felt right at home in an English classroom. He felt even better when his professor came in and smiled at the class. She was an adjunct professor, a public school teacher in town for forty years who had retired, but really didn't want to retire. To bide her time, she taught a few college courses and mentioned what a delight it was to see some of the local students in this class.

Her name was Ms. Wallace, and she spent the first thirty minutes of class talking about her philosophy, that all students could learn, and that it merely took hard work to accomplish their dreams. She reminded Vincent a lot of his senior English teacher, Mrs. Dean, in that Ms. Wallace seemed to care. He learned that he wouldn't need a textbook for this class, a relief. He would be writing ten compositions during the course of the semester, one research paper, and nine shorter works, one of which was due on Wednesday. So far, in three classes, he had to write a one page narrative on his life story and study for a biology quiz that wasn't even about biology. And that was just for

Wednesday. Tomorrow's classes included Psychology and American Literature Pre 1800.

In all Vincent carried nineteen hours, which his advisor told him was a large load for an incoming freshmen, but not insurmountable. Thankfully baseball counted as one credit hour, as did Freshmen Orientation. All he had to do for orientation was log in "Doughnut" hours so that the school could justify having all the library resources. Vincent knew that wouldn't be a problem as he intended to visit the library nightly. He was also given the passwords to the online databases for research purposes, which he could also log in toward orientation hours. Now that it was lunchtime, all he could think about was running back to the Cactus Cafe and grabbing some grub. Having missed breakfast, his stomach growled loud enough for others to hear it.

On his way he stopped at his dorm to drop off his books and to see if Evan wanted to go eat. Vincent had decided that he needed to befriend his roommate, be proactive in his approach, otherwise it would be a long semester. When Vincent opened the door, light from the open window in the hallway flowed into the dark cave. It was the work of a few seconds for Vincent's eyes to readjust, but when they did, he saw his roommate asleep on his bed, the girl he had brought in gone.

The lump under the blanket didn't move, and not knowing what else to do, Vincent dropped his book bag just inside the door and closed it as gently as he could. It was a strange way to end a strange morning.

Chapter Six

VINCENT SAT BY himself and ate as slowly as he could. He had hoped to see someone from the baseball team and sit next to him, but he didn't recognize any faces in the crowded cafeteria. In his seat at a corner table, Vincent tried to be invisible. He took deliberate bites of his hamburger and chewed slowly, wishing he had brought his backpack to lunch so that he could go over what he had learned that morning. He quickly decided that if he was going to have to sit alone for lunch, he would take advantage of the down time to be productive. Vincent had a whole round of thoughts on that subject until Evan surprised him, plopping himself down next to Vincent.

The prodigal roommate looked like he had dressed with the light on. He wore a pair of khaki shorts and a bowling shirt with flip flops, an ensemble that really showed off his tanned legs. His hair was a disheveled mess that appeared messy on purpose. The gel was still drying in his hair and made it look cool somehow. Nobody else in the cafeteria had hair as cool as Evan's because everyone else wore ball caps. Vincent noted the stares his roommate received from a table of girls behind him who he could only assume were basketball players, since most wore basketball shorts and tank tops with their hair up in ponytails.

"What's up roomie?" Evan said as he patted Vincent on the back. Evan's plate was filled with what appeared to be one food from each section. Before Vincent could say anything, Evan continued, "You check out the grub this place has? Disgusting stuff! I swear they must be trying to drum up patients for the infirmary. I mean, look at this pizza!" Evan held it up and took a big bite and dropped it back on the plate, right into his spaghetti. Either the spaghetti sauce or the pizza sauce splattered the table for a foot radius. "Disgusting stuff!"

Vincent smiled, wondering why Evan would take a bite if it were so gross.

"And the chicks here!" Evan laughed as he spooned a glob of cottage cheese freckled with bacon bits into his mouth. "They are off the hook!" Some bits of masticated food shot out of his mouth as he talked and Evan washed down what was left in his mouth with a glass of milk. "There was a party last night. Bunch of us met up and got a keg and took it out somewhere. I don't know where. Man, we howled at the moon. Girls dancing on top of hoods. I mean, it wasn't real swank, you know? No prissy girls here. It's just different here, you know? Lot of fun. Crazy stuff. You shoulda come!"

"I was busy," Vincent quickly chimed in, hoping his four syllables wouldn't be interrupted in the middle.

"Busy? Man, I've got to get you out tonight. I heard there's going to be a party by the dam. You game? Man, what coulda been so important last night?"

Vincent smiled and looked down at his empty tray. "I had that scrimmage."

Evan shoveled in a spoonful of some sludgy sugary cereal. He smiled with that bite and went silent for a second. "The scrimmage! I forgot. Hey man, how did you do?"

"I pitched pretty well." Vincent was just about to elaborate when one of the girls from the table behind him sat down next to Evan.

"So what's your name," the girl asked, giving a suggestive look.

Evan wiped his mouth and turned his attention away from Vincent and to this interloper. "It's Evan. What's your name, babe?"

"I'm Alexis," the girl said and looked back toward her friends who were all staring. She motioned with her head and the entire table got up and reparked their trays around Evan. Feeling uncomfortable, or maybe unwanted, Vincent got up and put his tray away. He didn't bother to look back.

Vincent practiced that afternoon, his mind abuzz. It was hard to focus on baseball. His first day of school had been full of difficulties, and it wasn't over yet. After practice and dinner, he planned to run to The Doughnut and log onto the computers for at least an hour. Without a laptop and Internet connection, he was going to just have to put in some seat hours at The Doughnut, especially with his first paper being due on Wednesday.

Thursdays were going to be a bear. After his two Tuesday/Thursday classes, each of which would take an hour and a half, he would have to grab a quick bite to eat before he rushed back to the main campus for a two hour afternoon biology lab. This would leave him very little time to get ready for practice. His attention was so taken with the stress of his academic schedule that he dazed out into left field during batting practice, and the pitching coach beaned him in the small of the back to get him to refocus.

The team ate together in the cafeteria, taking up a third of the available room. Vincent sat with them but didn't feel too compelled to speak. He nodded when others nodded and smiled when somebody cracked a joke, but from the time he went to practice to the time he made it back into his dorm for a quick breather, he had barely said five words. It seemed to be a groove he was settling in since his roommate seemed to have enough words for the both of them.

When Vincent returned to his dorm room, the first thing he noticed when he walked in was that three girls were sitting on his bed. The bed had not been made that morning since he had to dress in the dark, so he was instantly embarrassed.

"Hey roomie!" Evan belted from the other bed where there were two more girls. Vincent figured they must be from the basketball team, but was instantly corrected. "These girls are on the tennis team. Girls, this is my roommate, uh," Evan stopped and looked down at the ground.

"Vincent," Vincent reminded him.

"Yes! It's Vincent! Girls, this is Vincent. He's the best baseball player at the whole school. Here, look!"

He grabbed a copy of the school newspaper off his desk and handed it to Vincent. Right there on the front page was Vincent's picture on the mound, his stare locked in at his catcher. It made Vincent smile. He looked up to say something and stopped short. Evan had a beer in his hand and was chugging it. Upon closer inspection, all five girls had beers.

"Uh, Evan?"

Evan took another pull, burped, which made the girls giggle, then said, "Yeah, buddy?"

"Are you out of your mind?" Vincent pointed to Evan's beer.

"Awe, c'mon man! It's no big thing. Just getting a head start on the party tonight. Here, grab yourself one!" Evan reached into the mini fridge which was hidden under the desk and a tablecloth and pulled out another can. He offered it to Vincent who pulled his hand away as if the can were a diamondback poised to strike.

"Do you know what will happen if the RA catches you with beer in here? We'll both be kicked out of the dorms!"

One of the girls giggled at this suggestion and Evan said to her, "You laughed! You have to drink! C'mon, empty it!"

The girl obliged, tipping it, letting some spill down her cheeks and onto Vincent's comforter.

Vincent was speechless.

"Hey, what's going on in here?" The voice came from behind Vincent's shoulder. He just knew this was the resident assistant or worse, the head assistant. When he turned around, he saw two guys wearing NCA Tennis tee shirts. "You guys getting started without us?" the first one asked and slipped by Vincent and sat on Vincent's bed between two of the girls. The second guy parked it on the end and tickled the girl who had committed the party foul.

"Seriously, Vincent! Shut the door before we do get in trouble," Evan said and turned his attention back to the two girls on his bed, tipping the bottom of one of the girl's bottles. Vincent looked down at himself, still in his dusty practice uniform. He wanted to shower, change into something fresh, and head for The Doughnut, but where was he going to change? There was absolutely no privacy. He secretly wondered if he would ever have privacy.

Evan had ignored Vincent's simple request to get the beer out of the room and the eight continued laughing. Vincent grabbed his book bag off the back of his office chair and honored his roommate's request, shutting the door on the way out.

The sun was low in the desert sky, and the searing arid air radiated around Vincent. In an old pair of flip-flops, he slowly trudged to The Doughnut. He was glad that he brought his flip-flops because it would be very awkward click-clacking up the walk and into the library in his spikes.

When he finally sat down at a desktop computer, he wondered how he was going to get out of the mess he had inherited. This roommate was going to get him in trouble. There was no doubt about that. It was a mathematic certainty. The further into the school year he made it with his roommate, the better the chance would be of getting caught. Simple law of averages.

Vincent pondered this impossible situation. He logged onto the old desktop computer and opened a word document. He stared at the blank page for hours, hoping for some inspiration. Nothing came to him. He browsed on the Internet, checking his e-mail, dismayed to find that all he had in his inbox was junk. He closed down The Doughnut at 10:00, walking out without a shred of his work done.

The night sky was obscured with high clouds. None of the clouds would produce a drop of rain. Vincent was exhausted, ready for bed, but he really enjoyed the evening. The desert nights were always so cool, the air refreshing his spirit, which was pretty shot by now. Vincent snuck into the common area that he shared with two other rooms and stuck his ear up to his door. He heard nothing, so he entered.

The room smelled horrible. A case-worth of crushed beer cans was littered all over the floor, in the trash can, and even on his bed. His comforter reeked of stale beer, or maybe that was the overall stench of the room that had soaked into his nostrils. Either way, something had to be done, so Vincent opened a window and lit a few matches.

Still in his filthy practice uniform, Vincent reenacted a ritual he had done many times in his youth when his father went on benders. He cleaned the room, bagging up all the beer cans and spraying the room down with a bleach-based deodorizer. It seemed to help a little.

Vincent took a quick shower, hoping that he wouldn't emerge with the whole tennis team waiting with their camera phones at the ready. Vincent went back into his room and still noticed the stench of beer. Remembering his comforter, he stripped the bed and threw the linens into a trash bag. He would have to wash them tomorrow when he wasn't so tired.

He stood in front of his bare bed, the old, stained mattress not exactly greeting him. His alarm clock read 11:17. It was all the strength he could muster to close the window. With the room now smelling slightly better, he grabbed the towel which he used to dry off after his shower and covered up as well as he could. He was asleep in no time, forgetting his pledge to lay out his clothes for the next day.

Chapter Seven

AS LUCK WOULD have it, it didn't matter that he didn't lay out his clothes. He had gotten himself up half an hour earlier and turned on the light to see that his roommate had never made it in. Vincent didn't know where the guy was, and frankly he didn't care much. He hoped the guy would never come back.

On the way out the door a thought occurred to Vincent, so he walked over to where Evan had hid his mini fridge and opened the door. Other than twin bottles of ketchup and mustard, the fridge was bare. As he closed the door, one more thought raced through his mind, and as he peered under Evan's bed, he found the mother lode. Empty beer cans had been stored under his bed, probably kicked under there absentmindedly.

He picked up every can, four sacks worth, then found another dozen under his own bed! Clearly he would have to have a conversation with Evan, but he didn't feel he had the strength to confront his roommate. Besides, Evan seemed to be a nice guy and was even trying to plug Vincent into the social pipeline, which Evan seemed to have figured out already.

Vincent made a mental note to wash his bed sheets and comforter right after lunch, the only time he would have today. With a sigh, Vincent loaded his backpack onto his back, grabbed all the sacks, and walked out into the hallway. He had to make a beeline out the back door where the dumpsters were, and prayed he wouldn't meet the RA. Right as he got to the back door, his worst fears were confirmed.

"Hey, hold it right there!"

Vincent heard the voice come from behind and considered making a run for it, but a cool head took over. He opened the door and slipped the bags of beer cans outside, then shut the door and turned to face the RA.

The RA walked very quickly toward Vincent, and surprising him, the guy extended his right hand. Vincent shook it out of reflex, then quickly wondered if his own hands smelt of stale beer. The smell was burned into his nostrils.

The RA was a good six feet tall with a pimply complexion that looked like it had gone untreated for quite some time. That was the only feature Vincent could concentrate on because the rest of his concentration was taken up with the five sacks loaded with empty beer cans on the other side of this door.

"I don't know if you were at the dorm meeting the other night, but I wanted to introduce myself. My name is Michael Caughlin, and I am the first floor RA here at Newport." The RA beamed when he said this.

The handshake lasted longer than Vincent was comfortable with, and when he finally pulled his hand away, his RA said, "Just make sure you keep your nose clean, and I won't pull any surprise inspections on you. But if you are doing something stupid like drinking, I will find out." He raised his right hand to his face and sniffed. He wrinkled his nose at the smell, and Vincent's heart started racing.

"Say, what's that cologne you're wearing?" Michael asked.

Vincent thought quick and replied, "It's my aftershave. Pretty strong isn't it?" It occurred only after Vincent said this that he wasn't freshly shaven. In fact he hadn't shaved in a week because it appeared to be the cool look for the baseball players.

Michael took this in, looked sideways at Vincent, then the vise that held his neck in place must have released. He smiled and said, "Well Vincent, it was good to meet you. I expect I will be seeing you again very soon. Have fun at class." The RA walked away, and it was only at that moment that Vincent noticed the guy was in his boxer shorts and bare feet.

At first Vincent breathed a sigh of relief as he slipped out the door, picked up the sacks of beer cans and quickly disposed of them in the dumpster. But on the sidewalk up the hill to the campus, a thought occurred to him that he had been red flagged. Maybe the RA didn't get the handcuffs on him this time, but Vincent was sure that his room was now ripe for inspection. This was more weight on his shoulders. The guy was probably walking into his room that very second, so Vincent hoped he had done away with all the evidence.

This troubled him all the way to the other side of the campus to his first class at Burtner Hall, where all the history classes were taught. When he sat down, the first student in the classroom again, it occurred to him that he should have walked through the student union to see if the brunette who had smiled at him yesterday was there again. He vowed to do just that after Psychology.

Psych was great, mostly because the professor was really loose and relaxed. It gave Vincent time to get control of his nerves. This first week of college had been so hectic and confusing that Vincent felt as if he were trapped in a tornado, whirling out of control. He hoped the distractions like his roommate would just fade and leave him with a simple college life, but here he was, heading to the coffee shop to seek out another distraction with the girl.

As his eyes scanned the room, the butterflies in his stomach faded when he did not find her, so he instead went to the bookstore to buy a couple of textbooks, which would put him in financial strain for the rest of the year, despite buying them second hand. He knew that his lit class would require a textbook, so he just buckled down and bought it.

After such drama in his classes the day before, Vincent's Tuesday classes seemed to breeze by, which he was thankful for. After class, Vincent found himself on the outside of his room door, praying that his roommate wasn't in. He really was dreading talking to Evan about the drinking. Considering his upbringing, Vincent was morally opposed to drinking. Alcohol turned his father into a monster nightly, and the abuse that followed would always be seared into his memory. Alcohol caused his father to not just beat on Vincent, but also abuse Vincent's mother. Alcohol indirectly caused his mother to neglect Vincent out of fear for her husband's wrath. Alcohol was poison.

Vincent knew underage kids did drink—did it in high school and college would be no different—and that no matter what he said, it would continue to happen. His roommate would be no different. What really worried Vincent was drinking and driving, and he quickly wondered how often Evan got behind the wheel drunk.

In addition there was his scholarship to consider. If the RA had caught him with the beer cans that morning, it wouldn't have been Evan with his butt in a sling. Something had to be done. If self-preservation was at all important to Vincent, then he needed to have the talk.

With a silent prayer, he slid his key into the lock and turned the handle to the door. When his eyes adjusted, he saw exactly what he left behind that morning, an empty room that stank of stale beer.

Vincent exhaled and threw his book bag on top of his desk, relieved that he could put the speech off for another time, yet wishing he could just get it over with. He supposed that there was a slim chance that Evan was in class. To Vincent's knowledge Evan had missed all his classes yesterday, but then Vincent hadn't seen Evan's schedule. To be considered full-time Evan had to be taking at least twelve hours. Knowing what he knew about his roommate, twelve hours were probably about all he was taking. Evan seemed like the type to do the minimum amount of work possible. Shutting the door, Vincent went to lunch.

That afternoon's practice went much better than the day before. Vincent was able to concentrate much better, probably because he worked on his pitching, which was all concentration. He felt more than a little unsure about his hitting. He knew he shouldn't let one little strikeout in the scrimmage affect him so much, but after a stellar senior year in high school where he dominated at the plate, he expected himself to crush every pitch. He was soon finding that everyone on the team was good. Around here, Vincent knew he was…average.

After another awkward dinner at which he again felt like an outsider, Vincent retired to his dormitory room to get some work done on that essay that was due in his English Comp I class the next day. Without thinking, he opened the door to see the prodigal roommate.

"Just who I've been looking for," Evan said and stood to greet Vincent. Instinctively, Vincent took a step back when Evan approached him, but all that his roommate wanted to do was pat him on the back and welcome him home.

"There's a huge party going down at McEwan Bridge tonight. It's supposed to be real sick. Ten kegs, chicks galore, and I'm bringing something extra!" Evan gave Vincent a wink and let him enter. Vincent did so, stepping gingerly, not knowing what he was stepping into.

Sensing he had an opening to talk, Vincent opened up a round of questioning. "So Evan, where've you been?"

"Had to sleep one off at this chick's house last night. It was real cool though. I crashed on the couch and raided the fridge this afternoon when I woke up."

"So what time did you get back here?" Vincent asked.

Evan looked up and to his left to recall the time. When he finally did, he said, "Oh, around 2:00 or so. Came back and took a shower. Some serious funk growing on the walls of that shower. I wonder when the maid comes around?"

"Uh, I don't think we have a maid. I think we have to do it ourselves."

"What...?" Evan started, but Vincent butted in to keep the conversation focused.

"What about tennis practice?"

"What about it?" Evan countered, his tone becoming less cordial. His eyes sharpened on Vincent.

"Don't you have tennis practice?"

"Sure," Evan said, his countenance changing slightly. "I went to practice at 3:00 this afternoon." Evan sat back down on his bed, kicked his feet up and crossed them as he put his hands behind his head, a serious look on his face despite such a lax pose.

"Okay," Vincent said before continuing, "what about your classes?"

Evan was evidently annoyed by now. "What about my classes?"

"Are you making them?" Vincent asked, knowing the answer.

"Well, Mom," Evan said and sat up straight, "everyone knows the first few days are just syllabus and boring stuff. Besides, why is that any of your business?"

Vincent could easily sense now that he had crossed some line, so he changed direction. "I met the RA this morning."

"Yeah, and?"

"He about busted me carting off bags of your beer cans."

Evan sat back down and laughed. "I got the 411 on that dweeb. Don't worry. He won't be a problem."

Vincent was flushed, his voice rising, "Well I shouldn't have had to clean up after you and then almost get caught! Besides, my comforter and sheets were soaked with beer. I had to sleep with my towel as a blanket last night." Vincent was fuming now, and didn't feel as bad as he thought he would for yelling at his roommate.

Evan sighed and put his head down. "Sorry about that. Rachel kept laughing and spilling her beer. I finally sat her down in my desk chair, but then she spilled it on the floor—which I cleaned up myself!" Evan said this last part as if it were something to be proud of, a favor he did Vincent.

Vincent went for his comforter and sheets. The smell had gained strength from fermenting for a day in the bag. It made Vincent gag.

"Well, you should know that we've been red-flagged now. Expect the RA to come any day for a surprise inspection, so keep the stuff out of here!" Vincent said as he walked out.

"I guess you don't want to know what I have in my pocket then." Evan reached in and pulled out a baggy full of green stuff. Vincent took one look back in disgust and left for the laundry room with his trash sack of soiled laundry, slamming the door behind him.

Vincent mumbled under his breath all the way to the second floor laundry room. He didn't know what he was going to do with his roommate. Still, he was torn. Evan had tried to befriend him. It was just obvious that the two of them had very different views on morality and ethical behavior. Was Vincent being a prude? Did he need to chill out and go with the flow? Maybe this is how a person acts in college. He quickly passed the thought out of his mind. Still, Vincent had shown his hand. He had now burned the bridge with his roommate, and he doubted things would ever be the same between them. Maybe he just needed to switch rooms. He knew that there were some open rooms up on the fourth floor. Maybe he could get a room without a roommate.

Vincent cringed at the thought of using change on laundry that he had earmarked for washing clothes that next weekend. He didn't have much in the way of clothing, and did his best to reuse clothes that didn't appear dirty or smell bad. Every penny counted. He drew the line at socks and underwear, of course, and Coach Johnson demanded that the athletes practiced in clean uniforms. Thankfully the baseball team had a student assistant who was in charge entirely of laundry. It must have been a rough way to earn a scholarship.

Vincent hadn't had the presence of mind to bring his backpack with him to the laundry room. He had been so mad at Evan that he just wanted to get out of there. Well, sitting on top of a washing machine, he wished he could be shooting two birds with one stone. That paper for his comp class wasn't going to write itself, so he scoured behind the machines until he found a half-eaten pencil and a blank sheet of copy paper covered in an inch of dryer lint dust. He set to work composing his first college essay by using the washing machine as a desk. The spin cycle proved interesting.

Facing the music, Vincent went back to his room after his laundry was done to find it vacant. He threw the bundle of linens on his bed. He grabbed his backpack and lugged it up to The Doughnut to type and submit his essay. Just to be cautious, he printed it off, then worked on his other homework for the next day. When he returned late that evening, Evan was nowhere to be found, but both his and Vincent's beds had been made.

Chapter Eight

THE NEXT MORNING butterflies fluttered in Vincent's stomach. They made him feel as if he had to pee all morning long, despite frequent trips to the restroom. Evan had not come back last night either, and Vincent wondered if the butterflies he was feeling was a result of remorse about speaking so harshly to Evan.

The butterflies didn't fade when Vincent walked into the student union to look for the brunette. The smile she had given him the other day was haunting him, and he wished he could find her again.

High school had been a series of survival maneuvers, which left absolutely no time for girls. He had no friends, male or female, and the idea of any type of relationship was foreign. But the brunette had definitely caught his eye. Just thinking about her made feel queasy. If this was what love was all about, then maybe he was better off without it.

Vincent had stopped by the coffee shop and peered in before

his speech class, after his speech class, and before his biology lecture, and each time he caught no glimpse of her. His emotions were contorted. Each time he felt relieved that he didn't have to come up with something suave to say to her, but he also felt sad, like maybe he was never going to see her again. After all, there were over 3000 students who went to school there, which was roughly the population of his hometown. It was like trying to find a needle in a stack of needles.

Vincent had really never felt lonely because he hadn't ever known what it was like to be loved. Sure, Grandpa and Mrs. Dean had shown him love that summer while mentoring him, but other than that, he had never truly had companionship with anybody his own age. So it caught him off-guard every time some guy on the sidewalk would address him by name. "Hey, what's up Vincent?"

"Not much," he would say, lowering his head, hoping to avoid a conversation in which small talk was required. That was something of which he was definitely void.

"So, what do you think of the weather?"

"Hot as blazes."

"Yeah, this is Arizona after all."

"Yeah."

Awkward pause.

"Well, later."

"Yeah. You too."

Frankly, small talk didn't suit him. If he could build a relationship with his teammates, the people he assumed were being friendly with him on campus, then he wouldn't have to go to a discussion about the weather. But what then? What would he talk about? What did kids his age talk about? Would he be required to open up about his past? Tell his deepest, darkest secrets? Inform everybody how his father once broke a beer bottle over his head? Or would he have to tell them about the time he was bound in bed with his own tube socks tied to each wrist and ankle, to be beaten with a water hose? These were the conversations he wanted to avoid, and if letting people into his world meant letting people into his world then he would rather pass.

So small talk it was. Or a tip of the cap. Or a, "Whassup?"

He would rather hide out in his room and do his homework, but now that was off limits because of his roommate. There was always The Doughnut. Find some hidden corner back by the research stacks and just work on his school work. After all, that was why he was there. Really, between his past and his roommate, and his emotions that were all jumbled, college wasn't as liberating as he had hoped. It felt more like a prison. The only real place he feet at home was on the mound at Johnson Field. He would get that chance that night against South West Utah.

At 6:00 he was in the bullpen warming up with Tank catching him. Butterflies? Not a chance! This is where he excelled. This was what he was called to do. He felt it as strongly as anything he had ever felt, and when his fingers felt the laces on the ball in his glove and his eyes looked at his catcher's mitt sixty feet, six inches away, the world just seemed to make sense. All the complications of the real world were thrown out the window. All that mattered was the smell of leather and freshly cut grass, and a fastball that would burn a wormhole through the air. He heard nothing, said nothing, felt nothing. Even when Tank was giving him pointers, Vincent was in his own little place. If only baseball were the real world.

That evening Vincent didn't speak to anybody on the team, and they, in return, didn't speak to him. Being baseball players, they all knew the superstitions inherent in hardball, avoiding a player in the zone chief among them.

Vincent stood on top of the mound and allowed himself one glance at the crowd. The entire population of Page, Arizona seemed to be crammed into the ball park. The stands were filled to capacity and there was standing room only behind the fences along the baselines, despite the fact that the bleachers extended down each baseline, all the way to the fence where San Antonio Hill dropped off.

Vincent turned around and took a look down at Lake Powell a few miles away. The sun was still high enough in the sky that it didn't cast a glare off the water, and Vincent could make out boats zooming across the surface by the white wakes they left behind. He smiled and thought about those fly fishermen below the dam the other day, wondering if they were experiencing the same clairvoyance that Vincent enjoyed while on top of the mound.

Refocusing his attention, he turned around, and for the first time, he focused on the enemy. They wore white uniforms with red trim, each with pants that went all the way down to their cleats, with snaps that snapped into their shoes. Vincent didn't like the look of the pants much, looking down at his own blue pants with the red pinstripe that did the same thing. Every time he lifted his leg to pitch, he could feel it pulling. It felt restrictive, so he made a mental note to ask Coach if he could have more of a traditional pair of knickerbockers with high socks, the way ballplayers wore them in the golden age of baseball.

He shook his head and looked up at Tank who seemed to be perturbed. The batter was waiting in the batter's box, check swinging his bat, trying to gather a rhythm. The umpire behind the plate was crouched over in position, awaiting Vincent's first official college pitch.

With Vincent's attention in tow now, Tank showed one finger

and moved it from his left to his right, calling for a two-seam fastball which would tail away from the right-handed batter. Knowing better than to argue with his catcher who was a veteran at this point, Vincent quickly nodded and readjusted the ball in his glove to where his index and middle finger gripped the bottleneck of the ball where the two seams were closest together.

Vincent thought about Grandpa Dean's backyard lessons from that past summer, thought about the first time he ever threw the two-seam and how he couldn't control where it went at first, thought about how good it felt to have this secret knowledge from such a sage old man. He also winced at the memory of Grandpa Dean lying in that bed, half his former self, mere hours away from death. All of the sadness and rage and every other emotion he felt when his mentor died, all seemed to find itself into the potential energy contained in the little white ball with red stitching.

Vincent stared at tank's glove, looking for an identifying mark he could focus in on. Vincent went into the windup, grunted for all he was worth, and released, putting a little extra pressure on his middle finger to create the movement his catcher asked for.

Lightning!

The ball rocketed out of his hand and slid from the inside corner of the plate to the outside corner. The batter never lifted the bat off of his shoulder.

Thunder!

The ball clapped against the supple leather of Tank's catcher's mitt.

"STRIKE ONE!" the umpire behind the plate called out. The crowd went wild, half of them jumping up and down and pointing at the scoreboard. Vincent noticed this as he came out of his trance. He caught the ball from his catcher and turned around to look at the scoreboard and see the pitch's speed.

100 MPH

No wonder they are cheering, he thought. That was pretty hot!

Vincent shook his head at his reaction and promised himself that he would stop looking at the scoreboard after every pitch. He caught himself doing that at the state tournament and had paid the price.

"The faster you throw it, the farther the home run ball will go," Grandpa Dean had been fond of saying. Yup, Vincent had learned that one the hard way. It was the reason they had lost the state championship, but that was in the past, and Vincent wondered why he was bringing up all these old thoughts, emotions. He knew that being in the zone meant being in his own little world, but that was also a dangerous place to be if concentration on the job at hand weren't the main goal.

Vincent repositioned himself on top of the mound and waited for his catcher's signal.

Tank ordered up another fastball with the same movement.

At first Vincent thought that was not a good idea and thought about shaking his catcher off, but he relented. Going through the same ritual, Vincent delivered.

Lightning!

Thunder!

"STRIKE TWO!"

This time the batter had swung through but caught nothing but air. He had been behind, but not as slow as Vincent was used to seeing his opposition swing.

The crowd still cheered heartily, but Vincent tried to ignore it. He refused to look at the scoreboard, but the question of the pitch's speed was in the forefront of his mind. He was curious by nature and just wanted to take a quick peek.

No Vincent! Concentrate! Vincent repositioned himself on top of the rubber again to see Tank call for the exact same pitch.

92

Are you crazy? He'll time me! Ignoring his inner voice, Vincent dialed up all his energy and delivered the exact same pitch to the exact same location.

This time the batter let it go by, apparently expecting Vincent to try to lure him into swinging at a bad pitch. The pitch wasn't bad.

"STRIKE THREE! ONE AWAY!"

The crowd cheered lustily, but Vincent doing his best to ignore them, felt his concentration returning.

In the background his ears detected the loudspeaker announce the next batter, but Vincent's mind drifted to the aglet on the end of his shoelace on his left cleat. The aglet looked to be fraying a bit on the end. He stooped over, double-knotted it, and reassumed his position on the rubber.

Vincent looked up. The next batter, whoever he was, was a left-hander. Slender and fairly tall, he seemed to have an air of confidence about him.

Not wanting to humanize the batter anymore, Vincent instead concentrated on his catcher's hand which was showing one finger and pointing toward the batter.

Really? The same pitch again? Vincent thought really hard for an explanation as to why his catcher was giving the same pitch over and over, but came up with nothing. So spending half-a-second longer to nod to his catcher this time, a move that he shouldn't have done, he delivered another two-seam fastball.

Lightning!

Thunder!

The batter swung low, like he was wielding a golf club, and came up with air.

"STRIKE ONE!"

Vincent took the ball from Tank and repositioned himself, his mind only on the first two batters.

So, the first batter let the first pitch go by, but the second batter swung at the first pitch. What does that mean? Vincent came up with no answers, so he just placed his trust in his catcher, who finally called a different pitch, a changeup in the same location.

Making a show of it, Vincent grunted, only this time, with a circle grip on the ball, it came out much slower. The batter was taking all the way, but by the time he figured out it was a changeup, he lifted his bat and gave a check-swing.

Despite his neurons connecting, his swing was late.

"STRIKE TWO!"

This time Vincent turned around to see his pitch speed.

82 MPH

Vincent felt satisfied with the difference in speeds between the two pitches. That pitch was roughly one-fifth slower than his fastball. That pleased him, as did the fact that he had just used math. Also, the ploy had worked because when Vincent looked at the batter, he looked totally confused. Maybe Tank was smarter than he gave him credit for. Actually, there was no "maybe" about it.

In total confidence, Vincent took his catcher's sign and delivered a four-seam fastball on the outside corner, right across the knees.

Lightning!

Thunder!

The batter was much too astounded to swing.

"STRIKE THREE! TWO DOWN!"

Vincent caught the ball back from his catcher and turned around, but something caught his eye. He looked at the first row of the stands, just down the baseline from his dugout, and saw a kid hang a poster board from the top of the fence with a large letter "K" on it, which stood for strikeout. There were two of them side-by-side now, except that they were both backwards.

94

Vincent quickly deduced that it must stand for a strikeout where the batter doesn't swing at the last pitch.

The fans are keeping a count of my strikeouts! Another thing that I have to avoid eye-contact with! Still, deep down he thought that it was pretty cool. It was their way of honoring him, and he was touched.

Again, shaking his head, he made a few circles with his pitching arm to keep it warm, refocused on the plate, and gave a quick glance to the batter, a carbon copy of the last batter, only this time a right-hander.

Okay Tank, I am putty in your hands. Mold me.

Tank called for a four-seam fastball on the outside corner.

Lightning!

Thunder!

CRANK!

Vincent had hit his mark, but the batter had almost caught his timing, fouling one off into the stands along first base.

The umpire fired a new ball to Vincent, and he took his place on the rubber, hoping that Tank knew what he was doing. For most, a foul ball would mean nothing more than a strike. To Vincent, it meant he made a mistake. He knew he couldn't be perfect against college players, but he figured he would hold himself to this standard for as long as possible.

Vincent looked at Tank, who had a smile on his face of all things! He wouldn't give a sign until Vincent smirked back, under the mask of his glove that covered his face from the nose down. Apparently Vincent's eyes gave it away.

Finally Tank offered up a sign, a sinker. It wasn't Vincent's best pitch, but one he knew he had to master in order to save his arm with groundball outs. As Coach had told him in practice, there was a reason for having four infielders behind him.

Adjusting his grip, Vincent came home with a sinker. The

aggressive hitter swung for all he was worth, but was clean over the top of the ball.

"STRIKE TWO!"

Tank whipped the ball back to Vincent. He turned to the mound, and suddenly the brunette entered his mind.

Vincent, concentrate! He didn't know what on earth had come over him that his mind was all over the place. This was his safe haven. This little hill of dirt. *The bump.* What was going to distract him next? Still, his mind wandered to her smile, and it made him smile too. In fact his attention became so focused on the memory of her smile that he totally missed the sign. Vincent wiped the sweat from his brow and ran his right cleat across the rubber to make sure that it was properly clean of dirt.

When he refocused, he received his sign, another sinker. The ball sank at the batter's knees.

"STRIKE THREE! SIDE OUT!"

Vincent took his glove off his left hand and held it in his right hand while he walked off the mound to a standing ovation. The place was so loud that Vincent felt a little embarrassed. On top of the mound he was king, and at the same time, he was in his own world, safe from the pressures of the world. On his way to the dugout he felt a little vulnerable. Pitching a hat trick in the first inning, on nine pitches no less, only upped the high expectations placed upon him. He just hoped he wouldn't let the home crowd down.

He looked up at the student section above the dugout on the first base side and wondered if the brunette was watching him. The thought made him blush, so he put his glove over his face.

Tank was waiting for Vincent at the steps of the dugout and led him to the end of the pine so that they could have some privacy. They sat down, and Tank put his arm around Vincent and said, "That was a very good inning, Vincent. You're probably wondering about the pitch selection?"

Vincent nodded.

Tank chuckled a little and said, "Just wanted to take your arm out for a little drive. You know, push down on the accelerator." When Vincent looked questioningly at Tank, the catcher continued, "It's best to do that early on. You know, blow it by them while you have the arm. We will be a little more selective with the pitches the further in we get. We want them talking about how you rely on the fastball. That way we can work in more off-speed stuff to keep them off-balance. Make sense?"

Vincent nodded.

"Well, get your bat ready," Tank said.

Vincent looked at him strangely, so Tank continued, "You're leading off."

Vincent's butterflies returned. Leading off! Was Coach Johnson crazy? Vincent had never led off in a game before! He knew his job was to get on base however he could, and that he was seen as the rally starter. That was a lot of responsibility to shoulder. A ton of pressure. As fast as the butterflies arrived, they vanished as he grabbed his helmet and his favorite bat and walked out to the on-deck circle robotically.

Talking to Tank had given him no time to study the pitcher, so when Vincent had taken a few cuts, the pitcher threw his last warm up pitch, and the catcher fired the ball to the shortstop who was poised on top of second base, a perfect throw. It seemed everybody played perfectly in college.

The infielders tossed the ball around the infield, and Vincent stepped into the batter's box and took a couple of practice swings, entirely forgetting to check with Coach Johnson, who Vincent later found out, was in the third base coaching box trying to give him a signal to let the first pitch go.

A sign of perfect concentration, Vincent narrowed his focus

on the pitcher's eyes, which were as sharp as a hawk in the sky looking for a mouse in high grass. Vincent tried to read the corners of the pitcher's eyes, but they never changed.

Once the sign was agreed upon, the pitcher went into his windup. Something in the back of Vincent's mind said, *fastball...gotta be a fastball.* Vincent didn't know why he was thinking that and didn't pause to consider.

When the pitch came, it looked as big as a beach ball to Vincent, and the bat managed to swing by itself, robotically.

Vincent felt the slight tingle that accompanies a perfect connection, saw the bat out of his peripheral vision as it circled around to his left shoulder, all the while keeping his eye on the little white ball, which seemed to be getting smaller by the second. By instinct, Vincent dropped the bat and started trotting to first, watching the ball sail out to centerfield. Smaller and smaller it became until the centerfielder came to a running stop at the centerfield fence sign marked 400 and watched it sail way over his head. An incredible four bagger.

I creamed it! Vincent thought to himself as he touched the bag at first base. A huge BOOM! startled Vincent for a second, until he figured out it was a cannon that was shot to commemorate his home run.

I just hit a dinger! Vincent thought with a smile on his face and headed to second base, squeezing out all the excitement he could for the moment. When he reached second base, he picked up the pace so that it didn't appear he was rubbing it in the opposition's faces. When he got to home plate, the whole team was there to congratulate him, patting him on the helmet and fist bumping him.

The celebration headed back to the dugout, except that when he got there, Coach Smith, the bench coach, stopped him. Amid the loud voices and celebration, he said, "Vincent, you just blew off Coach Johnson's sign."

Vincent's smile peeled off. "His sign?"

"Coach Johnson gave you the take sign."

"Oh no, sorry Coach," Vincent said, some of the euphoria wearing off.

"Don't apologize to me. Do it to him. I know you probably just forgot, but it would be wise of you to say something to Coach Johnson. He has a specific philosophy that he sticks to. It's his way or the highway."

Vincent hung his head, and apparently sensing this, Coach Smith said, "But that was a heck of a hit."

Vincent looked out to where Coach Johnson was standing, but the coach was concentrating on the batter, his second baseman Ray Salinas, or "Steinbeck," as Vincent recalled. At that moment Steinbeck dropped down a perfect bunt along the third baseline and hustled out the throw to first.

A few people high-fived Vincent on the way to the end of the bench, but he wasn't feeling as euphoric about his towering home run shot as he had a minute before when he was getting mugged at the plate.

The game went much the same as that first inning. Vincent settled into a groove, and he and Tank focused on the sinker more, reserving the two-seam and the four-seam fastball to only one or two pitches during the at bat, so as to keep the batters on their feet. Vincent gave up a couple of groundball hits up the middle in the course of seven innings pitched. When Coach Johnson replaced Vincent for the eighth inning, Vincent had held South West Utah scoreless with ten strikeouts, as the fence clearly showed with the ten "K"s hanging, four backwards, so that the opposing dugout could constantly be reminded. The two base hits were the only two runners he allowed. On top of that,

Vincent went 3-3 on the night at the plate with a couple of singles added to that home run.

NCA also played a smart game on offense, getting the lead batter on base five out of nine innings and using a combination of sacrifice bunts and hit-and-runs to keep the runs coming across the plate. By the time the game was over, the Bulldogs had won 9-0, and the student section stayed in the stands, long after the last pitch, as if waiting for something.

The team sat in a circle in shallow right field. Coach Johnson praised their attitude and teamwork, and reminded the team that SWU was a quality opponent, so they should feel good about their performance.

When Coach finished talking, Vincent about rose to apologize, but stayed down when Tank stood to address the team. Vincent looked over to the stands to see the student section had moved closer, perhaps hoping to overhear what Tank had to say.

Tank, still wearing his catcher's gear and with his mask in his hand, looked at Coach Johnson, who nodded to his captain. Tank said, "That was a good game we played because you all put in the time and effort it takes this summer, hitting the weights, running hills, and staying away from alcohol and drugs. You kept yourselves clean and in shape, and it showed tonight."

He looked down at the grass beneath his feet and looked up smiling. "I think that was the difference between us and them. So tonight, no partying, no beer, none of that stuff. Go back to the dorms and get some sleep."

"Yes, Captain!" the guys all shouted. Vincent was amazed at the weight Tank pulled with the other ballplayers.

"Finally," Tank said, "I want you to stand up." He pointed right at Vincent, who looked behind him, not sure who Tank was pointing at. Finally, when Vincent stood, Tank said,

"Gentlemen, I would like to introduce you to Special K."

The ballplayers all stood, cheering and patting Vincent on the back while chanting, "SPECIAL K! SPECIAL K! SPECIAL K!"

Vincent was really embarrassed now as he realized he had just been given his nickname, a nickname he would assume for the next four years. Soon the student section, all of whom had been sticking around apparently for this moment, joined the team chant.

"SPECIAL K! SPECIAL K! SPECIAL K!"

Vincent felt goose bumps and smiled, plenty embarrassed. The commotion took up the better part of a minute, and after the guys finished patting him on the head, and he started walking off the field, he looked up at the student section. There in the front row was his roommate, a big smile on his face, pointing at Vincent and then thumping his chest with his fist. Vincent smiled back and nodded.

Then, halfway up the stands at the exit, Vincent saw her, the brunette. She was with four other girls who were all leaving. The brunette must have seen Vincent smiling at her and smiled back before quickly walking out with her friends.

Vincent felt his knees wobble. It was as close to a perfect night as he had ever had.

Chapter Nine

THE INTERNET. IT had to be the Internet. Vincent sat on his bed and looked at the note that had been taped to his dorm door. It was from the RA and it read simply,

As soon as you get this, call Elna Dean!

"She must have been listening on the Internet," he said to himself quietly. That had to be the explanation. "She probably found a link and listened online," he said, not worrying too much about his dirty, sweaty uniform on his freshly cleaned linens.

Vincent looked at the note again and smiled, wondering if he should first get a shower, but he took the note's message literally and walked to the front lobby to the payphone. He felt bad about calling collect, but he hadn't had a chance to buy a prepaid phone card, much less a cell phone. On his budget, he had no idea how he would do that. While everyone else typically stared down at their phones as they walked around campus, Vincent seemed to be the only one who was out of touch with technology.

He dialed the number and waited patiently as the operator

prompted him. Finally he heard a dial tone, and Mrs. Dean answered on the first ring, "Vincent?"

"Hi, Mrs. Dean! So you listened to the game tonight? Oh, sorry I had to call collect."

Mrs. Dean paused and said, "Vincent," then paused again.

"Yes, Mrs. Dean. I'm here." In her voice was a bit of a shudder, and he sensed immediately that something was wrong.

"Vincent, I am so sorry," she said and started crying. Vincent's smile vanished. He had never heard Mrs. Dean cry before. She had always been the perfect combination of poise and grace, even when her husband passed away. Now he was genuinely worried.

"Vincent," she started again when she composed herself, "I'm so sorry. I don't know how to tell you this."

"What is it?"

"Vincent, your parents passed away."

The train left Page, Arizona at 6:00 the next morning. Instead of sleeping that night, he waited at the train station. Though he was tired, sleep eluded him.

His dirty baseball uniform still on, Vincent sat in his seat immobile. He had plenty of time to think on the train ride home. He watched the high desert plateaus build into beautiful alpine mountains, and then watched as the mountains faded into high plains.

Since the train was half-empty, nobody sat next to him, so he didn't have to talk to anybody. That was just fine with him. First, he figured he stunk from the ballgame the night before. That didn't really bother him though. Really, he didn't want to have the added pressure of making small talk, since he didn't exactly excel at that in the first place. It was one of the scenarios he imagined on the ride home. Maybe stopping in Albuquerque, picking up somebody who would sit next to him and talk his ear off, then ask him why he was wearing a baseball uniform, why he stunk, why he was heading to Oklahoma.

"I play baseball. I haven't showered in a day. I have to go to my parents' funeral."

That would be a real conversation stopper. But again, Vincent was thankful he didn't have that opportunity.

Vincent had a duffel bag at his feet, all his money in his wallet, and he had found his way to the train station. Thankfully Mrs. Dean had paid for the train ride, called Coach Johnson to let him know the situation, and Coach Johnson was going to let Vincent's instructors know.

Vincent thought he had left his roommate a note, but for the life of him he couldn't quite remember. He didn't even know if his roommate was ever going to return? To this point Evan had spent only one evening in the dorm, and that was to drink with the girls' tennis team.

Vincent tried not to think about his parents, didn't know what to think about his parents. He hadn't even inquired how they died. The thought hadn't even crossed his mind when Mrs. Dean had called. Maybe Mrs. Dean had told him, and he tuned her out. Thinking about this on the way home was troublesome for Vincent. Maybe he had expected it. Maybe he was in shock. All he really knew was that it was probably his dad's fault.

Vincent slept here and there as the train plodded on. He arrived in Dallas at midday the next day and then had a long layover. Finally boarding the next train at 6:00 that evening, he didn't arrive in Oklahoma City until 10:30 at night. Mrs. Dean was waiting there to take him the rest of the way back home to Augusta.

Exhausted, Vincent slept in the car, and the two didn't arrive home until well after midnight, his last two days a complete blur.

Staying in Mrs. Dean's guestroom, Vincent woke with the sun the next morning. He hadn't slept much in the few days since getting the news, and he knew that his day was going to be extremely busy. He had to meet with the mortician, Mr. Strunk, and his father's CPA at 9:00. Mr. Strunk had done Grandpa Dean's funeral, so he would be good enough for his own parents. Vincent rose and started his robotic movements, not because he was in the zone like when he was pitching, but now out of necessity.

Mrs. Dean was cooking the two breakfast.

Vincent sat down at the table without a sound and recognized the letter he had just written to Mrs. Dean a few days before. It looked unopened. He peered out the window. A couple of robins flitted from one branch to another, a game of tag. Vincent envied the two birds for not being human, not having to deal with…all this. The heavy fumes of frying bacon hung in the air like cigarette smoke in a billiards parlor, and it occurred to Vincent that he hadn't eaten anything since before his baseball game three days ago. As if to acknowledge that fact, his stomach growled loud enough to startle Mrs. Dean.

"Oh, goodness!" she said as she jumped and turned around. "Vincent, I didn't realize you were up yet."

Vincent nodded, put his right elbow on the table, and propped his head up with his hand. He looked back out the window to see the robins had taken their game to another property. He found himself wondering why God allowed the two stupid birds to live while his parents were dead.

"Did you sleep alright?" she asked and turned back around to flip a strip of bacon with a fork.

Vincent nodded, without taking his eyes off the window. Again with the small talk. He really didn't know what to say. He raced his mind back a month before to when Grandpa Dean passed away and tried to remember how Mrs. Dean had acted then so he could take some pointers and act with such grace. The more he thought about it, the more he realized that he had been focused on his own grief, and that Mrs. Dean had taken care of him. That again seemed to be the case.

Knowing he must say something or appear rude, Vincent turned to her and finally said, "I wasn't gone a month." His own voice startled him, sounding foreign. He looked back out the window and now saw a squirrel scurrying across the top of a wooden fence. He wondered if the squirrel's mother and father were still alive.

"You want coffee?" Mrs. Dean asked without turning around.

Vincent nodded, again knowing that she full-well couldn't see his acknowledgement, then got up and helped himself to the coffee pot. He sat back down and slowly sipped, finding some comfort in the warmth that emanated through the mug and into his hands. It was late summer, still hot outside, but he felt cold on the inside. He felt…he didn't know how to put it into words. Just cold.

The two sat down to bacon and eggs, fried in the bacon grease. Vincent forked an egg. The yolks were perfect—not runny, but not solid either. Vincent didn't want to be hungry, felt that by not eating he was somehow mourning the way that he should, but he knew that Mrs. Dean would use her teacher voice with him if he didn't start chowing down. Vincent knew that there were some unwritten rules to how he was supposed to act or feel in the face of losing his parents. Perhaps others would be judging him, making sure he had the slow hitch in his step or the mournful expression and distant eyes. He shouldn't laugh. He shouldn't show any excitement. He shouldn't talk. If he did any of this, they might think that he held his parents carelessly. Too morose and he wasn't a real man. All of it was overwhelming, tiring, and he wished he were back in his dorm, writing an essay, or studying for a biology test, or yelling at his roommate for bringing in booze, anything other than dealing with this.

The two sat across from each other in silence and ate their breakfast. Mrs. Dean didn't seem especially willing to start a conversation. She probably was trying to be respectful of Vincent. Let him talk first. As Mrs. Dean got up to excuse herself, Vincent asked, "How did my parents die?"

Mrs. Dean paused for a moment, then took her dishes to the sink and refilled her coffee. She sat back down, this time next to him, and patted his hand. Exhaling, she quietly said, "Vincent, your parents..." and she paused, looking at the ceiling, apparently trying to force back tears. She took a deep breath again and said, "Vincent, your parents were in a car accident."

Vincent looked down and nodded his head. "He was drunk." It came out more as a statement than a question, but he still wanted to know, knowing full well he already knew.

Mrs. Dean sat back and gently said, "I don't know. Nobody does. The police haven't released their report yet, but," and she paused, again looking up, "it's suspected that alcohol was involved."

Vincent fixed his stare on a spec of peppered egg white on his plate.

"Vincent, how much do you really want to know about this?"

"All of it," Vincent whispered. He didn't want to know. He had to know.

Mrs. Dean sighed and continued, "The police found an empty bourbon bottle in the car. It was a one-car accident. They were out on Snake Road, and your father lost control of the car. The car went into the right-hand ditch, crossed back over the road and hit a big cottonwood tree in the left-hand ditch." Then she added, "It was over quickly," apparently hoping that last fact helped a little. It didn't.

"So, Dad finally killed Mom," Vincent whispered.

Tears streaked down Mrs. Dean's face, and she tried to hug Vincent, but he got up and went back to the guest room before she got too close.

Mr. Strunk was an odd duck. Vincent really didn't want to have to talk with him, but hey, Vincent didn't want any of this in the first place. A lousy bedside manner, Mr. Strunk cracked jokes, bad ones, as he described the cremation process to Vincent. Vincent knew the guy was just trying to keep things light, but Vincent wanted the meeting to end and even daydreamed about taking the frying pan that was hanging over the stove and bashing Mr. Strunk's face like a baseball bat to a hanging curveball.

When Mr. Strunk finished speaking, the CPA took his cue. He had introduced himself to Vincent when the two had arrived, but Vincent had already forgotten his name, or couldn't care less for that matter. The guy had a nasally voice that annoyed the heck out of Vincent, and he again looked at the frying pan.

"Vincent," Mr. Nasally said, "we need to go over your parents' finances."

Vincent nodded without looking up.

"Now, in most cases," the man continued, "the financial situation can get quite tricky, but this case is fairly simple, a few hitches aside."

For the first time, Vincent realized that he may have to take on debt. He had no idea how much his father owed, or to whom, but Vincent was pretty sure it was going to drown him.

"Let's start with life insurance," Mr. Nasally continued. "Since there are no retirement accounts in either of your parents' names, unfortunately, you will have to depend entirely on life insurance. Thankfully, your parents were insured for 250 thousand apiece."

For a moment Vincent couldn't breathe. He didn't want to go so far as to think that it was like winning the lottery, but that was half a million dollars!

"Now, the coroner has determined that the accident was just that, accidental. Therefore the insurance company should pay out, minus the death tax, of course."

"Death tax?" Vincent asked, looking up.

Mr. Nasally said, "The government taxes you for dying."

"For real?" Vincent asked defensively and turned to Mrs. Dean.

She patted his hand with hers and said, "I'm afraid that's true, Vincent. When Grandpa Dean passed away, we—or I—learned that the hard way."

Mr. Nasally continued, "Since your father was the owner of the policy at the time of death, by law the life insurance goes to the estate, which unfortunately gets taxed."

"How much?" Vincent asked.

"In 2010 there wasn't a death tax," Mr. Nasally told him. "People joked around that that was a good year to die." The annoying man chuckled, followed by Mr. Strunk. The other two present didn't crack a smile. "But now the death tax is in the neighborhood of fifty-five percent."

"Holy Cow!" Vincent said out loud.

"Unfortunately, you're right," Mr. Nasally agreed. "So a quick computation tells us that that leaves 225 thousand."

"That's enough to pay for school," Vincent said, and smiled for the first time in over two days.

"Well," Mr. Nasally said, "that's the easy part. Now we have to talk about debt."

Vincent's smile faded.

"As you probably know," Mr. Nasally continued, "your father

had quite extensive medical bills that he had been paying on, er, at least some of the time." Mr. Nasally blinked a few times. "In all, they total 148 thousand dollars. That leaves seventy-seven thousand dollars. Now comes loans—Vincent, just let me know if I need to go slower for you, or if you want to take a break."

Vincent shook his head, his anger flaring at this roller coaster ride.

"Okay, let's continue. Now there's your parents' house. Your parents bought it for sixty-five thousand and paid off thirty-one thousand of its principle. The remaining thirty-four thousand will be paid off with the insurance money, leaving forty-three thousand. Now on to the upside. You will own it outright and may sell it if you so choose."

Vincent thought that was a good idea. He didn't even want to step foot inside that house ever again. He had never had a good memory in it, so he should have no sentimental problem unloading it on the first buyer who showed interest.

Mr. Nasally finished, "That only leaves my fees and Mr. Strunk's fees. When it's all said and done, you will walk away with around thirty-five thousand dollars. That should leave a smile on your face!"

Mr. Nasally talked to Vincent like he was a child, and it made Vincent mad. He knew he should be happy with thirty-five grand, but when he considered that Uncle Sam took over half of his inheritance, thirty-five was a hard pill to swallow. Thirty-five grand was a slap to the face for what he had to endure at the hands of his father and his father's belt. At least he would be able to pay Mrs. Dean back for the train tickets.

Vincent signed on the dotted lines, and about the time Mr. Nasally and the mortician left, the church ladies brought them dinner, a casserole that looked pretty good, despite the fact that Vincent didn't feel much like eating. He and Mrs. Dean ate in silence again, Vincent's ponderous mind going in a million different directions.

Chapter Ten

IT WAS A small graveside service, attended by only a handful of mourners, many of whom were Mrs. Dean's church friends who had come to support Vincent. Not even any of Vincent's old teammates from the high school team were there. Most were off at college, but he figured that an underclassman or two might have shown.

There were a few of the town's drunks who had spent much time with Vincent's father at the Rusty Nail, the town's shady bar. Also, a few of the nurses who worked with his mother at the hospital showed up. As Vincent perused the faces, he noticed that not one tear was shed, not even his own.

The service didn't last long. Unlike Grandpa Dean's funeral where Coach Johnson had spoken kindly of the man Grandpa Dean was, no one, other than the preacher, said a word.

Afterward, a few of his father's drinking buddies came up to Vincent and told him what a "great chum" his old man was, how he always bought drinks for them, and about how he would, "give a stranger the shirt off his back." Vincent nodded at each gesture, wondering how "his old man" could care so much for these obscene drunks, but beat him, cussed him out, and didn't give him one dollar to go to college.

Concerning his mother, none of the nurses said anything to him, only turning back to their cars and leaving.

Vincent and Mrs. Dean stood at the gravesite after everyone else had left. Mrs. Dean, knowing Vincent needed a minute to himself, excused herself and waited in the car.

Vincent sat down and stared at the two urns, the best that money could buy. There wasn't a huge selection of urns, and he would have preferred that his parents weren't cremated, but it had been their wishes, so he honored them.

Vincent stared at the two urns, and instead of mourning, ran over the figures of the funeral costs in his head. It felt to him that he no longer had the luxury of letting his guard down. With an abusive dad and a mother who was, to put it nicely, in another world, Vincent had been forced to grow up way too fast. Maybe deep down he had had the security blanket of knowing his parents were still alive, and perhaps they might snap out of it and love him the way a child should be loved. But now that hope had faded, and if growing up too fast were a dark hole, he was falling faster and deeper.

The plot cost 3,500 dollars. That was the major expense. The urns were nothing really, but the arrangements with the funeral director would be steep. He figured that if he got out of this for less than 6,000 dollars, then he would be doing well. It felt like a final backhand from his father.

He stood up and walked back to the car, convinced that he had spent enough time at the grave to make it look like he had paid his last respects. He knew he should do the right thing, and deep down he even knew what the right thing was, but all he could think to do was leave without so much as a word of goodbye. His parents never loved him. Why should he love them?

Vincent didn't talk on the way back to the house, and Mrs. Dean didn't push it. Vincent knew that there was an elephant in the room, knew that Mrs. Dean wanted to help, but there wasn't anything she could do. He expected her to talk to him later that night, but when he finally went to bed, Mrs. Dean hadn't said more than ten words to him.

Vincent tossed and turned all night. He had a mammoth task in front of him now. He would have to clean his parents' house in order to prepare it for the estate sale. He had made up his mind that he didn't want anything. Sell it all. The house wasn't anything to look at and needed repairs. The foundation was sinking on the south side of the house and causing cracks in the walls around the outlets and doors that stuck and didn't latch properly. To fix that would cost an extra three to five thousand, something that he wasn't going to touch.

Speaking of outlets, some of them didn't even work. He had no idea if the whole house needed to be rewired, and he wasn't planning on finding out. Faucets dripped uncontrollably. Black mold decorated the walls and ceiling in the bathroom, and he even suspected that there would be a termite problem. He hoped not.

He figured that if he could sell the house and belongings "as is" and pocket the profits, he could unload the house and all its problems and never look back. But first he had to clean it. He spent the next three days scrubbing and vacuuming, trashing certain items, and arranging others so that the house looked clean, tidy, and ready for the inspector to give his report.

When the inspector came, the foundation problem was the first thing he found. That was to be expected. Then he nitpicked on things like the water heater, which by law should have been a couple of feet off the floor. Thankfully, no sign of termites had been found, and when Vincent locked the front door and walked to Mrs. Dean's house, he didn't look back. He planned on never again setting foot inside that house.

He had been gone a full week at that point, and he knew that his schoolwork had to be piling up. Plus, he didn't want to lose his spot in the rotation on the baseball team, though he suspected that Coach Johnson wouldn't do something so mean. He resolved to head back to Arizona that morning.

When he got to Mrs. Dean's house, he noticed that his insurance check had arrived. Knowing that he only had a certain portion that he could call his own, he went down to the bank to deposit it the next day, then went shopping for something he had wanted for a long time. He had to go to both of the car lots in town, but he finally found it, a Ford F150. It was a used model. A new model would have broken the bank. It wasn't fancy. White, an extended cab, and a little hail damage, but the engine was good, the miles were fairly low, and after haggling for two hours with the sales person and then the manager, the price was finally right.

He drove to Mrs. Dean's house that evening to surprise her. When he showed her what he had bought, she didn't say much. It occurred to him at that point that she hadn't said much at all since the funeral.

That night, as the last church meal, meatballs and cheesy potatoes, was served, Vincent decided he had to talk to her. About the time he went for seconds, Mrs. Dean beat him to the punch.

"Are you heading back tomorrow?"

Her words caught him off guard. "Yes."

"That's a nice truck. This way you won't have to buy a train ticket."

"Oh, that reminds me," Vincent said. He pulled out his check book. "How much did the train ticket cost last week?"

Mrs. Dean shook her head. "Don't you even think of paying me back for that. That was the least I could do to help you in your time of need." She paused, and when it was obvious Vincent wasn't going to say anything else, she continued, "Vincent, one of life's toughest lessons is knowing when to accept help when help is given. When you help someone, you set out to bless that person, but you end up blessing yourself. You are blessing me by letting me help you, so you just put that heavy checkbook back in your pocket."

This was more than she had said to him in the last week. She had been eyeing him, but had refrained from invading his space up until now. The way she spoke to him, it felt like things were getting back to normal. If only Grandpa Dean were there to enjoy dinner with them. Vincent missed Grandpa Dean dearly, and a pang of something invaded his stomach, perhaps his conscience reminding him that he just lost his parents and that he should miss them as well. No, that wasn't right. His mother might have given birth to him, and his father might have provided his DNA, but outside of that, they weren't his parents. Mrs. Dean was more a mom to him in that last summer in Augusta than his own mother had been in ten years.

Vincent put his checkbook away and took another bite.

"Just be sure to be smart with that money you have. It will go fast," she added.

"Yes, ma'am."

Mrs. Dean looked at Vincent and probed a little further. "What do you plan on doing with the rest of the money?"

"Well, pay off bills for starters. You heard the CPA."

"Yes," Mrs. Dean said, "but I'm talking about what's left

over. How much did the truck cost?"

It was kind of a personal question, but this woman had treated him like he was her own, so he figured he owed her at least that much. Obviously she wanted peace of mind. "I spent eight thousand on it."

Mrs. Dean flinched. "And how many miles?"

"Fifty thousand."

Mrs. Dean composed herself and took a bite of the potatoes. "Well, that's a pretty good deal. Actually, that's a really good deal, as long as the truck works."

Vincent smiled. That was as close to a complement as he was going to get out of her.

"I guess next time I buy a vehicle, I will call you back from Arizona to do my haggling."

Vincent chuckled under his breath.

"Insurance?" Mrs. Dean asked.

"Taken care of," Vincent replied. He had purchased the cheapest policy that Martin Insurance Agency offered and was perturbed at the idea that he had to make fifty dollar monthly payments. When he thought about all he could buy with fifty dollars a month, it felt like throwing money away.

"Well, are there any more major expenses you are planning on making?" Mrs. Dean inquired further.

Vincent chewed and swallowed before answering. "Actually I was thinking about getting a cell phone."

"Yes?"

"I know that cell phones and plans are expensive," he continued, "so I will probably just get a prepaid one. That will keep me out of trouble."

Mrs. Dean nodded, "A good idea."

Vincent knew the conversation wasn't over just with finances, so he wasn't surprised when she asked him the next question. In fact he had been waiting for it for a week.

"Vincent, how are you doing?"

"Fine," was his response.

"Vincent?" she asked, her tone deepening.

Vincent put his fork down and looked up. "What do you want me to say?" he asked with a gruff tone.

"The truth," she replied.

"The truth is that I don't feel anything. Those two people weren't my parents. Case closed."

Mrs. Dean jumped on him with her teacher voice. "Vincent, don't you ever say that! Now I know that your parents made their mistakes, but they will always be your parents. Don't ever disrespect their memory like that again!"

Vincent was taken aback. What right did she have to talk to him that way? Before he could respond, she continued, "Vincent, I know you're hurt. I understand why you are feeling this way. If my father had abused me like that, I might feel the same way."

Vincent flinched as if he were just hit with another backhand.

Mrs. Dean softened her tone a bit. "But you are better than what you just said. You are a better man than that. Now I know you haven't mourned much this week. I'm not about to tell you your business and how you should mourn. I just want you to know that you will eventually mourn your parents' loss. It will happen whether you like it or not. But I can tell you that the longer you wait to confront it, the harder it will be. It might hit you at the worst moment. Do you understand me?"

Vincent didn't say anything in response, acted like he hadn't heard her. In fact he couldn't wait to get out of there.

"Well," Mrs. Dean said, having spoken her peace, "all looks better with ice cream. I'll bring you out a bowl."

Chapter Eleven

VINCENT HADN'T DRIVEN since taking Driver's Ed back in his sophomore year. Like riding a bike, it all came back to him. With Augusta in his rearview mirror, he put the pedal down and left Oklahoma in the rear view mirror.

Like the train ride from Arizona, he had plenty of time to think, but he was thankful that this time he wouldn't have to worry about making small talk. He could just roll down the windows and let the cool September air run through the cab. He turned on the radio, finding only one station that played country music. Vince Gill sang, "Go Rest High on That Mountain." Vincent turned it up and sang along at the top of his voice, wondering if the red plateaus he was passing cared that he sang off-key. With the wind blowing through his hair, he drove toward the Rocky Mountains. In many ways he had never felt so free.

The station carried him well into New Mexico, or through about half of George Strait's number one songs, before turning to static. Vincent turned the stereo off and listened to the wind whip through the cab for a while. It led him to thoughts about what Mrs. Dean had said to him. He truly respected what she said, but he doubted she knew what she was talking about. The only difference between his relationship with his parents now and what it was two weeks prior was that now there was no chance of reconciliation.

Then it hit him. That was it. His father was never going to atone for all the beatings to both him and his mother. His mother was never going to atone for not protecting him. The more he thought about this line of thought, the more upset he became, so he tried the radio again, and still not receiving any reception, he just let the static fill the air.

He noticed that his new pickup guzzled gas, but he waited until he made it to Raton, New Mexico before gassing up, that way he would have a fresh tank as soon as he entered the mountains. He was excited about driving up into the alpine air. As he drove through town, he passed a fly shop that advertised the best breakfast burritos in town.

Even though it was well past noon, he wondered if they made them all day. Curiosity got the best of him. His stomach rumbling, he pulled over and decided to check it out.

He walked inside, and wonder instantly grabbed him. The store was narrow, maybe fifteen feet wide was all, but very deep. Rows and rows of rods stretched from floor to ceiling. Tables held bins of flies by the thousands. On one wall were packages of different types of feathers, everything from pheasant rooster tails to dyed marabou, and different patches of hair like a whitetail deer's tail and the side of an elk. Different styles of hooks, beads, synthetic fly-tying materials, and all sorts of hand-held tools that he had never seen before, most of which looked like they belonged on a tray accompanying a terrorist's interrogation of a hostage.

On the other side of the shop hung intricate woven blankets depicting alpine scenes with fly fishermen casting in tiny brooks and hooking monstrous trout. Above the shelving were stuffed fishes, all trout, or at least Vincent figured they were all trout. Tee shirts hung from the ceiling in the back of the store with catchy phrases like, "I'm Seeing Spots" on a shirt with a brown trout, and, "Don't Feed the Trout Bum" on a shirt that had a bearded fisherman in rags next to a mountain stream.

At Vincent's feet was a large female black Labrador retriever who didn't so much as look up at Vincent.

"Don't mind her. She don't bite."

The deep, scratchy voice came from somewhere deep into the store. Vincent carefully stepped over the dog, which rolled over, perhaps to make it more difficult on Vincent, perhaps to mark his territory in some lazy way. Either way, Vincent hurdled the dog and looked over the fly bins to see an elderly gentleman with a scraggly beard and an Elmer Fudd hat. The man was sitting at the table playing with some contraption. In one hand he held a bobbin with thread coming out the needle-like end. The thread attached to a hook that was held in place by some machine that seemed especially specific to that purpose.

Vincent marveled as the old man whipped the thread at lightning speed, adding a feather with his off hand, then wrapping the feather around the shank of the hook to make it look like the hook had wings. It was the work of a few seconds with yet another tool that whipped knots onto the hook shank just behind the hook eye before the other hand whipped out a short pair of scissors. With a quick snip, the man released the freshly tied fly from the vice into his hand and held it up to his bifocals to inspect his work.

"How does this look?" he asked and held out the fly to

Vincent. Vincent crossed the room and inspected the fly in the gentleman's hand. It was very small and very hairy. That's about all he could tell. It didn't especially look like an insect, but he wasn't about to insult the man's work.

"That's very nice, sir," Vincent said.

"On the Cimarron yesterday," the old man began. "Couldn't turn one with any of my standards, but there they were, sipping drakes off the top right in front of me. It dawned on me that they were probably taking cripples, so I came back to the shop and set out to whip out one with about a forty-five degree angle on the hackle so the butt would sink like a cripple, but it would still stand up high enough for me to see." Then the man dropped the fly into a pile of about ten flies just like the one he just made. "It's not much fun getting old," he finished, then took off his bifocals. "What can I do for you, sonny?"

Vincent looked past the old man and saw pair after pair of waders, with wader boots on one shelf. On the right was a glass case that held about twenty fly reels, all beautiful. On top of the case was a cash register, which looked like it belonged in 1955.

Finding his voice finally, Vincent said, "Well sir, I was wondering if you had any of those breakfast burritos left?"

The old man chuckled. "Sorry son. You have to get here no later than 7:30 to have a chance at my wife's burritos. Might have a little left in the coffee pot," he said, then looked at his watch. "But at this time of day, you would do better to drink a quart of motor oil than what's left in that pot!"

This made Vincent chuckle.

"Not from around here, are ya?" the old man asked.

"No sir. Just passing through."

"Where are you from?" the old man inquired.

Vincent thought it over, thought about just saying Arizona, but instead said, "I'm from Oklahoma, but I go to school in

Arizona. NCA."

"NCA?" the old man said and scratched his head. "You familiar with their baseball team? Pretty good team. Play here at Northeast least once a year. Make the tournament quite a bit. Good team." The man looked up at one of his stuffed trout, one with bright red slits under its jaw, a beautiful specimen. "I been out there to fish the Colorado. Pretty good stream. You fish it?"

Vincent shuffled his feet a bit and thought about how his father never took him fishing. Then quickly redirecting his mind, he thought back to the day he looked down into the canyon while writing the letter to Mrs. Dean and watched the two fly fishermen landing fish. "No sir. Never been."

"Never been to the Colorado, or never been at all?" the old man asked.

"Well, I…" Vincent stammered. He didn't want to sound stupid, or ignorant, whichever one it was, but he couldn't exactly swap stories with the gentleman.

"Okay, I got you. So you lookin' to get started?"

Vincent looked around the store and didn't know where to begin. He flipped the price tag on one of the fly rods within reach and saw five hundred dollars on it.

Five hundred dollars!

He released the tag and held up his hand so as to not disturb it, hoping it wouldn't drop to the floor and shatter.

The old man chuckled and apparently put it all together. "That there rod is for a serious fisherman. What you're looking for is a starter kit. Come with me." He got up from the wooden chair that made a creaking noise, or maybe it was the old man's back. Vincent followed out of curiosity, not exactly sure how to tell the old man that he wasn't in the market to buy a fly rod. Or was he? After all he had thousands of dollars in his bank account now, funds that would help him through school. Still, he wanted to know more about fly fishing. It looked so peaceful, and he reasoned that if there was one thing he needed right now, it was peace.

The store owner held up a rod and reel combo that was already put together, complete with bright, thick orange line that was strung through the rod guides. Attached to the end of the orange line was a piece of clear line that tapered to a smaller diameter, probably a good eight feet. On the end of the line was tied another hairy fly.

"This is a very popular starter rod. It's eight and a half feet, five weight, with a pretty fast action, but very forgiving. You know, the first time I ever fished, of course back then there was nothing but split bamboo, which if you know anything about fly fishing, is very slow. Well, I was on the San Juan just salivating about sticking a fly in the mouth of one of those chunky rainbows. Well, I buggy-whipped the line just like I thought I was supposed to, and when I dropped a bird's nest of gut on top of the hole, I had the audacity to be surprised. Ha! Didn't know a lick about fly fishing. In fact I wasn't much younger than you now, but I thought I knew the world. Well, I didn't have anybody to tell me any different. Wouldn't have listened if I had. But I can tell you that untying a bird's nests while other people around you are catching fish is a quick way to learn the proper method of how to cast."

Without skipping a beat, the old man went into his windup and delivered his pitch. "Tell you what. You buy this outfit from me, and I will give you a free casting lesson in the alley behind the store. What do you say?"

The old man put the rod in Vincent's right hand. Vincent held the soft cork grip and squeezed it a bit. He noticed that the simple action of squeezing it pulsed vibrations up the shaft of the rod, all the way to the tip and back down to the handle. It quivered with beating of Vincent's heart.

Vincent knew that the old man was giving him a sales pitch, and that he should thank the old man for his time and be on his way, but he somehow felt led to this moment. The longer he held the rod in his hand, the more comfortable he felt.

He looked at one of the blankets hanging on the wall, noticed the way the fisherman leaned back on the rod to force the fighting fish back into the water, and Vincent found himself daydreaming about being on a pristine mountain stream and doing the same. The fantasy lasted for the better part of a minute, until he looked at the price tag of one hundred and fifty dollars.

"I know what you're thinking," the old man said. "One fifty for a start-up rig. Well, that's actually a pretty good deal. This rod," and he pointed to the quivering rod tip, "when you buy it by itself is one twenty-five. The reel, another forty. Add the weight-forward fly line, the Five X leader, and you have two hundred bucks. And that's before you even buy a single fly or any of the tools you will need for the stream."

Vincent definitely felt overwhelmed. The old salesman apparently sensed this, so he sweetened the deal. "Tell you what young feller, I will throw in a fly box and five flies for free. What do you say?" The old man grabbed a fly box with his store's logo imprinted on the front of it. He opened it up, and five flies greeted them, each one looking a little different, one looking like a little worm.

"I don't know," Vincent said and he backed up a step toward the door, contemplating his escape plan.

"Okay, I need to convince you a little more," the old man said and looked at the shelving across the way. He walked over and grabbed a lanyard that had five clips coming off it. On one clip was a little tube of some waxy concoction. On the second clip was what appeared to be toe nail clippers. On the third was a hemostat, the kind one would find on an operating table. On the fourth was a little round compartmental storage container full of little tiny sinkers. On the fifth was two round little flaps of leather. Vincent could guess the purpose of the first four clips, but the fifth one was a mystery to him.

"Here's my deal. This lanyard, with all the tools, sells for twenty-five. I will throw it in for free. That's the fly rod and reel combo, fully outfitted, a fly box with five starter flies, and a lanyard with all the tools you will ever need. With the exception of waders, you now have everything you need to slaughter trout on the Colorado. Everything except my tutelage, which I will give in the alley upon completion of this sale, if you are interested. Believe me, this is the best deal you will ever find."

Vincent looked it all over. The guy was really trying to make the sale happen. Vincent looked at the fly rod in his hand and back at the blanket, and his mind drifted.

The old man, astute when it came to the human condition, said in a non-sales-pitch voice, "There's something going on in your life right now, isn't there, son? It seems like you're running from something. Am I right?"

This broke Vincent's trance. He looked the man in the eye and then down at the floor and didn't respond.

"Feel like talking about it, son?" The old man sat down at his table again and waited for a response. When Vincent didn't respond, the old man said, "Okay, what you need is a day on the water. Normally I wouldn't do this, but it looks like you need to stand in some running water something serious. It has healing effects, believe me, and it looks like you are in need of some healing. Am I right?"

Vincent didn't move. He just stood there, staring at his shoes.

"Well, son, I am heading over to the Cimarron tomorrow. I bet that's on your way to Arizona, isn't it? Stick around here for the day. My wife and I will board you tonight, and I will take you out fishing tomorrow, free of charge. I usually charge two fifty for a half day with a client, but my schedule is free tomorrow. Plus, I need to try out that new cripple I just tied. What do you say?"

Vincent thought he was going to lose it for a second and cry, but he forced it back. "Sir, that's awful kind of you, but I need to get back to school tonight for class tomorrow. Been gone a week already."

The old man nodded, as if in agreement, or as if he somehow understood Vincent's tragedy. "Well, then we will take a rain check. My offer will stand though. I promise you." The old man took out a business card and jotted his cell phone number on it. He walked it over to Vincent who took it with a nod.

"Well, let's settle up. You're a very persuasive salesman," Vincent said and took the rod to the counter. The man followed him and threw in another five popular flies in the fly box, to make a total of ten. Vincent paid for his goods and thanked the gentleman.

Vincent separated the fly rod into two pieces and put it on the passenger floor board. He watched the old man wave from the window, then he took off out of town and up into the alpine mountains of northern New Mexico, following the Cimarron River all the way. It looked just like his daydreams inside that fly shop, and he had to fight the urge to just step out of the truck and whip around his new toy. The same thought occurred to him when he arrived at Eagle's Nest Lake, the most beautiful lake he had ever seen. He drove on past, swearing to take up the old man on his offer, sooner, rather than later. The rest of the drive Vincent rode with the radio on, purposefully searching for country music stations to keep his mind focused. He watched the sun melt into the high desert in front of him. He made it back to his dormitory well after dark and was greeted by an empty room, which was just fine by him.

Chapter Twelve

VINCENT WAS SILENT through all of practice. He had plenty to think about, and again there was the issue of small talk with his teammates who all meant well. Most of them, at one time or another, came up to him and gave him a pat on the back, a "Sorry, man," or something similar.

Each time Vincent responded monosyllabically with, "Thanks," or with little grunts and nods to let the well-wishers know that their thoughts weren't falling on deaf ears. That's what it was all about though, making the well-wishers feel like they were making a difference. In all truth though, he wished they would all just leave him alone.

Coach Johnson pulled Vincent aside midway through practice and asked him if he wanted to take a break, obviously concerned about him, but Vincent politely declined and went about his business.

It was after practice that Tank approached Vincent. Asking

him to sit down as the rest of the players filed out to the parking lot, Tank didn't beat around the bush. He sat down next to Vincent, folded his hands, and rested his elbows on his knees and said, "Vincent, some of us guys are heading up to the Catholic Church tonight. Father Peterman puts on a meal for the college students one Wednesday night a month. It's good food, at least a break from the cafeteria. You interested? There'll be a lesson too. He's a really cool guy, real smart. And anyway, it will be fun hanging out with some of the guys. What do you say?"

Vincent looked toward the right field fence, the sun still high in the sky. It shined brightly, making him squint. A hawk soared lazily in the cloudless sky. Vincent looked down and saw a den of army ants a few feet away. A few of the soldiers had made a probe and sought to investigate his cleats. Vincent gently lifted his cleat and then came down on the closest one with one of his metal spikes. When he again lifted his shoe, he saw that the ant had been severed in half.

At least ten seconds had gone by before Vincent considered Tank's request. He had heard about half of what Tank said. What he took from Tank's words was that he was inviting Vincent to do something or go somewhere. Company was the last thing he wanted right now. Besides, he was overloaded with homework from all his classes that he had missed in the past week. With this built-in excuse, he said, "Thanks, but I have a lot of work. Maybe next time."

Tank nodded while looking at the ground and spit a shucked sunflower seed. The shell whacked the other soldier who quickly retreated to the ant hill to report to his leader. "I bet you are busy," Tank said. "Would you like me to stay behind and help you? What classes are you working on?"

Vincent didn't wait to respond to this request. He shook his head as he watched the soldier climb the mound and disappear down the hole. "No, I'm good. Maybe next time."

This standard answer accepted, Tank nodded again and patted Vincent on the back. "Gotcha." Tank got up to leave, then paused, "You change your mind, run by my dorm before 6:30."

Vincent didn't acknowledge his catcher leaving, only stared at the fence, thinking about the canyon below the dam. He wondered if he could scale the walls to get down to the water, and if he couldn't, would it hurt when he hit bottom?

When he got back to his dorm, his roommate still wasn't home. It was hard to tell when the last time was that Evan had been there. Vincent half hoped he had moved out, but he knew that not to be the case. The guy was seldom ever there, so it was kind of like having a single room.

That evening Vincent had all intentions of doing his homework, but he just couldn't concentrate. He watched an animal show about giraffes on his roommate's flat screen, and when that bored him to tears, he thought about just going to bed. He looked at his alarm clock which read 8:21 and knew he would wake up in the middle of the night if he went to bed right then, so he walked over to his closet and pulled out his new fly rod to examine it.

He ran his fingers up the shaft and watched how the emerald green rod shimmered in the light from the lamp. He daydreamed about wading in up to his waist and casting in that beautiful alpine lake he had driven past the day before in northern New Mexico. He wished he would have just stopped the truck, maybe even camped out in the bed. The idea of pulling out a fish from the mirrored surface of that lake fluttered romantically in his head.

He put his fly rod back into his closet and sat down at his desk to try to concentrate again, but nothing was coming to him.

His assignment was to write a three-page expository paper on something he was an expert in. He thought and thought, and the only thing he was expert in was suppressing pain while taking a beating from his old man.

Having run out of patience, and much too wound up to go to sleep, he got curious and went over to Evan's side of the room. He opened the door to the refrigerator, which was still poorly hidden under Evan's desk. He was greeted by empty shelves.

"Well, that's a relief," he said. Closing the door, Vincent took a peek inside Evan's closet and admired his roommate's collection of bowling shirts and the many, many pairs of shoes he owned. He picked up one pair of brown leather dress shoes and looked at the tag to see that they were two sizes too small, not that he would ever wear his roommate's stuff.

Closing the door, he walked back to his bed and sat down. He stared at nothing in particular, until something caught his eye. Between the box spring and the mattress was a little piece of clear glass. Vincent reached in between the mattress and box spring and pulled out a bottle of vodka. The seal had already been broken, but only a little bit had been taken off the top.

At first Vincent was very mad, but he paused. Curiosity got the better of him, and he opened the cap and put the bottle up to his nose and took a sniff. He about choked on the fumes and quickly capped it. What on earth would ever make a man want to drink what was in that bottle? He turned the bottle over and over in his hands, wondering if the taste was as bad as the smell. Already the smell had subsided, and only the memory of singed nose hairs stuck around. For no reason, he opened it again and took another sniff, this time a lot more reserved.

The same smell greeted him, and he capped it and returned it to its resting place, his face scrunched up. And not a second too soon, because there was the sound of a key in the door's keyhole, and the door opened.

"The prodigal roommate returns!" Evan exclaimed as he saw Vincent for the first time in over a week. "Where you been? Been meaning to congratulate you on that big win last week!"

Vincent shrugged.

"Well, I had given you up for dead. I figured you transferred or went pro."

Vincent lay back in his bed and said, "Parents died." It just came out.

Evan laughed out loud. "Dude, you been gone long enough that it…" but he stopped in mid-sentence. He must have looked at Vincent who sat there still. "Hey man, you serious?"

Vincent gave a short, one-syllabled answer, "Ha," and nodded without smiling. "Dad killed them both."

Evan was stone sober quiet for the first time since Vincent had known him. Apparently Evan didn't know quite what to say, so Vincent continued talking. "Got himself drunk and wrecked. Mom was in the front seat. Killed them both instantly. Would you like to know more?"

Evan stared at his roommate, apparently still not quite convinced that Vincent was not putting him on. "Uh, yeah man. Uh, I'm so sorry. Uh, I don't know what to say."

"Well that's a first," Vincent said and chuckled under his breath.

Evan apparently didn't hear that last comment, but just kept staring.

"Dad had it coming," Vincent said, then realized that he had said too much. He chided himself for divulging so much information, for even talking about his old man. He had been so businesslike in his approach to his parents' death to this point, not losing his poise and even convincing himself that it was a chapter of his book that was now mercifully over, hence not even worth talking about. Now it was just spilling out of him, and like the vodka bottle, he had to cap it.

Vincent walked over to his desk and picked up the pencil and once again considered his topic, but he couldn't bring himself to write about anything concerning his old man. Out of options, he turned around and asked Evan, "So, where is the party tonight?"

Evan was staring at the floor, apparently still at a loss for words.

"Yo Evan, where's the party? You got plans?"

Evan finally looked up at Vincent. "Hey man, you sure you want to go out?"

"No," Vincent responded. "I'm not sure at all, but I know that I'm going stir crazy here in this room, and if I don't get out, I will bust. So let's go do something. You got plans?"

Evan shook his head. "Nothing I can't break. What do you have in mind?"

Vincent drove Evan to the tree at the top of Glen Canyon Dam that Vincent had sat under a few weeks prior and written that letter to Mrs. Dean. The sun was setting on the other side of the canyon, and long shadows stretched across the west sides of Lake Powell, its red bluffs neutralizing under the fading light.

The two of them sat down under the tree in the grass, a cool breeze giving Evan goose bumps. Evan had brought along the vodka that he had stashed in his bed in his backpack. He knew how Vincent felt about alcohol and wanted to comply with his wishes, but he sure needed a pull at that very moment. He didn't know how he could handle what Vincent was going through sober.

Evan didn't know what was expected of him. So far he and his roommate had spent very little time together, and now that Vincent just lost his parents, Evan felt some sort of loyalty to

Vincent, as if he were responsible for helping Vincent through this tragedy. Though Vincent was naturally quiet, he seemed very peculiar now, and Evan even wondered if suicide were crossing Vincent's mind. Evan, again, thought about the vodka.

As the sun dropped below the horizon, the two sat in silence. It about drove Evan crazy. If only he were a little buzzed, he would feel better about being there for Vincent. Stone-cold sober, Evan couldn't think of a word to say to his roommate. He considered excusing himself to the truck and quickly and secretly taking a swig from the bottle concealed in his backpack, but before he could excuse himself, Vincent spoke.

"I like this spot. Been here a few times since I got here. I go here to clear my head."

Evan readjusted his weight and looked at Vincent who was staring off at Lake Powell. Evan looked into the distance, noticing for the first time the reflection of the thin cirrus clouds off the water.

"That is pretty awesome," Evan responded. When he was young, his father used to take him to Santa Monica Pier. They would sit at the very end where the fishermen all congregated to try their hand at catching shark or rays. The sun setting over the Pacific Ocean was beautiful. There would be a cool breeze coming in off the ocean, much like this one, so his father would put his arm around him and rub his shoulders, and the two of them would just sit there and watch the blue ocean turn indigo as first stars would appear. It was a happy memory to Evan. He realized he hadn't thought of that in years. Heck, he hadn't been to the Santa Monica Pier since junior high, about the time his father got the big promotion and started working late evenings and weekends.

"We have lakes in Oklahoma," Vincent said. "In fact did you know that there are more miles of shoreline in Oklahoma than in California? Check it out. It's true."

Evan chuckled. "Yeah, but I bet you don't have our waves."

Vincent chuckled back. "Tell me about them."

Evan looked at Vincent then crossed into his memory of another time he and his parents ate at a seafood restaurant right on a beach in Malibu, again, right after his father was promoted, and they could afford such a dining experience. "I do a little surfing."

Vincent looked up at Evan and nodded for him to go on.

"If there's one thing I love, it's the beach," Evan said and forgot all about the vodka in his backpack. "Girls in bikinis, surfing, girls surfing in bikinis! Man it's a blast! But you know, as much as I enjoy the big beaches, there's this one little beach in Malibu, not far from our house. It's a little rocky, and the seaweed churns up pretty good, but most of the time I get it all to myself. A lot of people think the beaches in Malibu are private property, but they are actually not, despite owners putting up *Keep Out* signs. Really, they only own the beach from the high-water mark up. So other than getting yelled at by some idiot owners, I would have the beach to myself."

"And what's it like to surf?" Vincent asked as he picked up a twig and started breaking it into little tiny pieces.

"Well, it's the best feeling in the world. The water is so powerful, and if you aren't careful, it could throw you right onto the rocks, or you could end up getting planted right into the sand and then have the next wave deck you from behind, but once you get up on that board," and Evan paused to think of the right metaphor, "well, you do a lot of horseback riding in Oklahoma, right?"

Vincent shook his head. "Sure there are cowboys, but I'm not one of them."

Evan chuckled at his misconception of his roommate. "Well,

I imagine it's like taming a wild bronco. It's something so wild, that you feel like master of the world for having conquered it. Something like that."

Vincent smiled. "Kind of like striking out a batter."

Evan smiled back. "Or hitting an ace."

"So how is your season going?"

Evan frowned a bit. "Well, I was hoping to play number one singles, but I lost a few challenge matches I should have won." Evan didn't tell Vincent the whole truth that he was entirely hung over in both losing efforts. He had a hard time admitting that to himself. "Right now, coach has me playing number three singles and number two doubles. It's the preseason, which means we are dueling other schools, and we will have the preseason national tournament coming up early next month, but as for records, nothing really matters right now."

Vincent nodded and flicked one of the little stick pieces he had broken off right over the edge.

The two fell silent for ten minutes, and Evan remembered the vodka. He wondered if Vincent would mind if he just pulled it out and took a swig. Remembering how Vincent's parents died, he reconsidered.

At about the time Evan was going to burst, Vincent got up and walked over to the edge of the cliff and looked down. Evan followed him and about fainted when he looked down. Hundreds of feet down a black river rushed by. Evan's knees buckled. "Whoa! That's a long ways down!" Evan said.

Vincent only nodded. "I want to go down there," Vincent responded.

"Uh, right now?"

Vincent shook his head no. "Not just now, but I plan to."

"And what would you do down there?"

Vincent nudged a pebble with the toe of his sneaker and

pushed it over the edge. It became invisible almost immediately. "Thought I would fish it."

Evan breathed a sigh of relief. For a moment he really thought Vincent was talking suicide. "So, what kind of fish are down there?"

"I heard they have trout," Vincent responded. "I don't know anything about it, but I wanna do it. Imagine standing in the water down there and looking up at the top of this cliff, or up at that big concrete dam! It just seems like such a relaxing thing to do. Kind of like surfing?" Vincent surmised.

Evan nodded in agreement. This was a pleasant conversation, and it made him think introspectively, recalling good memories, and he even had a touch of the warm fuzzies. He didn't realize he could feel so good without a drink or a joint.

The two backed away from the dam and sat back under that tree. Vincent lay down and stared up. Not wanting to be non-conformist in any way, Evan did the same and was startled. Now that it was getting dark, there were millions of stars coming out.

"Check out all the stars!" Evan said. "I didn't realize there were so many of them! You can't see anything but the moon most of the time in LA, because of the smog and all the lights." Evan smiled. "To be honest, I haven't looked up at the stars in quite a while."

"How 'bout all those parties you have been going to?" Vincent asked. "Aren't they at night?

"Yeah, I suppose so, but to tell you the truth, I don't usually look up."

The two were quiet for a few more minutes. A shooting star streaked across the northern sky, reflecting off the lake.

"So, what does alcohol taste like?" Vincent asked.

Evan was startled by the question. Vincent had maybe the clearest eyes of any athlete at NCA. Did Evan really want to give him a straight answer on this?

"Well Vincent, that depends on what kind of alcohol you are talking about." Evan hoped this sidestep would end the conversation.

"Okay," Vincent said and dropped it. Evan again thought about that bottle of vodka in his backpack. Should he bring it out and let Vincent have a taste? Should he call his buddy who was twenty-one and have him pick up a six-pack? Admittedly, he wanted something to bond over with his roommate, and it seemed that they didn't have anything in common whatsoever. Maybe Vincent would loosen up with a drink or two.

The guy had been extremely tight since the moment Evan had met him, so much so that Evan didn't even want to go back to the dorm for fear that Vincent would look down his nose at him, or yell at him, or maybe even lecture him. On numerous occasions, he had thought about just going to the Dean of Student Housing and changing rooms, but when Vincent disappeared, he stalled on the idea. Okay, honestly, he had been on quite the drunk binge and didn't really have the time to talk to the dean, much less go to class, but he had that worked out. That's what his tutor was for. All he had to do was tell his dad that he needed money for a tutor and then pay the tutor to write the papers for him. As for the mid-term, he still had a month to think about how to tackle that.

All this thought made him thirsty, and resolving to find a rallying point with his roommate, he reached into his backpack to pull out the bottle and offer Vincent a drink. Before he could, Vincent got up, wiped his fanny clean of any clinging grass, and said, "Well, this was just what I needed. Thanks for coming out here with me."

"It's my pleasure," Evan responded. "Anytime."

Vincent walked over to the truck. Evan wished he could have

brought up the topic of Vincent's parents, maybe dig a little deeper, but there would be time for that. He would continue to be Vincent's roommate and even try to look for the good in him. With his hand on the bottle, he unscrewed the cap, took a healthy swig, coughed a bit, and then put it back in his backpack and walked back to the truck.

Chapter Thirteen

VINCENT RECEIVED A zero for his assignment. No, check that. He earned a zero. Mrs. Dean had made sure that there was a distinct difference between the two verbs. She had a sign up in her classroom that read, "I don't pass out grades. You earn them." Repeated on a daily basis to her students, Vincent included, everyone knew that truth was singular. Vincent hadn't received a zero. He earned it.

Vincent didn't argue it any, despite what some might consider extenuating circumstances. After all the guy's parents were only a week in the ground. Coach Johnson himself was persistent enough to make sure that all of Vincent's professors itemized his to do lists, complete with instructions and due dates so as to make his transition back into the classroom as seamless as possible. The essay was the first assignment due upon his return, and he knew about it. He just plain didn't get it done.

Ms. Wallace seemed pretty stone-faced about the situation. She was big on teaching her students about how the real world operated. If Vincent were in a meeting with a Texas oil billionaire and was not prepared to give the sales pitch, then he would be fired. Not turning in a single essay was the same thing to her.

Missing this one assignment virtually guaranteed that Vincent wouldn't be able to make an A in the class. Surely Mrs. Dean would be disappointed in Vincent if she learned of this.

He went to practice that afternoon, not really caring about his zero, not really caring if he performed well. No, that wasn't the case. He really did care. Somewhere down inside he cared, but there was a hard outer crust like that of an over baked loaf of bread that barred him from admitting that he cared. After all, life was difficult. After practice he would go eat and then have a lot more homework to make up. He would go to sleep, then wake up the next morning and do it all over again. Class, eat, practice, eat, study, sleep. His version of death and taxes.

Vincent took batting practice, whiffing on half of his swings and only putting a few balls in play. He also fielded some fly balls, misjudging one so badly that it skipped off the top of his glove and whacked him upside the head, knocking off his ball cap in the process.

His energy level was zero, and now he had a splitting headache. Frankly, all he wanted to do was go back to his dorm room and go to sleep now, forsaking the rest of the day. The trainer looked him over and had him sit out the rest of practice with an ice pack on his head.

After practice was over, Vincent got in his truck and drove past tennis practice. Evan was on the outside court, whacking the ball back and forth with another teammate. They were hitting the little yellow ball so hard and controlled that it was a blur, like a comet bouncing off planets.

Vincent put the truck in park and watched his roommate. While Evan was a train wreck off the court, he actually looked really graceful on the court. A master of an art. His points the strategy of a chess master, Evan would think two to three shots ahead each time he stroked the ball. He would string together a series of shots that stretched his opponent to each corner, running down each ball that Evan crushed. Then when the opponent was running way behind the baseline, Evan would hit a drop shot, using touch that was light as a feather.

In the times when his opponent could actually run to the net and reach the ball, Evan would merely lob the ball back over his opponent's head. The strategy was brilliant, the execution was flawless. And best of all, after the point was over, Evan wouldn't pump his fist or chest bump the coach or anything that would draw attention to himself. He would simply return to his spot on the baseline and wait for his opponent's next serve. Sweat poured off him, dripping down his nose and onto the handle of his racquet as he awaited the serve, but nothing could waver his hawk-like focus.

Once Vincent got back to the dorms, he grabbed a sandwich from the cafeteria and took it up to his room. Despite his splitting headache, he sat down at his desk and worked on a take home test for his literature class. The topic was sinfully boring, writings about early colonization. Some guy named Smith.

It required a lot of reading, and a few pages in, Vincent's head pounded beyond control. He took some ibuprofen and pounded a few energy drinks that he found in Evan's refrigerator, but nothing seemed to help. Resolved to get rid of the headache so he could finish the test, he lay down and took a late afternoon nap. He figured he would have plenty of time later that night.

Vincent woke up at 2:34 in the morning, his pulse in his head still beating like a snare drum. After relieving himself, he opened the door to his room, the light from the hallway shining on his roommate's form in bed.

He about closed the door when something twinkling caught his eye. Vincent closed the door and crossed the room in the dark, carefully and quietly reaching under his roommate's bed to grab the neck of a clear bottle. He took it back to his bed and held it in his hands. It seemed to vibrate, warming his palm. For a brief minute, Vincent forgot about his headache.

He unscrewed the cork and held it in his right hand. In the other bed, Evan snored ever so faintly. Absentmindedly, Vincent put the bottle up to his nose and took a modest whiff. It didn't seem to smell so bad this time. Instead of putting the cap back on, he held it a minute at his lips and breathed in the fumes. Suddenly his headache came back with a fury, and the pounding at his temples increased. He put his bottom lip on the bottle and tapped it against his strong teeth a few times. He paused for another second, and then the snoring stopped. His roommate turned over in his bed and smacked his lips.

His arms stretching outward, Evan reached for the floor and groped about blindly. Vincent silently slipped the cap back on the bottle and scooted it across the floor to where it came to a rest, two feet under Evan's head.

Evan sat bolt upright. "What was that?"

Vincent thought quickly, came up with nothing. "What?"

"What was that noise," Evan asked and reached over to his lamp and turned it on. The soft white bulb lightly illuminated the room. Vincent sat there, trying to look innocent, but if his head felt like a snare drum with the light off, it now felt like a bass drum in a college marching band, so he covered his eyes with the palm of both hands and rubbed his temples.

"I have a headache," Vincent said, hoping this would somehow make sense.

Evan rubbed his eyes and looked down at the floor. He must have seen the bottle half-hidden under the bed, because through the pain, Vincent saw him take his heel and slide it completely under the bed.

Evan looked up at Vincent, questioningly.

To spare Evan the embarrassment, Vincent looked down and played like he hadn't seen a thing, hoping Evan couldn't figure out that he had held the bottle. This whole thing was awkward.

"What are you doing up anyways?" Evan asked.

"Had to pee. I have a headache. Got hit with a ball at practice."

Evan rubbed his eyes this time and chuckled. "You okay dude?"

"I guess," Vincent said and noticed he could still see part of the bottle's cap sticking out from behind the bed sheet that hung down.

"Well," Evan said, and he reached over and turned off the light, "Hope your headache gets better."

"I hope it does too." Vincent lay down. He tossed and turned for an hour before going to sleep, not remembering his unfinished take-home test, but very conscious of the bottle beneath Evan's bed.

Not only did Vincent flunk the American Lit test, but he also forgot that he had a biology lab that next afternoon. His headache still present, he went back to the dorm, turned the AC unit on high, and took a nap after lunch and didn't wake up until 4:00. In fact, he wouldn't have woken up at all if he didn't hear a knocking at his door.

He dragged his sorry hide to the door and cracked it open, the light from the hallway blinding him. "Vincent, what's wrong?"

This was the unmistakable voice of his catcher, Tank. Big muscled and barrel-chested Tank. Team captain Tank.

Figuratively speaking, the coach on the field Tank.

Vincent opened the door the rest of the way and closed his eyes. Tank was fully dressed, his practice uniform dusty. "Hey, Tank. Why are you here?"

Vincent walked back to his bed and lay back down.

"Why am I here?" Tank repeated Vincent's question with incredulity in his voice. "I'll tell you why I am here. You are late to practice! Coach wants to know where our star pitcher is. I ran my butt all the way down here because I am concerned about you."

It took a second for Vincent to realize that he was late to practice. He sat up and rubbed at his head, his headache finally starting to go away. He looked under his roommate's bed and noticed that the cap of the bottle was still faintly visible. He worried that Tank might see this, and he might get kicked off the team, so he stood up, stretched his arms to the sky and his feet out to the side until he could feel his pinkie toe slide the bottle a little farther under the bed. Now to come up with a lie.

"Well, I…" and Vincent realized that he didn't even need a lie. He got hit in the head with a baseball and probably had a concussion. If anything, he should have gone to the hospital to get checked out. No, check that. The team physician should have checked him out. "My head is still killing me from that ball yesterday. I think I have a concussion."

Vincent looked up at Tank who was staring at him, his arms crossed at his massive chest. His head was cocked to the side. "You make it to class today?" Tank inquired.

Vincent thought really hard about what day it was, figured out that it was Thursday and that he had indeed missed his lab. Looking up at Tank, he said, "I made it to my American Lit class." Technically, Vincent wasn't lying. He had made it to his 10:00 American Lit class. It just so happened that he had forgotten completely about the lab. Then he realized that the biology class met at 8:00, so not only did he miss a lab, but he also missed a lecture. Honestly, he didn't know if he was supposed to have something prepared for the bio lecture. He thought about looking at the homework makeup sheet his coach had so graciously had prepared for him, but he instead played it cool.

His arms flexing, Tank kept his stare on Vincent. "Vincent, I'm only going to tell you this one time." He leaned in for more effect. "I don't like being lied to."

"I'm not lying!" Vincent's voice raised, but he was immediately cut off.

"I'm not done talking!" Tank snapped back and took an aggressive step towards the star pitcher. "Now I realize that you have been put through the ringer these last few weeks, but I'm not going to cut you any slack. Do you see this big letter C?" Tank pointed to the C on the left breast of his practice uniform. "That stands for captain. Do you know what the captain's job is? It's my job to make sure I keep the team working as one unit. It's my job to make sure everybody plays at a level they are capable of. It's also my job to keep everybody in line." Tank leaned in even more to where his face was mere inches away from Vincent's. Vincent smelled aftershave. "Right now you are out of line. I think you need some help. I am not about to sit back and watch you destroy a beautiful future, so I am requesting that Coach put you on a plan of improvement."

Vincent recoiled. "What is it, and why?" His flippancy came easily despite his fear of this large man that was yelling at him.

"That means that you will have somebody assigned to you to check with your teachers, make sure you are going to class, make sure you are turning in your papers, keeping up your grades. You do know that you can't play next semester if you don't pass at least twelve credit hours, don't you?"

"Of course I know," Vincent said. "I plan on passing *all* of my classes."

"Oh, it's not just about you passing your classes. It's about you doing your best in all your classes. Every year, we are in contention for Team Academic All-American status, and we even won the national title last year. As a starter, your GPA will be figured into that team total, and I want to win it again this year, and I can guarantee that Coach Johnson wants to win it again next year! He takes more pride in our grades than our ability on the field, so you better get with it."

Vincent slumped back into his bed and held onto his head. The pounding came back in full force, just thinking about making up all that work from when he was gone for the funeral, making up the biology work he missed today, and doing whatever was due of him this coming weekend. On top of that, the team would be traveling to Farmington, New Mexico to play Northwest New Mexico A&M. When he was going to do all of this, he had no idea, and it made his head pound worse.

"Can you tell Coach that my head is killing me, has been since the baseball hit me yesterday?"

Tank straightened back up and exhaled. "You going to be better tomorrow?"

"I hope so," Vincent responded, still not opening his eyes.

"What are your classes tomorrow?" Tank asked.

Vincent had to think for a second, which made his head hurt even more. "Speech, Biology, and Comp I."

"And do you have homework in any of those classes that needs to get done for tomorrow?"

Again Vincent had to think. "No. I plan on doing some makeup work."

Tank nodded. "Tell you what I am going to do. I am going to

go back to Coach and tell him how bad off you are. By the way, next time you play hooky from practice, you better call or text Coach. You got that?"

Vincent nodded.

"Again, I will tell him that you are in a lot of pain. But tonight I don't have anything to do, so I will be checking in on you. And tomorrow I will be asking you some of the same questions I asked you today, and if you try to give me the same lame excuses or lies, I will put you on a plan of improvement myself." Tank flexed his forearms, each muscle clearly defined and fighting for space under the limited amount of stretched skin. "And believe me, I will be a lot harder on you than the coaches. Got it?"

His hands covering his eyes now, Vincent nodded.

Tank didn't say goodbye, only let himself out. He didn't even close the door behind him.

"Jerk," Vincent said when he was positive Tank was half way down the hallway and completely out of earshot. He closed the door and threw himself back down into bed. The pounding increased and he wondered for a moment if the bottle under Evan's bed would help his headache go away. He grabbed it, saw that it was now three-quarters empty, and put it back down under Evan's bed. He wondered if Evan drank continuously all day and night. Regardless, if Vincent were to even steal one small sip, Evan might notice, and Vincent didn't want that.

After pounding one thousand milligrams of ibuprofen and stealing a quick sip from the faucet just outside of the bathroom, Vincent fell back into his bed and slept.

Tank was true to his word. He even showed up to Vincent's 7:30 Speech class, having been given special permission from Dr. Vonnegut to audit that session. Vincent's headache now seemed to be completely gone, due in large part to the ibuprofen and the fact that he slept from the time Tank left his dorm room until 5:30 that morning.

Dr. Vonnegut had the students draw straws for speeches, and luckily Vincent didn't draw a short straw and was able to watch others struggle in front of the class. The whole time Tank was behind him, breathing on his neck.

Tank skipped Vincent's next class, Principles of Biology, which allowed him a moment to speak with Mr. Stillwell after class about his missing assignments. Mr. Stillwell was far from reasonable, informing Vincent that unless he made prior arrangements to be gone, then he had better get used to the zero he received for the lab he missed. Vincent thought about calling him a bad name to his face and just walking out, but he let the steam flee from his ears and walked up the aisle of the lecture hall and out of the room.

To Vincent's surprise, Tank showed up at his English Composition I class before Vincent arrived and was talking to Ms. Wallace. Tank raised his eyebrows during the conversation, saw Vincent take a seat, then whispered something in Ms. Wallace's ear. She nodded and Tank thanked her. He walked up to Vincent and said, "You better get in that next assignment Monday. Guess what you will be doing on the bus ride over to Farmington tomorrow?" With that he walked out and Vincent's headache returned.

Vincent gutted out practice. When Coach Johnson asked him how he was feeling, he didn't lie. The trainer checked him over again. To be on the safe side, he took Vincent directly to the urgent care clinic. The urgent care doctor looked him over really well, found no signs of concussion, other than the headaches, and prescribed for Vincent a heavy duty painkiller and ordered him to drink extra fluids. The doctor even suggested that the headaches might be due to dehydration, which he described as being the same as a hangover, as if Vincent knew what that felt like. Most importantly, he cleared Vincent for the game on Saturday.

Against his wishes Vincent was able to write his next essay on the bus, a persuasive paper over why teenagers need more sleep than the normal person. Vincent figured he was an expert in such matters as of late and wished that inspiration would normally hit him so easily.

As for the ballgame, Vincent never saw the field. In the doubleheader Coach Johnson elected to throw Sandy in the first game, and another pitcher that Vincent didn't know well enough to know his name in the second game. Vincent thought he might get to see the outfield, or even be a designated hitter at least, but Coach was obviously resting him or punishing him. Vincent really didn't know which. As it ended up, the team didn't need him as they earned the sweep and drove back into Page late that night.

Adding up all the games they had played to that point, including the games he missed for his parents' funeral, they were now a sparkling 10-0 on the season. This might have made Vincent really happy, but he considered that he was really only responsible for one of those wins and was concerned that Coach Johnson had lost all faith in him.

Just before the players shuffled off the bus, Coach Johnson reminded them to go to church that next morning. Vincent trudged down the hill, past campus and back to his dorm where his roommate was again absent. He crashed and slept in that next morning.

Chapter Fourteen

VINCENT'S GOOSE EGG and headache finally went away a few days later. Tank hovered over Vincent for the next week, so Vincent buckled down, attended his classes, and worked his tail off at night to make sure all his work from the funeral week was made up, at least everything he could still turn in for a grade. Evan had given Vincent permission to use his laptop, which saved Vincent from multiple trips to The Doughnut to use their computers. He was able to turn most everything in on his web portal, making Evan's laptop even more valuable. Vincent was able to put in a ton of hours towards making up all his work, turning it in while in his underwear, which he decided was very convenient.

Evan had been gone that whole week at a tennis tournament in Miami, Florida. It was a preseason national tournament. He explained to Vincent that any team that was serious about being ranked nationally in the spring season should go to this tournament, because the coaches that made up the rankings were always there.

Evan himself had high hopes of being ranked in the top fifty nationally but knew that was going to be pretty hard, nearly impossible. He had told Vincent that the spring national tournament was almost entirely dominated by foreigners, coming to the U.S. to take advantage of the education system and hopefully springboard themselves into a pro career. In high school, Evan had faced some of the toughest American competition in the junior circuits in California, so he held out some hope.

With Evan out of the picture, Vincent found it easier to concentrate. Though he still found his roommate annoying, Vincent was beginning to like Evan. Evan had tried at least to hide his drinking from Vincent the last few weeks, a gesture Vincent appreciated. Still, he didn't trust Evan.

Sitting at his desk burning the midnight oil, Vincent was working hard on his biology homework, specifically on the probability of inheritance, likely scenarios for crossing a male and female and seeing what comes out in the offspring. They were called Punnett squares. What percentages would suggest that this baby will have second digit knuckle hair? Attached earlobes? Big nose? Pug nose? It wasn't even remotely interesting to him, especially since he didn't want to think about his parents whatsoever, much less why he turned out the way he did. So instead, his mind got to wondering about other things.

Curiosity killed the mouse, right?

There was one thing on Vincent's mind: alcohol. His roommate had been gone for five days to this point, and Vincent hadn't snooped in the least. But he wondered if Evan had stashed some alcohol in the room.

My father was an alcoholic. What are the percentages that I will be too? Maybe I don't even have a choice? Is there a Punnett square for that?

Without Evan around, there was nobody to keep him honest, responsible.

When the cat's away, the mice will play.

Vincent stretched in his chair and turned around to see his roommate's bed still in the unmade state Evan left it five days ago. Vincent craned his neck to see if the bottle was under the bed, but he couldn't tell. He leaned back just past the chair's tipping point and crashed to the floor.

Ouch.

Vincent lay on the floor laughing out loud. He didn't know what had gotten into him. This was totally out of character for him. He was always so reserved. Perhaps he had finally snapped.

He stared up at the ceiling, wondering if his neighbors heard the crash. That question was answered with a knock at the door two seconds later.

Still laughing, Vincent picked himself up and opened the door to see the kid from 12A standing there. Vincent couldn't remember his name, partly because he couldn't understand the kid in the few encounters they had had. He was from Viet Nam and didn't speak English very well. He was more reserved than Vincent, never opening his door, slipping out only when Vincent or Evan wasn't around. It was strange. Vincent thought the kid said his name was Fong, or maybe Thong, but without ever having seen it written down, Vincent couldn't be sure.

"Loud noise," Vincent's neighbor said with a look that was either concern or annoyance. Vincent took this in and tried to figure out what was on Fong's mind. From the look in his eyes, he appeared concerned, so Vincent smiled and said, "Sorry, man. I fell over in my chair."

His neighbor cocked his head to the side and Vincent could see the gears turning, so he stepped aside and showed the chair, still laying on its back on the floor. The neighbor looked at

Vincent and said, "Boom?"

Vincent smiled again and said, "Fall and go boom." He gestured with his hand and whistled until he made a boom noise.

"You okay?" his neighbor asked.

Vincent again smiled and said simply, "Yes."

His neighbor, apparently relieved, held out his hand. Vincent shook it out of courtesy, and his neighbor nodded, gave a quick bow, and with that, he was off.

Vincent closed the door and chuckled. Fong or Thong was a really nice guy and had even shared food with him one night earlier in the semester, one of the only times Vincent had seen him. The neighbor had out his wok and stir fried fresh green beans. Vincent knocked on his door, and was ushered straight in. As if he had invited Vincent, the neighbor promptly made him a plate with rice paper and green beans, wrapped up like a strange kind of burrito. Vincent didn't know what he had put in them, but those were the best dang green beans he had ever tasted. Their language difficulties were a barrier, and Vincent didn't know if Evan had met the guy yet, but Vincent made a note to invite his shy neighbor over for a movie or something. Vincent was sure Evan wouldn't mind. After all, Evan was not such a bad guy, was he?

He keeps alcohol around. If that nosey RA comes around and really gets to sniffing, we're going to get busted.

"Alcohol."

Vincent said it out loud and startled himself. He was still standing at the closed door, looking down at the fallen chair, then up at his homework, then over at his roommate's bed, down at the mini refrigerator, over at Evan's closet...there could be alcohol stashed everywhere!

Should I be upset? After all, that is part of the college experience, isn't it?

Vincent stood there staring now at the upturned chair. Tank entered his mind. Tank had been making visits every night to check up on him, and each time he had left happy because Vincent really was getting a lot of work done.

Vincent looked at the alarm clock, which read, 8:34.

Tank has been visiting pretty early in the evening. Easily before 8:00. Does this mean he isn't coming around tonight?

Vincent stood there and pondered this, not knowing why he was even pondering this in the first place. He wasn't doing anything that would cause suspicion. If anything, Tank should be proud of him. Vincent had manned up this past week. Or around here, they called it, "cowboying up."

But what if Tank were to search around in here? What if he found the booze?

It made sense to Vincent now that he should search the premises for any contraband. Yes, that made sense. In fact it was Vincent's duty to know what was in his room. With Evan gone and not expected back for another few days, he would check out their dorm room. He could at least know what he was dealing with then.

But then what would I do?

He was stumped. What if he found something? Would he then need to throw it away? That might cause an issue with Evan. Vincent didn't know the answer, but trusted his logic to figure it out if it came to that.

Leaving the chair on the floor, Vincent walked over to Evan's bed.

Falling to his knees, Vincent looked under the bed only to come up empty-handed.

There. Satisfied, Mr. Nosey?

"There are plenty of places to hide," Vincent said out loud, his solitary voice acting as a dialogue to his thoughts. He walked over to Evan's desk and lifted the blanket that hid Evan's refrigerator under the desk. Vincent opened it and found nothing but a few packets of ketchup from a local fast-food restaurant.

Well, that should satisfy you then.

For some reason at that moment, he thought of his father. Not liking the thought of his father at all, he shook his head and walked back to his side of the room to pick up his chair.

Sitting back down, Vincent stared at his Punnett squares and felt his eyes crossing. He tried refocusing and worked one problem, the odds of a baby having a widow's peak. He filled out the squares, reported the results, then looked at the next problem.

But what if Tank or the RA dig deeper?

Back up, Vincent did an about face and walked straight over to Evan's closet. Vincent opened the closet and took inventory: designer shirts, designer jeans, slacks, tennis shirts, tee shirts all hung nicely from the rack. On the floor were about ten pairs of shoes, apparently two for each occasion he could run into in Page, Arizona. There were shoe boxes way in the back, and Vincent, just to be thorough, fell to his knees to check them.

In one box was a pair of golf shoes. Vincent didn't realize Evan even played golf and found it quite strange that Evan would have golf shoes but not golf clubs.

Must have left them back in California.

In the next box, he found a set of baseball cards. Knowing that there might be some expensive cards in the box, and not wanting to devalue any of them by accidentally bending a corner, he put the top back on the box and stood up bewildered.

No booze?

This was unlike Evan. Evan seemed to be very serious about his national tournament, so Vincent figured his roommate wouldn't be stupid enough to bring anything illicit on the trip with him. On the other hand, this was Evan he was talking about, and that's exactly like something his roommate would do.

Listen to yourself! You almost sound disappointed that you didn't find anything! You should be ecstatic.

Satisfied, and feeling slightly sleazy for snooping through his roommate's personal belongings, Vincent returned to his desk to get some work done, but a thought struck him. He returned to Evan's closet and this time looked up. The top shelf, which was about a foot over his head, was bare at first sight. When he stood on his tip toes, he saw in the very back corner what appeared to be the top of a little black plastic box.

"What the…" Vincent started then reached up, not really knowing what he was going to touch. His imagination even let him conceive that he might get bit by a spider or a venomous snake. Vincent touched the box, felt the molded plastic with a checkering pattern, and had a moment of regret, though he knew not why. Grasping the unknown, he pulled it down, a lot heavier and bigger than he first imagined.

Vincent walked over to his desk and put the black plastic box down and wondered if it might have a block of gold concealed beneath its cover. Taking a deep breath, Vincent unlatched the clasp, opened it, and discovered a handgun.

His first reaction was to take a step back, as if it were a spider or venomous snake.

Vincent's thoughts were jumbled in his head. He had never touched a gun before. His father had a few guns around the house, but the old man had never considered it part of his paternal duty to teach his son anything regarding guns, including safety. As far as Vincent knew, his father's guns were used to shoot beer cans on Saturday nights.

Without hesitation Vincent closed the lid and returned the gun, intact, to the top shelf and closed his roommate's closet door. It worried Vincent that Evan had a gun. Having a gun on campus was just as illegal as having alcohol or drugs. Why would Evan have a gun?

Vincent sat back down at his desk and tried to clear his mind and get to work. As soon as he put pen to paper, he heard another knock on the door.

Oh, Fong! I really don't have the time for this!

Vincent opened the door and saw the captain standing there. Vincent looked back at his clock, which read 9:01.

"Tank?"

"Hey Special K," his catcher said, looking tired. "How's your homework coming?"

Vincent stepped out of the way to let Tank enter and pointed to his desk. "Working on biology right now."

"What's the topic," Tank asked, a bit nosey, but he knew Tank was just doing his job.

"Punnett squares."

"And what is that?" Tank inquired.

"I think you know," Vincent said, but complying, answered, "They are used to determine what characteristics a baby will have, depending on the parents."

Tank nodded in approval and looked around the room. Vincent also checked out his room to make sure that it was up to all standards. From what he could tell, he was in compliance with any strict guidelines his catcher might have for him. For a brief moment Vincent wondered if Tank had to go through such rigorous scrutiny when he was a freshman.

Tank nodded in approval and asked, "Well, do you need any help with anything?"

"Just some caffeine," Vincent said and laughed. When Tank didn't smile, Vincent shook his head. "I'm doing just fine. Thanks though."

Tank nodded again and paused before leaving. "You know Vincent," he said and paused, "I'm sorry I had to be so tough on you, but it's my job to make sure that certain freshmen are doing what they are supposed to, and—"

"Tank, there's no need to apologize. I understand. I just thank you for caring."

Tank stood there in mid-sentence and closed his mouth, nodding again. "Okay. You ready for tomorrow's game?"

"University of California San Bernardino," Vincent responded, thinking about what a mouthful that was.

Tank nodded solemnly. "They're pretty good. All those California schools are. That's why we play here. To get the chance to take it to the California schools."

Vincent smiled.

Tank took another step towards the door and said, "You know, Vincent, Coach Johnson is going to test you tomorrow."

"Oh? How so?" Vincent asked.

"I hear you will be pitching one of the two games and playing outfield the other. That's what a little birdie has told me, anyways." Tank paused. "So, as soon as you're done with your homework, it might be wise to get your rest."

Vincent nodded and waited for any more advice Tank might have.

Apparently sensing that he had said too much, Tank walked to the door and nodded and was off. Vincent shut the door behind Tank and felt happy. He forgot all about his father, the gun, shooting beer cans, and only thought about how peaceful it was to be standing on top of the mound without anything else in the world to take up his attention. Some needed yoga. Others conducted Japanese tea ceremonies. All Vincent needed was a baseball and a small dirt hill.

He finished his homework and went to bed before 10:00. As

Vincent lay in bed, staring at the ceiling, he imagined himself, striking out all of his opponents the next day. The thought made him smile.

A thin light filtered in through the window blinds from the street lamp and illuminated the ceiling that Vincent stared at as he daydreamed. It also cast slight, broken shadows, and it was then that Vincent noticed that one of the ceiling tiles drooped a little, casting a longer shadow.

Turning the light on, Vincent scooted a chair over to the middle of the room and stood on top of it. He propped open the tile next to it, reached in, and pulled out a bottle of whiskey, the same one he had up to his lips the other day.

He sat back down on his bed with the bottle in hand and the lights off and tried not to think. Images of his drunken father came to mind again, but then again, images of Evan also floated in his mind. Evan with his pretty girlfriend. Evan with the girls from the tennis team. Evan with any one of his girls. What was it about Evan that attracted girls to him?

It's the alcohol, idiot. Evan is fun. You're not. There's a reason for that.

Vincent frowned and unscrewed the top to the bottle. He took a whiff, winced, and thought of his father yet again. Were there any times in his life when he loved his father? Respected his father? Surely there was something endearing about his father? Surely he held something in common with the man who provided half of his DNA, the man who provided half of the equation to the Punnett square that was Vincent Preston.

The smell of the liquor beckoned him. "Who am I?" Vincent heard himself say out loud.

You are a punnett square of your mom and your dad, that's who you are.

"I am my father."

The bottle was at his lips. And it was too much. It tipped. The liquid slid down his throat. It burned the whole way.

It was a practice in suppressing the gag reflex, but the shot went down fiery, not-so-smooth. Yet it still went down, settling in the pit of his stomach, burning like a fireplace that made him feel warm, maybe even a little safe.

That was not so bad.

Vincent waited and felt nothing revolt in his stomach. He waited a few minutes and decided that if he were to fill out the Punnett square for himself and drinking, it would come to a probability of holding his liquor. Not only that, it felt good to do the wrong thing for once.

Honestly, what is so wrong about this? Nearly every college kid in America is doing this right now. If my father were alive, this is what he would be doing.

Vincent shook his head the way Tank had nearly an hour before, but Vincent knew he was shaking his head because he had been oblivious for far too long.

The bottle tipped again, and Vincent took another pull.

Chapter Fifteen

VINCENT WOKE UP at 8:00 with a splitting headache. In fact he had never felt so bad in his life. He fumbled his way to the bathroom sink and popped some ibuprofen, slurping a few handfuls of water to wash it down, hoping that would take the edge off of the pounding. It was so consuming, that he could only think of one thing, a bible verse he had learned at Sunday school with Mrs. Dean just before he left Oklahoma. It ran through his head over and over. "And I looked, and behold a pale horse: and his name that sat on him was Death, and Hell followed with him."

It came from somewhere in the book of Revelations, though he couldn't remember what chapter or verse, or care for that matter.

Death. Hell. That sounds about right.

He walked back to his bed and saw the empty bottle on the floor.

The pale horse? I guess that would make me Death and this headache

Hell.

He tried to go back to sleep, this being a Saturday and a great opportunity to catch some much needed z's, but he just couldn't. It hurt more when he lay his head down, so he propped himself on his elbow, his head cradled on his hand. This seemed to help a little, at least for a while.

...and Hell followed with him.

Why couldn't he get the scripture out of his head? Think about nothing? Think about something else? Anything was better than what he was going through. He hoped the ibuprofen would work, but he really had no idea how to stop a hangover.

If Dad were still alive, I could just ask him. Lending on his expertise. A little father-son bonding. He would be so proud.

Frowning, he thought again about the verse, and realized that he hadn't been to church once since he had moved out to Arizona two months ago. It's not that he was against it, but it really just slipped his mind, he guessed. Sure, Coach Johnson was always reminding his players to attend Sunday service, and Tank had invited him a few times. Maybe this was why he had a headache. A karma of some kind? He doubted this, but was unwilling to rule out anything. If going to church was going to get rid of this headache, then he would resolve to do so tomorrow.

He managed to fall asleep for another hour, but when he awoke with nightmares about a white horse and a faceless rider, he was up, wiping the sweat from his face. His head pounded harder than ever, so he knew he had to do something right away. Obviously the medicine hadn't worked.

He got up and grabbed his roommate's laptop. When he got onto the Internet, he googled "hangover relief" and found an article about drinking electrolyte water for babies. Supposed to work like a charm.

He gave it a little thought, stumbled over to his window and peeked out to see a bluebird day.

"No way."

His head was not going to be able to take the bright sunlight, and the nearest druggist store was downtown, at least a fifteen minute walk from his dorm room. He wasn't about to drive feeling like this.

Vincent decided that it had to come down to dehydration of the brain, so he went back to the bathroom sink and held his head under the faucet for five minutes, painfully gulping luke-warm water. Choking, he barfed most of it up.

When he went back to bed, he felt sick to his stomach, had a bad taste in his mouth, and his head pounded even worse.

He felt like crying. For the life of him, he couldn't figure out why Evan did this to himself. Actually, Vincent had gained a little respect for Evan, for being able to put up with this kind of pain and nausea on a near-daily basis. Still, he had never seen Evan throw up or suffer from a hangover, unless sleeping in and missing class was a punishment. As for Vincent's own father, had he ever come down from his drunken state? Probably drank constantly so as not to experience a hangover.

None of that mattered to Vincent though. As he lay down and tried not to die, he thought, or tried to think about what had happened last night. He remembered finding the bottle, taking it down and taking a few sips of it. Beyond that, his memory was quite foggy.

Honestly, what is the allure of drinking?

Life experience. That was what he was going to chalk this up to. He now had an adult life experience on which he could draw later on to make wise choices. This was one choice he knew he was never going to make again. He thought about how he might be able to get an essay out of this for his composition class.

Surely he could find some benefit from such a lousy experience. Lemonade out of lemons. One sad thought air brushed over the essay idea. He now could not say that he had never drank before. He had lost some of his innocence, some of his purity, never to have it back again.

Then there was the thought about what Mrs. Dean would say. Vincent quickly decided that she should never know.

Looking at the alarm clock, Vincent closed his eyes again and managed to fall to sleep, hoping that the next time he woke, he would feel better.

When Vincent awoke, he did feel better. He wasn't hungry, felt a little icky in the stomach. When he looked at the alarm clock, it read 2:31. He had slept right through lunch and had to report to the ball field in a couple of hours. Tank had warned him that he would have a big night, that Coach Johnson was ready to put him back out there. He better get his act together, and fast.

He showered, the hot water feeling great on his skin and making him forget about his stomach pains, or what passed for a slight remnant of a headache. When he got dressed, he walked downtown, keeping his eyes closed against the glare of the sun most of the time before he got to the drug store and bought the magic elixir that the website had referenced. He also grabbed a hamburger from the refrigerated section along the far wall. They didn't have a microwave, so he walked home and ate a cold charbroil with cheese and washed it down with baby water that tasted slightly salty. It made him want to throw up all over again.

Thankfully it worked. By the time he got to the ballpark, he felt much better. He felt slightly off-balance, like the night's revels had affected his inner ear, but he passed it off as he ran a lap. His legs didn't seem to want to go like they normally did, and he felt a lagging resistance, like he was pulling a parachute behind him. Sweat poured from his forehead, and he wiped it with the bill of his cap. On the inside bill of the cap, he saw the scripture, blurry, but still legible:

Phil 4:13

Yeah, I know. I need to go to church.

It seemed more of a hassle than he remembered it being back home. He hated that, but he couldn't convince himself that he would actually get up in the morning, now that he knew he wasn't going to die.

When UCSB arrived and warmed up, the crowd got anxious. The stands filled more quickly than normal, which was usually pretty quick. Vincent figured it was because the early October weather was quite a bit more palatable. Or maybe it was because that this was their last home date until the spring when the real season began. They still had that road trip to California coming up next week, but he could feel a special magic in the air and knew he had to shape up quickly, or possibly lose his spot in the rotation and the batting lineup.

He had been given a pass already after his parents' deaths. This was undoubtedly Coach Johnson's way of easing him back into the swing of things, and Vincent didn't want to let him down, or the home crowd, especially given the ovation he received the last time he took the mound. So twenty minutes before game time when Coach Johnson told Vincent to warm up his arm, Vincent needed to cowboy up.

On the practice hill, he tried to focus, but everything caught his attention. Most annoying was the crowd's chanting of "Special K! Special K! Special K!" It came mostly from the student section, but seemed to be spreading through the stands.

The nickname was a source of pride before, when he made his grand appearance to the home crowd. They hadn't had a chance to see him play since that first pitching performance when he earned his nickname. But things had changed. Vincent felt like he had changed. Since his parents died, everything had changed.

Before he was a boy playing a boy's game. Now he was parentless, and essentially homeless. Now he was carrying around a ton of guilt. He was now no longer unstained. And somewhere in all of this mess, he seemed to have lost zip and location of his fastball.

Each pitch veered in a way he did not intend. It was a most annoying development, and he tried to concentrate on what the problem could be, but for that annoying, "Special K! Special K! Special K!"

I don't deserve that nickname.

After a good fifteen or twenty pitches, Tank got up and jogged over to him. As the chanting continued, Tank came face-to-face with the young ace.

"What's your story? The crowd getting to you?"

Vincent looked down and kicked at some dirt at the front of the rubber. He shook his head at the suggestion, though partly true. When he shook his head, he felt dizzy.

"The heat then? You know, it will cool off shortly. That's the great thing about autumn in the desert."

Vincent swiped the rubber with his foot, feeling very uncomfortable with the conversation, wishing Tank would simply return to his spot behind the plate.

"You stay up too late last night?"

"Yeah," Vincent said. That much was true, at least he thought it was.

Tank patted Vincent on the arm. "I really admire the way you've cowboyed up lately. You've been able to pull it together in ways I'm not sure I would have been able to. Actually, I can't imagine." Tank looked back to the dugout where Coach Johnson stood at the top of the steps, a look of puzzlement on his face. Tank nodded and dismissed his coach with a wave of his catcher's mitt.

"Keep your head up," Tank said and lifted Vincent's chin. Then his expression changed. "Why are your eyes bloodshot?"

Uh-oh.

Thinking quickly, Vincent replied saying way too much, "Stayed up too late. Didn't get enough sleep. I took a nap this afternoon, so I should be good. You just call the pitches, and I will get them to you. I have a feeling it will all come together quickly."

Vincent nodded at Tank who didn't seem very convinced. Tank paused a little longer, grabbed Vincent's chin again, and tilted his head from side-to-side, causing Vincent's head to throb a little more. Then he said, very gravely, looking directly into Vincent's eyes, "Do you have anything more to tell me?"

Vincent wrestled his chin from Tank's grip and backed up a pace. "No! Now just let me warm up!"

Tank didn't move a muscle, didn't flinch. He stood there for five more uncomfortable seconds before walking backwards to the bullpen home plate, keeping his gaze upon Vincent the whole time.

I think I just ticked off a very large man.

Vincent tried to ignore his impending fear, but he thought he knew Tank better than to worry about any repercussions. His attention refocused and a little angry, he burned a few more fastballs in there, this time with excellent control, then waved off his catcher much the way his catcher had waved off the coach. His head pounded worse than ever, so he headed straight to the dugout and drank cup after cup of water to quench his unquenchable thirst. When he was sure nobody was looking, he popped four ibuprofen tablets.

"There's something wrong with him," Tank whispered into Coach Johnson's ear. Even though Tank had drug Coach Johnson into the tunnel between the locker room and the dugout and away from everyone else, he wasn't going to risk letting anyone hear him.

Coach Johnson put his hand up to his chin in a thinking posture and said, "What makes you think so?"

"His head's not right."

"Well Tank, his parents did just die."

Tank shook his head, the truth irrelevant. "Sir, I think it's more than that. I think he's hiding something, and he won't open up to me."

Coach Johnson nodded and said, "Now Tank, would you want to be opening up to people right after your parents died?"

Tank pondered this for a second. Maybe Coach Johnson was right. Maybe he was reading too much into Vincent. Still, he couldn't shake this bad feeling. "Sir, I don't know why, but I think Vincent is under too much pressure, or too much stress, or is into something bad, or something." He wasn't making much sense, so he tried to clarify his thoughts. "What I'm trying to say is that he's about to snap. He's not ready to pitch tonight."

"Well," Coach Johnson said, "when will he be ready? We're running out of chances to get him on the mound this fall."

Tank nodded. "I don't know sir, but you asked me to stay on top of him, and I have. I have seen him lie to me, placate me, and even yell at me. You want my honest opinion? I say sit him. He's not ready."

Coach Johnson took in a deep breath and sighed. He closed his eyes for a few moments and finally opened them. He looked back to through the tunnel towards the field. "Tank," Coach Johnson said with resolve, "sometimes we just need to get back in the saddle. Now Vincent is more comfortable on top of the mound than he is anywhere else. I really think that pitching again will help him heal. Now do you respect my decision?"

Tank lowered his head in submission and said, "Yes, sir."

Coach Johnson patted his captain on the shoulder and said, "I appreciate all you've done for him. You keep up the good work, and we will be able to help him through this tough time." Coach Johnson waited a moment longer, nodded, then walked the length of the tunnel back to the dugout.

Still, Tank couldn't shake the feeling.

Try as he might, he could not plug his ears to the crowd's chanting when he was on the mound, so he tried to embrace it. The medicine had given him some reprieve from the pounding that had begun to come back with force, and with a new lease on his equilibrium, he focused on his first batter.

Vincent knew absolutely nothing about the UCSB lineup. He trusted in his catcher to veer him in the right direction in regards to pitch selection, but Tank hadn't said a word to Vincent since he had yelled at his catcher. Vincent felt a little bad about that, but a cool breeze fanned the back of his neck as evening approached, and he settled into what he hoped would be a groove.

Facing his catcher, he received his sign, a four-seamer on the inside corner.

Lightning and thunder, Vincent!

Vincent went into his windup, paused at the top of his knee kick, ever so slightly, and felt off-balance. He delivered, falling to his left a little bit. The ball followed suit, traveling right down the pipe.

Lightning!

Thunder!

171

CRANK!

Vincent turned around to watch the ball sail to left field, getting smaller and smaller. The left fielder turned and ran to the fence. The opposing dugout all yelled in unison, "I see numbers!" in reference to the number 21 on the left fielder's back.

He reached the fence and waited, but the ball never came down. It just seemed to keep going and probably ended up at the bottom of San Antonio Hill. On the scoreboard the clock read: 100 MPH.

Vincent stole a look at the batter who was jogging to second base with a smile on his face as he also snuck a peek at Vincent.

It angered Vincent that he had just given up a gopher ball on the first pitch, one so fast, he was sure no one could hit it. Also he noticed the crowd's chanting had stopped, and a few audible grumblings replaced it.

"Hey, don't hang your head," Hoover said from the shortstop position and clapped his glove. "It's just one run. We'll get it back!"

"No you won't," the batter said over his shoulder as he passed Hoover on the base path.

"You want to say that to me?" Vincent yelled at the guy who had just smoked Vincent's last pitch. Vincent stepped off the mound and walked in the guy's general direction.

"Whoa!" yelled Tank, but it was too late. Vincent was going to have it out with the wise guy.

The entire UCSB bench stepped up out of their dugout and walked towards the third base line to accept Vincent's challenge. Vincent kept advancing anyway and was halfway to the opposing team with his glove off and ready to go when his catcher tackled him like a linebacker hitting a defenseless wide receiver who had stretched out to catch a high pass over the middle of the field. It took Vincent's breath away. The crowd gasped.

"Vincent!!! You settle down right now!" Tank whisper-yelled at Vincent so that only those within a ten foot radius could hear. The rest of the infield ran over to the scene of the accident.

"Get off me!" Vincent managed to say, each word between breaths. Apart from having the breath knocked out of him, Tank was solid muscle, and very heavy, weighing down his chest.

"Not till you settle down!"

Vincent struggled but quickly found that he was going nowhere. Hoover stood over him, saying, "Just chill out, man! Don't let them get you down!" Then Vincent looked up and saw Coach Johnson standing above him.

"Let him up," Coach told Tank, who cooperated, jumping up and pulling Vincent off the ground. Vincent looked past Coach to the opponent's dugout where all the players still stood, now back to the top of the steps, but still ready to have a go at him. Both the home and field umpires were between the two teams, surely shocked that one pitch in they would have to referee a scrum. One held Tank back as he pointed his facemask at the batter and told him in an unkind way that he better not say another word to his pitcher.

Vincent's first urge was to run over there and just see how many punches he could get in before getting pummeled. Surely his teammates would have his back? Still, he didn't want to disobey Coach Johnson, so Vincent looked Coach in the eyes.

Tank walked back over to the huddle. Coach put a hand on Vincent's shoulder and applied a little pressure. It was a firm, reassuring gesture. "Vincent, what are you thinking?"

Vincent didn't have an answer. The fact was that Vincent had no clue why he sprang off that mound, ready to pound the leadoff hitter. That certainly wasn't a part of his regular demeanor, and now that Coach and the rest of the team were huddled around him, practically in a group hug, Vincent now felt very selfish, despite what that jerk had said to Hoover.

When Vincent didn't answer, Coach Johnson looked over to his catcher and said, "Tank?"

"Yes, sir." Tank replied, then he lit into Vincent. "Vincent, what good would it do for you to get thrown out of this game? Can't you see that is what they are trying to do? Man, they have heard of you. Everybody has. They are testing you, and you failed that first test. Now they know you're emotional. They think you're a hot head." Tank tapped Vincent on the forehead and said, "They are now living rent-free right here. Is that what you want?"

Vincent was furious. He knew deep down that everything Tank was saying was true, and Vincent was madder at himself for reacting the way he did than he was at Tank for tackling him in front of the home crowd. Still, he wished he could just turn back the clock. Now his coach and teammates would think he was a hot head. Now word would get around to other teams that they can rattle him. After all, baseball is so much more than a physical game.

Tank continued, "You have nobody to blame for that home run but yourself. I wanted it inside, and you put it right over the plate. This is a good team, one that will have batters that can hit the fastball. But none of that matters now. The only thing that matters is that you screw your head on straight and get back into this thing. We are all depending on you."

"You about ready, Coach?" the head ump asked. Coach Johnson ignored him.

Vincent looked down, now fully shamed. All his infielders patted him on the back with their gloves and said encouraging things as they returned to their positions. Vincent listened to none of them. Coach Johnson still held onto Vincent's shoulder and asked Tank to return to home plate. Since Coach had let Tank do all the talking, Coach must have wanted to get in the final word.

"Vincent," Coach Johnson said after the catcher had cleared out.

"Yes, sir?"

"Tank is right. Now forget about that last batter and get the next one." The hand patted him on top of the shoulder and moseyed off to the two umpires who had a conference with the two head coaches. Once Coach Johnson returned to the dugout, the game resumed.

The second batter, a lefty, stepped into the batter's box, a huge smile across his face.

Forget about it, Vincent.

Vincent looked down at his catcher who gave him the same sign. This time, being a lefty, the inside corner would be left. Vincent considered this and shook off his catcher.

What are you doing, Vincent? Listen to your catcher!

Tank was visibly mad, but called for a two-seamer to move from right to left, essentially the exact same pitch if location was the only thing that mattered.

Vincent went into his windup, forgetting about any mental preparation, grunted, and delivered with all he had.

Lightning!

Thunder!

CRANK!

This time the ball sailed to deep right field, and again, the opposing dugout yelled in unison, "I see numbers!"

The ball traveled at the same trajectory as the previous one, but hung up in a brief puff of wind. It hit the top of the fence and came back down into play. The right fielder corralled the ball and heaved it to Steinbeck, the second baseman who was the cutoff guy.

Meanwhile the batter was greedy and turning the corner at second, heading to third.

Steinbeck caught the ball in the middle of his stride, and in one complete motion, fired a laser to third base. The runner slid face first for a bang-bang play.

The field umpire was right on top of the call, "SAFE!" The call made Vincent's heart sink.

Now with a base runner on third, Vincent would have to pitch out of the stretch, not his favorite thing to do. It took away his velocity advantage, but if the first two batters were any indication, the advantage was nullified. His headache started to return.

As Vincent took the mound again, the opposing dugout yelled all sorts of demeaning things at him. He tried not to listen, but they were so loud that it was palpable. Everything from him having a weak fastball, to him being a hick from Oklahoma.

How did they even know that I'm from Oklahoma?

The crowd started to boo the opposing team's dugout, but that only seemed to spur them on more.

Vincent looked back at his catcher who shook his head as if to say to Vincent, "Stop listening," to which Vincent, if telepathy were possible, would have retorted with, "You first!"

The third batter stepped into the right hand batter's box and took a few practice cuts. Vincent didn't even bother to look at the guy's face, but to keep his stare on his catcher and try not to think about the pounding in his head.

Tank called for a fastball, high. Very high. He obviously wanted to see if the guy would chase a pitch out of the strike zone, since the first two batters were swinging away on the first pitch. Vincent went into the stretch, gave a quick glance at the base runner, then delivered home with a grunt.

Lightning!

Thunder!

The ball rose high alright, so high that it skipped off of Tank's glove and crashed into the screen behind the backstop. The base runner sprinted for home and easily scored. On top of it all, the batter never even took the bat off of his shoulder.

Vincent walked back to the mound and tried to look on the bright side. At least now he wouldn't have to pitch out of the stretch. Repositioning himself and wanting to speed up the pace, he waited for his sign, a circle changeup inside.

Agreeing with the sign, Vincent went into his windup and gave a fake grunt before releasing.

The batter started to swing before he realized what was happening and completely missed.

Now that's more like it!

Vincent forced a little smile while he hid his face with his glove.

See, Vincent. This game is supposed to be fun.

When Tank asked for another four-seam fastball, Vincent delivered, again feeling off-balance, and the ball this time sailed way outside and hit the dirt a foot in front of the plate. Tank had to dive to knock the ball down.

"Two and one," the umpire called out from behind the plate.

Yeah, I'm keeping count, buddy.

Vincent knew he didn't want to get behind three balls and one strike in the count because that was considered a hitter's count to swing away, yet he didn't know if he could even get the ball over the plate at this point. His confidence was totally shattered, and he cursed himself for even worrying about any of this.

You are your own worst enemy right now!

On the fourth pitch, Tank asked for a slider that ended up not sliding much. Not Vincent's favorite pitch to begin with, the ball sat over the plate and the batter crushed it, a line drive to the left center gap.

Again the opposing bench shouted, "I see numbers!" as the outfielders sprinted to the fence.

This time the centerfielder was able to get the ball back into the infield quickly to limit the batter to a standup double. He scored on the very next pitch, a single that burned right up the middle, Vincent diving to the dirt to avoid getting his head knocked clean off. It was in picking himself up off the bottom of the mound that he realized the first four batters collectively hit for the cycle against him: a single, a double, a triple, and a home run. Not a good start.

Tank called for time and walked out to the mound. Another uninspiring pep talk went in one of Vincent's ears and out the other. Vincent was stuck inside his own head, searching for answers and only receiving the pounding of his heartbeat thumping against the front of his skull. If he could pop some more pills and drink some more water, maybe he would be able to knock it out. Was all this due to drinking the last night? If so, then he vowed he would never do it again. He also vowed to go to church the next morning if God would only get him out of the inning. God's response came when the next batter hit another single.

Vincent tried to settle down and just throw, but his concentration was just plain off. The entire UCSB lineup batted the first inning, and it was from the work of a few nice fielding plays by the infield, including a double play, that he was finally able to walk off the mound and head straight for the water jug.

On his way in, he looked up in the stands and saw his roommate, sitting on the front row with a concerned look on his face. Vincent wondered why Evan was home a day early, but soon dismissed the question and focused on batting.

Coach had stenciled him in as the leadoff hitter again, a position he relished, but it left him no time at all to take more medicine or drink a cup of water. Besides, everyone patted him on the back and gave him little reassurances like, "Keep your head up." He felt he couldn't get away from his teammates fast enough.

When he dug into the batter's box, he looked at the pitcher for the first time, as he didn't have a chance to study the guy's pitches, much less get a plan. Remembering what happened last time, he looked over at Coach Johnson who gave him the "swing away" sign.

Good.

When the first pitch came in, Vincent was not ready for it. It was a fastball that started inside and rose towards his nose. Vincent bailed out and missed taking a dirt nap by mere inches.

The umpire stepped in. "Both benches have been warned!" he yelled and pointed to Coach Johnson and the opposing coach, then at the pitcher, who seemed to not even acknowledge the umpire. Finally, Vincent looked at the pitcher and recognized him as the leadoff batter.

What the heck? First he jacks me for a dinger and brags about it, then he flips me some chin music? Does this guy just have it out for me?

The pitcher's comments as he had been rounding third base now made sense at least. When Hoover had told Vincent that they would get that run back, the leadoff batter had been simply stating his case as a pitcher. Still it was uncalled for, just like the high, inside cheese that the guy had just flipped Vincent.

Vincent jumped back up and vowed not to get mad. He looked into the dugout at Tank who was staring back at Vincent, surely curious how Vincent was going to react. Instead of any reaction, Vincent looked back at Coach Johnson, got his sign, then waited for the pitch.

When it came, Vincent immediately recognized the changeup and knew the right call was on. Vincent held the bat gingerly in front of the plate and tapped a bunt down the third-base side. Like lightning he was out of the batter's box and booking it down to first, but unlike lightning, he noticed that the usual zip in his legs was missing. His thighs were mushy, his calves not giving much thrust. He dug in for all he was worth, but his legs felt more like gelatin than a bundle of high-twitch fibers.

Despite dragging a plow, Vincent gave it all he could, dove head-first into the bag, but was beaten by the throw from the third baseman by an eyelash. Vincent knew it, wasn't about to argue it. His head pounded too hard for him to dare.

The first baseman looked down at Vincent and laughed and innocently kicked a little dirt in Vincent's face before he threw the ball around the horn. It wasn't enough that the first base umpire saw, but Vincent's mouth was open. He tried to spit the dirt out on the jerk's shoe but missed. Sulking, Vincent retired to the dugout, again to a round of back patting from his teammates. He felt lower than ever.

The next two players grounded out so quickly that Vincent was only able to grab one glass of water to chug.

Catching his breath, Vincent ascended the steps again, trying not to think, trying not to feel. His only effort was to put one foot in front of the other. Breathe. Survive. Escape. He wished he were back in the showers with hot water cascading over his pounding head.

On the mound and waiting for his catcher to strap up, Vincent had a few moments to collect himself and go back over his training. Hard as it was, he sought to think without his head hurting. Naturally his thoughts directed him to Grandpa Dean. Grandpa Dean had taught him everything he needed to know, right? Had he ever taught him what to do when rattled? He certainly would have celebrated that high and tight fastball the opposing pitcher had flipped at him.

Grandpa Dean was old school, wasn't he?

Being old school meant that when one of your players is thrown at by the opposing pitcher, it is your job to return fire somewhere in the same game. The unwritten rule was that the pitcher only got one pitch to throw at the batter of choice. Of course it was a matter of picking a target.

That didn't seem too hard as up walked the leadoff batter, again. Vincent kept his glove over his face to hide any emotion and wait for the sign from Tank. Vincent saw that the batter was nearly standing on top of the plate and made up his mind what pitch he was going to throw well before Tank gave a sign.

Tank asked for a fastball outside, and Vincent smiled and nodded. Frankly, it didn't matter where Tank set up behind the plate. The ball wasn't going to touch his glove.

Vincent felt a ball of hot fire come up out of the pit of his stomach and manifest itself in his right arm. He held his breath, letting the hotness grow all over his body, until he pictured himself as having a force field of fire hovering not an inch from his silhouette. Forget Tank's words of encouragement. Forget Coach Johnson's easy way of calming him down. Forget Mrs. Dean's loving touch. Forget the goose bumps he felt when the brunette smiled at him. The fire gripped him like he gripped two seams of the ball, with hostility. His eyes widened, then sharpened. Vincent went into his windup, focused this time on balance, and strode forth with his loudest grunt yet. He put everything he had into this pitch.

Lightning!

Thunder!

CRACK!

The ball started inside and low and the batter had no time to get out of the way. The ball smacked the batter right on the knee cap and actually sounded like the ball had been hit by a wooden bat. Had Vincent cared, the sound of the shattering kneecap would have made him cringe. Instead he smiled and stared at the shrieking lump laying on top of the plate face down.

The batter rolled around in the dirt, clutching at his left knee and screaming like a jackrabbit in the jaws of a coyote.

The whole time, Vincent stood at the base of the mound, staring at his victim with that smile. Cold. Emotionless. That is until the umpire stepped into his field of view.

"You're out of the game!" he said and gave a sweeping gesticulation with his arm.

"What?!" Vincent said, incredulous.

"Get off this field!" the umpire responded, so Vincent took a step in closer for explanation. It didn't seem to make much sense to him. He had gotten thrown at, and he owed the guy one. That was how this game was played. Still screaming in agony, the batter rolled around, now being attended to by a trainer and a coach. The other coach was trying to coax the players back into the dugout. Vincent turned around to see his infield at his back, just in case.

"I said, 'Get off this field right now, young man. If you don't, I will file a formal protest with the governing body and have you expelled from playing college ball this year!"

Vincent kept walking towards the umpire until Coach Johnson jumped in front of him and yelled, "Get your butt into the locker room, right now!"

Vincent couldn't believe it. First, he had never heard Coach Johnson yell. This didn't bother him so much as the fact that Coach Johnson was not backing his play!

Just for good measure, Tank bear hugged Vincent and carted him off the field and back into the locker room, as Coach

Johnson had commanded. Vincent yelled at the umpire the whole way.

Tank didn't let go until he sat Vincent down in front of his locker. Then he laid into him. "Man, did you listen to me at all? What on earth could be going through your head? You are now out of the game and out for the second game as well! What good are you to us if you are sitting in the locker room? Huh?"

"BUT—"Vincent yelled back, but Tank wasn't finished.

"I'M NOT DONE WITH YOU!" Tank yelled. "What you just did was selfish. I did not call for that pitch. If I want you to flip a player, I will give you the sign. Otherwise, you are to do exactly what I say!" Tank's voice rose the angrier he became. "AND NO CALLING ME OFF ANY MORE! YOU HEAR ME? WHEN I CALL FOR A PITCH, YOU THROW IT! YOU ARE A ROBOT. I PROGRAM YOU. YOU DO WHAT I SAY. PERIOD!"

Tank stormed off, leaving Vincent to himself. Vincent's anger boiling over now after that excoriation, he slammed his glove into his locker, picked up the wooden towel basket, which must have weighed fifty pounds, and heaved it as far as he could, shot put style. Towels flew everywhere. It slammed into a locker against the far wall and splintered into two pieces.

"AAAAAAUUUUUGGGGGHHHHHHH!!!!!!!!!!!!"

Destroying the basket wasn't good enough. His head felt ready to burst, so he thought he would just help it along a little. He took a running start and head-butted his locker as hard as he could. His locker, as well as the other nine lockers that were attached to his, fell over with a bang loud enough for anyone in the stands to hear.

And still this didn't feel like enough destruction! There were no conscious thoughts running through his head. No conscience. No devil on one shoulder and an angel on the other.

Everything that he had been keeping inside of himself for so long came out. Grandpa Dean's death, his parents' deaths, the abuse he endured at the hands of his father all those years, being made fun of by his high school teammates, being treated unfairly by his high school coach, the extraordinary amount of homework he had to make up from being gone for his parents' funeral, being all alone in this world, and anything else that was to happen to him in the future of what he could only describe as a horribly unfair life. Everything came out at once in one, loud, atom-bomb-exploding moment. And he wasn't done yet.

Vincent turned around to look for the next victim of his madness when he saw Coach Johnson staring at him.

Vincent stopped, heaving heavily. Tears streamed from his face, and he had to fight against hyperventilation. The emotion was just too much for him to overcome.

He wiped his tears from his face and looked down to see that it was blood, not saline on the back of his hand. His headache, which had vanished for his ten seconds of complete madness, came back with a fury, throbbing at the point of impact, right in the middle of his forehead. Already there was a huge goose egg forming, and it bled profusely, running down the bridge of his nose like lava from a volcano.

Coach Johnson must have noticed, because he slowly walked over to the broken towel bin, grabbed a fresh towel, and threw it at Vincent. Vincent caught it reluctantly and put it on his forehead.

Coach Johnson continued to stare for another ten seconds, hands on his hips, before taking a breath. Finally, he said, "Put your uniform back in your locker and get back into your street clothes. I want you to report to practice Monday afternoon a half-hour early. Now get out of here." Coach Johnson left Vincent with whatever was left of his self-respect.

Twenty minutes later, Vincent was back in his dorm room. The towel was still on his forehead. The pounding in his head was fierce. The growing goose egg on his forehead had its own heartbeat. He couldn't shake it. It wasn't just the physical pain. It was the performance he just put on out on the field. His bad pitching. Tank tackling him. Tank yelling at him. The other team harassing him. The crack of the batter's knee cap when the ball met bone. The towel bin. The locker. The pounding.

For some reason thoughts of his parents also barged in. His father's drinking. His father beating him. His father calling him all sorts of names. Telling Vincent he should have never been born. His mother's apathy through it all. Their lovely drive that ended in blood. Unresolved feelings. Words never to be spoken. A dialogue to never take place. No notes left behind reading, "I'm sorry, Vincent." "I love you, Vincent." "You are a wonderful child of God, Vincent."

There was nothing for him, except a life insurance check. The best thing his parents ever did for him.

But there had always been baseball. His escape. The mound was the one place where the world made sense. The one place where all existence faded to a remote speck in the back of his brain. The one place where life was a game. The one place where he was perfect. The one place he had complete control of the outcome. His fate. Now there was just hate. Red-hot hate. And pounding.

The urge to scream. It was there again. He refrained, looked frantically around the room. For what? He knew not. His eyes developed x-ray vision, and he saw through Evan's closet door, to the corner of the top shelf, the black, plastic box.

"The gun," Vincent spoke, through his teeth and tears.

Just then there was a rattling of keys at the door to the room.

Evan entered, the concerned look still on his face. "Hey man, are you alright?"

Vincent gave another thought to the gun, and it scared him that he actually conceived the idea, as if the gun were an acceptable choice.

The feeling that everything was insurmountable was sobering. His impulsivity was sobering.

Deciding to pick the lesser of two evils, Vincent wiped more blood off his face and answered his roommate, "Let's get drunk."

Chapter Sixteen

VINCENT HELD A cold beer to his forehead. The dormitory building was absolutely dead, all its inhabitants either at the game or home for the weekend.

The cold beer didn't seem to help the swelling much. If anything, the goose egg was growing. Evan sat on his bed across the room from Vincent, silent, his face making little winces as he looked at his roommate.

Evan didn't know what to say to Vincent. A week ago when he left for Florida, it seemed like everything was going well and Vincent was healing, but after what he just saw on the baseball field, Evan threw away any misconceptions he had about his roommate. All he really knew about Vincent was that he best not tick him off!

The awkward silence saturated the tone of the room like a midnight fog. Evan looked down at the cooler he had brought in from his car. Filling the cooler was his first order of business when the team got back into town earlier that afternoon. He had texted his beer man when he hit town, and by the time he met the guy at the ball park, two cases of beer and a twenty-pound bag of ice greeted him.

It was easy for him to drink normally. He was a guy. Guys like beer, or at least that's what the beer commercials taught him. His plan was to get tanked at the game, cheer on his roommate, and then head over to the Red Pony to shoot some pool, maybe pick up a girl. Beer and a convertible seemed to work every time. He hadn't finished his first beer when the ruckus began, and now he was back in the dorm room with a cooler full of beer and his seemingly innocent roommate who was wanting to get drunk. He thought it best to let Vincent make the first move. So far, all Vincent had managed to do with the beer was put it to his forehead.

While he waited for Vincent to say something, Evan thought about this predicament. He felt guilty that he had given Vincent the beer in the first place. The guy had made it very clear that he didn't want to drink, and his parents had just died a few weeks ago from a drinking and driving accident. The move to give Vincent a beer seemed in bad taste after the fact. Maybe Evan should have said no. The little voice in his head started a conversation with him on this very topic.

No, I acted correctly in the interest of self-preservation. If I didn't give him one, who knows what he would have done to me!

Evan wondered if maybe he should have lied and said that he didn't have any beer.

No. Who knows what he would have done to me!

Evan sorted through the mess in his mind.

But Vincent's not in diapers. He's a grown man who can make his own decisions.

But a small nagging feeling told him that he was lying to himself. After all would he give a gun to someone who was suicidal?

But maybe this is something that is necessary for him. Maybe he needs to have the chance to face down his nemesis. Beat alcohol the way his dad hadn't.

Yep, Evan almost convinced himself that he was in the right.

At that moment, Vincent popped the top of the can and started to chug. Evan watched, half in amusement, half in horror of what he was sure to come.

Near the end of the beer, Vincent choked and spit out his last gulp right onto the floor. Evan took a sip of his beer and wondered if he would be cleaning up puke by the end of the night.

When Vincent's choking fit was quelled, he looked at the beer and attacked it again, this time in a more controlled fashion. Gulping it down, Vincent crushed the can with his hand and let out a belch.

Vincent tossed the empty to the trash can over by the door, a perfect shot, then opened the cooler and pulled another one out. It went straight to his forehead.

"Was it good?" Evan heard himself say.

"Not bad," Vincent replied and steadied the pressure on his forehead. Evan figured that a few more beers and Vincent wouldn't be feeling any pain at all.

"Well, if you get tired of beer, I have a bottle of whiskey in here that will dull that pain a heck of a lot faster," Evan said with a snicker.

"No you don't," Vincent replied with his own snort, keeping the pressure on his goose egg.

Evan wondered what that meant. Had Vincent found his stash? Thrown it all away? He was quite positive that Vincent wouldn't drink it, but then again, here was this guy sitting in front of him who until thirty seconds ago, hadn't ever had a beer.

"Well, you can help yourself to all of it. I certainly wasn't going to get it all drank tonight. Besides, if we drink it all, we will get rid of the evidence, just in case that dork RA shows up."

"What happened in Florida," Vincent asked, still not looking up.

Evan didn't even know if he was getting through to him at all. There seemed to be some kind of invisible wall Vincent had constructed around himself that made him impervious to everyone around him, with the exception of that catcher. The man was huge, and Evan had cringed when the catcher had tackled Vincent on the infield.

"Florida?" Evan asked. "Well, we got our butts kicked, that's what. Tough competition."

"Will you get ranked?"

Evan thought it over for a moment. "Yeah, I suppose. I made it to the round of sixteen in both singles and doubles, so there will be a good chance I make the top fifty. We'll see though. Whole thing's run by a couple of coaches from Florida schools, and I have a feeling they are pretty biased against anyone from outside of the sunshine state."

Vincent cracked open the second beer and took a big gulp, apparently tasting this one. He winced and Evan smirked.

"You know, if you're wanting to drink it faster, there are a few tricks."

Vincent looked at Evan and waited, so Evan reached into the cooler and grabbed a cold one.

"Well, this is called shot gunning it." Evan turned the beer upside down, grabbed his dorm key, and punched a hole in the bottom of the can. He looked over at Vincent who was so serious, he might have been in a class right now, taking notes for the big test.

"Then you just hold it upside down over your mouth and pop

the top. The air comes in through the top, and the beer goes straight down, but I gotta warn you, it will keep coming, and fast, so you just have to kinda open your throat and let it go down without tasting or gulping."

Vincent kept watching his roommate, so to model the expected behavior, Evan followed his procedures. The beer rushed out and burned straight down his throat. He drained it in less than five seconds. He even managed to keep from spilling a single drop.

"Ahhhhhhhh!" Evan sighed and threw the empty over to the trash can. "You want to give it a shot?"

Vincent took another pull of his beer, winced, and said, "Maybe in a little bit." Vincent continued to drink this beer slowly, and Evan began to wonder what was on tap for tonight. Sure, he was jet lagged and exhausted, but it was Saturday night, and he wasn't passing up a Saturday night to run out and have fun.

"Maybe after you've had a few, we can run over to the Red Pony and see if we can spot some chicks."

Vincent seemed to be mulling this over as he slowly drank the ice cold beer.

"So, Vincent, what exactly happened tonight?" Evan asked, afraid that he had stepped over some boundary. Vincent downed the beer, made another grotesque burp that sounded this time like a train whistle, and shook his head a little. He reached up and felt his bump.

"I can barely feel it now," Vincent said.

"That's good," Evan responded. "Best thing for sore muscles."

"I got mad," Vincent finally answered the question, "and it felt good."

Evan gave that some thought. He had watched the whole

thing, knew that Vincent was getting shelled out there. He just didn't realize Vincent had such a short fuse.

"Sure lit up that leadoff batter. And he deserved it!" Evan said.

"No he didn't," Vincent said, and took another swig. "I probably broke his knee. I put everything I had into that pitch, and I wanted it to hurt." Evan listened to Vincent speak, knowing that the magic elixir was now starting to take effect. Inhibitions were slowly drifting away. Truth serum. Evan figured that Vincent might end up being an interesting drunk.

Evan reached into the cooler, grabbed another one, and gave it to Vincent. Vincent poked a hole in the bottom, just like his roommate had told him to, popped the tab over his mouth, and gulped for all he was worth. A little poured down the sides of his cheeks, to which Evan laughed. Vincent wiped his mouth clean and burped again. "Yep, probably put him on crutches for the next six months. Got him back real good."

Vincent was becoming morose, so Evan decided to changeup the topic of conversation. "So, you wanting to head over to the bar with me?"

Without hesitation, Vincent said, "Yeah." He got up and headed toward the door.

"Uh, you need to take a shower or anything?"

Vincent shrugged and sniffed his underarm. "Smells good to me. Let's go. I want to see what I've been missing out on all this time."

Evan sighed, hid the cooler in his closet, and helped his roommate stagger to the door.

Tank felt terrible about the way he spoke to Vincent. Tackling him on the field? That was something Tank wouldn't take back. He told himself that Vincent needed to be restrained if he were to keep himself in the game, and darn it if Vincent didn't get himself kicked out of the game anyway!

Tank didn't stick around to speak with Coach Johnson after the game. Tank didn't have to be told by Coach to go speak with Vincent, now that both of them had probably cooled down.

Walking down to the dorms, Tank went over what he had said to Vincent, trying to remember exactly what had escaped his lips. All Tank could remember was that he yelled at Vincent a lot. Not that Vincent didn't deserve to be yelled at. Or maybe he didn't deserve to be yelled at. Vincent acted selfishly at the game, but he also was dealing with personal tragedy. What was the answer? The closer he got to the dorms, the less he knew what was the right course of action. All he knew was that he would approach Vincent in a much calmer fashion this time. Tank would establish a dialogue. He would open the lines of communication. What could that hurt?

A few minutes later, Tank stood at Vincent's door, listening for any sign of life. There was no light emanating from beneath the crack of the door, no sounds coming from within. Not knowing what to do, Tank knocked, rather quietly. If his protégé were sleeping, maybe it would be for the best. A few seconds more waiting, and there was still no sounds within.

Tank waited another thirty seconds and knocked harder this time, more determined. Still nobody answered. Tank's anger resurfaced. Either Vincent was not answering, which was disrespectful, or he was out and about. If the latter were the case, it would show just how little contrition Vincent felt.

Either way it was unacceptable to Tank.

The Red Pony wasn't much to look at on the outside or the inside. Set at the eastern edge of town by some low plateaus, the long building with the flat corrugated metal roof needed a paint job badly. The original color had been red at one time, but that was difficult to discern now with the Arizona sun having baked it to a pale pink. In fact, the only way a passer-by could tell that this was a tavern was by the faded beer posters on the marquee by the road.

At the door was a bouncer, a former basketball player who had washed out of school five years ago and decided he liked the college life way too much to leave while he was still in his twenties. Like all bouncers, he wore a tee shirt that was one size too small, had a mullet that was way too long, and crossed his arms at his chest to look mean every time a male wanted to gain entrance. When a female came to the door, the grim face turned into a smile, and surely he hoped that his general countenance would win him points with the ladies who didn't yet know him.

Evan addressed him as Danny and patted him on the shoulder as he slipped him some money with the other hand. He whispered something in Danny's ear and turned around to motion Vincent in.

His head a ball of fuzziness, Vincent obeyed, and he put one foot in front of the other with the utmost effort of concentration. Must not let anyone know he was drunk.

The inside was nothing impressive either. A bar greeted people when they first walked through the door. Like many nasty joints, the bar was wooden, properly greased by millions of drunken elbows to where it didn't exactly shine, but was protected from the elements better than if it had been polished with sealant. Each of the bar stools had, at one time, cushioned seats. Each cushion had been ripped off, and all that remained were the threads that hung from the uncomfortable plywood seats.

Just beyond the bar area was a short walkway to the dance floor, complete with handrails to keep the drunks on their feet as they ventured from a two-step to the beer tap. The dance floor was pretty large, taking up most of the area, minus tables along the edges. A large disco ball hung from the ceiling, and roving spotlights from all corners of the bar in all colors made it sparkle. The wooden floor was splintered with some boards sticking up as much as a half of an inch, ready to trip any boot scooter.

There was a hallway that led to another room off to the right of the bar. A man with sunglasses and a pinstriped suit stood at the entrance, looking straight forward. Vincent took one look at the man, decided it was polite not to stare, and refocused his gaze on Evan, which was hard. Vincent's eyeballs felt like they were floating in bowls of gelatin.

Evan went right up to the bar and ordered a couple bottles. The music was blaring loud, so loud that Vincent couldn't hear his roommate talking to him. Vincent stared at Evan with a dumb look on his face before being led over to one of the vacant tables. Again, Vincent looked down at his feet to make sure that they did what they were supposed to.

When the two sat down, Vincent watched for social clues. Evan would take a drink, so Vincent did the same. Evan would point and wave at someone he knew from across the bar, so Vincent would also nod, leaning back in his chair so as to be as cool as possible. Vincent had his ball cap pulled down over his eyes so low that he had to look way up to see anyone at all. It hurt the goose egg on his forehead, but sacrifices had to be made.

At present there was only one couple on the dance floor. It was a fully-registered cowboy. Stetson, western shirt, tight Wranglers, and shiny cowboy boots that glittered each time the purple light hit them. The cowboy was Texas two-stepping to an old George Strait song. Across the way there were a few couples hanging out at tables, one table with six guys chugging drafts in a race, and one woman who leaned against a support pole in the middle of the dance floor. She wore a tight mini skirt, a halter top that showed off her navel, and a pair of cowboy boots. She omitted the Stetson, and Vincent couldn't help but notice her sparkly hair in all the lights. Just looking at her hair was enough to make Vincent dizzy.

Finally the song ended, and Vincent realized that Evan had been talking to him all this time. Vincent picked up the conversation in mid-sentence, "...was out of her mind. I don't know what goes on here in Arizona, but I can tell you that that would even be considered weird in LA, and let's be honest. LA is the home of weird. Look at all we have out there in Hollywood alone! I try not to steer my car inland very often just because of that wacky stuff, but I can tell you that she takes the cake. You want a night of weird, she's your girl. On the other hand, you take that couple right there. They have no business being in this bar. I don't know why they even come. They always take up that table right there," and just like that, another George Strait song came on and flooded out Evan's voice.

Vincent tried to acknowledge his roommate, but it was hard, what with his gelatin eyes and loud music. All the cigarette smoke in the building didn't help any either. All it did was make his eyes sting. He rubbed them, nodding at his roommate in agreement with who knows what, and took another sip of his beer. He was far from a beer connoisseur, but he decided that this beer tasted exceedingly better than the ones he had drunk at the dorm room. On the label was a picture of an Old West saloon with a tumbleweed rolling down the street. At the top of the beer were the words "Tumbleweed Beer" and for a subtitle, "Good After A Hard Day On The Trail." It had been a hard day for Vincent, and this beer was a pretty decent reward; in honor of his monumental day, he emptied it, slamming it on the table in triumph.

Evan stopped in mid-sentence and said something inaudible, nodding towards the dance floor. Vincent looked up to see the cowgirl in the mini skirt standing in front of him, obscuring his view of the dancing couple.

"Feel like dancing?" she yelled at Vincent, plenty loud enough for him to hear. For help, Vincent looked across the table at Evan, who just stared at him in a half-cocked smile.

"Well do ya?" she persisted. Vincent had never danced before in his life. He had skipped the senior prom, and high school dances weren't tops on his priority list, at least not after his first junior high dance when Roy Walters, the class bully, slipped in behind him and gave him an atomic wedgie, all to the laughter of the popular crowd and all the girls. Vincent remembered thinking he couldn't get out of that gymnasium fast enough. That was his last social function before tonight.

Not knowing what else to say, he nodded. She pulled him up from the chair and led him over to a dark corner of the dance floor. Vincent again looked back for help and saw his roommate give him two thumbs up.

He stood there, trying to balance, hoping she would not notice how drunk he was. Quickly picking up on this fact and the fact that he had two left feet, she yelled into his ear, "It's simple. Left, right, left, slow right. Left, right, left, slow right."

This girl held up Vincent's left hand with her right hand then placed his right hand on her left hip. "Okay," she yelled into his ear, "One, two, three...four." And just like that, he stumbled out of the gate. He looked down at his feet and tried to remember the cadence. He figured that this was something he couldn't do sober. Then he remembered a lesson that Grandpa Dean had taught him about having rhythm, that pitching was about balance and timing, and that he should fancy himself a dancer if he wanted to be a good pitcher. That seemed to make things click, and before he knew it, his feet were doing what they were supposed to be doing. He admired them until she put her off hand on his chin and redirected his stare to her face.

"Now, that's better," she said, but all Vincent could really notice was that this girl used way too much makeup, and her breath smelt of smoke.

At that moment the song ended, and Vincent looked back to his table to see that Evan was gone. Before he could thank the girl for the dance, another song came on, so he danced with her again. In all they danced four in a row before she led Vincent back to his table. Evan was there again, and this time there were three beers, but only two chairs. It didn't bother this girl too much, as she picked up the beer, took a big swig, then sat right down on Vincent's lap.

Vincent must have had a shocked look on his face because his roommate was eating this up. In fact Evan had to turn away to keep from laughing. Not sure what the joke was, or why this girl he didn't even know was on his lap, he went with the flow and drank his beer. Before long he was back out on the dance floor, and the night's revels made the room spin.

For the second time in two days, Vincent woke up with a splitting headache. He had been dreaming about Lenny from *Of Mice and Men*. Vincent hated the ending, but couldn't stop thinking about how George ended up shooting his best friend in the head to put him out of his misery. It somehow seemed applicable to the present moment, but Vincent tried not to think about that.

There was a sunbeam that shone directly on his face, prompting him to turn over and pretend that the night before hadn't happened. The problem was that it had happened, and he really couldn't remember any of it. Slowly, Lenny faded, and his memory came back to him. The ball game. Tank. Beer. Bar. That's about where the memory ended, and the headache took over.

Remembering that recovery was a matter of drinking plenty of fluids and taking headache medicine, Vincent opened his eyes and got up to go to the bathroom. That's when everything became extremely confusing. He looked at his surroundings and discovered that he was not in his happy little dorm room. He was on a beat up old couch with a tattered wool blanket covering him. He still had on his underwear, but his clothes were piled on the floor at his feet. Realizing this little piece of information, he quickly covered himself with the blanket.

The room's walls were painted yellow and were peeling and had nothing else on them. There was a kitchen across the way, and he wondered if it were more domesticated than it appeared because a mountain of dishes lay discarded in the sink, as well as a trash can with refuse overflowing onto the floor. Despite feeling the need to vomit, Vincent trudged across the living room to the kitchen wearing his blanket, in search of a clean cup and ibuprofen. After a few minutes of searching, he found both.

Vincent went back to the couch and pondered his predicament. He remembered a girl, thought he remembered dancing, though that seemed highly unlikely. Then a thought jarred him. He knew how to both two-step and Texas two-step. The harder he tried to think about this, to put the pieces together, the more his head hurt, so he lay down again and went to sleep.

When he woke later, there was a woman staring at him. Her hair was disheveled. She wore a bathrobe and held a steaming cup of coffee in her hand. She offered it to him with a smile, and he took it very untrustingly.

"So, you sleep okay?" she asked him. Vincent took a sip and

nodded. The coffee had what appeared to be a touch of nutmeg flavoring to it. It kind of tasted like a pumpkin pie. It was good enough to warrant another sip, despite his nausea.

"You sure were out of it," the woman said and shook her head as she sat down beside him, forcing him to draw up his feet. He realized again that he was nearly naked in a woman's presence.

"But you sure did like dancing. I was a bit worried there that you wouldn't take to it, but you sure wore me out!"

Vincent, hurting, nodded and looked at his coffee.

The woman looked at him and smiled. "Do you remember much about last night?"

Vincent shook his head no.

She smiled and crossed her feet campfire style. "Well, you don't have to worry. You didn't do anything too stupid, though Evan sure set you up."

"Evan?" Vincent asked, remembering he went to the bar with his roommate.

"Yeah, Evan," she said and smiled as she shook her head. "He and I--" she said, then stopped in mid-sentence. "Well, that's not important, but I think he was trying to do you a favor. Don't worry. Nothing happened."

Vincent looked down at his tattered blanket to decide if she could see through it.

"Yeah," she said, "I kind of had to help you off with your clothes, but I didn't peek or anything. You were asleep in two seconds. I had to slip the pillow under your head. You were going to just sleep like that, and I didn't have the heart to let you."

Vincent heard church bells ring, thought hard, remembered that it was Sunday morning, remembered that he had told himself that he would go to church. Well, that didn't happen, obviously.

"Anyways, there's some cereal on top of the fridge. Bowls are above the sink. Sorry there's not much more selection. I don't get paid until Friday, so what you see is what you get," she said with an empathetic smile. Vincent sure knew all about that.

"How about I go to the bathroom to put on some makeup and while I'm doing that, you can get dressed. Then I'll take you back to the dorms. Sound good?"

Vincent nodded.

When she left the room, he shot straight into his clothes. His head felt a little bit better, though he knew he would need to make another trip to the drug store for some electrolyte water. A few minutes later, the woman sauntered back into the room with a pair of boxer shorts and a really tight tee shirt on. She slipped into her flip flops and said, "By the way, what happened to your forehead? Been meaning to ask you."

Vincent shrugged and touched it. It hurt to the touch. He replied, "Baseball game."

The woman looked at him as if he made no sense at all, grabbed her keys off a nail on the wall next to the front door, and waved him over.

Outside, Vincent still couldn't figure out where he was. He looked around for landmarks, but the sun blinded him and made his head hurt more. He followed her to an old Volkswagen Beetle, painted the same yellow as was in her living room. He got in, and she took a highway. It was then that Vincent found out he wasn't even in Page.

It took ten minutes to get to Page, and he was able to direct her to his dorm. As he was about to exit her car, she put her right hand on his left forearm and stopped him. "I have a question for you," she said.

Vincent was almost free and considered running for it, but what harm could one question do? He waited for her to ask it.

"Do you even know my name?"

Vincent looked down at his feet and sadly shook his head no.

"Well," she said and sighed, "I suppose the topic never came up. My name is Veronica." She lifted her hand off his arm. "Guess I'll be seeing you around, cowboy."

Vincent smiled and thanked her for the ride. When he got inside his dorm room, there lay his roommate, still asleep. Rather than get mad at Evan for apparently stranding him and leaving it up to a woman he didn't know to take him to her house, in another town much less, sleep sounded better. Vincent chugged water straight from the sink and flopped into his bed, ready to sleep the rest of the day away. The last thought that ran through his mind was that the gun was still just a few feet away in Evan's closet.

When Vincent finally woke late in the day, Evan was gone. Vincent felt a little bit better, but noticed for the first time that he stunk badly. He took a shower, and when he came back into the room, decided that it stunk also. Gathering up all his linens and dirty clothes, he went up to the laundry room. While there, his hunger got the best of him so he used a couple of quarters he had set aside for a load and bought himself a snack bag of stale chips and overloaded the washing machine instead.

Two hours later he was back in his room, hard at work on his biology, a candle burning on the desk beside him. It was well past six o'clock in the evening now, and the stale chips were the only thing he had eaten in over twenty-four hours. There was nothing to chew on in the dorm room, but there was beer. He grabbed a can and rested it on his forehead to ease the pain of the goose egg. Vincent wondered about the RA and what would happen if he came in right that second. Again, Vincent swore off booze, but his oath seemed to carry less weight than it used to.

As if on cue, the door opened. Vincent quickly put the beer between his legs and scooted his chair in. Evan walked in with a big cheery look on his face. "Roomie!" Evan announced and gave Vincent a big hug from the side, something Vincent largely tried to ignore.

Right behind Evan came in two blond girls Vincent had never seen before. "Ladies," Evan said, "I would like to introduce you to the best baseball player at NCA, my roommate, Vincent.

Vincent was embarrassed by this introduction, especially considering his last outing made that statement an outright lie, but stood and shook the two girls' hands. They said nothing in return but only giggled.

"If you would have a seat over there?" Evan asked the girls, and they found a seat on Vincent's freshly-made bed. Vincent might have cared before, but he found himself thinking that it wasn't such a bad thing now. He grabbed the beer between his legs and reapplied it to his forehead.

"So," Evan followed the girls, "you're both thirsty, right?" He walked over to his closet and grabbed three cans from the cooler. Most of the ice had melted and resembled the North Atlantic with ice berg beers floating with the holdover ice. "One for you Amber, and one for you Josie," he said and passed out the beers. Vincent didn't turn around, not even remotely interested in which was which.

"So, you two make yourselves comfy, and I am going to talk to Vincent about something personal," Evan said. He walked over to Vincent who was hard at work on his biology. He didn't want to get behind again, and it seemed like this class was keeping him busy constantly. He didn't want Tank on his case again.

Evan leaned in and whispered to Vincent, "So?"

"So?" Vincent replied.

"So tell me about last night?"

Vincent's pencil stopped moving, and he looked up, not really sure what to say. "Uh, her place was messy."

"What?" Evan said loud enough for the girls to hear. He leaned back in. "Tell me about Veronica. How did it go? You know, she kind of showed me around early on. Showed me the ropes."

Vincent pondered this for a while. He knew the details Evan was begging for, and he didn't want to disappoint his roommate, but the fact remained that nothing happened, and for that he was glad. Vincent had never had a girlfriend in his life. He was glad that he hadn't done anything stupid, other than getting drunk. Again, he considered how his moral line in the sand was bending.

"Well, what can I tell you?" Vincent started. "I fell asleep."

"You fell asleep?"

"I fell asleep."

Evan pondered this and gave a sly smile. "You're putting me on, right?"

"No."

Evan stood up, the smile gone.

It was quite evident to Vincent now that his roommate had set the whole thing up. In a way he felt honored, and in another way he felt that the whole thing was sleazy.

"But I don't understand?" Evan remarked.

"I guess I was too tired," Vincent replied, which wasn't a lie, just not the whole truth. It left in a little room for interpretation.

Evan looked over at the girls on the bed and said, "Drink up girls. There's plenty more where that came from!" He leaned in again and said, "Well, don't worry about Veronica. She'll be back at the Red Pony tonight. Besides, I have these two on the hook. I figure it will take about three or four beers to reel 'em in." Evan paused. "You mind if I take Amber? You can have Josie."

"I don't know," Vincent said, looking at his homework. "I am pretty busy. I have to stay ahead of this stuff." He looked down at his homework and knew he wasn't being totally honest. His homework would take no longer than half of an hour, then he would be twiddling his thumbs.

Maybe just one beer to be social.

Or two.

Or a six-pack.

As long as he got back to the dorm at a reasonable time so he wouldn't sleep in and miss class. "Okay," Vincent said. "Give me twenty minutes?"

"Now you're talking," Evan said and sauntered over to the girls. "Okay, which one of you are going to time me?" Evan popped the top and started chugging, and Vincent smiled. He was finding out that Evan really was a lot of fun.

Chapter Seventeen

VINCENT WOKE UP with not only a splitting headache, but a sore lower back and ribs. He tried to figure out why he was in so much pain, and once he opened his right eye, there he had his answer, for he was sleeping at the foot of his bed on the hard floor. All he had for comfort was a pillow and a sheet.

Vincent groaned ever-so-audibly and closed his eyes, wondering what on earth he had gotten himself into now. He thought back upon the night, putting puzzle pieces together, but a few of the pieces had been lost. He remembered chugging beers with Evan and two girls in the dorm. He remembered heading outside of town and attending a party. He remembered one of the two girls hanging on his arm the whole time. He remembered being held upside down above a keg of beer as he drank from the tap. Past that, he had nothing. It dawned on Vincent that he might not even be back in his dorm room, so he snuck another peek just to make sure he wasn't in a Steinbeck novel or something.

But why am I on the floor?

It hurt to sit up, and caused Vincent to use most of his remaining strength, but sit up he did. He looked at his bed and noticed somebody else sleeping in it.

Who the heck is that?

Vincent leaned in and got a closer look at the intruder. She was a girl. He could tell that by the blond hair, but it was messy and covering her face. She was fully clothed and laying on her stomach without so much as a blanket or a pillow. As the detective put the clues together, he reasoned that it might have been a compromise. She got the bed, he got the linens.

Vincent didn't have to look at Evan's bed to determine who all was in it, but he did anyway and wasn't disappointed. Two lumps were squeezed onto the same twin-size mattress.

What did I get myself into?

Vincent snuck a peek at the alarm clock and noted with dismay that he had already missed all of his classes. He knew that a shower would make him feel better, but he just couldn't move. As much as his back and ribs hurt, he decided that sleep was more important. Strangely enough though, he hadn't opened his left eye yet. For all the pounding in his head, he was now aware that his left eye hurt as well.

A new hangover symptom?

Closing his right eye, he went back to sleep.

It was two o'clock in the afternoon before the room woke up. Vincent was aware of movement in the bed above him, and then very aware of the foot that landed right on his left knee.

"Ugh!" he said, as the body fell over on top of the rest of him. Vincent looked up and saw his guest, face-to-face. Or maybe he smelled her first. Her breath was just horrible.

"Would you mind?" Vincent asked in the nicest tone he could

muster. He looked up at her and noted the disgusted look on her face. "If you're going to throw up, please do it in the toilet," Vincent said to her.

"Your eye looks horrible," the girl said.

"My eye?" Vincent asked.

The girl didn't answer but got to her feet and managed to avoid stepping on Vincent again. She stumbled to the bathroom.

My eye?

Vincent pulled his bones up off the floor. Everything hurt. He staggered to the mirror next to the bathroom and discovered that his eye was swollen shut. He almost didn't recognize himself. Not only was his eye swollen shut, but it looked like a purple balloon, ready to burst.

"Ugh!" he said again.

Vincent lifted his shirt to see his rib cage the same color as his eye. There was an acute pain in his ribs as he did this, so he put the shirt down again.

"Evan?" Vincent cried out.

Vincent walked back into the room and kicked Evan's mattress. The two lumps didn't move, so he did it again, which made his hip hurt now.

"What?" Evan asked and rolled over.

"What happened to me last night?" Vincent asked, hoping to get a straight answer, and fast.

Evan rolled back and squinted at Vincent. Evan winced when he did this and then rubbed his eyes. "Man, you got it good last night."

"What do you mean I got it good?" Vincent asked.

"Just what I said," Evan replied. "You hit on another guy's girlfriend, and he decked you. Then his friends gave you the boot treatment."

That explains the ribs.

208

"What do you mean I hit on some girl?"

Evan scratched his head, running his fingers through his greasy hair. "You were quite the Romeo last night. After about ten beers, you were doing keg stands, break dancing, you name it. Everybody was cheering you on, that is until you put your arm around that girl. Man, I don't even know who she was, but her boyfriend sure was mad!" Evan sat up and looked at Vincent quizzically. "You mean you don't remember any of that?"

Vincent searched his memory and found nothing.

"Wow," Evan said and chuckled. "That's something else. I've gotten so drunk that I don't remember much, and sometimes that's a good thing. In your case, I just don't know."

The bathroom door opened, and Vincent's bed guest entered the room. She seemed overwhelmed as well.

"Good morning," Evan said to her, but that didn't make her any happier.

"What happened last night?" the girl said while Vincent held his hand to his head and tried to remember her name.

"I guess I got in a fight," Vincent said.

"I remember that," she said and looked down at Evan and her friend. "Josie, wake up!"

On cue Josie looked up at her and smiled when she saw Evan. She pulled up the covers so as not to show anything. Vincent took it as a cue to exit the room. He grabbed a towel and headed to the shower.

Vincent took a long, hot shower and thought about all he had to accomplish that day. Classes were already out. First on the agenda was meeting with Coach Johnson before practice. Vincent only had a few minutes to get ready and out the door, and to maximize his time, he drank some hot water from the shower spigot, nearly vomiting in the process.

Vincent wondered what Coach Johnson was going to say to

him. Vincent was an absolute mess at the game on Saturday night, and he was going to show up at practice an even worse absolute mess. Shoot, he didn't even have any depth perception with the swollen eye, and he figured that the swelling wasn't going down in the hot shower.

When Vincent got out of the shower, he put the towel around his waist and went back in his room, hoping the two girls were gone. Thankfully he got his wish. Evan was still in bed, looking up at the ceiling.

"Wow," Evan said with a worried look on his face.

"Wow what?" Vincent asked.

Evan sat up in bed. "Did you know that those two chicks are still in high school?"

Vincent shook his head. "Did I do anything with, whoever that was?"

Evan shook his head. "No, you kept blabbering on-and-on about saving yourself, and you told her that you were going to be a gentleman and give her the bed, but you were taking the pillow." Evan smiled. "It made her want you more."

"But?" Vincent inquired.

"But nothing," Evan responded. "You grabbed your pillow and sheet and plopped right down and fell asleep on the spot. She fell asleep on your bed, and that's that. Boy, Vincent, you weren't kidding when you said that you like your sleep."

"High school?" Vincent asked again.

"Yeah," Evan said. "Amber said that they were both seniors. I don't know if I believe them though."

"What if they get caught by the RA?"

Evan shrugged. "Doesn't matter. It's two-thirty in the afternoon. The key is keeping them around until the dorms open back up for coeds at noon. We're totally in the clear."

Vincent walked over to his dresser and got into his practice clothes. He had heard enough. Everything was crazy, and he felt that he had absolutely no control over anything he was doing in his life, and he didn't like it. He again resolved to stop drinking. Zero tolerance this time.

Vincent was sure glad that he had his pickup. He knew he didn't have the strength to make it up that big hill to practice. He arrived fifteen minutes early and dragged his bones out of the cab. He pulled his ball cap down as low as he could get it and went over to Coach Johnson to face the music.

Coach Johnson had Vincent follow him to the coaches' office. When he got there, he was greeted by all the coaches, and Tank, all sitting around a table. In the corner of the room was a huge flat screen television. Vincent deduced that this was where the coaches all sat around and dissected film on upcoming opponents.

Before Vincent could look at the rest of the room, Coach Johnson spoke. "Vincent, I would like you to have a seat." He extended his arm to the seat at the end of the table, directly across from where he was sitting. On Vincent's right was Tank.

"Vincent," Coach Johnson started, "the reason I wanted to bring you in here was to just talk. I don't want you to feel intimidated in any way. We are all family in here, and I want you to be able to speak frankly with us about everything that is going on in your life right now. But first, I'm going to ask you to take your hat off like a gentleman."

Vincent obliged and heard audible gasps from the rest of the round table. Vincent didn't even look up he was so ashamed.

Nobody said anything for a good twenty seconds, so Coach Johnson started up again. "Well, maybe we should start with that black eye of yours. How did you get it? It wasn't from head banging the locker. That's the source of that massive goose egg on your forehead."

Vincent shrugged and considered for a short moment telling the truth. "Got in a fight." Short, concise, and truthful.

"Okay," Coach Johnson said. "With whom?"

"I don't know."

"Okay," Coach Johnson said again. "When?"

"Last night."

"And where were you?" Coach Johnson prodded further.

"Off campus."

Tank stepped in. "Vincent, you better start giving some straight answers!"

"Tank," Coach Johnson hushed his star catcher and offered a hand to Vincent to continue.

Vincent exhaled, which hurt his ribs. "I just got in to a fight. Guy forced me to. There was nothing I could do. There were probably five of them."

"And did you call the police," Coach Johnson asked. "It sounds like you got jumped."

"Kind of," Vincent replied, not answering Coach's question.

Coach Johnson exhaled and thought for a moment. "Okay, I want you to know that you can talk to me about anything. I don't want you fighting, but I don't have a specific rule prohibiting it. You're not the first of my players to get into a scuffle, on or off the field. But let's switch gears now. You want to tell me about the other night?"

Vincent shook his head. "Lost my cool."

"Yes?" Coach Johnson asked, prompting Vincent to continue. When he didn't, Coach Johnson exhaled again. "Well, Vincent, we could have used you pitching that game, and we also could have used your bat in the lineup. You do realize that you cannot help us if you are not on the field. You know we lost the double-header, don't you? Now consider if that were a game in

May, a regional game, or worse yet, a World Series game. We need you on the field, and that takes a level of professionalism you are sorely lacking right now."

Vincent sat there with his gaze fixed on his left shoelace, one of its tag ends longer than the other one. It bothered him somehow, but he didn't dare bend over to make them more symmetrical.

"Now, Vincent, would you rather I talk frankly to you, or would you like me to beat around the bush?"

Vincent shrugged and said, "Might as well give it to me."

Coach Johnson shook his head. "I see."

Coach Johnson got up from his chair and walked around the table over to where Vincent sat pitifully. Coach patted Tank on the shoulder and said to him and his coaches, "Guys, why don't you get out there and get practice started. I'll be right behind you."

Tank and the assistant coaches all got up, all but Tank patting Vincent on the shoulder on the way out. It made Vincent flinch.

When they were all out of the room, Coach Johnson sat where Tank was sitting and pulled the chair closer to Vincent, close enough that Vincent was uncomfortable. "Vincent," Coach Johnson started over again, "you are dealing with a lot right now. First with your mentor Leonard Dean passing away a few months back, but now with your parents..." Coach Johnson's voice trailed off. "Well, it would be a lot for anyone to deal with. Honestly, I don't think I would be able to deal with it so well."

Coach Johnson looked up at the ceiling, as if invoking the muse of compassion to give him his next words. "Right after your parents passed away, I thought it prudent to give you time to rest, mourn. I didn't want to throw you right back into the fray right away, but I knew that you needed to get back into the saddle, so to speak, fairly quickly. Perhaps I shouldn't have thrown you against UCSB. Maybe I should have thrown an upper classman like Sandy. The thing is, there was no way of knowing until I put you in there. Now I can see that it was a mistake."

"I could have beat them," Vincent said in defiance.

"Perhaps," Coach Johnson said, nodding solemnly. "Or perhaps not. They have a good team and excel at getting under their opponent's skin. I suppose that if anyone had a shot against them, it was you. Talent-wise, you got it. Where you still don't have it is upstairs, and that comes with time. Add on top of that pressure what all you've been through, and it should have been easily foreseeable what the outcome would have been, and I curse myself for not having the foresight."

Coach Johnson paused to give Vincent a chance to speak. When he didn't, Coach continued. "But I think that the issue is a lot deeper than the personal tragedies you have suffered as of late. I am pretty sure that there is something else going on in your life. Drugs perhaps? Alcohol? I have heard that there is a problem going on around campus with prescription drugs. Maybe you've been offered them? Yes? No?"

Vincent held his poker face and shook his head no.

"Well," Coach Johnson continued, "maybe it's just the schoolwork that is eating your lunch. I know that Tank is helping you stay focused in that regard, and I am ever-so-thankful that we have Tank. He truly cares about you."

Again Coach Johnson paused to see any reaction from Vincent that might give Coach some indication as to what was going on inside of that brain. But again, Vincent kept his poker face.

"Studies come first," Coach Johnson said, "and in speaking with your teachers, it seems like you are trying to get caught up. I am concerned about your attendance. That is the first thing you need to fix, and yes, we do have team rules about class attendance. By your truant behaviors alone, I have enough to keep you off the field this year."

This caught Vincent's attention as he looked up at his coach with his one good eye.

"Yes, grades are of utmost importance. Health is even more important though. Getting oneself healthy is so very important. And you know there are many kinds of health. For instance there's physical health, like keeping your eyes from getting swollen shut. But there's also mental health to consider. Now Vincent, this is very important. Bereavement counseling is something I would strongly recommend. Do you remember that list of services you paid fees on before school started?"

Vincent nodded his head yes.

"Well, Vincent, counseling is one of those services that you have already paid for. And how many people actually take advantage of the on-campus counselors? Not nearly enough." Coach Johnson smiled. "I am an old geezer and I tend to do things the old-fashioned way, but one thing I believe in that isn't so old-school is counseling. Fact is that we all need good counsel, but right now, you especially need to talk to somebody about what you are experiencing. Do you agree?"

Vincent shrugged.

"Obviously you are keeping a lot inside," Coach Johnson remarked. "And it finds its way to the surface, like lava working its way up. Sometimes it explodes, kind of like what happened the other night in the locker room. Or perhaps what happened last night? Yes? Well, that's not important. I want you to promise me that you will take some time off to visit the counselors. Will you promise me this?"

Vincent again shrugged, wishing he were elsewhere.

Coach Johnson exhaled. "You have talent, but talent alone

will not be enough for you to overcome your demons. I would love to be able to get you the help you need. It seems your schedule may be a little too packed, so I am going to make a very difficult decision, but one that I feel is the right one. This upcoming tournament in California is important, but not so important that I will sacrifice you. So I am going to have you stay behind and get the help you need."

"You can't do that!" Vincent burst out.

Coach Johnson didn't flinch, but he kept his tone level. "Yes, as the head coach, I can. You won't open up to me, you've cut off Tank, and you need to get healthy before you can start worrying about anything baseball related. You will just have to miss the rest of the off-season schedule. So, know that you are not suspended from the team. You are just taking a temporary leave to gather your affairs in order." And with the softest of voices, Coach Johnson expatriated Vincent.

Vincent was noticeably upset, but he knew Coach Johnson was right. Still, it stung.

I am the number one pitcher, one of the best hitters, and my life has deteriorated to the point that I have to be handled. Surely I could just work this out on my own?

Yet, he knew he really couldn't.

"So," concluded Coach Johnson, "effective immediately, you are on leave from the team. You scholarship will remain intact, and I will personally be checking up on you. Do you have any questions?"

Vincent stared at his shoelace, burning holes through it with his laser vision.

"Well then," Coach Johnson said, "Why don't you hustle down to campus and talk with your instructors from the classes you missed this morning as you were recovering."

Vincent looked up, wondering what Coach Johnson really

knew.

Coach Johnson filed past his star pitcher and to his team to get them ready for their tournament.

Chapter Eighteen

AS TIME QUICKLY moved days into weeks, Vincent was amazed at how fast he could spend money. At first it was essentials like school supplies and the pickup truck. Then he decided that ne needed a cell phone, since everyone else had one. He talked to a guy at the cellular store downtown who showed him all sorts of models, each equipped with life-changing applications that would connect him to the rest of the world, or at least help him catch up. At first he was cautious about signing a two-year contract, but Evan convinced him that it was the right thing to do because he could always upgrade to a new cell phone when the one he was buying became obsolete, which was always due to happen sooner rather than later.

The refrigerator now always had food in it. There was a stack of twelve-pack pop cans in his closet. Evan also helped him with his new wardrobe, and a person would swear that the two of them were twins when they left the dorm room together, especially since they adopted a no-shaving pact. They were going to let their hair grow out with their beards, at least until the spring season started when Vincent knew Coach Johnson would make him shave it.

And, of course, there was always beer.

In late October Vincent received a call from his realtor back in Augusta that there was a young couple interested in buying his parents' house. They made an offer, a fair one, and Vincent accepted without any haggling, for it was a memory he couldn't wait to get rid of. Besides, he was selling it "As Is" and knew that there wouldn't be too many people interested in taking that house and all of its problems on without trying to rope Vincent into paying for some of the repairs that needed to be fixed, especially the foundation issue, which was going to cost at least three grand.

The new couple closed on the house right after NCA let out for Christmas Break, giving Vincent a chance to go back one last time and salvage what he wanted and say good riddance to the rest.

Of course this also meant that Vincent was homeless for Christmas. His dormitory was closed down until the second week of January when the spring semester opened. Mrs. Dean graciously offered her home to Vincent for the holidays, practically begging him to move in for the month, but Vincent was impatient to get back to Arizona.

A new friend of his had offered his couch to Vincent. His name was Adam, another student who attended NCA. Evan introduced Vincent to Adam at a party one night, and the two of them hit it off, mainly because Vincent always bought the beer, and Adam was always thirsty.

Adam was heading home to Tennessee over the break and was happy to give Vincent a key as a way of paying him back for all of his generosity.

Adam rented a three bedroom, two bathroom party house on the east side of town, which had become a nearly nightly destination for Vincent and Evan. Vincent brought a case of beer with him almost every time. Most nights there would be the same five or ten people, sitting around and laughing, drinking, smoking, and not caring about a thing in the world. Sometimes someone would bring in marijuana and a bong would be passed around. Even though Vincent resisted each time, he knew he would eventually relent, especially considering the pressure he received from his friends who all said that it was the best feeling in the world. Watching them get high, Vincent often wondered if they were right.

Still, Vincent felt bad about rejecting Mrs. Dean's request that he stay the month of December back in Augusta with her. He knew that she was worried about him. She had asked him about his grades many times throughout the semester, and he was happy to share with her that he recorded a 3.31 GPA in the first semester.

Of course, he didn't tell her the whole story. His Monday/Wednesday/Friday speech class ate him up because he seldom made it to class at 7:30, and Dr. Vonnegut refused to let him in the room if he was a second late. Naturally he woke up later and later because he partied more and more at Adam's house, many times sacking out on his couch, the floor, or wherever he dropped. By the cutoff date for dropping classes, he was making an F, and didn't want to put in the effort to try to resurrect his grade.

Vincent also had to drop his biology class, which really hurt, because he actually tried hard to pass it. The tests just ate him up. When he dropped the class, he was making thirty-three percent, which was actually above the class average. Mr. Stillwell was convinced that in order to get full-time placement at the university, he had to be as tough and as unyielding as he could be. He also had to inject the curriculum with steroids, making it seem like a graduate course. Vincent felt a little bit better that he wasn't the only one who dropped the class, but that left him with thirteen hours, one more than the bare minimum he needed to be eligible for spring ball.

Tank checked up on him throughout the semester, but not with as much gusto as he had before Vincent's meltdown against UCSB. As far as Vincent knew, Tank didn't know about the dropped classes. Coach Johnson received a list of his players' grade point averages to make sure they were all eligible for the spring, and had the compliance officer double-check everything so they wouldn't be in trouble. Vincent slipped under the radar in this regard and looked forward to a very relaxing December of partying and sleeping on Adam's couch. In all that time, he didn't visit the weight room or exercise at all, and as a result, he had gained fifteen pounds. He reasoned that once spring ball came around, he could then get himself into shape. No need to work on that until it was absolutely necessary.

Evan went home to California to spend the break with his parents. When the dorms were finally opened in early January, Vincent was none-too-excited about moving back in. He had grown accustomed to his particular lifestyle. Worry free—focus on me. He concluded that that's what he needed after all. The campus counselor he was forced to see had even told him that. When Coach Johnson set up the first appointment, Vincent went reluctantly and found out from the quack with the bald head, grey beard, and hoop in his right ear that he needed to spend some time loving himself.

That was Vincent's first and last visit.

But love himself he did. At least he loved his lifestyle. The more beer he drank, the less he thought about his parents, or perhaps the less he cared about his parents. He wasn't too sure of which it was, and in the spirit of not caring, he didn't allow himself to think much about it.

Vincent soon found that hard liquor got the job done much more quickly than beer. When he drank hard liquor, his countenance took on a different feel. He wouldn't laugh or smile or be a funny drunk like when he drank beer. He would sit in one spot and sip on a bottle of Kentucky's best and think about what his father must have thought about when he had done the same. Sometimes, he even felt what he figured his dad must have felt, that is remorse. Not remorse for drinking, but remorse for his situation. When Vincent drank the hard stuff, it made a little bit of sense why his father didn't want Vincent or wished he had never been born. It made sense because Vincent had the same feelings about his father.

When Vincent tipped the bottle, it wasn't just his father that Vincent wished had never been born. It was his mother for allowing her monster of a husband to control her or beat Vincent like he did. It was Grandpa Dean for convincing Vincent to love him, only to die on Vincent after a couple of months. It was Mrs. Dean for having the audacity to care about him. Coach Johnson for seeing value in him. Tank for wanting the best for Vincent.

Don't they know that I'm a loser? I'll never be nothin' more than my father's son.

Each of these thoughts usually came on in order, his hatred for Tank usually arriving towards the bottom of the bottle. It was about this moment that Vincent would think about what lay on the top shelf of Evan's closet. So before Vincent vacated the dorms for Christmas break, he stashed the gun in its case at Adam's house.

Vincent found that the line in the sand that separated right from wrong was constantly being erased by incoming waves of hatred and self-pity. Each wave moved the line a little further from center like a rising tide until it was no longer visible. Really, all it took was broaching any particular moral or ethical topic for Vincent to start the erosion.

That's why he felt more and more comfortable around Evan's gun. If it hadn't been for the first time he found the gun, he wouldn't have had the guts to get it out again and again, each time daring himself to go a little further. One drunken night he would just touch it. The next drunken day he would pick it up. The next time he figured out how to take out the clip. After that it wasn't hard for him to load the clip and cycle a round into the chamber. He'd seen it done a million times on TV.

Right before Evan came back, Vincent was so comfortable with the feel of the gun that he would hold it in his hand, loaded, as he drank. Towards the bottom of the bottle, Vincent would consider what it would be like just to put the barrel to his temple. With each passing bottle, the sand eroded more.

In Vincent's sober moments, he longed to see his roommate, and ended up planning a huge party at Adam's house to celebrate the beginning of a new semester.

On the night Evan returned, Vincent had Evan's man buy a couple of cases of beer. Vincent put six in his backpack and brought it into his room, leaving the rest in the cooler in the back of his truck. There in the room, Evan was unpacking. He turned around and was very happy to see his old buddy.

"Yo, Vincent! How was your break?"

"Let me tell you," Vincent said and unzipped his backpack, pulling out two beers and throwing one to his friend. "It was awesome!"

Evan caught the beer and smiled. "Looks like you're picking up where you left off!"

"Naw," Vincent said and popped the top. He took a big gulp.

"I never left off! Been drunk since you left!"

Evan laughed and took a big gulp of his beer. "It looks like it," Evan said and pointed to Vincent's stomach.

Vincent looked down and grabbed at his added table muscle. "Yeah, I really worked on staying in shape. Six pack a day, sometimes more. Working on increasing my tolerance. Up to sixteen beers," Vincent bragged. "I plan on hitting that mark by dark tonight."

"You have something planned?" Evan asked.

"You know it! Got a few cases, talked around. We're going to head over to Adam's house and get plastered. He said that he is going to have some girls over. I don't know who they are, but it ought to be fun."

Evan looked down at his beer and then at his suitcase, still half-filled with clothes. "That does sound like fun, but do you think it's a good idea to party the night before the first day of school? I mean, don't you want to get a clean start on the semester?"

Vincent looked at his roommate with condescension. "Yeah right! If you'll recall, you are the one who said the first few days of school are only about the syllabus. Besides, I can make it to class just fine. I'm an iron man now." Vincent pulled off his shirt and flexed, the extra weight jiggling around his mid-section.

Evan laughed. "You are a wild man. You know, Vincent, when we first met, I thought you were going to be a real drag, but little did I know that you had a wild man lurking beneath your skin!"

"Oh yeah!" Vincent said and pounded the rest of his beer. He crushed the can beneath his feet and threw it towards the trash can by his desk. It hit the rim and landed behind the can, just out of sight. Vincent didn't give it any thought. "What do you say we get a head start on the drinking?"

"What are we doing?" Evan asked as he hung up another shirt.

"I don't know about you," Vincent said, "but I am one beer up on you as we speak."

"Oh yeah?" Evan said.

"Yeah!" Vincent replied, indignantly. As if a starter's pistol were fired, Evan pounded his can, and Vincent raced for his backpack and pulled out another one and started drinking. This contest lasted only a few minutes and Vincent came out ahead, finishing his three beers first. They both threw the empties in the waste basket and left the room, laughing. Before Vincent closed the door, he grabbed the keys to his truck, and they were off.

Adam was good to his word. When Vincent and Evan pulled up in Vincent's truck, the house was already rocking. They made their grand entrance and saw that, indeed, there were a lot of girls there, outnumbering the men at least three-to-one. Vincent held one case of beer on his right shoulder and Evan held the other case on his left shoulder, and the two of them parted the sea of partiers and deposited the beer on the back porch where it would keep nice and cold, being a January night in the desert.

The two of them chest-bumped party friends, and they all talked about what they did over the break. As the night wore on, Vincent worked on his beer tolerance some more, and before he knew it, they were down to only two beers, which was going to be a problem. Vincent grabbed both and headed back into the house.

A lot of the crowd had thinned out at this point, but there remained three girls. They were new to the house, second-semester transfers who came to play basketball. As they sat around the living room in a circle, the marijuana came out. One of the new girls passed a joint over to Vincent who tried to pass it on, holding his breath.

"Don't you want a hit?" new girl number one asked. Vincent had asked her what her name was earlier in the night, but even if he would have been listening to her, he wouldn't have remembered it or the other two girls' names for that matter.

"Naw," Vincent played it off. "Gotta keep the head clean," he said and pointed to his noggin.

"Dude," Evan said, "that ship sailed twelve beers ago."

Vincent considered this. He had lost track of how many beers he had consumed but estimated that number to be well over a twelve pack. He knew that he didn't feel especially drunk yet. Just tipsy. Pretty darn tipsy.

"Naw, I'm good," Vincent repeated and passed the joint on to Evan who greedily took it and inhaled deeply, choking on the smoke. He then passed it to girl number two.

"Well, if you don't like that, maybe you'll like this," girl number one said and pulled out a prescription bottle from her pocket.

"What do you have there? Aspirin?" Adam chimed in, looking very interested.

Girl number one laughed. "It's just something I took from Dad's stash. He gets these pain pills because of his back, but he never remembers to take them. I don't think he'll miss them." She opened the bottle and pulled out two little dark blue pills. She downed them and chased them with her beer. Vincent's beer that is. She smiled and took a couple more out and handed them to Vincent. "You've been so nice letting us drink your beer. Let me repay you," she said.

Vincent held the pills in his hand, looking them over, trying to get his eyes to focus on them. He looked up as girl number three took a deep drag on the joint and passed it over to Adam.

Well, it's better than pot.

Throwing caution to the wind, he popped the pills and pounded the rest of his last beer. He looked over at girl number one who winked at him. Five minutes later Vincent went from all smiles to somber. Something was happening inside of his brain, and he didn't know what it was. It was like being drunk and having somebody massage his brain, all at the same time. He felt an intense urge to sleep and had a hard time keeping his eyes open. It wasn't a feeling he especially enjoyed.

When the joint was extinguished and the beer was gone, the six lost interest, and the party officially ended. Despite offers to drive the three girls to their apartment, they left in their own car, so Evan and Vincent sauntered over to Vincent's pickup truck. Vincent fumbled with his keys and noticed for the first time that he was seeing double, maybe even triple. Try as he might, he couldn't see straight.

Vincent looked up at Evan who was standing in front of the truck, relieving himself. Evan managed to make his way to the passenger door, but when he reached for the handle, he missed completely and fell face-first in the cold, dead grass. A few seconds passed as Vincent tried to comprehend what happened. Then he heard a howling laughter. Evan pulled himself up, still beside himself with laughter, and this time managed to open the door and fall into the front seat. He pulled his feet up and managed to close the door with his face stuck to the center console.

Vincent laughed it off and thought for a moment that he should turn around and go back into Adam's house to sleep it off. He quickly dismissed the idea because he wanted to be able to make it to class on time in the morning. He pulled out his cell phone and checked the time:

1:32 A.M.

Vincent tried to compute how many hours of sleep this left

him, but gave up on his feeble attempt to subtract. At 9:00 the next morning, he would be neck-deep in algebra anyway, so he would save his brain usage for then.

After all tomorrow is a fresh start.

Then he remembered that tomorrow was today.

Vincent climbed into the truck, found the right key after three others wouldn't fit in the ignition, and the truck revved to life. From his console came the reverberations of Evan's snoring. Laughing, Vincent put it in drive and worked on putting what looked like three pictures into one. When that didn't work, he decided just to look at the middle picture.

Driving in this condition wasn't easy, but he had some practice at it the first semester and over the break. He reasoned that the key was to drive the speed limit, no faster, no slower. It was difficult though to take his attention away from the road to try to read the speedometer. When he did this, the numbers seemed all jumbled and fuzzy. He decided to just try to feel out the speed, as he turned onto Main Street.

The university was a mile ahead. That didn't seem like a very long ways to go. All he had to do was navigate straight and not arouse any suspicion. So far there was not another car in his path. As he cruised, his head felt fuzzier and fuzzier, and his windshield looked like it had frost forming on it right in front of his very eyes. He looked down to find the defrost button, then in the middle of doing that, forgot what he was doing and looked at his speed. Now his speedometer looked like it was frosting over.

He didn't know what the heck was happening to his truck, but he reasoned that he could just get it fixed. There was a little mechanics shop over by Adam's house. He would take it after practice tomorrow to have it looked at. Practice was going to be fun. He couldn't wait to get in the batting cage and hit some balls.

Baseballs reminded him of snow cones in July. He daydreamed about his father taking him to an Independence Day fireworks show and getting him a purple snow cone.

Baseballs aren't purple, he thought, but they should be. No one would be able to hit my fastball.

His smile was short lived when he heard the horn.

HOOOONNNNNKKKKKKK!!!!!!!!!!!!

Vincent looked up from the speedometer and saw a car coming in from the right. Reacting as fast as he could, he punched the gas to avoid the collision, but also had to swerve left. The truck veered into the oncoming lane, where there was another vehicle coming right for him.

HOOOONNNNNKKKKKKK!!!!!!!!!!!!

Vincent again veered left and gunned it, again narrowly avoiding the collision, but not the cottonwood tree that stood at the corner, right by the drug store. Much too drunk and high to feel pain, he was only faintly aware of the earth-shattering jolt of the truck smashing right into that cottonwood. As his head came forward to meet the windshield, the last thought Vincent had was of his mother and father. Then there was no sound.

Chapter Nineteen

THE FIRST THING Vincent noticed when he woke up was that he didn't have a hangover. Thank God for small miracles. But something was really off. It felt as if he were still in a dream. It was a dream about waking up. Or maybe he was dreaming that he was dreaming about waking up. He really didn't know. Everything just felt strange. It was like going to sleep at a different place and when awaking, not remembering where he had fallen asleep.

He didn't want to open his eyes, so he recalled his memory bank as far as it could go. Like many drunken escapades, flashes of what happened the night before crossed his eyes like a slide show in fast motion, but none of the images really connected the dots.

Drinking. There was drinking. There's a shocker.

He was confused as to whether he was remembering last night or the night before that, or a night last week.

Evan.

He put it together that he was remembering last night, the first day Evan was back from California. They had partied. There were girls. Some weed maybe? Probably. Adam was a pot head. There was always weed at Adam's.

Vincent smiled, then frowned.

First day of school! Gotta get out of bed early enough to make my first class.

Vincent was so comfortable that he didn't want to lift even one eyelid to check the time on the alarm clock, yet he knew that he needed to turn over a new leaf. He couldn't let what happened to his 7:30 speech class happen again this semester.

Okay, Vincent, just one eye. If it's before 7:00, you can keep sleeping.

With all the power he could muster, Vincent lifted his left eye ever so slightly to catch a peek at the alarm clock, but the room was bright, powerful bright. His vision was blurry, as if his eyeball were a white canvas and a painter had taken a fan brush and dabbed on heaping helpings of yellow paint. He was about to lift his right hand to wipe his eyes, but now he was aware of another sensation, an aching sensation. It hurt his chest and ribs really badly when he tried to move his right hand.

Wow, I must have slept wrong, or I'm getting older!

Vincent tried it again, more determined this time, but this time it really hurt, and he let out a soft moan.

"Nurse! Nurse!"

Vincent heard what sounded like Mrs. Dean's voice, and he knew he had to be dreaming now. No, it was a nightmare to be in so much pain merely trying to move a muscle.

"Nurse! He's waking up!"

Wait a minute!

Vincent felt that this couldn't be a dream. It was just too real. He tried to open his left eye, but again he found only bright blurriness. Extremely aware of his fright, he made a great attempt to move his left hand up to his eye and succeeded. He took a quick swipe at his eye before he let out a bellowing scream of agony.

"Whoa! Go easy there Vincent," he heard from a female voice he couldn't recognize. He didn't know what was happening to him, but it was scaring him. He opened his right eye, and again was blinded by all the light in the room, but this eye wasn't so blurry, and as his pupil adjusted through the insistent blinking, he saw a woman in pink scrubs standing over him, putting her right hand on his forehead and easing him back.

"You've been through quite a bit, so just calm down," she said.

"What the..." Vincent started, but his ribs hurt so badly with each word that he couldn't even finish the sentence.

"Vincent," the nurse said as Vincent's right pupil narrowed on her face. He noticed she had freckles across the top of her nose and her hair was red and curly like Little Orphan Annie. "Do you remember what happened?"

"What? When?" Vincent winced again.

"Do you remember anything?"

Vincent frowned, searching for answers.

"Vincent, you are at Saint Francis Hospital in Page, Arizona. You've been in a car accident. Three nights ago you wrecked into a tree downtown. You've been asleep ever since. Do you remember this?"

Vincent looked down at his right arm and saw he had an IV connected to the inside bend of his elbow. His first thought was to rip it out, but again, his left arm didn't want to move, and he ground his teeth in pain. He looked down at his left arm and saw that it was spotted black like an overripe banana. He looked up, and in the far corner of the room, he saw Mrs. Dean.

"Mrs. Dean?" he asked in a weak voice, wondering if he were

hallucinating, or if maybe he was having a nightmare. Mrs. Dean responded with a sob.

Oh, God! What happened to me?

Again, Vincent tried sitting up, but the pain through his upper torso was intense.

"Vincent," the nurse reiterated, "I need you to listen to me. Do you remember any of this?"

"What? No. I don't know what you're talking about! This has gotta be a dream." Every word hurt, but he was getting angry.

The nurse put her hand on his forehead again and applied a little pressure, and Vincent complied and lay back down.

"What's wrong with my eye?" Vincent asked. "I can't see out of my left eye."

"You have a bandage over your left eye. Your head hit the windshield and busted it. The doctor had to take bits of glass out of your left eye."

Vincent computed this as quickly as he could. "What else is wrong? Why does it hurt to move my left arm?"

The nurse put her soft hand on Vincent's left forearm. "You had quite a nasty accident, and you weren't wearing your seatbelt. Your entire body has been put through a lot, and you have many bruises, especially on your left side. All things considered though, you are lucky to be alive. You have no broken bones, only bumps and bruises, and of course your eye and forehead."

"My truck?"

"Sorry," the nurse said and shook her head no.

Vincent looked at Mrs. Dean, who was in full tears now. He reached up with his right hand and found only mild discomfort from his ribs and back. He felt his head, felt the bandage on his eye, and noted that the wrapping extended all the way around his head. Then he thought about baseball.

"How long will it take me to recover?" Again, every word

hurt, but he had to know.

The nurse checked his IV machine, and then injected a syringe into one of his tubes. "You have had a lot to take in, so it's best that you rest now. Your body needs rest. When the doctor is in, you will be able to ask him those kinds of questions. In the meantime, you just rest."

Vincent thought to ask for a mirror to see the damage, but that thought became blurred, and tunnel vision set in. The last thing he saw was Mrs. Dean, still looking helpless in the corner. He wanted to comfort her, but no words formed, and before he knew it, there was blackness.

When Vincent next woke, he had full memory of his conversation with the nurse, though he wondered if Mrs. Dean had really been a figment of his imagination. When he opened his right eye and looked to his left, there he saw the old lady, asleep in the chair next to him. For the first time something really dawned on him.

This is serious!

In his core Vincent felt the need to take a drink and could feel his right arm shaking.

"Vincent?"

The room was much darker than before. Vincent turned to his right and saw Coach Johnson. He was wearing an NCA warm-up suit. His silver hair was a mess, and by the look in his eyes, it appeared he had been sleeping as well.

"Hi Coach," Vincent whispered, partly because he didn't want his ribs to hurt when he talked, and partly because he didn't want to wake Mrs. Dean.

Coach Johnson just looked at Vincent and shook his head.

Vincent didn't know what to say either. Everything was just so foreign to him. All he knew was that he was in a lot of pain, needed a drink something awful, and wondered if there was a pill he could take for the pain. Then it hit him.

Pills!

Vincent's memory kicked in full gear and the slide show became vivid. Girls, beer, pills. Truck. Evan asleep on the console. Honking. The last image was graphic and Vincent winced again, which really hurt his ribs.

He had been in a wreck because he was drinking and driving, and he had no idea what was in those pills.

This fact hit him like a ton of bricks. Did Coach Johnson know? Did Mrs. Dean know? Shame. He felt so much shame that he prayed neither knew, but he thought better. Surely the doctor would know. Maybe the doctor didn't tell the two of them. Maybe it was a confidentiality thing. Before he could think any more on this topic, Coach Johnson spoke.

"Vincent, how could you have let this happen?"

Vincent lowered his head. Shame returned.

Coach Johnson waited patiently for an answer. Vincent had none, only shook harder and started sweating.

"How could you have ever considered doing something so reckless?"

You don't know the half of it, Vincent thought, not quite sure if he actually verbalized this.

Coach Johnson pushed further. "I want answers!" Coach Johnson was getting angrier by the second and Mrs. Dean wiggled in her chair. "I brought you on this team as a favor to your mentor. How do you think Grandpa Dean would feel about what you have done? And after what happened to your parents? How did you ever think it was a good idea to drink and drive? Huh? Answer me!"

Vincent was silent. He didn't want to disrespect Coach Johnson. It's just that he couldn't mount a defense because he knew his act was indefensible. Thankfully, a tall, skinny man came into the room to save the day.

"Well, Vincent, it's nice to see you awake," the man said. "I am Dr. Holcolmb. I'm the one who worked on you when you were brought into the emergency room about three days ago. You're quite the lucky man. Many people in your situation would have died from the impact without a seatbelt on, but you have sustained mostly bruising. How's the pain?"

"It hurts all over," Vincent whispered. He snuck a peek at Coach Johnson, who appeared to be praying.

"Vincent," the Doctor said, and he sat next to Vincent on the bed and started looking him over, checking vitals, "Do you have any recollection of the accident?"

Vincent slowly nodded,ing not to let his shaking be obvious. "I think it's starting to come back to me."

The doctor nodded and picked up Vincent's right wrist and put his index and middle finger on his pulse point and looked at his watch. "Do you remember what was in your body?"

"A burrito?" Vincent asked, slightly sarcastically. Coach Johnson peered up from his meditation with a look of disdain.

"Well, you might have had a burrito," Dr. Holcolmb said, "but you also had a pretty lethal cocktail in your body. When we had you stable, we pumped your body and found that you had taken some pain medicine. Did you have a prescription for any pain medicine?"

Vincent shook his head.

"Well, on top of that, you had a blood alcohol content of .15, nearly double the legal limit. With the combination and the wreck, I'd say that you are really lucky to be alive."

Vincent wiped the sweat from his forehead and found no comfort in the doctor's words. It seemed more like a guilt trip than a fact check.

"Now, you didn't have any broken bones, but there was plenty of bruising. We were very concerned about internal bleeding, but it looks like your rib cage did its job. Now it's paying the price, as you can tell by the pain, yes?"

Vincent nodded.

And then there's your eye. I had to pick pieces of glass out of your left eye. It's pretty scratched up and is going to need some time to heal." The doctor paused for a moment before softening the blow. "Vincent, your eye took a beating. It's hard to know how much vision you will have left.

"Will I be able to play ball?" Vincent asked, nervously.

"Well," the doctor replied and gave it some quality thought, "I'd say that the jury is still out on that one. It is going to depend on how well it heals, scar tissue, and so on. Is that your dominant eye?"

"No," Coach Johnson answered for Vincent.

"Well then," Dr. Holcolmb said, "I think we will just have to wait and see. If I were to guess, I'd say that you will have some depth perception issues that you will have to overcome."

The news hit Vincent as hard as his truck hit that tree. Depth perception was everything when hitting a pitch, catching a fly ball, heck, even in catching the ball that is being thrown back from the catcher.

How could I have been so stupid?

It just happened so fast. In the blink of an eye, his entire future might have been compromised.

How could I have let myself drink and drive? How could I have let myself drink? How could I have let myself take some pills when I didn't even know what the heck they were? Didn't I learn anything from my father? Why, yes. It would seem I learned a lot from my old man.

"But you never know," the doctor concluded. "You will have to see an optometrist to get that eye checked out."

Vincent, shaking harder than ever, couldn't seem to control his body. His head pounded, and his ribs hurt, and he couldn't keep from sweating. It seemed to be coming from deep down in his core, and all he could think of was alcohol.

"And that shaking," the doctor said, "your body is going through withdrawals."

Coach Johnson stared at Vincent.

"They'll hurt for a while," the doctor continued, "but they'll pass."

Vincent sat impatiently in his own sweat, trying not to think about it. Then a question hit him, and he became very scared at its possible answer. "Is Evan alright?"

The doctor looked puzzled at Vincent. "Who?"

"Evan, my roommate."

The doctor flipped through some notes and asked, "Did you have someone with you when you crashed?"

Vincent looked over at Mrs. Dean, who was fully awake, apparently taking in the whole conversation. Vincent looked back at the doctor, puzzled.

"We didn't treat anyone else. It was a one-car accident, and as far as I know, you were alone at the time. But then again, that's something for the police to speak about with you.

Vincent just knew that Evan was along with him. He had vivid memories of Evan passed out, with his head on the console. Maybe even snoring a little. Or maybe Vincent's imagination had gotten the best of him.

"Well, Mr. Preston," the doctor said, "Your injuries are minor, and I see no reason to hold you in the hospital, so I am discharging you. I want you to get plenty of rest over the next few days. The nurse will be in in a moment to help you with your things and your prescription. Also I would like for you to set up an appointment for next week with my secretary so we can change the bandage on your left eye."

The doctor walked out of the room, and the nurse came in. Mrs. Dean still hadn't said a word to Vincent, but excused herself as Vincent got back into his clothes, which stunk pretty bad of beer, sweat, and marijuana smoke.

Vincent was still shaking and was unsteady on his feet, so Coach Johnson helped walk him out into the lobby where Mrs. Dean was waiting. Every step hurt every inch of his body and he felt he might faint at any moment from the pain. The three of them walked outside where there were two police officers waiting at the bottom of the ramp. The taller of the two came up to Vincent and said, "Vincent Preston, you are under arrest for suspicion of driving while intoxicated." He took a pair of handcuffs out and cuffed Vincent's hands behind his back.

Vincent started to cry. No. He sobbed. He sobbed in shuddering spasms. He knew he screwed up, but that wasn't why he sobbed. At this moment he thought of his own Mom and Dad, not too long into the grave. He could have ended up like them. But even that realization wasn't what made him sob now. He thought back to the conversation he had had with Mrs. Dean before he left Augusta after his parents' funeral. She had told him that he would mourn, and the longer he waited, the worse it would be.

Boy was she right.

He cried his right eye out at everything his father had ever done to him, and to his mother. He cried that his mother never hugged him or told him that she loved him. He cried for a lost youth when he wasn't ever taken out fishing, camping, or even to the Pizza Barn to celebrate his birthday. He cried about never receiving gifts, birthday, Christmas, or any other. He cried about how his parents never took him to church, or to his elementary school plays, or watched him play baseball, or even walk in graduation. He cried that he wasn't ever loved or wanted, and he wanted to scream straight up, or straight down at his parents for why they couldn't just have loved him. And now they were gone without so much as a goodbye or an atonement of any kind, and all Vincent inherited from them was a predisposition to alcoholism.

Vincent wept like a little baby as the officers led him away.

Vincent, his shackles pinching his wrists, looked back and saw Coach Johnson shaking his head. Mrs. Dean broke down weeping, and Coach Johnson put his arm around her and gave Vincent a hard look that made him wonder if it would have been better if he had just died in the wreck.

The tall officer stuffed Vincent into the backseat of the police cruiser and promptly took him to jail.

Chapter Twenty

VINCENT HAD NEVER had a worse night of sleep. The whole ordeal was surreal, being treated like a criminal. Made to take mug shots, strip in front of officers to show that he didn't have anything he shouldn't. Thrown in a cell the size of a phone booth with a hard wooden seat and not nearly enough room to lie down, even if he pulled his knees up. Sweating and shaking, he was miserable. Even if he could get comfortable, there was a lot of light from the hallway, and all the other cells were full of guys who were loud, lewd, and willing to do anything to engage Vincent in a conversation so that they could threaten the new fish. Vincent's only consolation was that he didn't have to share his cell.

He was given a list of bond companies and told by the district attorney that he had to accept one particular company called Rosie's Bail Bonds. The DA said that he would reject any bail from another company and only set the price higher. This left Vincent no choice but to call Rosie, who turned out to be a guy with a gruff voice.

Vincent's bond was set at 50,000 and Rosie charged him ten percent interest, meaning that when he got out of jail, he had to scrape together 5000 bucks. He knew that it wouldn't be hard, just a simple bank withdrawal. He had the money from his parents' estate, but since his parents' house was in his father's name and not Vincent's, the government took about fifty percent of the sale as a death tax. Vincent figured that what was left over would pay for his left over schooling, but on his present course of action he was going to be broke in a year.

Then, to rub salt in his wounds, the DA informed Vincent that the police specifically didn't arrest him until after he was discharged, because if they arrested him while he was under the hospital's care, the city would have been responsible for his hospital bills. The DA said this with an air of arrogance, patting himself on the back for sticking it to Vincent. The DA wore his smile out the door.

Vincent met with a lawyer who told him that his fees right up front would be 5000 dollars to work out a plea agreement. Again, Vincent had no choice but to accept the lawyer's offer, knowing he was already down 10,000 dollars, and he hadn't even found out what the plea agreement would cost him. Then there was his truck to consider.

Not thinking anything would happen to his truck, Vincent had taken the cheapest policy Martin Agency offered, liability only, meaning his insurance would only pay for the other person's car in the event of a wreck. With his truck a total loss, he struck out. He would receive no check from his insurance company and would merely have to take it as a loss. Then there would be the hospital bill, ER bill, doctor's bills, and checkups with the doctor as his eye hopefully healed.

Man, I really screwed up.

Vincent tried not to think about all of this, but time in jail allowed him nothing but time for thought. He had to go somewhere inside of his mind with all the other jail birds hooting and hollering at him. In the end he thought about baseball, and it helped a little.

Finally, at 11:00 the next morning, he was released on bond to appear in a week for court. He left to a round of jeering from the others in lock up, and when he walked out the door, still stinking from his party clothes from four days ago, the bright sun shone on him, making him squint with his one good eye. He briefly looked for his pickup, but remembered his predicament, and slowly walked back to his dorm. Each step hurt his whole body. Sleep was absolutely essential at this point. All the way he tried to forget about his troubles, financial and other, and worried about Evan. He still had no idea what had happened to his roommate. Was Evan even with him in the first place? He knew it must be so, but he really didn't know. It just didn't seem to make any sense. He hoped Evan was okay.

Finally Vincent made it back to his dormitory. He walked straight for his room, and when he opened his door, he saw his roommate sitting on his own bed. The covers and sheets had been removed. His tennis racquet stringer was not in the middle of the floor where it usually was, and he noticed more than anything that the whole room was cleaned out.

"Evan?" Vincent asked, not really knowing what he wanted to ask.

Evan looked up at Vincent and then back down at his feet. "Hey buddy. How are you doing?"

"I'm tired and a little bruised up, but I'm fine. I don't know if you know, but I was in a wreck."

Evan looked up at Vincent. "You don't remember?"

"Remember?" Vincent asked. "Yeah, I think I do. I've blacked out some of the details, but it feels like it was a doozy. In fact, I swore you were with me in the passenger seat, but obviously I was wrong."

Evan looked back up at Vincent. "Man, you really don't remember, do you?"

Vincent looked quizzically at Evan, so he continued. "Sorry brah, but I had to run for it. I made it out of there before anyone knew better."

Vincent paused, his thoughts jumbling in his head. "So, you were in the truck with me?" Vincent asked.

"Uh, yeah. I have no idea how you could have hit that tree, but we were lucky we weren't both killed. Have you seen your truck? Brutal, man."

"You ran?" Vincent asked as if he couldn't muster the capacity to comprehend that thought.

"Sorry, man. I couldn't afford to have anything alcohol-related on my record. I had a DUI my senior year, and I'm on probation. If the cops found me in that truck with the open containers and everything else we had, my butt was toast. I had to run for it."

"And the police really don't know?"

"No," Evan replied. "Hey man, you didn't tell them, did you?"

"I don't think so," Vincent said, feeling very slighted. Here he was in the hospital and then taken straight to the slammer, and his roommate got off totally free and didn't even have the decency to come and see him.

"Good," Evan said. "Look man, there's more to this you probably aren't aware of. Word got around pretty quick, so that dorky RA with the head resident stormed our room and found our stash. They found everything, the beer, bourbon, and some weed."

Quickly, Vincent's thoughts turned to Evan's gun, and

Vincent realized that it was still at Adam's house, his first lucky break. Vincent sighed and tried to take everything in, but had a hard time comprehending the big mess he had come back to. All he wanted was a good rest, and now, after being in trouble with coach, after being in trouble with the law, he was now in trouble with the school. Was he going to be kicked out? Had Evan already been kicked out? Is that why all his stuff was gone?

"Man, Vincent, I am really sorry. I hope you understand what I had to do and why I had to do it. I just couldn't have anything else on my record."

"What are you talking about?" Vincent inquired, trying his best to remain upright and awake.

Evan exhaled. "They asked who all the stuff belonged to. Sorry man. It was either you or both of us. Since you were in the hospital and they had you painted already, I had to lie."

"What did you tell them?" Vincent asked, not believing his ears.

"Sorry, Vincent. They wanted me to move to another room where I wouldn't have to deal with alcohol and drugs. Sorry I had to throw you under the bus."

Evan stood up and shook his head as if he were disgusted with his behavior. "I gotta go now. I will understand if you never want to talk to me again."

Evan walked up to Vincent and paused for a moment. Vincent considered punching out his roommate for this ultimate betrayal and the obvious lies Evan told, but Vincent knew it would hurt too much just to lift his fist. So instead he took a step to the side to allow his ex-roommate a chance to leave unharmed. Evan slid past Vincent and out of his life.

Vincent's head hit his pillow, and he fell fast asleep, but he was wakened fifteen minutes later by a knock on the door. Vincent didn't move a muscle, but the door opened anyway. It was the RA, What's His Face. Vincent never could remember what the kid's name was, and he wasn't about to in his present condition. Behind him was the head resident, who spoke first. "Vincent, you have been evicted for breaking the drug and alcohol policy. You have twenty-four hours to leave the premises with all your belongings or we will have to get the police involved."

Vincent turned over and asked, "Where will I go?"

"That's not my problem," the head resident said, staring at Vincent. The RA stood next to his boss with his arms crossed at his chest, a smug smile playing about his lips.

"But sir, you don't understand--"

"No," the head resident interrupted, "it's you who doesn't understand. We have a zero-tolerance policy for drugs and alcohol in the dormitories. You knew the rule. You broke it. You have only yourself to blame."

The conceited RA chose this time to get in his barb. "In my time as RA, I have never seen a worse tenant!"

Vincent chuckled at this ridiculous hyperbole, yet he knew the comments were fairly germane. He wasn't exactly a paradigm of the successful college student.

Vincent attempted to marshal his concentration, but his mind was fuzzy from not having slept. He knew he should defend himself, but the words that came out didn't exactly fit fluid sentences. "But I don't have a house. It just sold. My truck's gone too. I have nowhere to go."

The head resident shook his head. "That's not my problem, buddy."

"Isn't there an appeals process or something?" Vincent asked, finally saying something intelligent.

The head resident stiffened and inhaled. "Yeah, you can make an appeal to the housing board." He then crossed his arms at his chest like his compadre and said, "But unless I have that appeal form on my desk by this time tomorrow, you are expected to be out. Is that clear?"

Vincent nodded and turned back over. He heard his door close, and his tears welled up in his eyes. It hurt, especially his left eye, and he wasn't sure if he was doing damage to it by crying, but cry he did, like when he was arrested.

Vincent could feel the saturnine sector of his personality taking over, and there wasn't a thing he could do about it. "I have—nothing! Vincent said out loud. "Nobody! Nowhere to go!"

Vincent shook and cried some more as he whispered out loud in the middle of his sobs, "I wish I—had never been—born."

Again Vincent thought of Evan's gun. He knew he could walk to Adam's house, go to the spare bathroom, pull it out from under the sink where it sat loaded in its case, andnd all the pain. He closed his eyes and thought about the first time he touched the gun. He could feel the cool, hard steel press against the soft pads of his fingers. His thumb wrapping around the handle. Its awkward weight unbalanced in his hand, foreign to him, like love.

It seemed the only option. There was no other way out. His father had been right after all.

Vincent turned back over. With decision he got up and grabbed his old high school baseball cap off the desk. The time was now. It could all be over in half an hour.

As he put the hat on, he paused and looked at the inside bill. Faded as it was, it still read:

Phil. 4:13

Automatically, Vincent sat down with the ball cap still in his hand. He just stared at the verse.

I can do all things through Christ which strengtheneth me.

"Lies!" he shouted. "I can't do a damned thing right!"

He put the hat on, and he stood up again, but something stopped him from taking the first step to the door. He felt no way out of his situation, felt his fate was certain, but instead of a picture of his father entering his head like it normally would in his miserable condition, this time it was a picture of Mrs. Dean, sitting in that hospital room, tears falling from her cheeks.

Suicide seemed the only option, but the word had a nasty connotation to it. Yet try as he might, he couldn't come up with a euphemism to soften its blow. Then it hit him.

If Mrs. Dean was so hurt by seeing me in a hospital bed, how hurt would she be if I killed myself?

It was a question he had never pondered before. Whereas before all he could think about in his self-pity was his own pain, he never gave any consideration to what pain his suicide would bring others who loved him.

Do others actually love me?

Try as he might to take the negative, it was undeniable. There was Mrs. Dean and Coach Johnson. Tank, and his other teammates. There were his teammates back home who he came to eventually call his friends. There were even teachers that had invested their time in him who would be crushed by such a selfish act as suicide. Each of these people, and probably more who he couldn't think of at the moment, would be crushed. He knew deep down that his life had touched countless others'. Is that really what he wanted to leave behind? A whole host of hurting people, each asking "Why?" Each bearing the burden of responsibility? Each wondering if there were something they could have done to prevent it? Each feeling guilty?

But I'm in such big trouble. There seems no way out.

And there it was, the word "seems." He had felt his situation to be so dire and had considered making an impulsive decision to end it all, but he never even looked into possible solutions. Sure, at the moment it felt like all was lost, but was it really? Suicide was such a permanent solution to a temporary problem.

His head hurt, so he took off his ball cap and sat back down on his bed and looked at the faded writing again.

Can I do all things?

Then he heard a voice in his head say, softly, yes.

Finally, amazingly, he felt a small twinge of peace. For the first time since his parents had died, he felt peace. Not the numbness that went along with drinking, which was a temporary feeling of bliss, but actual peace. He didn't know why or how he felt it, or where the little voice came from that whispered the affirmation in his ear, but as surely as his heart beat in his chest, he knew it to be true.

Vincent closed his eyes and focused on Mrs. Dean's tear-streaked face. It ate him up inside to know that he caused her pain. How could he possibly consider causing her more?

Vincent lay back down on his bed and sought to sleep. The small twinge of peace seemed to be spreading like tentacles to the rest of his body. As peace led to drowsiness, his mind's eye pictured a dark and deep forest in front of him, and it made him frown. But he focused harder on the forest and was able to pick out an individual tree. As he looked farther, he saw that the forest was comprised of nothing more than individual trees. Lots and lots of individual trees.

His mind's eye peered down at his hands which weren't shaking now. They held an axe. Sprinting towards the first tree, he took a big swing and toppled it in one swoop. He could hear the crashing of the shadowy leaves and branches, and it made him smile, so he took aim at another, and another, and slowly blazed a trail through the forest. In a matter of seconds he was fast asleep.

The next day Vincent woke with determination. Never mind the fact that he still felt the alcohol withdrawals here and there. He cowboyed up and acquired the appeal form and filled it out. He was told that he would have a chance to defend himself in front of the board, and with all that was going on, he decided he must make a "to do" list. Never mind school. Cleaning up his mess seemed like a full-time job. He was granted a hearing in front of the board the next week, which bought him some time to get his affairs in order.

In the meantime, he moved money around and paid his lawyer and Rosie the bond bully, wondering how much of a kickback the DA was going to receive. He went back to his dorm and checked his mailbox, which was full since he hadn't checked it in quite some time. The usual junk was crammed in there, but on top was a bill from the hospital. When he opened it up, he saw that he owed 22,000 dollars! The thought made him faint. Knowing what the DA told him, Vincent wished that the cops would have chained him to his bed. He had no health insurance. He didn't even know if he had health insurance when his parents were alive. He figured that his father never thought to care enough about him to insure him. Even if he did, that policy would have lapsed by now. Any way he cut it, he owed the hospital 22,000 dollars.

Vincent went back to his dorm room and pulled out his cell phone and got a hold of a receptionist in the billing department at the hospital. He worked out a billing plan that would slowly bleed him to death. Right as he got off the phone with the hospital, there was another knock at his door.

"Geez, what now?" he said loud enough for the visitor on the other side of the door to hear. Vincent didn't really care. When he opened the door, he was greeted by Coach Johnson, Mrs.

Dean, and Tank.

Vincent stuttered, so Coach Johnson asked, "May we come in?" in a gentle voice.

Vincent stepped out of the way and pulled out his chair for Mrs. Dean to sit on. Tank sat on Evan's bare mattress and Coach Johnson remained standing. "Vincent," Coach Johnson said, "I need a moment of your time. Would you please sit down?"

Vincent obeyed, sitting down on his unmade bed.

Coach Johnson seemed to be looking for the right words to say. When they didn't come, he grabbed the other desk chair and sat on it backward, leaning forward on the back rest for support. When the words finally found him, he said, "Okay Vincent. You've gotten yourself into trouble. I feel partly to blame for it. Tank could see it coming. He warned me, and I didn't do a good enough job as coach to make sure you had a supporting cast after your parents passed away. Is it fair to say that you've taken it pretty hard?"

Vincent stared at his feet and didn't answer.

"Well," Coach Johnson continued, "you have quite a mess on your hands. I understand that you are set to be evicted, pending the outcome of the housing board meeting next week, am I right?"

Vincent nodded.

"And you have some legal issues to contend with, correct?"

"Yes sir."

"And I assume hospital bills?" Coach Johnson further prodded.

Vincent looked at Mrs. Dean who had composed herself. She stared straight at Vincent, unwavering, and Vincent thought about her crying in that hospital room. It made him sad. Tank stared at him as well.

"Yes, sir. I got the bill in the mail today," Vincent answered.

Coach Johnson rubbed at his chin, scratching his five o'clock shadow. "So, how are you going to get yourself out of this mess?"

Vincent shrugged. "One tree at a time?"

Coach Johnson looked sideways at Vincent, apparently not comprehending the inside nature of the answer, so Vincent continued.

"I've paid the bond fee and my lawyer's fees. He said he would work with the DA to get me a plea deal so I can avoid prison time. He seems to think I have a good case since this is my first offense."

"Okay," Coach Johnson said and scratched at his chin some more. "Now, how focused are you on changing your lifestyle? Before you answer, I want the truth, and I don't want you to say it to me. I want you to look Mrs. Dean in the eyes and tell her what your future holds. I think she deserves it after all that she has done for you."

Vincent gulped.

Moment of truth. Guess I will have to make a decision.

But Vincent knew that it really wasn't a decision. There was only one option, and that's what he wanted anyway. After yesterday's revelation, he had already made that decision. He turned to Mrs. Dean and said, "Ma'am, I am so sorry. I got in over my head, and one thing led to another. I promise to change my life. I want to be the man you knew last year, not what I've turned into."

Mrs. Dean nodded, got up, and walked over to give Vincent a big hug. "I forgive you, my son."

For the first time in a long time, Vincent felt loved again. He hadn't felt love since he left Oklahoma, and he wished Mrs. Dean would move in with him, protect him from all the evils of this world, never stop hugging him. He certainly had a better chance with her guiding him than he did by himself.

"Good," Coach Johnson said as Mrs. Dean resumed her seat. "Now," Coach Johnson continued, "do you mean it?"

"Yes, sir," Vincent said.

"Tank," Coach Johnson said, "do you believe him?"

Tank sat there, staring at Vincent, appraising him. "I don't know," Tank said. "I want to, but he's lied to me before. What's stopping him from lying to me right now?"

Vincent shook his head, the truth coming out as easy as all his previous lies had. "I'm sorry Tank. I need your help too."

Coach Johnson looked over at Tank, who nodded back at his elder. "Okay," Coach Johnson said, "I believe you. I will vouch for you with the housing board. See if I can convince them to let you stay on a probationary status. You'll need constant contact from your mentor, so Tank has agreed to move in here with you for his last semester of school."

Vincent looked up at Tank who kept his stare back on Vincent.

Coach Johnson continued, "I have no influence over the court system, so you are alone in your battle there. Saying your lawyer does work out an agreement, you will probably have a million service hours to complete, which will be good for you. In the meantime, you will need to get caught up with your studies. School has started already, but Tank will help you out there as your full time accountability partner."

Coach Johnson paused. "Now, we have a question about your left eye. Remember, Vincent, that a baseball player's eyes are more important than his arm. Let's say it heals properly, like the doctor thinks it will. That puts you back on the field by the first game of the season."

Vincent smiled.

"But," Coach Johnson continued, "I'm not about to let that happen."

Vincent frowned.

"I have a list of conditions for you before I am willing to grant you the privilege of playing for NCA again," Coach Johnson said as Vincent leaned in. "First, you have to be totally healed from your injuries as determined by our team physician. Second, you will have to maintain at least a 3.0 GPA throughout the semester without dropping any classes. Third, you will have to fulfill all of your legal requirements. You won't so much as practice with us until you are square with the state of Arizona. Finally, I will need Tank's approval, and as you've undoubtedly figured out by now, he's tougher than I am. And he will be on top of you all the time. If your captain says no, it's no."

Coach Johnson looked over at Mrs. Dean. "Does that cover everything, Elna?"

Mrs. Dean replied, "I would like a weekly report. Is that too much to ask?"

Coach Johnson shook his head no and said, "I am sure Vincent will be more than happy to keep you up to date, and Tank will verify everything Vincent says." Coach Johnson looked at Vincent. "Perhaps you think we are being harsh? A tad unfair?"

Vincent shook his head no. He knew that Coach Johnson couldn't trust him, and all the safeguards he was putting in would surely keep him on the straight and narrow path. He didn't want to go back to that drunken lifestyle, but in the back of his mind, he relented to the dark side, thinking that he would be unfaithful to his friends like Evan and Adam. Vincent quickly brushed the thought aside. Evan had double-crossed him to save his own neck, and Vincent never recalled seeing Adam at the hospital in Vincent's time of need. Those two facts spoke volumes. If they were real friends, they would have cared about him. Vincent was quickly figuring out what it meant to be a real friend. Supporting someone in a bad lifestyle was not being a friend. On the other hand, Tank was going to be tough on him, the mark of a true friend.

"I will not let you down," Vincent said, looking into his coach's eyes.

"Good," Coach Johnson replied. "So we are in agreement that you are still on scholarship, but are suspended until you have resolved all of your issues and completed the terms of our agreement." Then Coach Johnson paused. "But," and he paused again, leading Vincent's heart to climb into his throat, "I want you to know that I have never given any scholar-athlete a second chance like this before. Not many coaches would. In fact, you can thank Mrs. Dean for persuading me."

Coach Johnson paused again as Vincent lowered his head in submission. "Now I want you to know that you are on permanent probation. If I so much as catch word that you touched a beer, went to a party, looked at drugs, skipped class, or anything that you shouldn't do, you will immediately lose your scholarship, and I will personally go to the board of academic affairs and ask to have you kicked out of school. Do you understand how serious I am? You have lost all of your credit with me. Understand?"

"Yes, sir," Vincent replied.

"Tank? Your turn." Coach Johnson said and looked over his shoulder at his captain.

"Yes, sir," Tank said and approached Vincent with serious eyes. "Vincent, as a penalty, you've lost your nickname. When such a time comes, you may get another one. As for now, you're no longer "Special K." Understand?"

Vincent nodded, staring down at the ground. Of all the blows he had taken, that one hurt the worst.

*

Coach Johnson was true to his word. He spoke on behalf of Vincent to the housing board and was able to convince them to allow Vincent to stay on a one-semester probationary period. Tank moved in the very evening they all spoke with Vincent, and the two of them spent that night talking about all the issues in Vincent's life: his parents, his high school life, Grandpa Dean, and of course, Mrs. Dean. Tank asked Vincent to lay it all out in front of him so that he could understand Vincent better. Knowing it was important, Vincent obliged. It was actually a bit freeing.

In addition, Vincent's lawyer was able to have his charges reduced. He would have no prison time, but there would be a reckoning for his wrong. In this regard, Coach Johnson was correct about community service. Vincent was sentenced to 100 hours in the community, and was ordered to seek counseling, twice a week for the rest of the school year with a therapist in town. Vincent owed the court another 2000 dollars, but after all he had been paying out as of late, including another grand to the doctor who cared for him after his wreck, this didn't seem so bad. Also, if Vincent had plans on buying another vehicle, it would be of no use because the judge revoked his driver's license for one year. Now that he was used to driving everywhere, this was going to be tough.

When Vincent returned to the doctor, he was able to lose the bandage around his head and let his eye heal. His vision was plenty blurry, but the doctor thought it would take a few more weeks for it to heal properly. Vincent was referred to the only optometrist in town. He remained hopeful, but cautious. His baseball career depended on it.

With Tank's help, Vincent was able to start getting caught up in his studies. Tank had strict rules on school nights: lights out at 10:00 every night with a wake up at 6:00 A.M. for conditioning.

Of course Vincent was expected to accompany Tank on all early-morning workouts. Though it was hard and Tank was every bit the drill sergeant, Vincent quickly lost that extra weight he had put on from his first semester.

Vincent called Mrs. Dean once a week, sometimes more frequently, to keep her updated on his progress. Tank, as Vincent's accountability partner, verified all that he said to her, keeping a close ear on his conversations.

The biggest change came on weekends. Vincent had been used to sleeping in late on Sunday mornings. Tank didn't instruct Vincent, but rather invited him to his church again. Acting on free will, Vincent agreed. That's where, to his surprise, he finally met the brunette he had seen in the coffee shop on the first day of school.

Chapter Twenty-One

HOPE BROWN WOKE up with the alarm clock promptly at 7:30 Sunday morning. There were mornings when she wished she could sleep in like anyone her age, but she felt the same sense of duty that she felt every other morning of the week. Even on Saturday mornings she would wake at 7:30 and gather with her girlfriends in the lobby of Flagler Hall at 8:00 to run over to The Wheel, the town's local doughnut hut, to have a maple frosted, Bavarian cream-filled long john. It was something she looked forward to all week long, even daydreaming about it as she went to sleep on Friday nights. There, the girls would gather around one of the little round tables with barstools and talk about their week, highs and lows.

They all came from different places but had migrated to each other through their faith. Hope, a freshman, came from Amarillo, Texas. Her best friend Grace, who was a senior, hailed from Albuquerque, New Mexico. This made it easy for Hope to go home for a weekend since Albuquerque was on the way.

Charity was home grown in Page, and Amie, the fourth, came from Salt Lake City. Hope never stopped marveling at how neat it was for the four of them to have found one another and become friends. As she saw it, it was only possible by the awesome power of God.

Every Saturday morning at The Wheel, one of the girls was responsible for a short devotional, an encouraging word, usually with a story or anecdote to go along with it with encouraging words from the Bible. Yesterday it had been her turn and she chose a verse out of Ecclesiastes, her favorite book of the Bible. "So I concluded that there is nothing better than to be happy and enjoy ourselves as long as we can. And people should eat and drink and enjoy the fruits of their labor for these are gifts from God."

She remarked about the importance of these Saturday mornings where they could be happy, enjoy themselves, and eat doughnuts. She then prayed for each to remain strong throughout the next week.

Each of her friends had their own churches to go to on Sunday mornings. They all met for various gatherings during the week, though, to hang out and encourage each other. Monday evenings they met at the Christian Church for evening meal and a word from their preacher. Wednesday lunch they would meet at the Baptist Collegiate Ministry Student Union across the street from the basketball arena for their weekly lunch and speaker. Friday lunch they would meet at the Wesley House, which was across the street from the tennis courts. Once a month they would meet at the Catholic Church for supper and an inspirational word from the priest, Father Danny.

In Hope's mind, each of these opportunities was very important because of the encouragement it brought. She knew that there was an element to college which was wicked, evil, intent on promising pleasure but only delivering pain. She was susceptible to it every day. She had been asked many times to go to parties, and even went once, but ended up walking home when she found out it was just an excuse to drink, smoke, and do other things to which she would not let her imagination wander. Hanging out with like-minded people only encouraged and strengthened her, and she was thankful for these opportunities.

Her inner circle of friends was there not only for friendship, but also as accountability partners, and each weekly function was important in her mind because of the encouragement it gave her to keep on the straight and narrow path. So with her Saturday morning Doughnut rush and church and Sunday school included, the only days she wasn't involved with and encouraged by other Christians were Tuesday and Thursday.

Waking up early was her duty as she saw it, to enjoy as much of the day as possible. She pulled herself out of bed and got ready for church, fighting off the urge to sleep in.

At 8:45 she met Grace in the lobby. Both of them wore loose curls in the back of their brunette hair. They both sported long dresses and flats, but wore wool coats over their dresses to survive the chill of the desert on a winter morning. It had snowed a foot a few days prior, and despite the parking lot having been cleared off, there was still ice, especially from the snow melting during the day and refreezing overnight. Both of them had the same thought. They verbalized it in unison when they saw each other. "Flats!"

They both smiled.

"I'll lean on you and you can lean on me," Grace said. "Maybe we will be able to keep from falling."

"Deal!" Hope said. The two of them walked out of the lobby. Hope held her NIV Bible in her hand, and Grace clutched onto her iPad. They made it through the slippery parking lot to Grace's car unscathed.

"Tank meeting us there?" Hope asked Grace, waiting until the road was ice free not to distract Grace's attention.

"Yeah, and he was very excited!"

"Oh yeah? Why?"

Grace followed the highway to the south end of town. "He is bringing someone."

"Who?" Hope asked, intrigued.

"He wouldn't say. Spoke with him on the phone last night before I went to bed and all he would tell me is that he had prayed for a long time, and his prayer had finally been answered." Grace pulled into the parking lot of their church and she parked the car. "You know how Tank is. He keeps his emotions to himself most of the time, but he seemed about ready to burst last night. Really, I had to laugh at how he talked, all giddy, so I am really interested in who he is bringing."

"Well," Hope said, "Tank has a big heart."

The two got out of the car and leaned on each other again. When they got inside, they waited in the lobby for Tank and his visitor.

Vincent stood in front of his closet in a pair of basketball shorts and couldn't decide what to wear. He had no dress clothes at all. He had some nice Polo shirts, but no pants, only jeans.

"Vincent, just pick something. I already told you that the dress code there is very lax. In fact, in the summer people come in shorts and tee shirts. I guarantee you will not go to Hell for wearing jeans in church."

Vincent looked back at Tank who wore khakis and a baby blue button-down shirt. "But look at you," Vincent protested.

Tank looked at his clothes and sighed. "Okay Vincent, if I put on a pair of jeans, will you do the same? I'm betting Grace is already waiting for me."

Vincent nodded. He finally picked out a redshirt that went well with a pair of jeans and put them on, tucking in the shirt for extra measure, then putting on his brown loafers.

In the meantime Tank dressed casually to make his new roommate feel more comfortable. Tank tried to keep his gruff exterior so that Vincent would know that he wasn't let off the hook. He didn't know how long he could keep up the act, or was it an act? Tank wondered if he was really just that gruff on the exterior. It didn't bother him any because he knew it was out of necessity. He had a lot of burden on his shoulders, helping Vincent. This poor kid had so much potential but needed Tank's help to fulfill it. This morning was a big step in the right direction.

They both put on their coats before going out into the frigid morning air and getting into Tank's truck. As he rolled out of the parking lot, he glanced over at Vincent, who was looking out the window. Tank cranked the heater and waited impatiently for it to warm up as he rolled down the highway. He thought about talking to Vincent, but he didn't know what to say. Vincent looked like a scared little puppy that had just been taken away from its mommy. Tank didn't want to scare the little puppy away, so he just said, "I think you'll like this church. It's really laid back, and we get into some really good conversations in Sunday school." Vincent didn't respond, but only looked out the window, so Tank left Vincent to his thoughts.

When they arrived, Tank got out and started for the front door. He looked back and saw Vincent still in the truck passenger seat, staring out the window. He appeared to be pondering something, so Tank went back to Vincent and opened the door for him.

"Am I giving you the VIP treatment this morning?" Tank

asked Vincent.

Vincent looked thoughtfully for a moment and broke out of his trance. He shook his head and said, "I'm not good enough to go to church."

Tank rocked back on his heels. "Why is that?"

Vincent shook his head. "Look at everything I've done! I don't belong here. I would be a hypocrite! I can't even look at myself in the mirror!"

Tank shook his head this time and said, "Vincent, you have it all wrong." Then Tank paused and pondered the next thing to say, for it was very important. He prayed quickly, "God, give me the words." Then he just spoke.

"Do you think I am perfect?" Tank asked Vincent.

Vincent didn't respond.

"Well, I'm not. I sin on a daily basis. We all do. But by your line of logic, I don't belong here either."

"But you're a lot better than me!" Vincent said.

"In whose eyes?" Tank asked.

"In mine." Vincent replied. "In Coach Johnson's. In everybody's!"

Tank shook his head. "Well, first that isn't true. It's just that you've made some recent mistakes and are paying the penalty for those. Believe me; I've done some stupid things over the years myself. But none of that matters. God doesn't look at me and say that I am better than you. God loves us both the same. We all come here to church as broken, sinful people. We need God's grace, because his expectations for us are so high, so grand, so lofty, that we could never live up to them. Ever. We just can't be perfect. That's why he has extended us his grace. He gave us Jesus, so that everything bad we had done can be erased. We just have to ask for forgiveness."

Tank paused, wondering if he had said way too much. Then

he decided that he wasn't the one talking, so he continued. "Listen Bud, you have to forgive yourself, and by the looks of it, that won't be easy. If you think that people will think you're a hypocrite, then prove them wrong today. Prove them wrong tomorrow. You've already declared to Coach, Mrs. Dean, and me that you plan on changing your ways. Prove it. It all starts here, because as I see it, you can't start to heal until you let Jesus back into your heart."

Tank stepped away from the truck door and said very seriously, "And I will be with you every step of the way."

Vincent shed a tear, then quickly wiped it away. Tank didn't know what Vincent was thinking about, but he knew Vincent had many more tears to shed as he healed.

Taking a deep breath, Vincent got out of the truck and followed Tank to the front door. Vincent paused a second before walking in, but as soon as he did, he was greeted by the preacher. He offered his hand and said, "Welcome! I'm Reverend Paul Smith."

"Vincent," Vincent responded, still a little chilly.

"Well, it's good to have you. You go to NCA?"

"Yeah," Vincent said. Tank thought Vincent looked a little uncomfortable, so he stepped in.

"Vincent is one of our star pitchers, Reverend."

"Oh, baseball! This town just loves baseball," the reverend remarked and beamed, looking up and over Vincent's shoulder, apparently reliving some great NCA baseball moment.

"Yes, sir, " Vincent responded.

Tank spotted Grace across the lobby and excused himself. He went up to his girlfriend and gave her a quick kiss on the cheek. "How's my favorite girl?"

"I'm awesome," Grace said and smiled up at her boyfriend.

"Hi Hope," Tank said and gave her a hug. Both ladies looked

stunning.

"Hi Tank. You're looking casual today," Hope responded.

Tank smiled.

"Well, it looks good on you. Looks like you have loosened up a bit," Hope said.

Tank smiled.

"So where's your friend?" Grace asked.

Tank smiled. "He's right behind." Tank turned around to see Vincent walking up to him. Ten feet away, Vincent stopped in his tracks, looking like he'd seen a ghost.

Tank cocked his head sideways at him, wondering what came over Vincent. He turned to Grace and Hope, and saw that Hope had the same look on her face. Within a split second, Hope's stare turned into a big smile. Tank turned back to Vincent and motioned him over. Vincent somehow found the ability to move one foot in front of the other, despite his condition.

When Vincent finally arrived, Tank said, "Vincent, this is my girlfriend, Grace."

"Hey!" Grace said as she extended her hand, and Vincent shook it.

"And," Tank said, "Grace's best friend, Hope."

Vincent smiled really big and said, "It's, uh, uh, a pleasure meet you. Meeting you." Vincent couldn't keep his eyes off of her.

"The pleasure is all mine," Hope smiled and said in her sweet southern accent.

Tank stole a peek at Grace, who was also smiling really big. Tank winked at her and said, "Well, let's get off to class."

Chapter Twenty-Two

VINCENT FELT HE was struck by lightning. As he stood in that lobby, staring stupidly at Hope, he went back over his chance encounters with her over the year. There were two such instances.

There was that first day of school at the coffee shop at McSorley Student Union when he tried ordering coffee, only to find out that he couldn't afford it, then tried to gracefully back out of line. That was awkward to say the least. Still, he remembered how beautiful she looked with the white bow in her hair, sitting at that table all alone, an inviting smile on her face, a picture of perfection. He couldn't get her out of his mind, and he had sought her in that same place many times after to try to strike up a conversation, only to be let down every time.

Then there was his first pitching performance, when he earned the nickname Special K. That was his mountaintop, his Super Bowl moment to this point in his life, and she was there to see it. He even remembered that she smiled at him as their eyes met. Forget his team practically putting him on their shoulders and serenading him around the infield. Forget the student section chanting his name. All that mattered was that their eyes met.

And she smiled at him.

He blushed.

All that school year he had been looking for her. It's just that he had been looking in all the wrong places.

And now here he was staring at her, she smiling at him with those big brown eyes. And again, like that first awkward encounter, he felt...well, stupid for lack of a better word. Heck, there he was, mouth agape, drooling like a cave man and not being able to move a muscle for fear that she might vanish into thin air again. When he was introduced to her, he tried to come up with something smart to say, something charming, but cave man mode held on. He was sure she thought he must be dumb.

They went to the Sunday school class for college-aged students and singles. There were twenty chairs set up and most of them were taken already. Vincent recognized a few of the guys from the team, who all smiled and waved at him. Everyone managed to make room so that the four could sit down next to each other, Tank and Grace in the middle with Vincent next to Tank and Hope next to Grace as bookends. Vincent snuck a quick peek behind Tank's back to see if Hope was looking at him, but she wasn't.

An elderly gentleman addressed the class and asked for prayer requests from the audience. A few had requested prayers for sick family members, for their schooling, or for personal issues, and Vincent thought about raising his hand and requesting prayers for the difficult road he was about to travel, but he was too shy and in the end, just listened. Church still felt foreign to him.

The class was talking about Jesus' "Sermon on the Mount"

from the book of Matthew. As they discussed the various topics Jesus hit on in this passage, Vincent remembered that first Sunday he went to church with Mrs. Dean last summer, about how interesting the discussion was, and about how he felt like he were part of a college setting. The memory came back to him, and he thought about how Grandpa Dean was still alive, though doing poorly at that point. He thought about how his parents were still alive at the time, and wondered briefly if he might have been able to mend fences with his father, even be able to speak with his mother. He wondered if he might have even been able to persuade them to go to church. All of these thoughts were painful for him, and he blocked them out as usual, but he knew that he had just opened the door to his pain. He knew that those memories weren't just going to go away, and that he was going to eventually have to confront his demons. He decided that would be a good thing to do in counseling.

When class was over, Vincent was already feeling energized, the same feeling he had when he would make the sign of the cross with his bat across home plate, prior to cranking a pitch over the fence. He spoke with a few of his teammates, each wishing him well, telling him that they were praying for him, which made him feel awkward, like a circus attraction.

Hey, come one, come all! See the alcoholic kid with unresolved parental issues!

Still, he knew that they were just looking out for him, like teammates should, a band of brothers. He left the classroom and went into the main auditorium to find Tank and the ladies. Sitting mid-way down the right side, Vincent came up to them. Hope was on the outside of the pew this time, and Vincent thought for a moment that he should go around the outside of the pews and to Tank's side, but before he could, Hope turned around and smiled. That's all it took to get the butterflies going in Vincent's stomach again.

"Would you like me to scoot over?" Hope asked in the sweetest voice he had ever heard, her big, brown eyes inviting.

"Sure!" Vincent said, hoping he didn't sound too anxious. Hope smiled bigger and moved over to make room for him. As Vincent sat down, he tried to remember if he had put on deodorant that morning and wished he would have dabbed on a little cologne.

After Vincent sat down, he still tried to come up with a topic of conversation, but no topic seemed perfect, like she was.

Thankfully, she broke the ice. "So, Vincent, you're a pretty good baseball player."

Vincent smiled and blushed. "Well, I'm okay, I suppose. Tank's the best player on the team. In fact Tank will probably be drafted and be playing in the big leagues this summer."

Hope smiled. "Yeah, he's good, but I've seen your fastball. I think you're too modest."

Vincent blushed again and wondered just how red his cheeks could get. To get off the topic, he turned the conversation to her. "How 'bout you? Why did you decide to come here?"

Hope pondered a moment before speaking, "I don't know," she said plainly. "I mean, all my friends stayed in Texas to go to college. I guess I just wanted to get out, see the world a little bit. Arizona sounded like an interesting place, and NCA specializes in my major, so I decided to give it a shot."

Vincent was starting to feel more at ease now, keeping the spotlight on her. "Where in Texas you from? What is your major?" He hoped he wasn't coming off as too nosey.

"Amarillo, and Elementary Education. I want to be an elementary teacher.

Vincent smiled. "A teacher! That's pretty great. I thought about becoming a teacher too."

"If your baseball career doesn't work out?" she asked.

"Well," Vincent said, "I really don't know what baseball holds in store for me. But my favorite teacher was my English teacher last year, and she really looked out for me, so I thought I owed it to her to pursue a degree in English."

"Oh," Hope said. "I suppose I should mind the way I talk then. Use proper grammar and such."

Vincent blushed again. "No, you probably speak better English than I do."

Hope smiled again. "Well, I'll try to speak good around you. Or is it well?"

Both laughed. Vincent thought about mentioning the first time he saw her in the coffee shop, but the music began to play and the church service started. Vincent wondered why she didn't ask about the bandage on his left eye or the fading bruises on his face and what was exposed of his left arm. He respected her for respecting his privacy. He figured she knew. Word got around fast about that kind of stuff, especially with social media, texting, and word of mouth. Vincent had avoided all three as much as possible, but surely she knew about his accident? Surely she knew about his poor decisions? Well, if she did, she gave no indication, and he respected her for allowing him to keep his chin up. Really, she could have shunned him because of his decisions, but instead she chose to be kind to him and he took note of that.

After church was over, the four decided to go to the local pizza joint. They sat at a booth, and Tank and Grace took one side, forcing Hope and Vincent to sit next to each other on the other side. Vincent didn't know if this was on purpose, if they were trying to play matchmaker, but he wasn't going to complain.

Hope was not only beautiful, but she had such a bright, optimistic spirit. He had seen it in her smile the first time in the coffee shop. Vincent thought about the relationships he had made since coming to NCA, and it was only natural to make comparisons. His roommate did everything possible to get Vincent to defile himself, which happened. When things went bad, Evan cut the cord and let Vincent fall to his own death. Adam was the same way, not caring for Vincent, only looking for a good time and free booze. Sure, he could argue that Adam opened his home to Vincent, but didn't it come at a price? Didn't Vincent keep his fridge stocked in beer? And after the accident, neither had come to the hospital to see if he was okay. They were probably at Adam's house getting baked.

Tank, on the other hand, truly cared about what was best for Vincent, even if that meant being tough on Vincent. Amid the talking and laughter at the table, Vincent found himself wishing he had latched onto Tank when he first got to campus. Surely he would have made better decisions if he had hung around with the right kind of people?

After dinner, when they parted ways, Hope asked Vincent if he had ever been to the weekly meal at the Baptist Student Union. Of course he hadn't, and he accepted her invitation and planned to meet her there Wednesday. When he and Tank walked to Tank's truck, Vincent found himself thinking that Wednesday was a long ways away, and he didn't know how he would ever wait that long to see her again.

Monday was a busy day for Vincent. He had his first day of classes, getting used to his new schedule and asking the instructors personally for everything he needed to make up. Tank woke him up at 6:00 and took him for a pre-sunrise run around campus. Still out of shape, that about killed Vincent.

That afternoon Vincent got his eye patch off at the doctor's office. His left eye was extremely light sensitive, and the doctor gave him some really uncool sunglasses to wear to help his eye adjust. He could see out of it, but it was pretty blurry. The optometrist couldn't say for sure if Vincent's vision would return to normal, cautioning him that he may never again see the same out of that eye. Vincent's first reaction was to worry, but he instead decided to pray about it, silently as the doctor finished up his paperwork. Whatever would happen would happen. He just prayed his poor decision wouldn't affect his ability to play baseball. He knew that was a tall order, but he also knew that he must trust in God's plan for his life, whatever that was.

While the rest of the team reported to practice, Vincent reported to the court-appointed therapist in an office downtown, a fifteen minute walk in the cold. He surely had reservations about talking to a counselor, mainly because he didn't know how judgmental the guy would be. To his surprise, the two merely engaged in pleasant conversation and Vincent thought he could trust the man.

The topic of forgiveness came up, and just as Vincent expected, the therapist told Vincent that he had to forgive himself before he would be able to move on. That was a tall order, Vincent well knew, but he didn't fight the advice. He knew it to be the truth, Tank's words to him in the church parking lot ringing in his ears. Vincent wanted to talk about his suicidal thoughts, mainly to see if the guy had any suggestions to keep him from ever considering something so horrible again, but before Vincent knew it, the hour was up and he was released. Counseling wasn't going to be so bad.

Vincent wanted badly to show up at practice and beg Coach to let him prove himself again, but Vincent knew he must prove himself by being true to his word first. He had made an arrangement with Coach Johnson, and he must honor it. So instead, Vincent walked over to Pleasant Hill Retirement Home, another five minutes in the wrong direction from campus, to start the first hour of his penance.

Again, he was pleasantly surprised by what he encountered there. After checking in at the front desk, he sat in the sitting room next to an elderly gentleman who was warming himself by the fire. His name was Robert, and he was a World War II veteran, like Vincent's mentor, Grandpa Dean. Robert regaled him with a tale of sailing through the Panama Canal on the way to the South Pacific. He talked about sailors getting sick on the open seas with the rocking up and down, and spending most of their time with their heads hung over the railing. He talked about how he once pulled up a jellyfish with a fishing pole, and then one of the sailors got stung by touching one of the tentacles and got deathly ill.

Vincent played chess with Robert, getting whipped in no time flat. The man's legs might have been failing him, but he was still as sharp as the fishing hook that snared the jellyfish. Vincent asked for chess pointers, and Robert told him that he would just have to learn through repeated beatings. It sounded good to Vincent.

About the time the guys at baseball practice were finishing up and going to dinner, Vincent was in the Pleasant Hill Retirement Home's kitchen, peeling potatoes, dicing tomatoes, and taking orders from a grouchy cook. Vincent found this to be less gratifying than spending time with Robert, cozy next to the fire, listening to war stories, but as part of his penance, Vincent took his medicine with a smile. If he ever got down, he would just think about Hope.

After eating leftover beef stew with a few of the staff members, Vincent signed his time sheet and left. By the time He was walking back to the dormitory, it was already dark and getting colder. He practiced using just his left eye to guide him, and though it was still blurry, he thought his vision was improving a little bit. His depth perception was way off though, and he kept tripping on the curb. If a police officer were to watch him stumbling around, he figured he might get cited for public intoxication.

The thought of intoxication got him to thinking. Did he miss his previous life? Partying till all hours of the night? No worries on his mind? Sure, there was a little piece of him that longed for a beer. Just one. He hadn't fancied himself a beer connoisseur before, but he had adjusted to the taste of beer and even longed for one. It was just a little part of him, a hibernating demon. His own father had fallen victim to this demon and never recovered. Vincent knew he must make the right choices, and that would be accomplished one day at a time. One hour at a time. One minute at a time. One decision at a time. Alcohol would always be available to him. It was so easy for a minor with the right connections to score a case of beer. Vincent knew that he would have weak moments. How would he handle these moments? That was the question that was foremost in his mind.

When he got to the dorm, Tank met him at the door and ushered him to The Doughnut to study. The library also offered free tutoring--one of those services he had already paid for when he paid all of his fees-- and Tank introduced him to an algebra tutor named Becky. Algebra was by far Vincent's weakest subject. Vincent was enrolled in a zero-level algebra class to prepare him for Algebra I, and he still found the elementary concepts frustrating. His brain just didn't work well that way. But he found out that Becky was just as tough as Tank and that she wasn't going to let him off the hook or do it for him.

Tank and Vincent returned to their dormitory room at half past nine. Vincent fell straight into bed, totally exhausted from his day. It had started at 6:30 when Tank woke him up and ended at 9:30, with only a break for lunch. A fifteen-hour day of work, work, and more work, and this was his first of many days.

Vincent was exhausted but satisfied with himself and all that he had accomplished. Again he thought about how easy life had been when he was just a student, going to class, practice, and doing homework. He didn't know just how great he had it. Now life was going to be difficult until the debt was paid, and paid in full.

Tank was talking to Vincent about something, but Vincent blocked out his roommate's voice and fell fast asleep while still in the clothes he had worn that day. He didn't even get his shoes off.

Chapter Twenty-Three

VINCENT SETTLED INTO his new schedule. Tank would wake him at 6:00 every morning and work Vincent hard. Some mornings it would just be a run. Some mornings they ran to the indoor pool that was attached to the basketball arena, and he and Tank would swim laps with the basketball players, whose coach made his players do in-season workouts early in the mornings. Some days they would lift weights. It wasn't long before Vincent was in great shape and stronger than ever. He worked his pitching arm hard, hoping that he was adding velocity.

All of the workouts would have been hard for the normal athlete, but add all the pain from the accident, and Vincent was often miserable. His left side had received the brunt of the impact, and his left arm was still not as strong as it had once been, but the swimming seemed to loosen and strengthen it, and each day brought with it renewed hope that his body would eventually heal. Then there was the eye.

He worried about his left eye, which had improved to a

certain point but no further. He could see out of it now, but the crispness was gone. When he closed his bad eye and looked out of his right eye, it was like looking at a brand new, HD television. When he closed his good eye and looked out of his left eye, it was like staring at an old box television set on a partially snowy channel. He did eye exercises to strengthen it per the doctor's orders, but in the end he knew he would always be handicapped by his left eye, a constant reminder of his poor decisions. It made Vincent wonder if it would eventually lead to his exclusion from baseball. After all, Coach Johnson repeatedly told him that a baseball player's eyes were far more important than his arm.

Another part of Vincent's complete makeover was his social activities. He did enjoy the weekly lunch at the BSU. That first Wednesday, he met Hope there and the two of them played a friendly game of table tennis in the game room as they waited for her friends to arrive. She introduced him not only to Charity and Amie, but to at least twenty others who were very friendly, many complimenting him on what a great pitcher he was.

They all ate the dinner, provided by the ladies from the First Baptist Church, and listened to a speaker, a former student who was now a state representative. He spoke with them about the dangers of living in and of the world, and about their duty of being Christians in everything they do. He told them that just because something felt good, that did not make it good. It was a message Vincent took to heart and had learned the hard way.

Vincent loved that he and Hope were becoming good friends. There was no doubt that he found her very attractive, not just in a physical sense, but really everything about her. He had never met anyone like her, so willing to give of herself for another without any thought of personal gain. It was as if she actually gained her endless energy by helping others. When Vincent was around her, he felt he never wanted to leave her. When he was away from her, he felt the urge to call her up, just to talk to her. He was a better person around her, and he knew it.

Vincent thought often about the contrast between his friends from the first semester, and Tank and Hope. The former only cared about what he could do for them. They only cared about what he could buy them with the money from his parents' estate. They wouldn't stand with him in his moment of need. They wouldn't even visit him in the hospital.

On the other hand, Tank and Hope spent countless hours with him, trying to help him, especially in his faith. Neither of them ever asked for money from Vincent, and they both found fun in innocent activities like going bowling, or shooting pool, or sitting around the dorm lobby and having a devotional. Vincent had no doubt that both Tank and Hope would be there for him through thick and thin.

There was no doubt that Hope was Vincent's friend, but Vincent had further thoughts about her. He wondered if he should ask her out on a date but didn't know how he would accomplish that. If he asked her to the movies, she would think he was asking as friends. If he asked her and specified that it was a "date," that might make things awkward between them. Besides, he had no vehicle. What was he going to do? Walk her to the movies? Another kink in this idea was that he had very little spare time for a life. She had invited him to all of the evening meals at the various churches, and he unfortunately had to decline because he would either be doing community service at the rest home or hanging out at The Doughnut studying. It left very little time for a social life, which was good in keeping him out of trouble, but not so good when he wanted to surround himself with quality people.

By February, the baseball team was ramping up for the regular season. Again Vincent wanted so badly to be a part of the team, but the only way he could do that was during his weekly meeting with the coaching staff to discuss his progress. He had already bitten off forty of his community service hours but had plenty to go, which made him sad. He was looking at rejoining the team around April, easily half-way into the season. Then he would have to earn his spot all over again, without much help from his left eye. It wasn't how he had envisioned his first year of college.

Vincent also stayed true to his commitment to calling Mrs. Dean and keeping her abreast of his progress. She, too, was gruff with him, using tough love, but he was used to it with her. He knew that she only cared about his well-being, and he had made himself untrustworthy to her. After all, she and Grandpa Dean had invested a lot of hours into him without asking for anything in return. He owed her.

Vincent's body was fully healed, and he was in the best shape of his life now, which made walking uphill to campus easier. He hoped that this increased fitness would benefit him when he did return to the team. At first he hated getting up at six to work out, but the more fit he became, the more he found himself looking forward to waking up early. He had never fancied himself an athlete. He didn't go out for any school sports in high school, and summer baseball was his only pursuit. His former coach never took conditioning very seriously, so Vincent had really never known what it was like to work out, much less be in shape. Alcohol was his addiction before. Now he had found an alternative addiction in working out.

Speaking of addictions, Vincent saw Evan around campus every now and then. It was never in the same place at the same time, though. Vincent could be counted on to be in one particular place at one particular time, living his life strictly to his schedule. Tank saw to this, and it was the only way Vincent could survive. He found he liked knowing his place, knowing he had to be somewhere and that he couldn't be wasting time doing nothing, because idle hands were indeed the Devil's playground.

Vincent sometimes saw Evan on Tuesday mornings before Vincent's British Literature class, but only every now and then. Vincent attempted to approach Evan the first time, but his former roommate made an escape maneuver through McSorley Student Union.

All Vincent wanted to do was tell Evan that he forgave him. It was what Vincent's therapist suggested he should do. The doctor explained to Vincent that forgiveness is not for the one who has done the wrong. Forgiveness actually relieved the one who has been hurt, freeing him from the burden of the pain and allowing him to move on with life. Evan was one of the people Vincent needed to forgive, and even if Evan was going to avoid him, Vincent felt he had forgiven Evan and was ready to let that part of his life go. As for his own father, Vincent hadn't mustered up enough courage to forgive him yet. Vincent prayed for that day, though.

One Saturday morning in mid-February, Tank woke Vincent up at 6:00 like usual, only Saturday was generally their morning to sleep in. Vincent got out of bed, stretched, and started to get into his workout clothes. Just as he put both arms through his tee shirt, he stopped and said, "Hey, it's Saturday. Why are we working out today?" Vincent didn't mean it rudely or anything. It was well known that a day of rest was important for muscle growth, and the two of them had hit the weights really hard the morning before.

Tank grabbed a pair of hiking boots and said, "I have a different workout planned for you today." When Vincent stood there wanting more, Tank only said, "Trust me, you'll love it. By the way, grab your fly fishing gear."

Not asking any more questions, Vincent fished out the fly

fishing gear he had bought from the old man in New Mexico way back in the fall when he was returning from his parents' funeral. The gear had been sitting in the back of the closet, and Vincent had forgotten all about it since then. Actually, he half-feared that it was gone, his former roommate having pawned it for beer money. Thankfully, that was not the case.

The two of them put their gear in the backseat of Tank's cab and drove out to Glen Canyon Dam. The sun was just starting to rise behind them, creating a gray complexion on Lake Powell. Vincent loved this spot and hadn't been here since he and Evan had a deep talk after his parents had died. This was the same spot in which he had written a letter to Mrs. Dean the first week he was on campus. The same place he went to get away. Vincent wondered why he hadn't been back since.

After ten quiet minutes with the truck on and the heater running, Tank said, "Okay, time to get out. By the way, I have a surprise for you in the back."

Vincent went to the bed of the pickup and saw a pair of old waders. "They might be old," Tank said, apparently reading Vincent's mind, "but they will keep you dry. I promise."

"Thanks, Tank."

"Don't mention it," Tank said. "There's no way you would be able to stand that water down there. It's icy, especially this time of year.

"You mean--"

"Yep," Tank cut him off. "We're going down there."

His breath visible in the pre-dawn light, Vincent walked over to the edge of the canyon and looked straight down, just like he had done that first week he was at school and had admired the two fly fishermen wading the river, casting gracefully. It was such a beautiful, poetic moment, and now he was going to climb all the way down there and try it. Butterflies invaded his stomach, although not as strong as the ones he had whenever he was around Hope.

"Hey, you better get ready," Tank yelled over at Vincent. "Otherwise, I'm going to leave you up here, and I am going to catch all the fish."

Vincent ran back to the truck. Tank was sitting on his tailgate, slipping into his waders.

Once the two of them were snuggled into their waders, Vincent pulled out the lanyard the old man in the fly shop in New Mexico had given him and put it around his neck. Vincent looked at each tool, wondering if Tank was going to teach him how to use each one. Then he assembled his fly rod and attached the fly reel to the seat. Tank helped him string it up, and when the two of them were set, Tank reached into a cooler in the bed of the pickup and grabbed a couple of waters. He handed one to Vincent and said, "Long way down there. You won't want to drink river water. Trust me."

Tank walked over to the cliff and picked up the trail. Vincent followed. The going was treacherous. One false step and Vincent would end up in a free fall. The two took their time. There was a reason Tank had waited ten minutes in the truck before getting out. They needed all the light the rising sun could muster.

The hike down was taxing on the legs and difficult in waders, but after thirty minutes, Vincent was at the foot of the bank of the mighty Colorado River. The air was frigid down at the bottom of the canyon, cooled, no doubt, by the rushing water, and Vincent wished he would have brought his coat along. The sweatshirt he had on just didn't do the job, but before he could complain, Tank motioned him over.

The two stood staring at the water, not another soul in sight. They both looked up at that massive wall of concrete that held back Lake Powell. "Can you imagine if the dam broke right now?" Tank asked.

Vincent reasoned that they were easily 300 feet below the surface of the lake. "I forgot to bring my surfboard," Vincent replied. Tank chuckled, which caught Vincent off-guard. Tank hardly ever smiled, much less laughed.

"Okay," Tank said, "there are about a million rainbow trout in front of us right now, and all of them are hungry."

"How do you know that?" Vincent asked.

"Because they are," Tank snapped at him. "Anyway, they will be in the deeper runs, but most of this water is ankle-to-knee deep. Doesn't sound very deep, but as long as there's enough water to cover a trout's back, that's all it takes." Tank looked over Vincent's rig. "That's a nice fly you have on."

"Thanks," Vincent beamed. It was one of the five flies the old man at the fly shop had given him.

"Unfortunately, that fly won't work here."

"Why not?" Vincent inquired.

"Because it's a dry fly," Tank responded. "That means a fly that floats on top of the water. Now take a look out across the water."

Vincent looked out across the water as instructed, not knowing what he should be looking for.

Tank continued, "Now, what do you notice? Do you see any flies buzzing around?"

Vincent peered, closing his left eye, and said, "Nope."

"Okay," Tank continued. "Now do you see fish splashing the top of the water?"

Again Vincent looked out over the water with his good eye and shook his head no.

"Okay," Tank said. "That's why you shouldn't use that fly. Now let me see your fly box."

Vincent pulled out his brand new fly box from his front pants pocket beneath his waders. Tank looked over the other flies, shook his head, and then got out his own fly box. He pulled out four flies and transferred them to Vincent's box. "That will serve you. If you run out, I will give you some more." He handed the box back to Vincent.

"What are they?" Vincent asked, looking them over.

"Scud patterns."

"What's a scud?"

"A freshwater shrimp."

"There are shrimp in here?"

Tank chuckled again. "Yeah, but don't get excited. They're about the size of your pinkie nail. They might not look like much, but these trout gorge themselves on them all day long and get really big because of it." Tank knelt down and picked up a rock about the size of his head from out of the slack water. He turned it upside down and showed Vincent. Five little shrimp-looking insects clung to the rock and wiggled in place. Each had a ginger hue in the early morning light.

Vincent accepted this explanation, and using the clippers on his fly vest, clipped off the dry fly he had on and set about to tying on one of the flies Tank had given him, an orange one that seemed to match the bait he was trying to imitate. Tank waited on Vincent, and when he was set, Tank helped him take a small split shot out of the little compartment that hung on his lanyard and pinched it into place about eight inches above his fly with the hemostat that was also on his lanyard.

"Okay, follow me," Tank said.

They stepped out into the water. At first it was a weird feeling. The water was cold, but with the thin rubber protection over his legs, the water seemed to vacuum to his leg like a python grabbing onto a small animal.

The two of them waded out into the middle of the river where it was thigh-high. As a last touch, Tank pinched on a little sticky foam float four feet up the line from the split shot and said, "Okay, now all you have to do is cast and watch the indicator."

"What's the indicator?" Vincent asked.

"It's that little pink thing I just pinched onto your line. Now if you see it move left, right, down, or even pause, then set the hook."

"How do I set the hook?" Vincent asked.

"Just lift up on your rod in a jerking motion like this," Tank said and demonstrated for Vincent with his own rod. "That's what embeds the hook in the fish's mouth."

Vincent pulled out some line from his reel and started whipping it around romantically like he had seen in the movies. When he finally dropped it on the water thirty seconds later, he saw what appeared to be a tangled up mess of line that resembled a bird's nest land far from where he was aiming. Vincent pulled it in, not knowing what went wrong.

Tank stood five feet away, false-casting gracefully, all of his attention apparently taken up with his target. When he finally let the fly land in the water, he lowered his rod and stared intently at the spot. "You see, Vincent, when you do something carelessly or not paying attention, you'll find yourself a mess to contend with."

Vincent didn't know whether Tank was talking about Vincent's mess of line or his past indiscretions. Either way, it took Vincent ten minutes to untangle the wind knots he had tied in the air. For all the grace and peace that fly fishermen looked to behold in the pictures, Vincent was thinking that attaining that peace was something that took time and patience.

Just then, Tank hooked into a fish. His rod came to life, convulsing with the pull of the unseen fish fifteen feet in front of him. Enamored, Vincent spent more time watching Tank than working on the kinked up line of his own fishing rod.

Tank kept the pressure on the fish and slowly stripped the line in. Two times he almost had the fish to his hand when it went on another run upstream, searching for freedom despite the unrelenting tug at its lip. "You see, Vincent, there are times in life when you have an opportunity, but patience is a must. You have to wait for the time to be right before you can pull in your reward." Tank lifted up on the rod and brought in his trophy, a fat rainbow trout that splashed him in the face when he tried to dislodge the hook. Finally the fish went free, scurrying straight upstream.

"About sixteen inches," Tank said. "Not a bad fish, but there are bigger here. I promise you." He looked at Vincent. "Hey buddy, the most important rule to fly fishing is that you can't catch a fish unless your fly is in the water."

"Sure," Vincent said, untying the last of the wind knots.

"Hey, use that leader straightener to smooth out your line," Tank said. Vincent looked at his lanyard, and by process of elimination, grabbed the two little leather flaps. He ran his leader between them and saw the kinks from the knots magically disappear. While he did this, Tank continued his soliloquy.

"Technique is everything," Tank said. "Tell me, when you're on the mound, do you just get up there and throw as hard as you can, or do you focus on your technique?"

"I focus on your mitt and think about balance."

"Yes," Tank said. "You said it perfect. Balance is so important. You must learn to balance, which is difficult when you feel the burden of life bearing down on you. That's one of the reasons we are here and not studying at The Doughnut or lifting weights or running. Balance. Learn how to balance work and play, and you will be a happy man."

Vincent released his fly line a few feet out in front of him and watched as the little strike indicator slowly drifted back towards him without making any strange movements that Tank warned him about when a fish strikes.

"You want to know how to cast now that you've tried it?" Tank asked.

"Sure," Vincent replied.

"Let the rod do the work," Tank responded.

"Am I not?" Vincent asked.

"No, you are not. You are flailing your arm about. All you have to do is snap your wrist. The rod will do the work for you. Work smarter, not harder."

Vincent tried to snap his wrist, but still he wasn't able to cast it half as far as Tank.

"Next is timing," Tank said. "You have to allow time for the fly line to extend fully on your back cast before you snap your wrist forward. It's the same on the forward cast. Let the line extend all the way. It's like dancing. Have you ever danced?"

Vincent thought about his time at the Red Pony, shook his head, and lied, "No."

"Well," Tank said, "think graceful, like a lady. Ladies are full of grace in everything they do, and your cast must be the same, full of grace, not manhandled. Try it."

Vincent did as instructed and watched his line extend back and forth. He noticed that now he could actually get the fly out there about as far as Tank was casting. It reminded him of two-stepping to a country song, and he started counting out a four-count beat in his head to keep the timing. Four counts on the back cast, four counts on the forward cast.

"How's that feel?" Tank asked.

"Graceful," Vincent replied.

"Okay, speaking of graceful," Tank said, "what do you think of Hope?"

Just the mention of Hope caused a hitch in Vincent's back cast and the line coiled up on the water behind him, causing him to start the process all over. "What about her?" Vincent asked.

"You know what I am asking you. Do you like her?"

"Yeah," Vincent replied. "She's really nice."

"She is that," Tank agreed. "Have you asked her out yet?"

Vincent didn't respond right away. He took his time to craft his answer as he practiced his timing, responding in tetrameter to keep with the rhythm of his graceful rod. "No sir, I haven't asked her out. I don't know if I should or not."

Tank was now silent for a second. "Okay. Why not?"

"I guess I don't have a reason. Maybe she is too good for me?"

"I can see that," Tank said and chuckled again. Vincent could really tell that Tank let his guards down when he went fishing. He enjoyed seeing this side of the captain, despite the interrogation.

"What if it screws up our friendship?" Vincent asked.

"You planning on being a jerk to her?" Tank answered the question with another one.

"No," Vincent responded, screwing up his rhythm.

"Well then, what do you have to lose? Can you really see Hope getting all weird on you?"

"No, not really," Vincent responded, and he picked his line back off the water to try again.

"Well then, what do you have to lose?" Tank repeated.

Vincent considered what Tank was saying and finally said, "I think she is too good for me." Vincent's pace had picked up, and fearing another bird's nest, he stopped casting for a moment and considered this, losing all poetry and grace in his haste. "Think about how messed up I am and how perfect she is. Tell me how that would be a good thing for her to do?"

Tank didn't respond at first. When Vincent looked over to

see why, he noticed Tank had another fish on.

"Well buddy," Tank finally said and finished the next sentence while holding his breath, the fish taking up quite a bit of his mental capacity, "I recall you saying the same thing about me." The fish went on another run, and Tank grunted and leaned back on his rod, his reel's drag singing a shrill song in the chilly morning air. When Tank finally slowed the fish and turned it, he continued. "Was Jesus perfect?"

Vincent said, "Yes."

Tank continued as the fish made yet another run for deeper water. "Whoa, buddy—Okay, Vincent...do you...do you deserve Jesus' love?"

Vincent thought that over for a moment before answering, "No. I screwed up pretty bad."

"But He gives it to you freely anyway," Tank said as the fish finally came off the end of the line. Tank reeled in the slack to inspect the hook, a contemplative look on his face. "I don't deserve Jesus' love because I screw up pretty bad, but I accept it. You see the difference?"

"I suppose so," Vincent said.

Tank looked up from his battered fly and stared at Vincent. "You suppose so?"

Vincent nodded. "Yes. I see the difference."

Tank looked back down and cut his line with his teeth just above the fly. "Jesus extends his grace to all sinners. None of us deserve it, but we have the option to receive it all the same. That's how God wants it." He searched in his fly box and decided on another fly to tie on. "Now I understand that you may still be working a few things out in your life, and if that's the case, you are right in not asking Hope out. You need to clean your own backyard first. That is true. But if it's just a matter of you thinking that you aren't worthy, just remember that God's grace is extended to everybody. You only have to accept it. When you accept that Jesus loves you despite your sins, you will ask Him for forgiveness and stop judging yourself so harshly. Then you will see yourself the way that Hope sees you." Tank cinched the knot down on his fly and concluded his sermon. "Besides, Hope is not perfect. Nobody is."

These words hit Vincent hard. He didn't know how Tank was so insightful. It reminded Vincent of Grandpa Dean. Tank was right. Vincent had spent his entire life being told that he wasn't good enough. His dad said it to him. His high school coach said it to him. The kids in his class said it to him. Even some of his teachers had said it to him. The repetition really led to the affirmation that Vincent was indeed, a loser. Now in Tank's words, coupled with what Grandpa and Mrs. Dean had preached to him, Vincent saw a revelation, an understanding of truth. Vincent was a child of God, and thus loved by God. The rest was just details.

When Vincent didn't respond for a few minutes, Tank said, "Did any of that make sense to you?"

Vincent smiled. "Yeah, it makes perfect sense." Omitting the details of his revelation, Vincent changed back to the original topic, "I don't know how to do that, you know, ask her out. I've never had a girlfriend before. I've never even been on a date. I don't have the first clue about how to approach her."

"Do you think she likes you?" Tank asked.

"Well," Vincent thought about it as he started false-casting, attempting to get a little extra distance on this next cast. It landed about thirty feet in front of him and a few feet farther to the right than he had been casting. "I think she might." Just then Vincent saw his strike indicator pause. He lifted on the rod to set the hook like Tank showed him.

The fish surged on the end of his line and Vincent could hear

Tank whisper, "Yeah!" under his breath. Vincent was scared now. He didn't know what to do, how to reel in the fish, and his immediate reaction was to let the fish do whatever it wanted. In this case, it was to let it swim upstream like a Jet Ski racing up Lake Powell.

"I think you know she likes you," Tank said, "and I think you have nothing to lose by asking her. She'll be your friend either way."

Just then, the hook slipped free of the fish's mouth and the rod unbent.

"When you have a fish on the line," Tank said, "don't be scared to reel it in."

Chapter Twenty-Four

IT WAS THE hardest phone call Vincent ever had to make. He had the same feeling of butterflies he usually felt before a baseball game, only magnified to the point of insanity. The biggest difference between the two types of butterflies, outside of the intensity, was that he knew what to do on the baseball mound to control them. Here, he was clueless.

Tank sat in his chair at his desk, working on a research paper. If he knew what Vincent was going through, he sure didn't seem willing to offer any advice. The two of them had enjoyed a wonderful morning. Fly fishing cleansed Vincent's soul, and he needed it since learning how to cope with burning the candle at both ends. Vincent only landed one fish that morning, which was the fifth one he had hooked. The first four were on for a split second or two before they threw the hook. He had trouble learning all the little nuances of fly fishing's art and science, something Tank told him was normal for every beginner. To Vincent, netting that first rainbow trout, holding the fish under the stomach as he unhooked the fly, and letting it swim upstream from his hand was an experience that seemed freeing to him. A step towards recovery, and he couldn't wait to go again.

But first he had other business. Homework was done. There was no tutoring on Saturday nights to go to. The room was sparkling clean, his bed was made in a military fashion, and all his laundry was folded or hung up. Vincent tried to think of an excuse, something, anything that would keep him from having to make this phone call. After Vincent stared at his cell phone for twenty minutes, Tank finally turned around and said, "Oh will you just call her! She's a girl, and girls like to be asked out on dates."

This didn't make the butterflies go away. Fearing Tank's wrath, Vincent found Hope's name in the Contacts tab of his phone and hit the send button.

Five long seconds went by before the first ring.

Then there was a second ring.

Then a third.

Three rings, he thought. *There! She's not around her phone.*

Just as Vincent was going to hang up, thanking his lucky stars that she didn't answer, there was an audible click and a delicate "hello?" on the other end of the line.

Think of something to say, Vincent.

Vincent forgot how to talk. His tongue felt swollen and his throat closed up.

"Hello?" The sweet, innocent voice said again.

Vincent finally pulled it together and said one syllable, "Hope?" His voice cracked in doing so, but he was relieved that he was at least monosyllabic.

"Well, hey Vincent! How are you doing?"

"Uh, I am good, er, well. I am doing well. Quite well. And you? Are you well?"

Oh, that was smooth!

There was laughter on the other end of the phone, and Vincent wondered how Hope could have it all together so well. It was probably because she wasn't calling him, asking him out on a date, her first date ever. It was probably because she didn't have time to panic nor think about this phone call all day.

"Yes, I am quite well myself." She chuckled and said, "I had to ask my English teacher if that was the correct way to say it so I could speak correctly to you."

Vincent laughed, already feeling better.

"How was your fishing this morning?" she asked.

Vincent smiled and wiped the sweat from his brow. "Oh! It was a lot of fun! It's hard to explain it. I don't want to say a spiritual experience, but it kind of was."

"That sounds about right to me," Hope said. "You watch someone fly fishing; it's like watching a graceful dancer, or reading a poem, or painting a picture. It's--"

"Art," Vincent finished her thought when she ran out of words.

"Yes, like art. Are you an artist now?"

Vincent smiled. Hope always had a way of making him smile by the interest she took in him. Heck, who was he kidding? Just listening to her voice made him smile. "Well, I wouldn't consider myself an artist, more like a first grader with a box of crayons."

"Well, I have seen some first grade art that is spectacular."

She always had a way of making him smile.

"I caught my first fish."

"That's great. What was it?"

"Uh, a trout," Vincent said. "You should have seen all the colors, the way it shimmered. There's a reason they call it a rainbow trout. Where I come from, we have catfish. Catfish are ugly, but trout are beautiful."

Why am I talking about slimy fish to a girl?

"Yeah, but catfish taste really good!" she said.

Vincent laughed.

"So what are you doing tonight?" Hope asked.

Uh...

"Uh, well," Vincent stammered.

"Oh, I'm sorry. Do you have plans?" Hope asked.

"No!" Vincent blurted out, making sure he very clear on this point.

"Well, I was thinking about trying out the bowling alley at McSorley. Do you want to come? It would be lonely just going by myself, because Grace is busy with her homework."

Vincent couldn't believe his ears. Did she just ask him out? Was she only asking him out as a friend? Vincent was now a little more confident. "That sounds like a lot of fun," Vincent said. "Actually, I was going to see if you wanted to do something."

"Oh, that's so funny," Hope replied. "I guess brilliant minds think alike!"

"I guess so," Vincent responded, not knowing what the next step was.

"Well, would you like to meet me in my lobby at 7:00?"

"It's a date," Vincent said, then smacked himself on the forehead for being so forward.

Oh, you're smooth!

"It's a date!" Hope repeated. "See you tonight!"

"Oh, okay. See you tonight."

Hope hung up the phone first, and Vincent stared at his phone in bewilderment. He had no idea what had just happened, but he now felt in over his head.

"Now was that so hard?" Tank asked.

Vincent was embarrassed, but said, "She asked me out."

"How about that?" Tank said. "It's like she knew you were

going to ask her out and wanted to save you the embarrassment."

"Actually, it kind of was like that," Vincent said. Then he turned around and said, "Wait! Did you say something?"

Tank ignored the question and said, "Make sure you pay for everything and open doors for her."

Vincent stared at Tank's back and just smiled.

Vincent showed up at Hope's front lobby at 6:45. He checked in at the front desk and waited on the couch as the RA on duty went up to Hope's room to let her know he was there. His palms were sweaty, and he constantly wiped them on his pants. He donned his nicest pair of jeans and a blue collaredshirt that he hoped showed off his blue eyes. If there were one thing he had learned from Evan, it was how to dress fashionably.

Sitting there waiting felt a lot like a job interview. He had to wait the full fifteen minutes he was early, but when Hope came down the stairs, Vincent's heart started beating harder than ever and the darned butterflies returned.

She too wore a pair of jeans and a blue blouse. When she got to him, he stood, and they both started laughing.

"Okay," Hope said, "Did I copy you or did you copy me?"

Vincent shrugged and smiled. "You look really nice," he said, thankful he was now polysyllabic, but wishing that those syllables were more romantic.

"Well, you look pretty sharp. That blue shirt really brings out your baby blues," she returned. Flipping through a magazine, two girls behind the counter giggled a little, trying to act like they weren't listening in. Hope must have taken the hint. "Let's get out of here. What do you say?"

Vincent nodded, and the two walked out the door. The night air was cool. Spring wasn't quite in the air yet, and winter was trying its best to hold on. Neither brought a coat, and Hope crossed her arms in the cool night breeze. Vincent noticed and put his arm around her shoulder. "Is that better?" he asked.

Hope smiled up at him, her brown eyes shining. "Thanks," was all she said. He couldn't tell if she were okay with him doing this, but took the risk anyhow.

The two walked up the sidewalk to McSorley Student Union, only a few minutes by foot, and when they entered the building, the place was abuzz. Vincent thought back to that first time he had seen her, sitting in that booth, watching him make a fool of himself. It made him cringe that he made such a poor first impression on her, but maybe she didn't remember. "Say," he said, "do you go to that coffee shop very often?"

"Actually, no," she replied. "Their coffee is too expensive. In fact I went there the first day of school back in August, and I haven't been back there since."

Vincent felt really stupid. All the time he thought he had acted like an idiot in front of her in their first meeting when he couldn't afford the coffee, and she had felt the same way the whole time! He really wished he would have at least said hi to her. So much wasted time not knowing. So much regret. Maybe she even would have been able to keep him from making such big mistakes?

Plus, Hope had no problem mentioning that she couldn't afford the coffee, and he had actually felt ashamed of his financial situation. He loved how honest Hope was and hoped that he would profit from such an example. After all, he was a college student. He was supposed to be poor.

"Well," Vincent said, "I am up for coffee if you are. My treat, of course."

Hope smiled and said, "That's really nice of you."

Vincent noticed that he still had his arm around her, even though they were in a controlled environment, but he was reluctant to take it off because he didn't know if he would have the guts to try something like that again. Then, without thinking, words just came out of him, naturally. "You know, the first time I saw you was at this coffee shop."

"Oh yeah?" she said and looked up at him, her eyes twinkling again.

"Yeah," Vincent said. "You were sitting at that little booth right there. You had a white bow in your hair and you looked like an angel."

Hope kept her stare straight ahead. "Uh-huh. Tell me more."

Vincent scarcely knew that the words were coming out of his mouth. He felt so vulnerable telling her this, but went for broke. "Yeah, and I wanted to talk to you, introduce myself."

Hope looked up at him with those big eyes. "Well, why didn't you?"

"I guess I was too scared. I'm not really good at that sort of thing."

Hope giggled, "Well, looks like you've gotten better."

Vincent's heartbeat rose again.

"I remember that," Hope continued. "I saw you too. I guess God has a funny way of working things out. He made sure we would meet one way or another."

Vincent spent the next few moments wondering if Hope would elaborate on what she saw in him, but she didn't.

There were only a few others at the coffee shop, one couple talking quietly in a corner, and a guy in shark pajamas, wearing a beret, and working a Sudoku puzzle. Hope said, "I am going to take a seat at our booth. Would you get me a white chocolate mocha latte?"

"That's quite a mouthful," Vincent said.

"There'll be a quiz later," she said and smirked. She sat down, and Vincent went up to order. The same girl that waited on him way back in August was again his barista. He recognized her, but was shocked that she recognized him.

"Good evening, Vincent. Do you know what you want?"

Vincent was taken aback. "You know my name?"

"Sure. Everybody knows you," the barista said. "You're famous here."

Vincent didn't know if she were talking about his baseball skill or his recent indiscretions. Maybe she even remembered him from the first day of school. Anyway, he didn't proceed with that conversation. "Okay, I will take a medium white mocha chocolate latte, and a medium coffee."

The barista laughed under her breath, and Vincent replayed what he had said over in his mind to see if he got it right. From what he could tell he got out all the key words but thought he might have gotten them out of order. He didn't really care though as long as the barista got it right.

He looked back at Hope who seemed to be studying him. He paid for the drinks and took them back to the table. With a drink in his hand, he felt more confident, and he didn't know why. It made him feel more social. Then it hit him. He felt the same way whenever he had a beer in his hand. It saddened him to think that he couldn't shake off thinking about alcohol, even now while on a date with the most beautiful girl he had ever met.

Regardless, the two sat across from each other, sipping on their drinks and making small talk. What they talked about wasn't important to Vincent, because he spent most of his time being an attentive listener, soaking up not just everything she said, but the way she said it, wrinkling up her nose when she smiled, a little tress of hair in the middle of her forehead playfully teasing him by wisping the wrong direction. On himself he might have found that to be an imperfection, something to be combed, but it matched her personality. Not only what she said, but how she

299

said it. It spoke to him of a joyful innocence and hope.

When they finished their coffees, they went downstairs to the bowling alley. Again, the place wasn't exactly hopping. A few college students were playing, including the men's basketball team who took up three of the lanes.

Both commented on how groovy they looked in those ridiculous bowling shoes, and per Hope's suggestion, both chose balls for the other, just to see if they could get it right. Hope ended up with a ball that was way too heavy for her, and Vincent ended up with a ball that was way too light for him that he couldn't even get his fingers into, so they just switched.

Hope also thought it would be a great idea to place a bet on the game, the winner deciding what they did next. Vincent had never bowled before, but that didn't stop him from the friendly wager. It was kind of embarrassing to Vincent that he was not so good, because Hope turned out to be an excellent bowler. When all was said and done, Hope beat Vincent 162 to 110, including rolling three strikes in the tenth frame. Had Vincent been less of a man, his ego may have smarted from such a shellacking from a woman, but he trusted that from her calm demeanor, she still respected his place in this world, whatever that might be.

If there were any question of pride lost, she answered the query by letting him pay for the game. Outside now, he asked her, "Okay, you won the bet. What do we do next?"

Hope smiled at her date and said, "Come with me."

They walked over past the Doughnut to the other side of campus and up San Antonio Hill. Vincent—to keep her from getting the chills—kept his arm around her the whole time. Some of Vincent's nervousness left him. Maybe it was because she was so easy to be around, or maybe it was a calming effect from the coffee. He doubted that. Either way, he felt more comfortable as the evening went by. Still his voice showed some tenseness.

When they got to the top of the hill to the ball park, they entered the gate and walked onto the field. It was the first time Vincent had stepped foot on Johnson Field since being suspended at the end of the fall season.

Hope led Vincent onto the infield. Everything was dark, only a few distant light poles turning blacks into indigos. She took Vincent's hand and led him to the top of the mound. Why she chose the ball field or specifically the pitcher's mound, Vincent did not know. He couldn't take it any longer, so he finally asked, "So, what is this all about?"

Hope smiled at him. "How do you feel?"

Vincent didn't exactly know how to answer, so he shrugged.

"Well, you look comfortable on the pitcher's mound," she said.

Vincent nodded, smiled.

Hope said, "I just wanted to take you somewhere you felt confident." She paused and looked up at the stands. "You know, I've watched you pitch."

Vincent nodded. "Yeah, I saw you up in the stands," another admission that put him out there.

"Well, you were pretty impressive when I watched you. I wasn't at your last game though. I understand you had it tough."

Vincent looked down and nodded.

"You want to talk about it?" Hope said.

"About what?" he said.

"About your parents?" she said. "I know that we haven't been friends very long, but I do want you to know that you can talk to me about anything."

"I doubt that," Vincent replied with a frown and took a quick mental inventory of all the bad things he had done and all of the dark moments he had experienced over the past year.

"Why?" she asked.

"Well," he started, then lowered his voice, "there are a few things I'm not so proud of, in the way I handled my parents' death. I don't want you to think any less of me."

"Oh, Vincent, I wouldn't be much of a friend to you if I didn't accept you when you're vulnerable."

Vincent sat down on the pitching rubber and looked up at the stars, millions of them making their way across the sky on a constant track.

How much can I tell her? How much should I tell her?

This was his worst fear, acceptance. He dealt with a lion's share of it back home, and now his past was about to catch up to him. He just didn't know how someone so perfect as Hope could accept him, all of him. From his limited viewpoint, he knew she would be off like a leaf in the wind as soon as he bared his past to her naïve ears, yet he dared for some unknown reason. Perhaps it was hope.

He patted on the ground and Hope sat next to him, heedless of the dirt. "Thank you, Hope. Do you want to know what makes you so special?"

Hope shook her head, no.

"That you care about others before yourself," he replied. "That's what I can't get over. Sometimes I think that I am so selfish. Then I look at you and see just how unselfish you are. It makes me wish I was more like you."

"Oh, I don't think you give yourself enough credit," Hope replied.

Vincent sighed and began, his shame aside. "Losing my parents was harder than I let myself admit."

"Oh?"

"Yeah," he said. "I didn't have much of a relationship with them. I lived in their house, but they didn't really take care of me. Dad was a drunk. When he drank, he would look for an easy target to beat on. That target was my mother usually, but every once in a while I would instigate a fight with him, egg him on so that he would take it out on me instead of her. Then there was this one night when he pulled me out of bed in the middle of the night, but I raised my fists against him and he backed down."

Vincent paused. He could feel tears welling up. "That was the last time he ever touched me." Vincent took a moment to compose himself in Hope's silence before he continued. He had spoken to the counselor about all of this, but it was a different feeling to do so in front of this beautiful woman.

"I was in high school and big enough to defend myself at that point." He paused again. "Well, when they died, I fought against mourning them, because I didn't think they deserved to be mourned. I held onto my anger for a long time and made a bunch of mistakes after that. I hit rock bottom a couple of times," and he paused to look for the right words. "A couple of times I thought there was no hope. All I really needed to do was--"

"Forgive him?" Hope finished his sentence.

"Yeah, forgive him."

Hope nodded, staring at the ground.

"I'm working on it," he said.

"Well," Hope said, "just remember that forgiveness doesn't let him off the hook. Forgiveness lets you off the hook. Takes the chains off of your wrists, the weight off your chest."

"You're right," Vincent said, but changed topics. "How much do you know about me?"

"Oh, a little," Hope replied.

"Do you know how I got in trouble?" Vincent asked.

"Oh, a little," Hope replied.

Vincent omitted any details and continued, "And you still want to be my friend?"

"Oh, a little," Hope replied, and the two of them laughed.

Vincent shook his head. "I can't believe I was so dumb. I did things I swore I would never do. Things my dad did. Even worse."

"And now you're paying the price."

"Yeah," Vincent said. "That's sure true."

"Well, did you learn a lesson?"

"I hope," Vincent replied. "You still want to be my friend after knowing how badly I messed up?" In his mind he saw the image of Evan's handgun and shuddered.

"Well," Hope said and paused, "Vincent I just want you to know that there is nobody perfect out there. We all make our mistakes, and we pay for our mistakes. It's part of life. But if you ask God for forgiveness, he gives you his grace for free."

Vincent didn't know what to say. Before he could utter a single word, Hope put her hand on his chin and lifted it so that she could look into his eyes. "Vincent, Christians are not perfect, just forgiven. Remember that."

Vincent shook his head. "Hope, how do you do it? How is it that you make me feel so special even when I am not?"

Hope put her hand on top of Vincent's and squeezed. "Because you *are* special." Hope emphasized the "are" and squeezed Vincent's right hand. The moment lasted a few seconds and Vincent thought about leaning in for a kiss. Instead, Hope spoke again. "God has a plan. You just don't see it yet," and she paused before continuing in a whisper, "but I'm guessing that you will."

Vincent smiled at her. She was amazing. They sat out on top of the pitcher's mound and looked up. She told him about many of the stars and planets that they could see with the naked eye, of times in her youth when her late grandfather had taken her outside of Amarillo to the countryside to teach her about the night sky. Before they knew it, midnight was fast approaching, and Hope didn't want to be locked out of her dormitory, so they started walking back.

The whole time on the pitcher's mound, Vincent felt at ease and he put away the notion to kiss her. It almost seemed to him that it would ruin such a perfect evening, though he didn't know why. He questioned his sanity and started working up the nerve to kiss her.

When he got to the front door of her lobby, she turned around and said, "Vincent, I had a great night. Thank you for taking me out."

Vincent mustered up all the strength he had and put it all on the line. "Can, er... may I kiss you goodnight?"

Hope smiled at him. She instead put the back of her left hand up to his face, and he took the hint. He took hold of her hand and kissed the back of it.

She exhaled deeply. "Good night Vincent." She smiled one last time at him turned toward the door. In a flash she was up the stairs. Vincent chided himself for throwing caution to the wind, wishing he had trusted his instincts, and trudged back to his dorm where Tank would surely be waiting up for him.

He was.

Vincent tried to keep his composure. He walked over to his bed and started undressing. Tank was at his desk, looking over some papers with his laptop open to a new word document. When Vincent couldn't take it anymore, he finally burst out, "Okay, I know you want to know how it went."

Tank didn't answer or even acknowledge that Vincent had spoken.

"Well, it went pretty well, I suppose. She is quite the amazing girl."

"Lady," Tank corrected him.

"So you *are* listening," Vincent said.

Again, Tank didn't respond.

"Well, like I was saying, she is amazing. What is so cool is that she makes me feel welcome, no matter what. We went bowling, had coffee, then watched the stars." Vincent paused, wondering if he should include his rejection in front of her dorm. It got the better of him, and he wanted some insight, so he continued. "I asked her if I could kiss her goodnight, and she said, 'No.'"

Tank chuckled. "Yeah, I should have told you."

"Told me what?"

"Their pact."

"What are you talking about?"

Tank put down his papers and turned around. "Look, Vincent. It's pretty simple, and smart, and I don't know if you will agree with it, but I am sure you will respect it. Both Grace and Hope made a decision early on. They won't kiss a man for the first ten dates."

"You're kidding me?" Vincent said. He couldn't believe such foolishness.

"Do I look like I am kidding?" Tank replied.

Vincent thought it over, ran it through a few times, and couldn't fathom why to have such a rule. Surely they would never have a guy wait that long to kiss them.

Before Vincent could verbalize any of his thoughts, Tank clarified it. "Vincent, how much do you like Hope?"

Vincent thought for a second and said, "A lot."

"But how much?"

"I don't know how much," Vincent said. "Is there some scale? From one to ten? I'd say that she tops the scale. A ten. She is perfect."

"Okay," Tank said. "Now, how much do you respect her?"

Vincent again had to think about this. "A lot," he said. "I guess ten again."

"Okay," Tank said. Vincent hoped Tank was getting somewhere. "Now look at your former roommate, Evan. How much did he respect ladies?"

"Not very much," Vincent said.

"Are you a better person than him?" Tank asked.

"I hope so," Vincent replied.

"But how do you know?" Tank asked.

Vincent thought for a moment, started to say something, paused, thought again. Finally, Tank jumped in. "You ever hear of a man named Petrarch?"

"Is that a first name or last name?" Vincent asked.

Tank ignored the question. "He lived a long time ago in Italy. Shakespeare was very devoted to his teachings. Anyway, Petrarch's ideals of courtly love suggested a period in which the man's devotion is tested."

"Well that's stupid," Vincent said, but Tank put up one finger to shush the freshman and continued.

"I know you are a better person than your former roommate, but women are really trusting. Trust can easily be broken. If a lady wants to know how devoted a man is to her, how much he respects her, she must test him. That's what the ten dates is all about. Would your former roommate wait ten dates?"

"Ha! Evan? Not a chance!" Vincent blurted out.

"Okay," Tank said. "Now here's the really big question. Are you willing to wait ten dates? Is Hope worth it?"

Tank had a point. Vincent knew now that he must earn her trust. The more he thought about it, the more he appreciated Hope and Grace for making this decision to make the man wait to kiss them. It gave good guys like Vincent the opportunity to outlast a man who had dishonorable intentions.

"How long have you and Grace been dating?" Vincent asked.

"118 dates," Tank said, already busy again in his work.

Vincent was amazed. Tank was one of the most honorable of men he had ever known. "So after ten dates?"

"We kissed," Tank said.

"And now?" Vincent asked.

Tank dropped the papers. "Now? We still kiss."

"Nothing more?"

Tank stared at Vincent. Vincent began to wish he hadn't asked such a personal question, but then Tank answered. "Were you present for this conversation we just had about respecting ladies?"

Vincent nodded. "Thanks, Tank." Vincent smiled at the idea of winning Hope. That's what he had to do. Win her over. She had plenty of reasons to make him wait to kiss her. Considering his past? That terrible first semester? He had given nobody a reason to trust him. He was just now starting to earn back Tank's and Coach Johnson's trust, much less Mrs. Dean's. Losing her trust really killed him. What was one more person, especially somebody for whom he cared so deeply?

Vincent pulled the sheets over his head and went to bed with a smile on his face. The problem was that he couldn't sleep. He couldn't get the night's revels out of his head. Every time he thought about Hope, he softly giggled like a middle school girl talking to her bestie about boys. He just couldn't help himself and tried to keep it down, hoping that his roommate couldn't hear him. By the sound of typing on the laptop now, it appeared that Tank was in his own little world.

Finally Vincent centered his thoughts on Tank. Tank was so much older than Vincent, so much wiser, so much more mature. Had he always been so? It was so simple to see why Grace was so in love with him. But this also bothered Vincent. As far as he could see, Tank never made a mistake. Tank always did the right thing. When others were out partying, enjoying their last moments before the real world came calling, here was Tank, diligently sitting up at his desk and doing his homework. The reason it bothered Vincent was that Grace had nabbed a real winner. In contrast, what could Hope possibly see in Vincent?

Throwing caution to the wind for the second time that night, Vincent lowered the sheet and blurted out, "Have you always been perfect?"

The typing stopped.

Tank let out a sigh and turned around to face Vincent now. Vincent looked at the laptop and saw that Tank was typing a research paper. He had stopped in the middle of a sentence.

"I'm sorry, Tank. I shouldn't have asked that." Vincent convinced himself that he had offended his roommate, but Tank quickly corrected him.

"No, no. It's alright." Tank stared at the floor for a few seconds, then at the ceiling tile, apparently to collect his thoughts or invoke some muse. Vincent too looked up at the ceiling and thought about the whiskey he once stored up there, quickly trying to purge the thought from his mind.

"First," Tank started, "let's get one thing straight. I'm not perfect. I think I made that much clear to you already."

"I don't believe that," Vincent said. "You always do the right thing. I have never known somebody who always made the right decisions and never took the easy way out."

"Well, don't believe everything you see," Tank said.

Vincent was silenced at this.

"I was major trouble in high school," Tank continued. Vincent didn't say a word, so Tank qualified that statement. "About the time I hit fifteen I started to rebel against my parents. I started doing some things that I shouldn't of. At first it was chew. A couple of guys on the team chewed because they do it in the majors, so I naturally thought that in order to be a good baseball player, you had to chew."

Tank cleared his throat, making a pained face. "And, man, it was nasty stuff! I don't know if you've ever tried it, but I can tell you that it's nothing special. Nasty habit and very addictive. I started out with chaw and was introduced shortly thereafter to snuff. That stuff really kicked my butt. The nicotine high was overpowering. Made me want to sit back and close my eyes and just enjoy the moment. Of course I would get really sick to my stomach after the high subsided, and I told myself each time that this would be the last time, but it became an addiction, and I didn't want to be caught dead around my friends without a dip in."

Tank nodded as if in agreement to something Vincent hadn't said. "It was a social thing. Acceptance. Well, the sick feeling started to go away, but then the high went away as well and I found myself craving a dip, going out of my mind if I didn't have a dip in my mouth. That's how it started."

Tank kept his stare away from Vincent, but if he had looked at his roommate, he would have seen Vincent's mouth wide open.

"I became flippant with my parents. Anything they said, I would do the opposite. I disrespected their wishes, said all sorts of things I regret, all sorts of things that I have apologized for profusely in the years since." Tank paused again and regrouped. "Then it was cigars. Really nasty ones that left the taste of ashes in my mouth. We thought it looked cool to be puffing on a stogie. Try to make smoke rings. But then one day, a buddy of mine brought a pack of cigarettes to practice, and we snuck behind the bathrooms and lit up, and that feeling I used to get from chewing came back strong. I suppose it was then just a matter of time before I got hooked on cigarettes. By the time I was sixteen I was chewing and smoking, and since I had my own car, I was going out to parties. This is where I drank my first beer. Before I knew it, Friday and Saturday nights were all about drinking, smoking, and having 'a good time.'"

Tank used the air quotes with his fingers to emphasize the last three words. To this point his voice was matter-of-fact. Now his voice lowered to a whisper, softened and remorseful.

"That was my life for the next year. Then during my junior year, somebody got the great idea that we should break into a liquor store and steal a keg. Since I was one of the bigger guys, I was selected for this little mission. It was a stupid thing to do, and I should have known better, but peer pressure got the best of me."

Tank chuckled sorrowfully, shaking his head. "I actually had the audacity to be surprised when the alarm sounded when I broke the window. The sad thing is that I went through with the mission. I grabbed a full keg and put it on my back. But when I walked out of the door, the others had driven away. Left me there."

Tank exhaled. "I didn't make it a block before the cops grabbed me. That was a rough night."

Tank didn't elaborate on the "rough night," but Vincent knew all about that.

"Anyway," Tank caught his breath, "Mom and Dad freaked out. They had seen such a change in my behavior, in the way I was treating them, and now this. Well, I suppose that they didn't have a choice."

"A choice?" Vincent finally spoke up.

"Military school," Tank responded.

"Oh!" Vincent said a little too loudly. He was finally starting to put the puzzle pieces together.

"Yep," Tank nodded, and Vincent swore he saw a teardrop on Tank's cheek. Still, Tank continued, "and I was mad at them.

You better believe it! I could not believe that they would send me away, despite the judge's order. I mean, after all, so many of my 'friends' had done so much worse." Again, Tank used the air quotes, this time around "friends," and Vincent knew exactly what that meant as well. Vincent was well aware of the true meaning of a friend. He had learned it the hard way.

"At first it was tough, especially not having any chew or cigarettes. Man, in military school, they don't worry about some twelve-step program to help you kick an addiction, at least not this school. It was cold turkey detox, and man, I had never felt worse in my life!

Again, Vincent knew exactly what Tank meant.

"But, you know, I survived. Military school gave me structure, and I soon learned to rely on that structure. Up before the crack of dawn with a forty-pound rucksack on my back for a five-mile run. School for eight hours. Studying until lights out at nine. Repeat." Tank smiled and looked at Vincent. "Kind of what you're going through right now."

Vincent smiled.

"Well, I had to grow up quickly," Tank continued. "So I did. After I graduated, I enlisted in the Marines. It seemed like the right thing to do, and I think it was. I wanted to serve my country and relied on the structure that the military provided."

Tank stopped abruptly and looked back to the ceiling, apparently at a loss for words. "I'm not really going to talk about that though. What I will say is that after a while I missed baseball. When I returned from Iraq, I was discharged, I contacted a bunch of colleges, but nobody was willing to take a chance on an old man like me, especially with background checks so easy."

At the mention of "old man," Vincent chuckled.

"In fact Coach Johnson was the only one who replied to my letter. He invited me to a tryout. I was forthcoming about everything I had done, and he was really cool about it. He didn't have any scholarships left to give out, so he asked me if I would walk on my freshman year with the possibility of earning a scholarship my sophomore year. I jumped at the chance. I had plenty of money to get me through one year and set my mind to working hard and proving to Coach that I deserved a scholarship the next year. And that's how I made it here."

Vincent considered the story for a moment and noticed all the parallels to his own life, namely that he didn't start out doing bad things, but once he relented just a little bit, compromised his virtues a fraction of an inch, the slow fade ensued. It happened to Tank, and it happened to Vincent. It was a slow, inevitable fade.

"That's quite a story," Vincent finally said, blinking.

Tank nodded. "Yes it is. But I told you this to remind you that everything that glimmers isn't gold. Nobody is perfect Vincent. We all have our pasts to contend with. I left mine in the past where it belonged. I got myself right with the Lord, and now what you perceive as 'perfect' is just wisdom gained through experience and applied to present situations. That and a lot of hard work." Tank paused then said, "Whatever you do, work at it with all your heart.' Colossians 3:23."

Vincent didn't know what to say. He had the utmost respect for Tank and all he stood for, but now, after hearing about Tank's checkered past and all that he overcame to make it to where he presently was, Vincent held him in hero status.

"Grace know?" Vincent asked.

"Well of course!" Tank responded. "Think I would keep something from her? She loves me despite my past, just as I love her despite her past." Tank looked at Vincent for a few more seconds. When Vincent didn't ask any more questions, Tank turned around and resumed typing the sentence he had left unfinished.

Vincent laid his head back on his bed and took all of this in. He had a lot to tell Hope. "Hey Tank?"

"Yes," Tank said without stopping.

"Thanks."

Chapter Twenty-Five

VINCENT WORKED HARD to learn how to play chess. His daily trips to the retirement home to play Robert, the WWII veteran, sent him home a loser every time. Robert wouldn't take it easy on Vincent at all. If it took ten moves to beat Vincent, ten moves it was. Eight moves? Let the beating begin. Vincent tried his hardest against Robert to give him a good game, and sometimes he actually made Robert think hard about a move, but Vincent still had a long way to go before he was giving the old gentleman a challenge.

Vincent looked forward to going to the retirement home. He loved the smiles it put on the residents' faces. At first Vincent didn't know how he was going to have enough energy to keep up with the demanding schedule, but once he found out that he had the inner strength to survive, then enough inner strength to thrive, he found that the work he did at the retirement home wasn't work at all, but a way to replenish his spirit. Exercising at six A.M.? Vincent really never got excited about that, but his community service truly made him happy.

Speaking of making him happy, Hope was so inspired with Vincent's tales of his service to the retirement center that she rearranged her schedule so that she could volunteer when he was there. Vincent would be getting his tail kicked in chess and look up and see Hope across the room with a female resident, holding her hand and just listening to her tell her life story. That's what Hope was good at. Listening. Vincent knew that better than anyone. Vincent would be scooping out the old ashes from the fireplace and look up to see her helping a resident walk. They would befriend the residents, and every so often, both would look up at the other at the same time and share a smile.

In the brief off-moments in Vincent's schedule, he would take out his old burlap bag of dirty and fraying baseballs and haul them out behind his dormitory parking lot to a vacant field with an old chain link fence. He would count off sixty feet, six inches and with the aid of a shovel, create a mound and practice throwing against the fence. It wasn't easy at first, with the damage done to his left eye from the accident back in January. He tried to retrain his eyes, but thoughts went back to his senior year, of having eyesight so clear that he could pick out a single thread hanging from the webbing on his catcher's mitt. Such a miniscule target to throw at necessitated exact precision, surgical precision. Now that was gone.

Eventually he decided on glasses. His optometrist fit him with a pair of sports glasses that helped him to see a lot more clearly, yet he couldn't quite get his perfect vision back. The glasses helped though, and he ordered another pair of the same frames, this time with smoke lenses to help with the light hyper sensitivity he acquired through the accident. With the aide of his sunglasses, and his probation from the team about over with, Vincent was hopeful that he could again impress the coaching staff and regain the trust of his teammates.

Outside of class and community service, Vincent and Tank spent most of their time together. Tank continued to tutor Vincent in fly fishing on Saturday mornings, and Vincent felt he was getting the hang of that art. Though it was true that Tank would fish circles around him, Vincent became better adept at focusing on the strike indicator and recognizing a strike, something he reckoned would help him reel in his eyesight. At least he reasoned that it didn't hurt.

Tank would also accompany Vincent to the empty lot where Vincent had created the makeshift pitcher's mound, and he would help Vincent with his pitching, playing the role of coach since Vincent wasn't allowed back at practice at present. Most of Tank's comments were constructively critical, which Vincent appreciated. Though the two of them were becoming good friends, Vincent still needed Tank to be the team's captain, his mentor.

The baseball team won more games than it lost. Vincent watched all of the home games from the stands, taking a spot in the upper corner of the stands, hoping not to be seen by the other spectators. The new prescription shades helped a lot, and he cheered on his team, anxiously awaiting the moment when he could finally rejoin his teammates.

Vincent's court review was on April Fool's Day. He had met all of the requirements that the court set out for him to meet, and quickly to boot. His fine was paid in full, all one hundred hours of community service had been worked and signed for by the retirement home manager. In truth, Vincent had worked well over one hundred hours, and had no plans to stop if for no other reason than that it meant spending more time with Hope.

At the review, Vincent appeared in a suit and tie, accompanied by Tank, the whole coaching staff, a few of the other baseball players, and Hope. They sat a few rows behind him to support him.

The judge asked Vincent a series of questions, and Vincent answered them honestly, with much contrition. The judge spoke harsh words to Vincent about how the results of his actions could have cost him, "and more importantly, other people their lives." Vincent agreed with the judge on everything he said, and there was a moment when Vincent thought he might be sentenced to more penalties, but the judge, having thoroughly scared Vincent back to reality, released him on probation for a period of one year, during which time, if he were to be caught with so much as a beer in his hand, he would be thrown in jail and all of his community service hours would be for naught.

Vincent wasn't worried though. He knew that the temptation would always be there, but he also knew that he had a great support team around him. He would not let them down, or more likely, they wouldn't let him.

When Vincent stepped down from the stage, he shook Coach Johnson's hand. Coach Johnson said only, "See you at practice." It was Four. Golden Words. Though Vincent was sad that he wouldn't be able to spend those afternoons at the retirement home anymore, he vowed to find a way to get there, weekends or something.

The others shook his hand and congratulated him, and Hope gave him a big hug. It was the first time they had ever hugged, and Vincent held on for dear life. He felt closer to Hope than he had ever felt with anyone before. He had wondered what the lack of intimacy would do to their dating life and relationship, but he found that much tenderness, if not more, could be found in merely holding her hand and having a conversation with her. They had been on five dates to this point, and Vincent no longer waited impatiently for date number ten. He found that the journey was more fun than the destination.

That afternoon, all the players welcomed Vincent back with no questions asked. He was dazzling all throughout practice. He threw off the mound with a ton of zip on the ball and had to be reminded by the coaches that he shouldn't go full speed. He had some trouble at the plate. This was where he was most worried. With his eyesight compromised, he had trouble seeing some pitches. His dominant eye was still good, and he was able to make a pretty good showing from the right side of the plate, but he switched over to the left side where his left eye had to do most of the work. Any pitch came in like a blur. Though Vincent knew his decision to drink and drive was a bad one, his inability to hit showed him the permanence of his mistake.

Forever.

It seemed that in a land of second chances, he was only given one in this case. Still he considered himself fortunate. Fortunate to still be on the team. Fortunate he was alive after the crash. Fortunate he didn't kill anyone else. Fortunate he didn't lose his scholarship. Fortunate he had a group of people around him that loved him and wanted to see him succeed. His schoolwork was always done on time, he was making all A's in his classes, and he was in the best shape of his life, thanks to Tank and their six A.M. workouts. Vincent quickly regained the reputation as the team's ace.

In his absence the team had seventeen wins against eleven losses. This was respectable, but Vincent quickly learned that some serious ground needed to be made up if they intended to be invited to a regional for postseason play in late May. He hoped to be able to help out immediately. In this regard he was deeply disappointed.

Vincent practiced the entire month of April and never saw the field in a single game. Not as a pinch hitter. Not in mop up duty in a blowout. Even with one bad eye, he was considered one of the best hitters on the team, and by far the best pitcher they had. He felt he had proven himself to Coach Johnson over and over.

All the service hours? Check.

3.0 grade point average? Check.

Square with the state of Arizona? Check.

Kept his nose clean? Check.

Worked his tail off? Check.

Physically able to play? Check.

After a month of being reinstated back on the team and only practicing, Vincent began to lose faith. Tank apparently saw it because he spent quite a bit of time telling Vincent to be sure to wait his time, to be patient. Patience was something Vincent was running out of. A week into May, NCA had a record of 25 wins and 18 losses. Still, Vincent sat the bench. Not once did Coach Johnson speak to Vincent about this.

Finally, when Vincent thought he could stand it no longer, he looked into transferring to another school. He really didn't want to, especially since he and Hope had been on eight dates now. School was out, and Hope went back home to Amarillo. Dates number nine and ten were definitely up in the air. From a baseball standpoint, he was about to waste a year of eligibility. His only other option was to redshirt so that he would still have four years to play. Since he hadn't played in a single game that spring, he was certainly eligible. On the other hand, if he transferred to another school, collegiate governing rules would dictate that he would have to sit out the next year as well. Vincent decided that the best thing to do was pray about it.

NCA hosted Stansfield University, a tough team from Oregon that was as successful as NCA was at making the World Series every few years. Stansfield had a quality team this year, and the NCA players knew how important it was to try to sweep them on their home turf. If NCA failed to win their postseason tournament to gain entrance to the regional, these two wins might give them an outside shot at an at-large bid.

In typical fashion with such good schools, pitching dominated the first game. NCA had managed to squeak out one run in eight innings of play, on Tank's thirty-fifth home run of the season. As they batted in the bottom of the eighth inning, Coach Johnson calmly walked up to Vincent and said, "Warm up."

At first Vincent thought Coach Johnson was talking to someone else, until Tank elbowed Vincent in the ribs and said, "What are you waiting for?"

Vincent snapped out of it.

Yes!

He sprang off the bench as if a firecracker had been lit under his bottom. He raced out to the bullpen, reminding himself to calm down, and then focused on easing into his pitches. With the nerves at an all-time high, the last thing Vincent wanted to do was throw out his arm.

This was Vincent's first official ball game. All the autumn ball games he had played in did not affect his eligibility since they were just considered scrimmages, so just thinking about this made the butterflies even worse. Even though he was not nearly ready, the third out was recorded, and NCA took to the field to close out the game in the top half of the ninth.

Vincent sprinted to the mound amid a chorus of cheers from the student body. Tank warmed him up, only asking for four-seam fastballs so as to not give anything away.

The early May air was perfectly tepid. Vincent thought about back home where all the trees would be flowering. It made him smile. He took in a panoramic view from atop his mound, the highest place on the baseball field feeling slightly foreign to him. His eyes wandering across the landscape, over to beautiful Lake Powell and across the red plateaued backdrop, he felt a tapping at his shoulder.

"You've waited a long time for this. You ready?"

Without turning around, Vincent recognized this as Tank's voice. Vincent smiled and closed his eyes, picturing instead his first strike. Once he visualized it, he turned back around and focused on his catcher.

When the first batter stepped into the right-hand batter's box, the crowd didn't exist. The other players didn't exist. Even the batter didn't exist. All was quiet in Vincent's ears as he prepared to take that last step forward in completing his penance.

Tank called for a splitter, a pitch that Vincent didn't throw very often, but had learned that past summer with Grandpa Dean's instruction and honed while working in the empty lot with Tank that winter.

Vincent nodded, strained his eyes to see some small detail in Tank's glove, and when he couldn't find anything, he went into his windup anyway. His concentration was on the center of the mitt. When Vincent delivered the ball, it started about waist high and sank to the batter's knees. The guy never even tried to swing.

"STRIKE ONE!"

Vincent took the ball back from Tank and repositioned himself on the mound. The ball went where he wanted it to. He didn't have as much confidence in himself as he was used to having without his laser eyesight, but he figured he could still hit his mark, and that would have to be good enough.

Tank next called for a four-seam fastball, outside. Vincent accepted the sign, went into the windup, and gave it all he was worth.

Lightning!

Thunder!

The ball popped leather, a little inside of where he was aiming, hitting the corner of the plate.

"STRIKE TWO!"

Tank threw the ball back to Vincent, and Vincent began to wonder. Yes, it was nice that he threw a strike, and in turning around and looking at the scoreboard, he saw that he threw that last pitch ninety-four miles per hour. A nice pitch. Not Mr. Nasty, but really dang fast all the same. Still, he knew he could throw harder, and more importantly, he knew he could hit his mark better. He just really had to concentrate.

Vincent leaned in for the sign. Tank called for a changeup on the outside corner, and Vincent nodded. He stared as hard as he could at Tank's glove, hoping to see anything that he could laser focus his attention on. The more he stared, the less he seemed to be able to focus without his vision becoming blurry. To alleviate this, Vincent stepped off the back of the rubber, took off his hat, and wiped his brow. Just as he was about to put his hat back on, he saw, written on the inside of the bill, the Bible verse Colossians 3:23.

Colossians 3:23? What is that verse? I know that verse. I know I've heard it somewhere.

Vincent paused while looking at the verse. He had been going to church with Tank every Sunday. He went to the Noonday lunch every Wednesday. He had reestablished his faith, but he realized that he had truly forgotten to bring his faith onto the baseball field. "Cast all your burdens away," Vincent said to himself. He had failed to do everything in Christ's name, and being the stubborn person he was, he was relying too much on himself. He didn't know who wrote the verse on his hat. It didn't matter at the moment. What did matter was that he lean on Jesus for his strength. He could always look it up after the game.

He put his cap back on and refocused on Tank, whispering a short prayer, "Lord, help me to lean on you in all I do."

Vincent went into his windup, threw his circle changeup, and the batter swung right through the ball.

"STRIKE THREE!" the home plate umpire called.

Vincent turned around and caught a peek at his infielders who were all clapping their gloves and holding up one finger.

Okay, that's one down, Vincent. Lean on The Lord.

The second batter came up to the plate, and Vincent felt more focused than ever. He still could not see Tank's mitt with precision, but he didn't worry about that and just threw. With lightning and thunder erupting from his arm, the second and third batters also went down on strikes, Vincent's last pitch hitting ninety-eight miles per hour.

The crowd came to their feet with applause, Vincent recognizing them finally with this last out recorded.

Tank ran out to Vincent, handed him the ball in his glove, and shook his hand. "Like riding a bike," Tank said.

"Do you have a Bible with you?" Vincent asked. The others in the infield came in and started giving high fives.

Tank smiled and nodded.

When the team made it to the dugout, Coach Johnson stopped Vincent, shook his hand, and said, "'Whatever you do, work at it with all your heart.' Colossians 3:23. Welcome back, Special K."

It finally dawned on Vincent that he had heard Coach Johnson say that verse at one of the first practices way back in August. He may have even heard Tank utter the verse once or twice.

Coach Johnson pointed into the stands. In the upper corner of the stands sat an elderly lady. "She came a long ways to see you play."

"Mrs. Dean!" Vincent said.

Above the dugout, the crowd chanted "Special K! Special K! Special K!"

Vincent was able to speak only briefly to Mrs. Dean in between games because he had to cool off his shoulder. Game two saw Vincent riding the bench again, with an ice pack on his shoulder. Though it was only a few pitches, rules were rules, and he couldn't take a chance with his shoulder. Again the game played out like a chess match with Sandy on NCA's team working the corners of the plate and inducing ground ball outs, and the opposing pitcher doing the same. This time in the bottom of the ninth inning, neither team had been able to score, and both coaches were too stubborn to take out their starting pitchers. Vincent knew that Coach Johnson wanted this game badly for the all-important sweep, so Vincent shouldn't have been surprised when Coach Johnson inserted Vincent as a pinch hitter.

Vincent unwrapped the bandage with the ice pack on his shoulder and selected a bat. He walked out to the on deck circle and the "Special K!" chant started up again. Vincent tried to tune it out, instead replaying the bible verse Coach Johnson had given to him.

"Whatever you do, work at it with all your heart."

Vincent again felt confident. He didn't know how he had forgotten to include God in baseball, but there in the Colossians verse it was written, seemingly just for him. That meant, everything he did.

Vincent strode up to the right-hand batter's box and made the sign of the cross with the bat across the plate. He felt more confident than ever. He had watched the opposing pitcher pitch the whole game, knew his tendencies. He knew that the pitcher

325

liked to start the batter with a strike on the outside corner, which this guy did.

He then knew that the next pitch would be off-speed, which it was.

Now down two strikes in the count, he expected a high fastball. This was tricky for Vincent because high heat was his kryptonite, but he stood in there, slightly forward in the batter's box, hoping to catch it before it rose too high to swing. With two strikes he knew he needed to protect the plate, which meant opening up his stance and taking a short, abbreviated swing. This would deprive him of all his power.

The ball came in a little high anyway, but Vincent managed to get a bead on it, forsaking the conventional wisdom of protecting the plate and giving a huge home run swing. He was a little behind the ball, but it rebounded off of his bat and into right centerfield. He knew he got a lot of the ball, but thought that he might not have gotten enough, so he took off in a sprint.

The centerfielder raced toward the ball, but it tailed away from him, hitting the bottom of the fence at an awkward angle and shooting back toward the infield. Neither the centerfielder nor the right fielder was ready for this as it managed to burn them on the way to the fence and then back past them the other direction. Vincent knew he would be able to get a triple out of it if he really booked it, so he turned on the after burners. He rounded second and saw his coach looking intently into the field, not giving a sign. Halfway to third base, his coach gave him the sign to round the bag and head home.

The crowd jumped up and down and screamed with delight as Vincent found one more gear and cut the corner of third base on his way home. He had no idea what was happening in the field, only that he was going to need to slide. The opposing catcher had his left foot blocking the plate. He looked ready to catch the ball and apply the tag, so Vincent took an outside angle and dove head first to the left of the catcher. Just as he feared, the catcher caught the ball right as Vincent hit the dirt, but with the angle Vincent took, he was able to slide past the catcher and swipe the plate with his left hand. The catcher swiped his glove at Vincent but missed completely.

"RUNNER'S SAFE! RUNNER'S SAFE!" the home plate umpire called, both of his arms out to the side.

The crowd went wild as Vincent jumped up, losing his helmet in the process before getting mobbed by his teammates in a huge dog pile. The crowd again chanted his nickname "Special K! Special K! Special K!" This went on for at least ten minutes until the majority of the crowd finally dispersed.

Vincent didn't know if it was Mrs. Dean's calming presence in the stands or the patience that he had acquired through his adversities, but Vincent's confidence soared. His return to the field energized the team at a point when energy was badly needed. Vincent resumed his normal spot in the rotation after that game and was counted on to pinch hit, playing the field sparingly because of the limitations of his eye. NCA went on to rip off ten more games in a row, winning their league and their conference tournament, advancing them to into the regional tournament.

Chapter Twenty-Six

THE SAME WEEK as the eight regionals across the United States were going on, the pros also held their draft. NCA held out hope that a few of their juniors and seniors would be drafted. Unfortunately for Vincent, freshmen and sophomores were not eligible according to the rules. NCA's big hopeful though was Tank, whose stock soared throughout the season. It was obvious to everybody in the stands who the scouts were. In such a small town as Page, Arizona, everybody knew everybody. At the beginning of the season it was just one or two scouts showing up here and there with their notebooks in hand and fedoras keeping the sun off their necks. Ttoward the end of the season, as word spread about Tank's abilities, it was nothing to see ten to fifteen different scouts in the stands, some with notepads, some with their cell phones, recording Tank's every move.

Coach Johnson was mum when it came to discussing Tank's future with anybody but Tank. Having been trained by Coach Johnson, Tank, in turn, was mum when discussing his future with anybody, even Vincent. Coach Johnson had played in the pros, and then scouted in the pros in his younger days before taking over NCA's baseball team, so he knew the inner workings of the business of selecting the right player for the organization. Having that respect with the other scouts, he was on a first-name basis with every one of them, chatting with them after games. This intrigued Vincent to no end. He was excited for Tank's future in baseball, and only wished Tank would share with him everything he was experiencing. Still, Vincent wondered if any of the scouts had noticed his play.

The first day of the draft was set for June 3rd, the very day that NCA played in the first championship game of their regional at the home field of Nevada Western University. Each regional, eight in all, had four teams. It was a simple double-elimination format, and on June 3rd, NCA found themselves at 2-0, playing the winner of the Nevada Western versus Arizona A&M loser's bracket game. NCA had played both teams in the course of the year, AA&M being in their conference, so NCA knew all about them. NCA had defeated them five times out of six in the course of the year, including the first game of the regional, and they hoped to play them again. Unfortunately, Nevada Western dispatched them rather easily, so NCA set their sights on winning their next game and advancing to the super-regional. In a worst-case scenario, if they lost, they would still get another chance the next day. The problem was that Nevada Western was the home team and would have a decided emotional advantage.

Nevada Western was a dangerous team, especially at home. NCA had played a double header at their place in early March, escaping with a split. Of course this was before Vincent was playing with them. Simply put, the team was better with him in the lineup and vastly better when he took the mound. The issue remained his inability to see the ball in the air as well as he had before the accident. Coach Johnson wanted Vincent in the outfield, but not at the expense of being a defensive liability, so he worked Vincent hard on fly balls. Though Vincent still couldn't see the ball as well as he had liked, he found that he could overcome his disability to an extent.

The worst was seeing the ball off the bat. With his myopia, he always got a late start on the ball. The ball might pop straight up in the air, and Vincent, mistakenly thinking it was going over his head, would run backwards, catch sight of the ball's trajectory in mid-flight, whip a U-turn, and burn rubber to make a fantastic sliding catch. While this was good for highlight reels, it was simply a pop fly out for an outfielder with good eyesight. The same would be true of the ball going over his head. He might start moving in, plant with his foot when he discovered it was going over his head, and then it was a matter of using his amazing speed to track it down. Vincent made most catches, but it was an unmistakable fact that there were just some balls that he couldn't get to. Vincent figured that his circus show must cause Coach Johnson quite a bit of heartburn.

Incidentally, Vincent must have shown himself to be good enough to take the chance of putting him in left field, because that's where he landed against NWU. Coach Johnson not only rolled the dice with Vincent in left, but he also let Zach Crawford, the number four pitcher in the rotation, take the mound. It was Zach's turn to pitch. This was true, but NCA had been given an extra day of rest while waiting for the loser's bracket to work itself out. Zach did have a few wins on the year, but he was used only sparingly during the season when Coach Johnson knew his other pitchers were tired or banged up.

With Vincent out of the rotation, Zach was the number three pitcher, but with Vincent in the rotation, Zach dropped to number four, and was more relied upon as a middle-innings relief pitcher than a starting pitcher. Vincent had pitched the first game of the regional and was ready for action, but Coach had made up his mind, and at worst, Vincent knew that he would get the ball on the mound if they lost that first game.

As expected, the game was a slugfest. Zach's fastball lacked zip, and he didn't mix up his speeds as well as he should have, so it was easy for the NWU batters to time. Similarly, NWU's pitcher faced a team whose batting average since Vincent had returned was well over .300. Going into the bottom of the ninth inning, NCA clung to an 11-10 lead.

To this point, Vincent had played a great game. Thankfully most of the balls he had to play were singles that rolled to him. There was one ball, a line drive he got a late start on, but he made up ground and laid out to make a spectacular catch. Vincent hoped he'd made Coach Johnson proud.

All NCA had to do was collect three outs in the bottom of the ninth and they would be moving on to the super-regional, but with the way the game had gone to this point, Vincent knew it wasn't going to be that easy. It started with a leadoff walk and a single to move the tying run over to third base. With no outs and runners on the corner, the next batter was induced into a pop up in the infield that Hoover, the shortstop, easily took care of.

Now with one out and a chance for a double play, the runner on first attempted to steal second base on the first pitch. Tank caught the pitch, faked a throw to second base, then considered throwing to third to try to catch the runner off the bag. The runner on third base stayed put which allowed the man on first to steal second base. With no base runners on first, the double play was now off the table, and there were two runners in scoring position, the tying run and the winning run. That's when Coach Johnson's worst fears were realized.

The next batter belted a hard line drive to left field. Vincent managed to get a good start on the ball and caught it on the run. Then all in one motion, zipped the ball to Tank at home plate. The runner on third base was tagging up, but halfway home, figured out that he wasn't going to make it, so he put on the brakes and ran back towards third base. Tank caught the ball, and just like Vincent, whipped it in one motion to the third baseman who applied the tag just a split second too late. The runner dove headfirst into the bag and cradled it for all he was worth.

"SAFE," the third base umpire called.

NCA was a mere inch away from the double play they needed to earn a trip to the super-regional, and though Vincent wished they would have gotten the batter out, he still was happy with himself, telling himself that he was back fully now, confident in his ability to make any play.

Confidence is a funny thing. It's easy to mistake it for arrogance. On the very next pitch, the batter flied a ball to what looked to Vincent like short left field. Vincent came bolting straight ahead to make what looked like an easy play, but then the ball kept sailing and sailing. Before Vincent knew what was happening, he was turned on his heels and booking it toward the fence.

Yet the ball kept going.

Vincent neared the warning track at full stride and stabbed his glove in the air to catch it. The ball hit the top of his webbing and bounced once on the warning track dirt before hitting the wall and bouncing past Vincent, who couldn't slow down fast enough. He slammed into the wall with his left shoulder and landed with a thud in the dirt. The ball bounded away, and though Vincent knew the centerfielder was coming on, the ball had been in the air too long. The batter must have had too much time to run. Meanwhile he could hear the NWU fans cheering. When Vincent looked up, there was a play at the plate, but the throw was off line and the batter crossed home plate for an improbable walk-off win.

Vincent was stunned, but okay. He rattled a few bolts loose in his head when he slammed into the wall, and was picked up by his teammates who helped him into the dugout. The other team celebrated while Vincent and his teammates licked their wounds. They filed into their locker room and helped Vincent to his locker. He shook his head to clear the cobwebs and knew he would be dealing with a headache tonight.

Coach Johnson let them sit and whisper quietly to themselves for the first ten minutes. Then he and the other coaches came in and attempted to console the team. Coach Johnson bunched up a towel, put it on the floor, then kneeled on it. He looked up at the team, who all waited for his words of wisdom, and said, "Well, we won't be sorry, because we played one heck of a game. They just had the last punch." Then he looked to Vincent who held his head in his hand.

I sure don't take very good care of my head.

"Vincent," Coach Johnson said, "you have nothing to be sorry about. That was one heck of an effort on that last ball." Coach Johnson exhaled. "Besides, without that great play and throw you made just before, we wouldn't have even been in that situation. We would have been in the locker room five minutes earlier doing the same thing we're doing now.

"And that goes for all of you. You all made plays tonight that staked us a lead or kept us in the ballgame. Your effort was top notch, and for that I thank you."

Coach Johnson groaned as he got back up off his knee. He wiped it off, as if it had dirt on it, surely an old habit of his, and said, "Season's not over yet. We'll get them tomorrow. They know they were lucky, but that's not what I want to talk with you about right now. We'll get to that tomorrow.

"Right now we have reason to celebrate. I wish it came in better circumstances, but we weren't in control of that, now were we? What I'm trying to say is that I think you all know that the baseball draft started this evening, about the time Zach threw the first pitch."

Everybody leaned in. Steinbeck put a hand on Tank's shoulder. Tank didn't look up.

Coach Johnson smiled, "Well, I won't beat around the bush. I just got off the phone with the general manager from Charlotte, and they informed me that they took Tank with the fifth overall pick."

A locker room that was solemn just a minute ago now erupted with cheers. Coach Johnson came over to Tank and shook his hand. The rest of the team followed suit, Vincent bringing up the rear. The whole time, Tank kept a straight face and thanked everybody for their support.

Coach Johnson stepped out of the way and let Tank have the floor. A man of few words, Tank simply said, "Thank you everybody. I don't really know what to say in a case like this, so instead let's just focus on coming back tomorrow and taking it to those guys. What do you say?"

The room erupted in cheers again, and Vincent wondered what the team within earshot in the other locker room must be thinking. Before he could wonder long, Coach Johnson came up to him and said, "They also wanted to know more about a few other players who were underclassmen." He walked off leaving Vincent to wonder.

Vincent called Hope that night. With the semester over, she was back in Amarillo, and he was stuck in western Nevada having to play another game to advance to the next round. Vincent hadn't talked to Hope in a few days and really missed her. He hadn't seen her for nearly a month now, since the second semester ended in the first week of May. He hated not being able to see her every day, and the phone was just no substitute. Vincent still hadn't any idea where he was going to live that summer. He just figured something would come along.

When he dialed the number, she answered on the first ring. "Vincent? How are you?"

"I'm doing okay. How are you?"

"I'm doing fine," Hope said. "Just getting used to my new summer schedule."

"What have you been doing?"

"Well, I got a job at the front desk at the Y."

"Really? That sounds like fun."

"Yeah," she said, "I like it. I get to greet everybody who comes in the door, ask them how they are doing, wish them a good day. It's a lot of fun to meet everybody."

Vincent smiled. "I bet you are really good at it. Sounds right up your alley."

"I think so," she said. "But enough about me. I listened to your game on the Internet tonight. Tough loss. Sorry."

Vincent sighed, "Oh, don't worry about that. We had to lose eventually. We were on something like a ten or twelve game winning streak. Maybe more. We'll just have to get them tomorrow."

"I'm sure you will."

"Did you hear about Tank?" he asked.

"No... is he okay?"

"Oh yeah," Vincent said. "Tonight was the draft."

"Oh, I totally forgot," Hope said. "Grace was supposed to call me if anything happened. Did he get drafted?"

"Number five to Charlotte!"

"Oh! That's great. I'm so happy for him. He totally deserves it."

Vincent nodded and smiled, forgetting that she couldn't see him. There was a pause and he didn't know what to say, so he just said what was on his heart. "I miss you."

There was silence on the other end of the line. It persisted for five seconds, and Vincent felt his heart drop. He said, "Hope?"

"Yeah, I'm here. Did you say something? I'm sorry. I dropped my phone."

Vincent chuckled, the pressure let out of the balloon. "I was just saying that I miss you."

"I miss you too. When I went away to Arizona, I was so afraid that I wouldn't make any friends and become homesick. I didn't know that my homesickness would now be for Page! I miss all of you."

"Well, I guess it's settled. You'll just have to pick me up at the train station."

"Deal," she said. "Well, you better go get your sleep. I understand you are pitching tomorrow."

"Probably," Vincent said.

"Hey," Hope said.

"Yes?"

"You will be awesome tomorrow!"

"Thanks. Good night."

"I'll be listening. Good night."

It helped knowing that Hope was listening to the game. As he threw his warm up pitches, he imagined her hugging her computer as the announcer talked about him. Vincent knew that was a stupid idea, and apparently his lack of concentration on baseball didn't go unnoticed.

"Hey, do you want this to be my last college game?" Tank yelled at Vincent.

"Sorry."

"Stop daydreaming and throw the ball," Tank yelled.

Vincent burned one in there and Tank nodded. It amazed Vincent how Tank was reacting to the news that he would soon be playing professional baseball. A person would never know that Tank just got the best news of his life just by looking at him. He was the same gruff guy he always was, barking orders like an extra coach and making sure that everything ran smoothly. Vincent realized at that moment just how lucky he was to be able to call Tank his friend. Vincent took off his ball cap and looked at his verse:

Colossians 3:23

Vincent was all business during the game. His fastball was, well, fast, and his two-seamer hit the locations Tank demanded of him. His splitter sank sharply, and he was able to use his off-speed pitch effectively. In all, Vincent pitched seven scoreless innings, allowing only two hits, both singles, before Coach Johnson pulled him to save his arm.

The Nevada Western crowd had nothing to cheer about all game long, and as Vincent walked to the dugout to all the high fives by his teammates, the home crowd also gave him an ovation, a particularly classy move considering that he was solely responsible for keeping their home team from advancing to the super-regional.

When it was all said and done, NCA won 8-0. The players celebrated, but in a muted fashion because their road to the World Series wasn't complete yet.

That night, they traveled back to Arizona by bus. While most of the players slept on the bus, Vincent kept his stare out the window at the moonlit desert landscape. He didn't feel tired, knew he should sleep, but he had a million things on his mind. He thought about Tank and his future in the big leagues. He thought about the mistakes he had made and how much they had affected his life. He thought about how thankful he was for second chances. Mostly though, he thought about Hope.

Vincent didn't know what the future held for the two of them. They were really good friends, and he loved that. He loved that he could talk with her, and she would make him feel good when he was down. He loved that she brought out the best in him. He loved that she didn't give up on him before she had the chance to know him. He was lucky that she had a pure heart, and he knew it.

On the other hand, he wondered if she would like to see him exclusively. He hadn't known her to have a boyfriend that year, but the topic never really came up. Considering her ten dates rule, he doubted if anybody even tried. He wanted to be the one to prove to her that he was honorable, but he also worried a little bit about what being "boyfriend and girlfriend" might do to their relationship. It was a recurring thought that about drove him mad. Maybe they would never make it that far, but he felt he had to at least give it a shot.

Leaning his pillow against the window, Vincent finally made it to sleep about two o'clock in the morning, only to be awakened by a text. He hoped it was Hope, but considering that it was so very late into the night, or very early into the morning, he doubted it. When he saw the number, he instantly recognized it as Evan. Vincent read the text, not really knowing what to expect.

Hey, heard ur game 2nite. Good job. UR really awesome i am so sorry i messed things up 4u good luck will be rooting 4u.

Vincent was surprised by the text. He really thought he would never hear from Evan again. When Evan had shunned him before class early in the semester, Vincent had closed that painful chapter in his book.

Vincent felt the mandatory counseling had really helped him to move on from what the therapist called "a string of bad decisions," revolving around a perfect storm of conditions set against him, starting with his parents' deaths continuing through the constant pressure from Evan, and ending with thoughts of suicide.

Vincent's therapist urged him to forgive all who had hurt him, not an easy chore. In fact, Vincent's first reaction to the text was anger at Evan for having the audacity to contact him now. The thought quickly passed though. Vincent had forgiven Evan already. Evan just didn't know it yet. In fact, Vincent imagined Evan was stepping out on a limb to text Vincent. He replied to Evan's text.

i forgave you long ago. blessings.

Vincent shut off his phone so that he could get some sleep. He didn't know if Evan would text him again, and didn't really care. Their friendship was over. Just because Vincent forgave Evan didn't mean that he would let his former roommate off the hook. Forgiveness lifted the burden off of Vincent's shoulders. He would pray for Evan, though, that very moment.

Vincent only wished he could do the same for his own father.

Chapter Twenty-Seven

VINCENT WAS CHOMPING at the bit to get back on the field, especially when he found out his next opponent. There were a great many things he was not proud of in his life, the first semester of his college career being one of them. He thought back to the poor decisions he made, his bad attitude, and the lack of respect he had shown to both himself and to the people who cared for him, and it sickened him. Now under Tank's tutelage, Vincent had found the straight and narrow path and was determined to show the world that his recklessness was a thing of the past.

As luck would have it, the University of California, San Bernardino also won their regional and advanced to the Southwest Super-regional to face NCA. The last time he had seen them, marked the moment Vincent had cemented his downward spiral. He was hung over at the start of the game and was ejected for throwing at one of the batters. He got into a fight with the umpire. He yelled at both Tank and Coach Johnson, and he trashed the locker room. He got drunk and stopped going to classes. He stayed out all hours of the night and partied. He got himself mixed up with the wrong crowd. He wrecked his truck and now had irreparable damage to his left eye. He even had holes in his memory that he couldn't replace with information. It was fair to say that when he last saw those guys, it was not a good time for him.

Of course the UCSB team had absolutely no class about them. No topic was off-limits, and Vincent wasn't strong enough to ignore them the first time around. He knew that times had changed, and he would be better able to withstand their verbal assault, except that he had surely given them more ammunition now. How he performed in this game and how he reacted to their vileness would be an indicator of just how far he had come.

Unfortunately, the selection committee awarded UCSB home field for the super-regional. After three days of practicing back in Arizona, the team loaded the bus again for the trip out to San Bernardino.

The two teams were to play a best of three game series, the winner advancing to the College World Series. It was immediately apparent that NCA was not welcome in San Bernardino.

When the bus first pulled into town, college students were ready by the side of the highway at the first stoplight. Each had a carton of eggs and the NCA bus was pelted with what had to be over 200 eggs. When the egged bus pulled into the hotel they were staying at, more students met Vincent and his teammates there to boo them as they grabbed their luggage and equipment and walked into the hotel. Worst of all, the opposing fans prank called the players' rooms at all hours of the night, keeping them awake. It was no wonder then why the next day, NCA came out so flat in the first game.

Even Tank played a poor game. He went 0-4, Vincent only managed a single, and the rest of the team followed suit.

All game long Vincent had to endure chants of "DUI! DUI! DUI!" If he was playing in left field, the student section would all gather outside of the left field fence and chant it. If Vincent ran in at the end of an inning, the student section would follow him in, running and chanting at the top of their lungs. When he went up to bat, the chanting only increased. When he was sitting on the bench, they stood on top of the dugout chanting and stomping their feet.

Heckling was part of the game, Vincent well knew. Trying to stay positive, he had to admit to himself that their fans did have a lot of energy. All Vincent's teammates told him at different times during the game to forget about it, which was impossible. After a while the "DUI!" chant began to sound to Vincent like locusts on a hot August afternoon, and he took that imagery with him, hoping the sound would soothe him.

Regardless of any meditation he might have done, the team just stunk and UCSB handed them an 11-0 loss. The NCA players were shell shocked as they filtered into the locker room to avoid the awful student section, and if there was any silver lining, it was that Coach Johnson had saved Sandy for game two, and hopefully Vincent for game three.

For another night, the phone calls interrupted sleep until Coach Johnson finally had all the players pull the cords out from the walls. Undeterred, the UCSB students stood outside the hotel hooting and hollering until about three o'clock in the morning when other hotel guests who couldn't stand to be kept up any longer, called the police and had them escorted away.

This time with half a night of sleep under their belts, and with a pep talk from Tank before they left the locker room, NCA fared much better. Sandy was his usual deft self, working the corners of the plate, pitching around UCSB's best hitters and focusing on ground outs. In all, NCA recorded seven double plays and tied the series at a game apiece with a 3-1 victory.

Now the ball and NCA's World Series fate rested in the hands of a freshman, who up until a month ago, wasn't even an official member of the team.

That night Vincent didn't need the rowdy UCSB students to be obnoxious to keep him awake. His own brain did that. He spoke with Mrs. Dean who told him to forget about everything and just pitch. He spoke with Hope who informed him that the game was going to be covered live on national television. He worried that he might screw up and it would end up being Tank's and the other seniors' final collegiate game. The draft was now over and none of the other upperclassmen had been drafted, which didn't necessarily mean that they were out of luck. There was always free agency, but it was apparent to Vincent that this might be the last game of baseball that half of the team ever played. He had to be great for them, and in order to do that, he had to go to sleep.

But how does a guy order himself to sleep? The more he thought about how important it was for him to sleep, the more he worried that he wouldn't. He would stare at the alarm clock, watching the numbers slowly add one-by-one, until Tank, who was also Vincent's hotel roommate, told him to stop wiggling in that bed over there and just daydream about baseball if he was having trouble going to sleep. Vincent tried it, thinking about the natural beauty of the throwing motion, about standing in the batter's box and watching opposing pitchers throw fastballs that looked more like beach balls than hard balls. It worked, and Vincent was fast asleep.

It was a beautiful early summer evening in San Bernardino,

California. The temperature was in the mid-eighties at game time, and as the sun descended towards the horizon, Vincent marveled at the cirrus clouds that turned to yellows, oranges, pinks, and eventually indigo. The stands were packed with UCSB fans, and they were especially pumped for this game. A win and UCSB advanced to the World Series.

From the second Vincent stepped onto the field, he was again serenaded with chants of "DUI! DUI! DUI!" Knowing that this game was going to be on television across the entire country, Vincent was embarrassed that every American tuning in would be privy to his personal failings. Surely the announcers had to explain to the viewing audience why the fans were chanting that?

Tank apparently could see this a mile away, so he made it a point to take Vincent back into the locker room where it was quiet and sit him down for a little last-second advice. When the two were comfortable, Tank exhaled and said, "You know, Vincent, I've been pretty tough on you this year."

Vincent nodded. He looked down at his forearms, watching the veins popping out. All those early morning workouts had their positive effect on him.

"And next year you will be a sophomore. We are losing a lot of seniors off the team this year, and Coach Johnson will be looking for leaders to step up. Do you know what happened to me when I was a freshman?"

"Did you also get into trouble?" Vincent asked.

"No. I had just come back from pulling a tour in Iraq with the Marines. College and baseball were easy compared to what I faced over there. No, I didn't face the problems you faced this year because I was twenty-two when I was a freshman. As you know, I had already faced down those demons. What happened to me was that Coach Johnson sat me down early on and told me to listen to everything the seniors had to say, because it's easier to learn from listening than to learn from making mistakes. To that point I had made plenty anyway. So I learned. Even though these guys were my own age, and some of them a little younger, I gave them the respect that experience requires, and I learned how to pass their wisdom forward."

Tank shifted in his seat and rubbed his knees a little above his shin guards. "That is why I am talking to you now. If we lose this game tonight, I fly out to join Charlotte's farm club. And you will have to readjust to your new role as the leader. Now I've taught you everything I know, and this semester you've been an apt pupil. Next year you will have to take over that role for me, so I want you to promise me you will do that."

"Tank," Vincent interrupted, "you're talking like we are going to lose tonight!"

Tank shook his head. "You never know, Vincent. We'll go out there and give them all we have, and if it's enough, then it's enough, and we pack our bags for one more tournament. If it's not enough, at least we will know that we put everything into it that we could, that we left it all out there on the field. Either way, we leave this dump with our heads held high. Agreed?"

"Agreed," Vincent said.

Tank stopped and considered one last thought. "Vincent, winning and losing doesn't define us." Tank paused for a moment and continued. "Vincent, baseball doesn't define us. Life is much more important than some baseball game. There are so many things about life that are more important. Faith, hope, and love being three. It's your job to make the distinction between what is and isn't important." Then Tank stared straight into Vincent's eyes. "Always remember that."

Vincent nodded.

"That comes from First Corinthians," Tank said. He shook Vincent's hand, an iron-firm grip. "'Whatever you do, work at it with all your heart.' Colossians 3:23. Now, let's give them everything we got!"

"You got it," Vincent agreed.

The two walked side-by-side out to the dugout. Tank stopped Vincent a step from the dugout and said, "Oh, yeah. One final piece of advice. Hope likes yellow roses," then Tank walked on, saying over his shoulder, "She is from Texas, you know!"

Back in little Augusta, Oklahoma, the whole town gathered at the high school basketball gym. The tech guys wired the projector so that it shot the NCA game on the side wall, an extra-large big screen for everybody to watch. They also piped the sound through the speakers, and the whole town packed into the gym and watched their hometown product, Vincent Preston, warming up on the mound. Vincent's teammates from last year sat on the front row, each sharing their stories from their freshman years of college, each marveling at how this relative unknown had turned from rags to riches. There was a lot of pride in the building, and everybody pulled for this kid they barely knew a year ago.

Mrs. Dean sat down on her couch and turned on her television. She figured that she was the only person from Augusta who was not crammed into that basketball gym watching Vincent pitch for a national audience. She was so proud of him. Not for making it to this level of competition. She knew he had the natural talent to go even further. She was proud of Vincent for facing his demons and keeping them at bay. She knew he would be tempted again. Temptation was always out there. As he burned in pitch after pitch, Mrs. Dean hailed up a silent prayer for Vincent.

Hope sat in her chair behind the front desk at the YMCA,

watching the television on the wall across the room. Everybody who came in that day was told how this young man she was friends with was going to be on national TV, pitching to go to the College World Series. Now a crowd had gathered around the television, and Hope smiled and prayed.

Vincent threw his last warmup pitch and walked off the mound as Tank whipped the ball right to the shortstop covering second base. Hoover caught it and flipped it to Steinbeck who tossed it around the horn. When the ball finally made it back into Vincent's glove, he paused at the back of the mound and looked out at his teammates, each of them excited. Vincent took off his hat and saw the Colossians verse staring right back at him.

Whatever you do, work at it with all your heart.

Vincent prayed a simple prayer, for God to grant him strength. And with that, he turned around and faced his first batter. The pitches came out of his hand robotically. Vincent tried not to think at all, only obey Tank's signs and deliver the goods. UCSB's team tried to get into Vincent's head, but Vincent wouldn't let them in. The fans heckled him, and it didn't faze him a bit. A picture of perfect concentration, he stood on top of that mound and fired away, flirting with triple digits on the radar gun.

The first five innings flew by. Though Vincent was unhittable, the opposing pitcher had stymied the NCA hitters as well. To that point, Vincent had made solid contact with the ball, putting it in play, but in his two plate appearances, both times he grounded out sharply to the third baseman. Tank had been intentionally walked in both of his plate appearances, rendering his bat useless with the other hitters not breaking through.

In the sixth inning, Vincent finally made a mistake. Tank had Vincent working a batter on the inside corner, and when he asked for a four-seam fastball in the same spot, Vincent missed his location and put it right down the middle.

The batter swung for the fence. He made contact with the ball and it sailed deep to left and way out of the park, much to the delight of the rabid fans.

It was the only hit Vincent had given up in the game to this point, but it was a big one, and it worried Vincent, since the team wasn't advancing runners. Vincent managed to close out the side, using a good combination of two-seam fastballs and sliders. When Vincent needed a fastball, he reached back and found something deep inside of him to put a little extra mustard on it. When he needed movement on the ball, he concentrated and directed it well.

Still, NCA couldn't manage to get a run across the plate. They had their base runners, but all of them were left stranded on base. So when the top of the ninth inning rolled around, UCSB clung to a puny one-run lead, and Vincent aimed to do something about that. He came to the plate, fully knowing that this might be his last at bat that year. Since he had given up the game's only run, he felt a personal responsibility to do something about it.

First up in the lineup, Vincent practiced his swing in the on-deck circle and worked to get the pitcher's timing. As he stretched out, his mind wandered. He got to thinking about his parents again. Though his faith was strong, Vincent wondered why God let him have his father. Out of all the fathers out there, why that man? And what about his mother? Surely she had feelings. Surely she was more than the person who Vincent knew, a turtle who barely stuck her neck out for fear of getting her head cut off.

Vincent had been carrying these issues around for too long, and the night was far too beautiful for him to feel sorry for himself. He had been counseled to let go of that hatred for his father. He felt it was time to move on, free himself from the shackles his dad had tied on him. He didn't know why this very second was that important moment, but he felt it stronger than ever. Vincent bent for a moment in prayer, chants of "DUI! DUI! DUI!" in the background.

Dear Father, please give me the strength to move forward and the ability to take the positives from my parents and use them in my life. You are in control of all, and I praise you. Through Jesus' name, amen!

"Dad," Vincent said, with determination, "I release you."

When Vincent stood, he smiled. This was just a game. The TV cameras meant nothing. The UCSB fans meant nothing. There was no pressure on him because this wasn't life or death. There was something more important out there, and it revolved around his faith.

The catcher whipped the ball to the second baseman, and Vincent stepped into the batter's box.

This is a kid's game, and if I am lucky, I will share this passion with my own kids.

Vincent smiled and thought for a second about Hope.

Now, let's play some baseball.

Vincent made the sign of the cross with his bat across home plate and took a couple of practice swings. Vincent then studied the pitcher's eyes. They were concentrated on his catcher. Then the pitcher agreed on the sign, and when he released the ball, it started inside and kept going.

Vincent was poised to swing, but he never had a chance. The ball thudded as it hit his lower back and lost all kinetic energy.

Vincent dropped his bat and winced. It hurt, but he wasn't going to give the pitcher any satisfaction, so he headed to first base. He knew what this was. Retaliation from their very first meeting. Apparently Vincent getting kicked out of that game way back in October wasn't enough for UCSB. They had to retaliate for the star their star that Vincent put on crutches, even if it meant putting the tying run on first base with nobody out and clinging to a one-run lead in the ninth inning.

UCSB's coach yelled at his pitcher from the dugout. It was obvious to Vincent that the pitcher and/or catcher had acted without their coach's consent. It was a stupid move, a selfish one. In order to exact revenge they would put the tying run on first base in a one-run game in the ninth inning with the World Series riding on the outcome? It was beyond selfish.

Vincent knew it was his responsibility to get into scoring position and apparently Coach Johnson read his mind. As Vincent had hoped, Coach Johnson gave him the sign to steal, as soon as he was able to get a good lead. This was difficult because the pitcher threw three different pickoff moves at Vincent, trying each time to catch him leaning. In all, the pitcher threw to first base six times before he threw a single pitch to the batter.

But that seventh time, as soon as the pitcher's foot extended for home plate, Vincent shot off like a rocket. He dug into the soft dirt with his tunnel vision on the outside corner of the bag. Lightning shot out from his fresh legs. Grunting for all he was worth, he dove in head first and touched the bag just ahead of the throw.

"SAFE!" the second base umpire called from a perfect angle to see the play.

Vincent stood up and brushed off the dirt from his pants and shirt. For the first time since the first pitch, two things dawned on him. First, the student section was finally quiet. A little drama will do that. Second, the television camera was on him right now for all to see. He wondered who all was watching, but quickly closed out that thought and concentrated on the pitcher again.

Again the pitcher worked his pickoff moves on Vincent. Vincent hadn't been given the steal sign, and he knew Coach

Johnson was going to keep him at second base in the hopes that somebody would be able to knock him in with a base hit. It was the percentage play, and though Vincent wanted to steal an extra bag, he knew he had to be a team player. The opposing pitcher hadn't been a team player, and that was why Vincent was on second base now.

The move didn't seem to work out so well as both Hoover and Steinbeck went down on strikes, leaving Tank as the last hope. Vincent just knew that the pitcher would automatically walk Tank to keep him from being a difference maker, but to his, and apparently everyone else's surprise, they elected to throw to him. Vincent could only describe it as hubris.

Tank stepped into the batter's box with a look set on the pitcher that could pierce steel. He took a couple of practice swings and awaited the first pitch. The pitcher threw a fastball off the outside corner of the plate that the umpire called a ball. Throwing in a few more pickoff moves, the pitcher again threw the ball a bit outside.

As a pitcher, Vincent knew the guy on the mound was hoping to lure Tank into taking a swing at a bad pitch. It was the equivalent of an intentional walk, pitching outside of the strike zone on purpose. Both pitches had been hittable, but neither were where Tank apparently wanted, so he remained motionless in the batter's box for the next two pitches, the first which was again outside, and the second which barely hit the outside corner for a strike.

Vincent clapped a few times and said, "C'mon, Tank. Take this guy out of here!"

The pitcher apparently didn't like the comment, because he threw another pickoff move at Vincent, but this time neither the shortstop nor the second baseman were there to cover the bag. It skipped into centerfield, and Vincent picked himself up and raced to third and stopped on the bag. He had a slight inclination to round third and go for home, and he knew it would have been close, but he was given the hold sign. Again, he knew his role and he had to let Tank do his job. This was Tank's moment. Tank's team. Tank's chance to be the hero.

UCSB's head coach called for time and stepped out to the mound to conference with his entire infield. The conference lasted for a couple of moments, enough time for Vincent to study Tank. He was laser-focused on the bat in his hands. Vincent wondered what must be going through Tank's mind. Was it excitement? Anxiety? Fear of failure? Was Tank supremely confident that he would park the next pitch somewhere over the outfield fence? And if Vincent were Tank, how would he be feeling? Finally the conference broke up and play resumed.

The pitcher took his time on the mound, breathing heavily enough for Vincent to notice. Vincent felt calm in that moment, amazingly, and wondered if the pitcher would be able to control his nerves. He knew that Tank must have seen the same thing.

With the count three balls and one strike, the hitter's count, the pitcher finally leaned in for the sign. He shook off his catcher a few times, and Vincent saw Tank smirk under his helmet. Finally the pitcher and catcher agreed on a sign. Vincent took a very short lead off third base just off the baseline, just in case a line drive off Tank's bat was to hit him.

The pitcher inhaled deeply, focused his vision on his catcher's mitt, which was positioned on the outside once again. His leg kicked up and then back down toward home. He delivered a fastball slightly outside the strike zone, only this time Tank wasn't taking a ball four.

Crack!

Tank put a charge into the ball and it sailed high into the night sky to dead centerfield. Vincent slowly jogged toward home plate, watching the white ball get smaller and smaller.

That's it! Tank did it!

The centerfielder took to his horse to try to chase it down. A moment of euphoria, a moment more, and Vincent raised both hands in celebration. There was no doubt that this was a home run!

Just then the centerfielder stabbed for the fence, timed his jump, and reached up a good foot over the fence and came back down. For a moment or two, nobody in the stadium knew whether or not the centerfielder had snared it.

Vincent paused a foot from home plate. Tank was still at full gallop, rounding second.

Then, the centerfielder held his glove in the air and pointed his index finger on his free hand up in the sky, proclaiming that they were number one.

Not convinced, Vincent stomped on home plate as Tank rounded third. None of the umpires on the field made so much as a motion to declare it an out or a home run.

As Tank slowed his sprint into a jog and touched home plate, the two roommates kept their stare on the centerfielder, who met the second base umpire halfway into the outfield. The fielder opened his glove, showed the umpire what was in the webbing, and the umpire raised one fist into the air.

Immediately the UCSB bench sprinted to centerfield in celebration.

Tank stood there with Vincent, both with their hands on their hips.

No. Surely not. That's not how it ends for us! That's not how it ends for Tank!

Yet through the pain, Vincent knew deep down that this wasn't Tank's big moment. It was hard to admit, because Vincent wanted to go to the College World Series so badly, if only for Tank's sake, but God had bigger things in store for Tank. Vincent had no idea at the time how much of an understatement that was. He would eventually.

Tank dropped to a knee and put his head down. Vincent dropped to his knees and put a hand on each shoulder of his captain. Soon he was followed by the entire NCA team, each dropping to a knee around their star catcher, honoring a man who would be flying out that night to start his professional baseball career.

The student section, as well as many of the older UCSB fans, ran onto the field and celebrated with their home team and the hero centerfielder who had just sent UCSB into the College World Series and NCA home for the summer.

Vincent watched, the scene burning itself into his permanent memory. With the celebration commencing in the outfield, Tank kept his head down and said a prayer of thanksgiving for this season, these teammates, and their futures. All said, "Amen," and walked back to the dugout, ushered by chorus of jeering and profanities from the students who had stormed the field.

Chapter Twenty-Eight

TANK'S TEAMMATES DIDN'T have a long time to tell him goodbye. It was a tough way to end the season, being a mere inch away from making the College World Series. Vincent at first felt bad for Tank, but the more he thought about it, the more he realized that it was somehow poetic. Nice guys finish last. It felt so very familiar.

Vincent didn't have a chance to say goodbye, but that didn't matter to him because he knew Tank had spoken his peace to him prior to the last game. Tank had made sure Vincent knew what was important before he left his protégé.

The team drove all through the night, as Tank flew out to North Carolina.

Vincent went to his dorm room with nothing to do now but ponder his first year and all the trying times he had encountered. He had a knack for making things hard on himself, and he hoped that by his sophomore year he will have learned from all his misery.

Vincent looked up at the ceiling tile where he and Evan had stored alcohol. The temptation to drink would always be there, but Vincent knew he could handle the temptation if he put his faith in God. All things were possible through Jesus, as long as he put his entire heart into it, because God's grace and forgiveness was extended to everyone, himself included. As for the state of Arizona, they had their own set of rules.

Vincent had spurned Mrs. Dean's offer back during Christmas Break to stay with her. Now he knew he needed to go back to Oklahoma and atone for that. In fact he had a lot to atone for with Mrs. Dean and three months to do so. Before going home though, he had a few plans. He made a phone call to the old gentleman in the fly shop in Raton, New Mexico, and took him up on his offer to guide Vincent for a day on the Cimarron River. They set a date for later in the month, and Vincent smiled as he hung up.

Vincent spent the rest of morning cleaning out his room. With duffel bag on his shoulder, he walked to the retirement home and said his good byes, promising Robert that he would work on his chess game before next fall. When he left, teary-eyed, he trudged down to the same train station he had when he had learned that his parents died. The pain was still there, no doubt aided by the heartbreak of last night's loss and the sentimentality he had gained for his new home.

His steps were slow and deliberate. He had plenty of time for a slow walk in the cool morning's air before his train departed, plenty of time to think about what pain really was. Vincent thought back to the final pitch he had thrown his senior year of high school. That home run just seemed to keep going and going. That one mistake meant the difference between winning the state championship and being the goat. That feeling was horrible. To that point in his life, he would have classified that painful moment about a nine on a scale of one to ten. The thought made him chuckle. What did he know of pain back then? Better yet, what did he know of forgiveness?

Losing the game last night with a chance to go to the World Series? Was that really pain? Vincent used to think of the pitcher's mound as his place in this world. It was his everything. When he was suspended from the team, he felt he didn't have anything. Now as he neared the train station, he realized just how unimportant last night's game was. Sure, it would have been really nice to win it, but all the trials he had been through his freshman year taught him that it was merely a game. There was so much more to life than some baseball game. These trials, along with some good friends, taught him to hope for the future.

That's a statement he once thought he would never be able to make.

As Vincent waited on the bench for his train, he reminisced on his freshman year of college. He learned that college isn't about how smart a person is, but about how hard that person is willing to work. He learned that he wasn't all alone in the world, but he still had better start caring for himself. He learned that he had the capacity for love, and that others loved him. Most importantly, he learned that just because a person is friendly, that doesn't make him a friend. True friends are willing to let you know when you are doing something wrong and then stick by you to help you change for the better. The year had gone absolutely wrong, and yet Vincent was able to make the better of a second chance. Funny enough, he came to Page, Arizona with a pair of tennis shoes as his only mode of transportation, and in the course of the year's travails, he had come full circle.

As a man selling flowers walked by, Vincent recalled Tank's last piece of wisdom.

Vincent, baseball doesn't define us. Life is much more important than some baseball game. There are so many things about life that are more important. Faith, hope and love being three. It's your job to make the distinction between what is and isn't important.

Vincent took off his ball cap to rustle his hair and saw the faded verse:

Colossians 3:23

Vincent smiled, put his hat back on, and bought a single yellow rose, then went to the ticket booth to exchange his ticket.

ABOUT THE AUTHOR

Ryan Shelton's faith in God and love of writing both grew from a young age, but it wasn't until adulthood when he decided to put the two together with his first novel *The Mentor*. It was then that he realized this outreach ministry.

As a high school English teacher for the last fifteen years, Ryan has seen it as his mission to help his students in their daily struggles. With his novels, Ryan realized he could reach outside the walls of his classroom to minister to teens with issues like peer pressure, alcohol and drug abuse, and even suicidal thoughts. His mission in life is to show others that through Christ, all things are possible.

The Captain is Ryan's second published novel.

ryanmshelton.com
@ryanmshelton